“Any sign ... ges?”

“None.” Josh ... t move off the bed. H ... over her.

And he was naked.

Jaycee did a double take.

Okay, not naked. Just shirtless.

She had a good view of not just those toned abs and pecs but also the scar. It was several inches long and gashed across his otherwise perfect body. Even though it was well healed, she figured the ashy white line would never go away.

The memory of it certainly wouldn’t.

Any sign of the men or the hostages

JOSH

BY
DELORES FOSSEN

Published in Great Britain 2014
by Mills & Boon, an imprint of Harlequin (UK) Limited,
Eton House, 18-24 Paradise Road, Richmond, Surrey, TW9 1SR

ISBN: 978 0 263 91354 5

46-0414

Harlequin (UK) Limited's policy is to use papers that are natural, renewable and recyclable products and made from wood grown in sustainable forests. The logging and manufacturing processes conform to the legal environmental regulations of the country of origin.

Printed and bound in Spain
by Blackprint CPI, Barcelona

Imagine a family tree that includes Texas cowboys, Choctaw and Cherokee Indians, a Louisiana pirate and a Scottish rebel who battled side by side with William Wallace. With ancestors like that, it's easy to understand why *USA TODAY* bestselling author and former air force captain **Delores Fossen** feels as if she were genetically predisposed to writing romances. Along the way to fulfilling her DNA destiny, Delores married an air force top gun who just happens to be of Viking descent. With all those romantic bases covered, she doesn't have to look too far for inspiration.

Chapter One

This was exactly the kind of *homecoming* that Deputy Josh Ryland had wanted to avoid.

Just the sight of the guy with the gun caused his head to start pounding, and his heartbeat crashed in his ears. The flashbacks came.

Man, did they.

Flashbacks of another surveillance, another gunman. And the three .38 jacketed slugs that the gunman had fired into Josh's chest. The wounds had healed, for the most part anyway, but still the flashbacks came.

"You okay?" his cousin whispered.

His cousin was Grayson Ryland, sheriff of Silver Creek, Josh's hometown where he'd been born and had spent his childhood. Not a town where Josh had expected to see a man carrying an assault rifle. It wasn't exactly a standard weapon for a Texas cattle rancher.

"I'm fine," Josh lied. And he tried to level his breathing. Tried also to ignore the healing gunshot wounds on his chest that had started to throb like a bad toothache.

"I can call one of the other deputies to come out here," Grayson offered.

There was no shortage of them. Like Grayson, four of the deputies were Josh's cousins, too. And if Grayson had thought for one second that he would encounter a rifle-toting man on what should have been a routine call, then he would have almost certainly brought one of the others and not Josh.

"You made me a deputy," Josh reminded him. "This is part of the job."

That sounded good. Like something a small-town deputy should say to his boss.

It was pretty much a lie, though.

The truth was, Josh had come back home after taking a leave of absence from the FBI so he could avoid gunmen. Assault rifles. Bullets to the chest. And the tangle of bloody memories that he fought hard to keep out of his head.

So much for that plan.

Using the binoculars, Josh watched the rifleman pace across the front porch of the two-story ranch house. He was clearly standing guard.

But why?

Too bad Josh could think of several reasons why a rancher would need a guard with an assault rifle, and none of those reasons involved anything legal.

Josh handed Grayson the binoculars so he, too, could have a look. "You think they're hiding drugs in the house?" Grayson asked.

"Drugs or guns, maybe."

Whichever it was, it had created a lot of traffic, because there were plenty of tire tracks on the gravel driveway in front of the ranch house.

It was that unusual traffic that had prompted someone to make an anonymous call to the sheriff's office to report possible suspicious activity at the ranch. It didn't help that no one knew the tenants. The place had recently been rented by a couple from nearby San Antonio who'd yet to turn up in town.

Josh could see the source of some of that traffic. There were four vehicles—two trucks, an SUV and a car, all parked around the grounds. No tractors, no livestock or any signs of any ranching equipment.

That didn't help the knot in Josh's stomach.

"The gunman's not the new tenant of the place," Grayson explained.

No. Josh had glanced at the couple's driver's license photos in the background info that he'd pulled up on them before Grayson and he had even started the half-hour drive from Silver Creek out to the Bluebonnet Ranch. A peaceful-sounding name for a place that was probably hiding some very unpeaceful secrets.

And speaking of hiding, the front door of the ranch house flew open, and Josh didn't need the binoculars to see another armed man step into the doorway.

Yeah, this was definitely a bad homecoming.

Grayson and he stayed belly down on the side of the hill dotted with spring wildflowers that overlooked the ranch, and Grayson returned the binoculars to Josh so he could take out his phone and call for backup. Unfortunately, they were going to need it.

Josh zoomed in on the second guard who'd stepped onto the porch. Both men were dressed in dark clothes, and both carried the same type of assault rifle. Maybe they were part of a militia group, though Josh hadn't heard of any reports of that kind of activity in Silver Creek.

The second man glanced around. The kind of glance that a cop or criminal would make to ensure he wasn't being watched. Josh was pretty certain that Grayson and he were well hidden, but he ducked down lower just in case, and he watched the man motion toward someone else in the doorway.

A woman stepped out.

And Josh's pulse kicked up a significant notch.

He adjusted the zoom on the binoculars. Hoping he was wrong. But he wasn't.

Josh instantly recognized that pale blond hair. That face. Even the body that was hidden beneath a bulky pair of green scrubs and a gray windbreaker.

Jaycee.

Last time he'd seen Jaycee Finney was the morning of his shooting when she'd been half-naked and skulking out of his bedroom. He hadn't stopped her, that was for sure, because he'd already figured out that a weekend affair with a fellow agent was a bad idea. After the shooting and after he'd realized what she'd done, Josh knew it hadn't been just bad. It had been one of the worst mistakes of his life.

"You know her?" Grayson whispered when he finished his call for backup.

Obviously, something in Josh's body language had clued Grayson in to that possibility. Probably the narrowed eyes or the veins that Josh could feel pulsing on his forehead.

"Yeah. She's Special Agent Jaycee Finney." And if Jaycee was here, that meant the FBI was already aware of something illegal taking place on the ranch.

Josh took out his phone and called his brother, Sawyer, who was an FBI agent in the San Antonio office. "You ready to come back to work, little brother?" Sawyer said the moment he answered.

"Not exactly. Fill me in on SA Jaycee Finney."

Unlike his cheerful greeting, Sawyer didn't jump to answer that, cheerful or otherwise, but Josh heard what sounded like keystrokes on a computer.

"Please tell me you're not involved with her again," Sawyer implored.

"Not like *that*."

"Good. Because she's bad news."

Oh, yeah. No arguments from him on that.

Josh had learned his lesson when it came to Jaycee. She would do any- and everything for the badge, and while Josh had once put himself in that same super-troop category, he never would have risked another lawman's life.

As Jaycee had done.

Josh kept his attention fastened to her and watched as the second gunman grabbed her by the arm. She didn't fight back, though he knew she was capable of it. She didn't appear to be armed, either. Jaycee just let the goon practically drag her off the porch and into the yard.

Even though Jaycee and he didn't have a good history together, it still took everything inside him to stay put and not bolt out there to help a fellow law enforcement agent. This was obviously some deep-cover assignment, and playing knight in shining armor could get her killed. Grayson, too.

"Seems like you're not the only one who wanted some downtime," Sawyer finally said. "I just checked the computer, and it says Jaycee's been on a leave of absence for nearly four months now."

That didn't mesh with what was playing out in front of him. Either Jaycee was doing her own rogue private investigation or else she'd been taken captive.

Josh watched as the guard shoved her in the direction of a barn that was almost the same size as the house. "Any ransom demands for her?" he asked Sawyer.

"Ransom? None. Why? What in the Sam Hill is this all about?"

"I'm not sure, but I'll get back to you." Josh pushed the end-call button and slipped his phone back in his jeans pocket.

The guard gave Jaycee another shove just as she reached the barn door. It was impossible to get a decent look at the interior even though there were overhead lights, but it appeared to be some kind of living quarters. The guard shut her inside the barn, slammed the door, engaged the slide lock and walked back to the house.

"Want to let me in on what's happening?" Grayson asked.

"I'm not sure. That agent down there is supposed to be on a leave of absence like me. How long before backup arrives?"

"Twenty minutes at least."

That was an eternity if those men were torturing Jaycee. And that was a strong possibility. The man hadn't exactly handled her with kid gloves when he'd maneuvered her into that barn. It was highly likely that her identity had been blown and that she was being held and forced to give information.

Which she wouldn't give easily.

Not Jaycee.

She wasn't just married to the badge, it was her soul mate. The only thing she actually cared about. She'd die—and get others killed—before giving up anything that would compromise an investigation. Even an unauthorized one.

He knew a lot about that, too, when it came to her.

Josh cursed under his breath. "Cover me. I'll move in for a closer look." And then he remembered that he wasn't talking to a fellow agent but rather his new boss. "I'll stay low and out of sight."

Grayson stared at him, his lips pressed together a moment, but then he nodded. "Call me if you spot trouble."

His phone was already on vibrate, and Josh drew his gun. That simple gesture gave him another jolt of flashbacks, but he wrestled the images aside and made his way back down the hill. It wasn't much of an elevation, but thankfully just enough to keep him hidden.

Grayson had left his truck parked on a ranch trail about a quarter of a mile away. That was no doubt where his brothers would park when they responded to the scene. They were all experienced cops and would know to do a quiet approach, but Josh wanted to finish his surveillance and be back in place with Grayson before they arrived. That way, they could discuss the best way to handle this.

Whatever *this* was.

He didn't see any guards on the side of the barn that wasn't facing the house, but he stayed low and used the vehicles for cover to make his way from the road and to the barn. No windows, of course. So he went to the back and spotted the door. It wasn't the type that'd normally be on a barn. More like a house door with a padlock on the outside.

But it wasn't locked now and was open just a fraction.

Still no sign of any guards, so Josh went closer and peered inside. It was dimly lit, the only illumination coming from an exposed bulb dangling in the center of the barn and a TV that'd been mounted high on a stall post. An old black-and-white movie flickered on the screen, but the sound was barely audible.

It took Josh a moment to pick through the darkness and shadows and spot Jaycee. She was sitting on an army-style cot, her elbows on her knees, her face buried in her hands.

She wasn't alone.

Josh saw two other women, both also on cots. One was reading a paperback and the other was staring up at the ceiling. What he couldn't tell was if there were any guards inside.

He didn't make a sound or move, but Jaycee's head snapped up, and as if she'd sensed he was there, her gaze zoomed straight toward him. Josh didn't need a lot of light to notice the relief in her eyes.

Quickly followed by something else.

Fear, maybe.

She shook her head, barely moving it, and she looked down, her loose shoulder-length hair sliding forward to conceal the sides of her face. She put her finger to her mouth in a stay-quiet gesture.

At least that was what Josh thought she was trying to do.

"What the hell's going on in there?" a voice boomed through the barn.

Josh glanced around and soon spotted the source. A large speaker mounted on one of the crossbeams. Next to it was a camera.

Hell.

Had they seen him?

Still no sign of either of the guards, but he got ready just in case he had to grab Jaycee and the others and run for cover.

"Nothing's wrong," Jaycee shouted. She stood, her back to Josh, and she put her hands on her hips. The sleeves of the bulky windbreaker billowed out like wings as she stared up at the camera. "What, I can't scratch my nose now without getting interrogated?"

The tone was the same old Jaycee. Smart mouth. In charge. But Josh could see that her hands were trembling.

"It looked like more than scratching your nose to me," the man on the intercom fired back. "You girls aren't trying to plan something, are you? Like another escape attempt? Because the last one didn't go so good, did it?"

So they were being held against their will. But why? And who was doing this?

"We learned our lesson about that already," Jaycee said, and the two others bobbed their heads in agreement.

The women were at the wrong angle to see Josh, and Jaycee made it even harder for them to spot him by stepping to the side. Positioning herself and that bat-wing windbreaker between the camera and him.

"So do I have permission to scratch my nose?" Jaycee yelled.

"Yeah. For now anyway. But if you try to break any more cameras, this time your roommates are gonna pay for it."

The moments crawled by, and there was a slight crackling sound. Jaycee's shoulders slumped, and she blew out a barely audible breath.

"I'm getting some air," she said to no one in particular, and she turned and headed toward the back door.

And Josh.

He saw it then. When she turned to the side and the windbreaker shifted. Her belly. Not flat as it'd been the last time they'd crossed paths.

Jaycee was pregnant.

Oh, man.

Josh forced himself to stay quiet and calm. And he also forced himself to think about the timing of all of this. It wasn't hard to remember the only time Jaycee and he had slept together. Because that was the same day he'd nearly died.

Five months ago.

Like the flashbacks, that hit him darn hard, like a heavyweight's fist to the gut. But he bit back any sound of surprise because if the guards heard him, it would likely get them killed.

Jaycee didn't look at him. In fact, she gave no indication whatsoever that she knew he was even there. She strolled to the back door, eased it open several inches farther than it already was and took a deep breath—like someone indeed getting a little fresh air.

"Don't move," she mouthed, her chin still lifted slightly in her fresh-air pose. "I broke the lens a couple of days ago with a rock, and they haven't gotten a replacement yet." She tipped her head to the tiny camera mounted on the eaves. "Right now, you're out of camera range for the one inside, and you need to stay that way."

He nodded, didn't move, except to drop his gaze to her stomach. "Whose baby is that?" he asked in a whisper.

She opened her mouth but then closed it just as quickly. Her attention sliced to the front door of the barn, and she whirled around to step in front of him.

Not a second too soon.

The door flew open, and Josh got just a glimpse of the armed goon as he rushed in.

And he pointed his rifle right at Jaycee.

Chapter Two

Jaycee cursed the panic that shot through her.

After months of being held captive, she should be used to having a gun pointed at her, but maybe that was something that never got *old.* Especially since each time one of the guards pointed a gun at her, they aimed at her stomach.

The one place that they knew would get her to cooperate.

She'd risk her own neck, but not the baby.

However, there was a new reason to do whatever they wanted so she could get the guard out of there. Josh's life depended on it, and sadly, so did hers and the other two women's, Marita and Blanca.

Her cell mates spoke only Spanish, but they understood enough English to know what they had to do. When the guard came in, they got to their feet, cowering. Both pregnant, like Jaycee, and both willing to do anything to protect the babies they carried.

"You sure you ladies aren't up to something?" the man growled.

Jaycee didn't know his name, but he was bald, ugly and big, which described every guard who'd been at the ranch over the past month.

This one came in at least several times a day, and he always made a repeat visit after bringing one of them back from the house. Maybe because he thought they were going to discuss whatever they'd seen or heard in there. Or maybe he thought they'd break some more cameras.

On each of these visits, Jaycee wished she could punch the guy in the face, take that rifle and get herself and the others out. But so far, escape had been impossible.

Maybe it still was.

She couldn't risk verbally warning Josh to stay put, but hopefully he would. He was a good agent. At least he had been before the shooting that'd nearly left him dead. If they survived the next few minutes, maybe she would be able to ask him how he'd found her and how he planned to get them all out.

And he'd better have a plan.

A darn good one.

Keeping herself directly in front of the door, Jaycee lifted the leg of her scrub pants to remind the jerk that since her attempted escape, she had been wearing an ankle monitor. One that would alert him if she did manage to get out of the barn. So far, she'd had no luck in getting the monitor off or disabling the Big Brother camera inside that watched them 24/7.

The jerk stared at them awhile longer. Jaycee didn't prolong his stay by glaring at him as she sometimes did. Her glare would rile him, she knew that for a fact, but a riled man just stayed longer.

She wanted him out of there *now*.

Finally, he mumbled something and got moving. So did Jaycee. She knew the angles of the camera and the blind spots. Well, one blind spot anyway. Even the bathroom that'd been added in the corner had no door. But she had learned that any time she moved into the remains of the horse stall just to the left of the back barn door that one of the jerks came running to make sure she was still there.

Definitely a blind spot.

"Stay low," she whispered to Josh, "and go in there."

Jaycee tipped her head to the stall. She had to get him out of the yard because the guard would soon be making a sweep of that area. Maybe he wouldn't come upon the backup that Josh had hopefully brought with him. If Josh had come alone, well, they were in trouble.

Without making a sound, Josh slipped through the bottom part of the door and into the stall.

"Keep your voice at a whisper," she warned him, angling her head away from the camera. She couldn't do that for long, either, or it would prompt another look-see from the guard. "There's a listening device on the post by the camera, but I've crammed bits of hay in it to muffle the sound."

She was sure he heard what she said, but his smoky blue eyes were planted firmly on her stomach.

Oh, *that.*

She owed him an answer to his question.

Since she'd first eyed that little plus sign on the home pregnancy test over four months ago, she'd wondered how she would spill this news. Josh wasn't exactly a family man. Thirty-four and had never even lived with a woman or been engaged. Jaycee didn't consider herself a relationship expert, but she figured that meant he hadn't planned on becoming a father this year.

And she didn't care.

This was *her* baby. She'd spent the last three and a half months protecting it, and she didn't intend to stop now. The only thing she needed from Josh was his help in getting them all the heck out of there.

Jaycee moved back to the door, propped her shoulder against the frame and pretended to examine the split ends on her hair. She spent a lot of time pretending to do mundane things that concealed her eyes and mouth just so the guards wouldn't be alerted that she was looking for a way out of this Hades of a prison.

"Well?" Josh prompted.

Since an answer to that question would only waste time and distract him, Jaycee went in a different direction. One that would fully occupy his lawman's attention.

She hoped.

"There are four guards total," she explained. "At least two are on watch at all times. And right now, there's a doctor inside. He's already given me and the two women here checkups, but he'll examine the other four women who are also being held captive in the house."

She risked a glance at Josh, and judging from the way he looked at her—as if she'd lost her bloomin' mind—he hadn't known those details.

"You did know about the captives, right?" she asked. "And that this is a baby farm, and they're holding us against our will?"

He shook his head.

That sucked the breath right out of her.

He didn't know. So why the devil was he here?

Josh shucked off his black Stetson and generally looked as if he wanted to throw up in it. That only lasted a split second, and he became the tough FBI agent again.

Or rather the hot cowboy cop.

That wasn't an FBI shield on his rawhide belt. It was some kind of local badge. And he was wearing jeans and a denim shirt that looked as if he'd been born to wear them. Ditto for the rumpled chocolate-brown hair. Definitely not FBI regulation length. Later, if she got the chance, she'd tell him that it suited him.

Later, she'd tell him a lot of things.

And maybe he would listen.

Josh eased his phone from his pocket and fired off a text. "Will these men kill you if you try to escape?" he mouthed.

"Oh, yeah." She didn't have to think about that.

Jaycee had had enough experience with killers to know one when she saw one, and the guards were killers. She figured their boss was, too, though she'd yet to lay eyes on him. What she wanted to do was put a gun to his head and pull the trigger a couple of times. Harsh, yes, but he'd put a lot of women and babies through way too much misery.

"They've had me for three and a half months." She glanced at the other two women, who were pretending to do anything but look at her. "My Spanish sucks, but from what I've gathered, they were here about a month before I arrived."

"How'd this happen? How did they take you? *Why* did they take you?"

All good questions. Too bad her answers were somewhat lacking.

She moved to another section of her hair for the fake split-ends check. "I was coming out of a clinic after an OB visit. Another woman was walking out with me. Someone I didn't know. But she was close to her delivery date, and we were talking. Two men grabbed her. When I tried to help her, they hit us with Tasers."

Those memories were almost too painful to recall, but Jaycee had tried to brand every detail into her brain so she could catch the monsters once she was able to get free.

And she *would* catch them.

"I don't know what happened to the other woman," Jaycee continued. Again, a painful memory that clawed at her. She hadn't been able to save her, and now heaven knew what had happened to her and her baby.

"Why did they take you?" he repeated, his attention on her belly again.

"From what I've been able to find out, they kidnap women or force them into surrogacy and then sell the babies on the black market."

She let go of the hunk of her hair and moved on to nail-biting to cover the movement of her mouth. Except she was shaking enough that nail-biting didn't exactly seem like a pretense.

"They don't appear to know I'm an agent," Jaycee added.

And that was probably the only reason she was still alive.

This operation might not be huge, more like a sicko cottage industry, but it carried with it all sorts of felony charges. If the brains behind this thought she was FBI, they might not let her draw another breath.

And that would mean her baby wouldn't stand a chance.

Or maybe they knew she was an agent and were planning to use that in some way. Maybe to get information from her.

Josh's phone vibrated, and he glanced at the screen before answering it. "We're going to need a lot of backup," he whispered to the caller. "This is a black-market baby ring. At least four armed guards in the house. Four captives, too, and another three captives here in the barn."

Jaycee couldn't hear a word of what the caller said, and Josh's body-language clues shut down, too. No more emotion in his eyes.

Sometimes, like now, she got just a flash of the heat that'd once been between them.

Okay, more than a flash.

She got a full shot of the attraction that'd landed them in bed. Of course, with Josh's alarmingly handsome looks and long and lanky body, the attraction was a given. Even after all the bad that'd gone on between them.

He dropped his phone back in his shirt pocket and got into a crouching position. His gun ready. She hoped he had some kind of backup weapon that he could let her use.

"When I tell you and the women to get down, do it." Even though Josh whispered that order, it had some snarl to it. As if he'd considered that she might refuse. At this point, she wasn't refusing anything that would get her and all the captives out.

Jaycee managed a nod under the guise of more nail-biting, and since she didn't know what Josh's plan was, she stayed put. Waiting.

Praying, too.

"Is that baby mine?" he whispered.

She'd been expecting the question, of course, but Jaycee wasn't prepared for the suddenly clammy hands and her knees locking.

"Yes," she said.

She purposely didn't look at Josh because if he had another wave of nausea or some other unmanly response, he wouldn't want her to witness it. And besides, she didn't need the distraction of his response, either. Apparently, something was about to happen, something that would require her to shout to Marita and Blanca to get down before she did the same.

Something that would likely be dangerous.

Later, Josh and she could talk about the baby. Yelling would no doubt be part of that discussion, but for now, everything inside her screamed for her to do something—anything—to help with this escape.

And soon.

Jaycee felt useless standing there and waiting. Fortunately, she'd had a lot of practice with that during the past months, and she'd learned some other things that Josh needed to know.

"As far as I can tell," she whispered, "there are no working exterior cameras, and the computer inside the house seems to be rigged just to monitor the camera here in the barn and our ankle bracelets."

"How long will the doctor be here?" he asked. It was a logical question, no hint of the baby bombshell she'd just dropped on him.

"Maybe awhile. I think one of the women inside is in labor."

That brought on some muttered profanity from Josh. With good reason. It would be hard to escape with a woman delivering a baby. As it was, it'd be difficult for some of the women to run for cover. At least Marita, Blanca and she weren't megapregnant, and they all appeared to be in decent shape.

It seemed as if time practically came to a stop. Jaycee couldn't say the same for her breathing. It was gusting now, and there were beads of sweat on her face. The camera wouldn't pick up the sweat, but the breathing would no doubt alert one of the bald goons.

As would her continued stay near the door.

Soon, very soon, one of them would show up to make sure she wasn't up to no good and to order her back to her cot.

Hoping to buy them some time from the guard check, Jaycee partially closed the back door, leaving just a one-inch gap—the way it usually stayed during the day. At night, the guards locked them in with deadbolts. She went back in the direction of the cot but didn't sit.

Best to stay on her feet, ready to react.

Marita and Blanca obviously picked up on her nonverbal cues. Maybe the verbal ones, too, if they'd heard Josh and her whispering. Blanca studied her from over the top of her paperback, and Marita kept volleying glances between Jaycee and the movie that she obviously wasn't watching.

Finally, Jaycee saw the movement in the gap in the back door. Not one of the guards. This was another cowboy with a badge. She got just a glimpse of him, but he had the same hair coloring and body build as Josh. A strong enough resemblance that this could be his brother.

The man peeked in, his gaze briefly connecting with Josh's, and Josh motioned for her to move to the door. She did, though Jaycee tried not to give anything away that the guards would detect.

"It's hot in here, huh?" she said to the others as a ploy to cover up why she was headed back in that direction.

She cracked opened the door again and saw that it was just the one lawman, *one,* and while he looked capable and in charge, that meant they were still outnumbered and outgunned.

As Josh had done, this guy dropped his gaze to her belly before he glanced in at the other women. Jaycee wasn't sure exactly what they wanted her to do, but she figured they had a minute at most before the guard would check to see why she'd reopened the door.

But she was wrong.

Not even a minute.

Just a couple of seconds.

The front door flew open, and the guard bolted inside. Not the one who'd come in earlier. This guy had a serious mean streak and had even slapped Blanca when she hadn't in his opinion moved fast enough.

"Hands in the air!" he yelled at the top of his lungs, and he shifted the gun not toward her but to the stall where Josh was hiding.

Jaycee braced herself for the guard to move closer so he could do a thorough search.

But that didn't happen.

The man pulled the trigger, and the shot blasted through the barn.

Chapter Three

The shot was deafening, and it roared through Josh's entire body. The flashbacks started again, but he shoved them aside. No time for that now.

"Get down!" he shouted to Jaycee, but she was already dropping to the floor. From the sound of it, so were the other two women.

He had no idea if they were out of harm's way because the *harm* just kept coming. The man fired another shot into the barn.

And then another.

Grayson threw open the back door just as Josh bellied out of the stall. Both of them fired at the shooter. Josh had no idea who'd taken down the man, but he fell, his rifle clattering to the ground.

"Let's move," Josh ordered the women.

Jaycee sprang up darn fast for someone who was pregnant, and she hurried to the other side of the barn to latch on to the two women. Josh stayed put, guarding the now-open front door where he was certain that it wouldn't be long before the other guards responded and came in firing.

"Mason and Dade are covering the house," Grayson let him know.

Mason and Dade were Grayson's brothers. Both were experienced deputies, but covering the house would be next to impossible with the gunmen inside. Unless there was some way to get the captives out so the guards couldn't use them as human shields.

Jaycee made it to the door, and Josh looked out, checking for those guards. By now they'd heard the shots, so why weren't they running to the barn in order for Mason and Dade to pick them off?

"Go ahead," Grayson insisted. "Get them out of here. I'll cover you."

Josh nodded, reached into his ankle holster to retrieve his backup weapon so he could give it to Jaycee. But it wasn't there, of course. He hadn't carried a backup since he'd left the FBI.

Big mistake.

But then, he'd never thought that he would run into something like this in the middle of nowhere.

With Grayson behind them and Josh in the lead, he maneuvered them out of the barn and to the corner away from the house. He glanced around first to make sure they weren't about to be ambushed. No one in sight. However, that didn't mean someone wasn't there, hiding.

"Don't use any of their vehicles," Jaycee warned. "I've seen the guards rig them with explosives."

Great. The guards had no doubt done that so the women couldn't use them to escape, but that was exactly what Josh had had in mind. One of those vehicles would have been the fastest way to get them out of there. Now they had to hoof it a good quarter to a half mile away.

And each step could be a fatal one.

He refused to think about the pregnancy now. Refused to think about anything that didn't involve survival.

"More backup's on the way," Grayson added.

They'd need it. Josh would have liked to have stayed with the women until they arrived because it was a risk to be outside like this. But staying put was just as much of a hazard as moving.

With his gaze firing all around, Josh led them to the front of the barn. No guards. But he spotted Mason and Dade on the hill where Grayson and he had been earlier. It was a good vantage point if anyone came out of the house, but no one appeared to be doing that.

The other two women were crying now, their breaths making hiccupping sounds with the sobs. Unlike Jaycee. She wasn't crying, and if Josh hadn't noticed her bleached-out color and jerky movements, he would have thought this was routine for her. But she also had one of her hands on her stomach.

Protecting her unborn child.

No, this wasn't routine.

She was scared spitless. And so was Josh—scared that he wouldn't get them safely out of there. He'd already faced death and made peace with it and his maker, but there'd be no peace if any of the women and their babies were hurt.

He glanced around at the position of the cars. There was a road and a heavily treed area on the backside of the hill.

"Have you ever seen guards in the surrounding woods?" Josh asked Jaycee.

"No. But sometimes replacement guards come in from the pasture on all-terrain vehicles. It's not time for the shift change, and I don't know where the replacement guards stay when they aren't here."

Later, that would need to be investigated, but they were a heck of a long way from the *later* point. For now, he just watched and made sure one of those ATVs didn't come barreling up on them from behind.

"Stay close and let's move," Josh ordered.

They ran the ten yards to the first vehicle so they could use it for cover.

But not for long.

If the kidnappers had indeed rigged it with explosives, then they might have a remote detonator. Josh hurried them to the next vehicle, a truck. And then the third, the only one left that would give them any protection if the gunmen in the house started firing.

"Move fast and don't look back," Josh told them, and he did exactly that.

Grayson would keep watch behind them. Dade and Mason would do the same to the right side. Josh would need to cover anything else, and that included those woods ahead.

Lots of places for gunmen to hide in there.

One of the women stumbled, but Jaycee latched on to her and kept her moving without missing a step.

He hated that he had to put them through this—a blasted footrace. This kind of stress couldn't be good for the pregnancies. But then the women had no doubt been through hell and back while in captivity. There was plenty of stress associated with that.

When they maneuvered away from the truck, Josh took a deep breath before he moved out into the open. He picked up the pace, jogging now, and they made it to the side of the hill.

Before he heard the shot.

It hadn't come at them. But it had come from inside the house.

Hell.

He prayed that none of the hostages had been hurt. His cousins must have feared the same thing because the shot sent Mason and Dade scrambling down the hill. They ran toward the same vehicles that Josh and the others had just used for cover. He knew the deputies couldn't wait any longer for backup. They had to move in and hope for the best.

"Go help them," Jaycee said to Grayson.

Josh met his cousin's gaze. It was a split-second glance, and he gave Grayson the nod. According to what Jaycee had told him, there were four women inside, and they were in grave danger. Mason and Dade would need all the help they could get.

Grayson tossed Josh his truck keys. "If you don't see me in ten minutes, go ahead and get them out of here and back to town. More backup should be here soon."

Josh didn't waste a second. It wasn't easy jogging with two sobbing pregnant women, but Jaycee helped. She pushed them from behind while she kept watch around him. When they made it to the road near the wooded area, Josh shifted positions, putting himself closer to the trees.

"If something goes wrong, get them in the ditch," he told Jaycee. Even though it was filled with several inches of water from the spring rains, it would still act like a bunker against flying bullets.

Each step seemed to take an eternity, but Josh finally spotted Grayson's truck ahead. He'd parked it just off the road, partially hidden beneath some towering oaks.

They had to run some more.

That put his heart higher in his throat, and the blasted wound on his chest started to throb again. But there was no way he'd give in to the pain and let it slow him down. Josh took one of the women by the arm and practically dragged her along those last yards.

Once he reached the truck, he used the keypad to unlock it, and even though it'd be a tight fit, he threw open the door and pushed them inside and onto the floor of the truck. The women stayed there, still sobbing, still praying in Spanish.

But Jaycee didn't stay down. She immediately threw

open the glove compartment and pulled out a Colt .45 and some extra ammunition.

"Was that man your brother?" she asked, tipping her head toward the house.

"Cousin. His brothers were on the hill."

She rolled down the window and got the Colt ready in case she had to fire. "Please tell me they all know what they're doing."

Josh did the same with his own weapon. "They do."

Grayson might have been sheriff of a small town, but Josh knew that he and his brothers had dealt with plenty of trouble over the past couple years.

Unfortunately, this was trouble of a different kind.

They waited, their attention pinned to the road ahead, their breaths bursting in and out. Josh hadn't checked the time when Grayson had given him that ten-minute rule, but he knew the minutes were ticking away.

"I don't want to leave them here," Josh said, more to himself than to Jaycee.

"Agreed. We have to get those other women out." Her gaze met his, and he saw her bottom lip tremble. "I think they kill the birth mothers once they're finished with them."

Oh, man. That did *not* help. Because there was no way he could drive back to safety when others were in danger.

Except Jaycee and these women were in danger, too.

And so were their babies.

Even though he didn't want his thoughts to go there, Josh couldn't stop them this time. "Why didn't you tell me about the baby?"

"I would have, but I didn't get the chance. I was kidnapped immediately after the doctor confirmed that I was pregnant." She had such a fierce grip on the Colt that her knuckles were turning white. "Are you going to ask me if the baby's really yours?"

"Don't have to." Josh looked away from her and put his attention back where it belonged—watching the area for any sign of one of those guards. "The baby's mine. You have a lot of faults, but lying's not one of them."

Any response she might have had to that was cut off when they saw Mason. He was flat-out running, and he was carrying a woman with a huge pregnant belly.

"I don't know her name," Jaycee said, "but I'm pretty sure she's the one in labor."

Josh looked for any signs of injury or blood. Didn't see any. Thank God. He jumped out of the truck and hurried over to his cousin.

"Take her," Mason growled and dumped her into Josh's arms. He turned as if to run back and help his brothers, but his phone vibrated, and cursing, Mason yanked it from his pocket.

Josh heard the footsteps behind him and reeled around as best he could, but it was only Jaycee.

"Here, I can help," she said, and she eased the moaning woman from Josh's arms to a standing position. Jaycee looped her arm around her waist and got her moving to the truck.

Josh was about to head there, too, but Mason's profanity stopped him. It wasn't unusual for Mason to curse. He wasn't a very friendly sort, but this bout of profanity was worse than his norm.

"The guards have one of the captives at gunpoint in the yard," Mason explained. "Get these women out of here now in case shots are fired."

"We can help," Jaycee repeated.

Mason shook his head, turned and delivered the rest

from over his shoulder. "One of the gunmen escaped out back. He could be headed your way."

There wasn't much color in Jaycee's face, but those words rid her of what little she had. She hurried, dragging the woman toward the truck.

"Go with them now, Josh!" Mason insisted.

That and the pregnant woman's sounds of pain spurred Josh to move. Jaycee maneuvered her into the truck, and the others helped pull her onto the seat.

"I can ride in the back," Jaycee said.

"You'll do no such thing," Josh argued. "Get inside and stay down."

She did. Well, she got in anyway. But she didn't stay down. Jaycee aimed the Colt at the bend of the road where Mason had darted out of sight. It was probably the route a gunman would take if he was coming after them.

Josh started the engine, threw the truck into Reverse and had just put his foot on the accelerator when he heard the sound. Not a shot from a rifle. Not this.

No.

It was much louder, and it literally shook the ground beneath them.

Something had exploded.

Chapter Four

Jaycee felt the vibration of the blast and saw the fear and concern jolt through Josh. It went through her, too, and she wanted to go back and try to save the others.

But that could be dangerous for the women Josh and the others had already managed to rescue.

Plus, the woman stretched out across Marita, Blanca and Jaycee's laps was clearly in labor. She was moaning and clutching her stomach. Jaycee had never been around anyone in labor, but she figured the woman was close to delivering.

Josh glanced at the woman, then at Jaycee. The worry and questions were still etched on his face, and she had to wonder what this was doing to him. Agents suffering from posttraumatic stress didn't usually have an easy time in a gunfight.

Or the shock of something totally unexpected—like fatherhood.

But Josh had gotten a double dose of both today. Hopefully, he'd be able to keep it together. She hoped the same for herself, too. She didn't have the nerves of steel that Josh had once accused her of having.

He'd accused her of a lot of things.

And sadly, most were accurate.

"Hang on," Jaycee told the woman in labor when she

made another of those loud moans. "You're safe, and we'll be at the hospital soon."

Jaycee hoped that was true on both counts. Josh was certainly driving as fast as he could, and both of them were keeping watch for those guards. So far, no one was following them.

Including any of Josh's cousins.

She prayed they hadn't been hurt, or worse, in the explosion.

"What's your name?" Jaycee asked the woman in labor. She'd need to give it to the doctor, but talking might also distract her from the pain. If that was possible.

"Grace Levitt," she answered through a sharp breath.

"All right, Grace, just hang in there a few minutes longer." Jaycee tried to sound calm. Failed miserably. But after everything she'd been through, she wondered if she would ever be calm again. Normal seemed way too far out of reach.

Jaycee put her hand on Grace's stomach so she could feel the contractions and time them. Yet something else the doctors would want to know. And Jaycee felt a contraction almost immediately.

Grace clamped her hand on Jaycee's shoulder. Her bruising grip was paired with more moans. Louder this time. And she lifted her hips. Jaycee didn't have to tell Josh to hurry. He no doubt knew they might have to deliver this baby in the cramped space.

The contraction finally subsided. Jaycee didn't have a watch, so she had to use the clock on the truck's dashboard to keep time. Barely two minutes had passed before Grace had another contraction.

Josh's phone buzzed, the sound shooting through the truck, and he managed to fish it from his pocket despite the fact that Marita was squished against him.

"Grayson," Josh answered, sandwiching the phone against his ear and shoulder. There was still no relief in Josh's expression, but thankfully at least one of his cousins was alive.

Jaycee couldn't hear what Grayson was saying. Couldn't tell if the news was good or bad. She could only wait and keep watch. They were getting close to the town of Silver Creek now, but that didn't mean the guards couldn't catch up with them and start shooting.

Josh finished talking with his cousin, but instead of telling her what was going on, he made another call.

"I'm calling the hospital," he said to her, and he told whoever was on the other end of the line that he was en route with four pregnant women who needed medical attention.

Jaycee opened her mouth to say that she was fine, but she didn't know that for sure. She'd been held captive for months, and even though she'd gotten plenty of checkups during that time, she couldn't trust any doctor working for black-market baby brokers.

Josh finally finished the call with the hospital, put his phone away and took the turn toward town. Just as Grace had another contraction.

"The house blew up," Josh relayed to her. "My cousins are okay. They weren't hurt in the explosion."

"But?" Jaycee asked because there was definitely a bad-news tone in his voice.

Josh didn't jump to answer, but his jaw muscles were stirring like crazy. "The guards escaped with the other three women."

Jaycee groaned. It was better than hearing they'd been killed, but it was still a major setback. "All the women who were staying in the house are close to delivering.

Once they have their babies, the guards will probably kill the women."

For once she was glad Blanca and Marita didn't understand a lot of English, though both women had no doubt figured out what was going on. They'd all seen the guards leave with babies, but never once had they seen one of the new mothers walk out of the ranch house.

Jaycee suspected they were being carted out in body bags at night.

"Grayson and the others are looking for them," Josh added.

Though it was the only thing they could do, it didn't seem nearly enough. The women were very pregnant and were no doubt being forced to run and do other things that their bodies and babies might not be able to handle. The guards wouldn't care a flying fig if the escape led to the women's deaths. They only cared about getting their hands on the babies so they could be sold like cattle.

"After we get Grace to the hospital," Jaycee murmured, "I want to help find them."

Josh made a sound. Definitely one of disapproval. "Going off half-cocked hasn't worked well for you or others in the past, has it?"

That stung. Because it was true.

Jaycee choked back her own moan. Barely. And just like that, the memories came.

All bad.

The old mixed with the new from her captivity. Five months ago, she'd been conducting her own investigation into some money laundering and hadn't been aware the operation already involved several undercover agents. Jaycee had only wanted to catch the piece-of-slime launderer who'd killed two women who happened to stumble upon his operation.

Instead, Jaycee had endangered the agents.

Josh had been shot and had nearly died during surgery. There'd been no *nearly* for his partner, Agent Ben Sayers. He'd been killed.

Someday she might learn how to live with that.

Might.

But for now it was just more bad memories added to the new ones from being held captive. She hadn't been beaten, but only because it could have caused her to miscarry. However, she'd certainly been slapped a few times and threatened daily. And yet the slaps and the threats hadn't been the worst of it. The worst thing had been not knowing what the abuse would do to her baby.

Grace moaned again, causing Jaycee's attention to snap back to the woman. Another contraction, and this one seemed even harder and longer than the others.

"We're almost there," Jaycee told her.

No lie this time. The town of Silver Creek was just ahead, and next to the sign for the city limits was one for the hospital. Josh went in that direction, and it was less than a minute before he pulled into the E.R. parking lot where there was a team of medics waiting for them.

The moment Josh stopped the truck, Jaycee hurried out. Blanca and Marita, too, so the medics could get to Grace.

"There's less than a minute between her contractions," Jaycee told them, and they got Grace on a gurney and whisked her away.

Jaycee was about to follow them when she found herself being placed on a gurney, too. The medics did the same to Blanca and Marita and wheeled them through the hospital doors. Josh was right there, hurrying along behind them.

"The doctor will be with you soon," a nurse said, and she put Jaycee into one of the E.R. cubicles. The nurse paused and looked at Josh. “Stay with her until I can get someone in here.”

Josh nodded, though Jaycee was sure that staying with her was the last thing on earth he wanted to do. He no doubt wanted to check on his cousins or go after those escaped guards and missing women.

Anything that didn’t involve having close contact with her.

She heard Grace’s moans fading. Not because the woman had gotten quiet. But probably because she was being taken to Labor and Delivery and out of earshot. Jaycee hoped that she’d deliver a healthy baby and that she could soon put this nightmare behind her. Jaycee wished that for all the captives. Especially for those three who hadn’t been rescued.

Soon, very soon, the quiet closed in around them, and because the room was small, Josh had no choice but to look at her.

Correction: he looked at her pregnant belly.

She saw the questions in his eyes. The doubts. Not about the baby’s paternity. He was right about that—she wasn’t a liar. Even though she had considered it. Briefly. After all, she was the last woman on earth who Josh would want carrying his child, and for a fleeting moment she’d wondered if he might want her to lie.

“I really did intend to tell you about the baby,” she repeated, trying to answer some of those questions in his eyes. “I was worried that it’d cause you to blow a gasket or two, but I would have told you.”

He nodded.

That was his only reaction. He certainly didn’t deny that he would have been seriously upset to hear the news months ago. But then, Josh wasn’t a liar, either.

“When’s the baby due?” he finally asked.

"In four months."

Nine months after their weekend together in San Antonio. Their only weekend together. Yes, it'd been good.

Darn good.

But their last morning together, she'd seen that look in Josh's eyes and known he hadn't been looking for anything other than a short-term hookup. Old baggage, no doubt, since Josh had a love-'em-and-leave-'em reputation. So Jaycee hadn't given him an out and walked away.

Six hours later, he'd been shot.

And they'd learned about her rogue investigation that had collided with Josh's authorized one. If she had thought for one second that other agents were involved, she would have backed off. Of course, she hadn't asked a lot of questions when she'd gone after those money launderers and killers. Jaycee had only been thinking about justice.

Josh kept staring at her. Kept those questions in his eyes. She wasn't sure what he expected from her. Wasn't sure he'd tell her if he knew. But after all these months of being held captive, Jaycee had had time to figure out what she would say to him if she ever got the chance.

Well, now here was her chance.

"Look, I don't expect anything from you," Jaycee firmly stated. Giving him another out that he looked like he desperately needed. "I just wanted you to know because, well, because."

No reason to get into her old baggage. Or tell him that her own mother hadn't told her birth father that she was pregnant with Jaycee. Not until it'd been too late anyway. Jaycee had never had the chance to know her dad, and even though he was a less-than-stellar person, she'd sworn she would never do that to her child.

Even if the pregnancy was unplanned, like this one.

Josh's mouth tightened. His nostrils flared a bit. "It's my baby. Expect something."

That didn't sound like an offer of child support or shared custody.

It sounded like a threat.

And maybe it was.

Josh hated her. But she couldn't go back and undo this baby, and even if she could, she wouldn't. Though Josh might not believe her if she told him, she loved this baby with all her heart and would do anything to protect it.

"Expect something?" she repeated.

"Yeah," he snapped. And that was all he said for several moments. "Don't expect me just to walk away. I slept with you knowing there could be consequences, and I'm man enough to accept it."

She lifted her shoulder, ran her hand over her stomach. "But you probably didn't expect this consequence. We did use protection."

And clearly something had gone wrong. Jaycee had had a lot of time to think about every detail of that weekend, and while becoming pregnant had been the last thing on her mind, Josh was right. Sex, even safe sex, could make babies. And in this case, it had.

She waited to see if he intended to say more about consequences and expectations, but he didn't. He just kept staring at her and looking far better than he should have. His good looks weren't something he worked at. They were just there. And even now, she felt that little tug that she always felt when she looked at Josh.

Even when he was glaring at her.

"How are you?" she risked asking. Normally it was a polite, rote question, but this time, she truly wanted to know. And she figured he wouldn't want her to know.

"Fine," he snapped.

Translation: he was *not* going to talk about this. But she had five months of catching up to do.

She glanced at the badge clipped to his rawhide belt. "You left the FBI?"

"For a while." His jaw muscles went crazy again. "I'm on a leave of absence."

"Because you're recovering from the gunshot wounds," she finished for him.

He made a sound, a rumble deep in his throat. No doubt a back-off warning. But Jaycee didn't listen to that warning. "You're a deputy sheriff?"

He nodded.

Getting information from him was like pulling teeth. "Well, the job seems to suit you."

The clothes, too. She'd known about his cowboy roots but had usually seen him in a suit or his undercover outfits. Now he wore jeans, a black T-shirt and boots. He had his Stetson in his left hand as if he'd always carried it there.

"Something wrong?" he asked. Definitely not a friendly question. "You're looking at my clothes."

Actually, she'd been looking at the man in the clothes, but it was best to keep that to herself. "I want to thank you again. If you hadn't discovered where the baby farm was—"

"I didn't discover it." His words were clipped. Almost angry. But Jaycee got the feeling that this particular anger was aimed at himself and not at her. "I got lucky, that's all. But I didn't get lucky enough to save those other women that the guards took."

No. But maybe that'd be remedied soon if the sheriff could find something at the now-destroyed ranch. Yes, it was a long shot, but it was the only shot they had unless the woman in labor could give them some much-needed answers.

Before Jaycee had a chance to rile Josh further with more questions, a nurse came back in. According to her nametag, she was Lillian Renfrew. She took Jaycee's blood pressure and temperature—both were normal. That was a good start, and Jaycee hoped everything else proved to be normal.

"The doctor wants you to have an ultrasound," the nurse said, and she started to wheel Jaycee out of the cubicle. However, she stopped when Josh followed them. "You can wait outside."

"He's the baby's father," Jaycee volunteered when Josh didn't budge or say anything. "If he wants to come, I don't mind."

It was another risk, saying that out loud, but Josh kept the same expression that he'd had since they arrived at the hospital.

He was one angry, confused man.

"I want to see the ultrasound," he insisted, not like an argument but more a declaration of war.

Nurse Renfrew nodded and took them to a room in another hall. There was a tech waiting for them, a middle-aged woman with brunette hair, and she didn't waste any time hiking up Jaycee's scrub top all the way to her breasts. The scrub pants came down too, all the way to her panty line.

Even though Josh had seen her stark-naked, this seemed way more intimate.

"You don't expect anything from me?" Josh mumbled under his breath. And he repeated it, using that same "declaration of war" tone.

Oh, so that was what was still eating away at him. Jaycee tried to make eye contact with him, but the tech moved between them and squirted some cold goop all over Jaycee's stomach.

"I've heard you say plenty of times that you weren't looking for marriage or a family," Jaycee reminded him.

The tech finally went back to the other side of the gurney. Josh's and Jaycee's gazes met.

Collided, actually.

"I wasn't looking to be a father," he stated, enunciating each word as if she were mentally deficient, "but I'm not running from it, either. That's my baby, and he or she should expect everything from me. Because he or she will get just that—*everything.*"

He stopped, muttered some profanity. Rubbed his forehead. And got his teeth unclenched. "I'm glad you made it out of there." His voice was a lot softer than before.

"Yes. Thank you for saving me."

He nodded, and she hoped that meant they'd reached a tentative truce. No time to linger on it, though, because the tech started moving the wand over Jaycee's stomach. She immediately saw something.

Maybe the heart beating.

The images weren't very clear so Jaycee didn't know exactly what she was looking at, but it was her baby. And she hadn't expected that seeing all those blurry images would pack such a wallop.

"Is the baby okay?" Josh asked.

Jaycee was glad he had said that because her mouth was suddenly bone-dry, and her heart was pounding. She was terrified that this ordeal had been too much for her precious child.

"Everything appears to be okay. Good, solid heartbeat. Good movement." The tech stopped, volleyed glances at both of them, her attention finally stopping on Jaycee. "How much did your doctor tell you about the pregnancy?"

Oh, God. Just like that the fear returned. "Is something

wrong? I had other ultrasounds, but they kept the screen hidden from me. Did they do that because something's wrong with the baby?"

The woman shook her head. "I don't think anything's wrong." She glanced at the screen again. "But the doctor will need to see the images and talk to you." She paused, cleared her throat. "Some people just don't want to know the sex of the baby, and sometimes we can't tell. This time, we can."

The relief came as fast as the fear. Nothing was wrong.

"Do you want to know the sex of the baby?" the woman asked.

"No," Jaycee said at the same moment that Josh said, "Yes."

"I've just had too many surprises today," Jaycee added. "I'd like to hear it at a time when I'm not about ready to jump out of my skin. But you can tell him," she said to the tech. "I'll just cover my ears."

Jaycee did. Closed her eyes, too. And when she opened them, she couldn't detect a darn thing from Josh's expression.

"I'll show the ultrasound to the doctor," the tech said, turning off the machine. "Someone will be in shortly to take you back to the E.R."

The tech had hardly made it out the door when Josh's phone buzzed. Just like that Jaycee was reminded of the three missing women and the nightmare that wouldn't end until they were all safe.

Josh looked at the phone screen. "It's Grayson," he told her. And he clicked the speaker function.

"How are the women?" Grayson asked.

"One's in labor. The other three are being checked out now."

"Good. Stay there with them, and if they're feeling up

to it, get statements from them. I'm trying to get a CSI team out here ASAP."

Josh shook his head. "What's going on?"

"I'm not sure." Grayson paused a heartbeat. "But we found something."

Chapter Five

Something.

Yeah, it was that all right. Josh looked at the items that had been collected from the rubble of the house that had exploded.

A laptop.

Or rather, what was left of it.

Josh wasn't sure they could recover anything from it, but there was a tech from the crime lab already working on it.

There were also bits and pieces of paper. Several coffee mugs that would be processed for prints. Some shoes.

And a badge in its black leather case.

It was pretty beat up, as if someone had used it for a mini punching bag, but Josh had no trouble recognizing it as one issued to FBI agents.

Beside him, Jaycee pulled in her breath when she saw it. "Is the badge mine?"

Grayson nodded. "There's enough of the identification card for us to confirm it's yours."

"Oh, God," she murmured and sank down into the chair next to the desk. "I didn't have it on me when they took me. That means they got it from my apartment."

And more than that, it meant they knew who she was.

She looked up at Josh as if she expected him to have

some answers, but he didn't. The only thing that he was certain of was they would have indeed killed Jaycee once the baby was born. No way would they let an agent go free.

"But why steal my badge?" she asked, volleying glances at both Grayson and him.

"We're not sure." Grayson motioned to the laptop. "But we're hoping the info's recoverable. Plus, we've contacted your supervisor, Philip McCoy, to let him know what's going on, since he thought you were on a leave of absence this whole time."

"I did let him know I was taking some time off," Jaycee said. "I was trying to deal with what happened so I told him I wasn't sure when I'd be back to work—if ever," she added in a mumble.

"That's why he didn't push to find you," Grayson continued. "Now that he knows what happened, he'll check to make sure no one used your badge to get into the FBI building."

Where the person would have had access to all sorts of files and people. Of course, the San Antonio office where Jaycee was assigned wasn't that large, so someone would have noticed a stranger trying to use Jaycee's badge to gain entrance. If that had happened, it would have been a red flag for McCoy that something was wrong.

Grayson opened his mouth to add more, but his phone rang. It was the third call that had come through since Josh arrived with Jaycee ten minutes earlier.

Josh looked down at her. At her exhausted face. Her shoulders were slumped. There were dark circles under her eyes. She was biting her bottom lip. Every part of her body language told him she was tired and worried. Heaven knew what all this stress was also doing to the baby.

"I'll get you out of here soon," he let her know.

But that was another problem.

He'd learned on the drive over that Jaycee no longer had an apartment. Since she hadn't paid her rent, her things had been moved to storage and the place had been rented out to someone else. She had no family to speak of. And he wasn't sure how she would feel about going to a hotel with the armed guards still at large, especially since those guards knew her identity.

Heck, Josh wasn't sure how he felt about it. After all, if Jaycee was in danger, so was the baby.

His baby.

Those two words kept running through his head. It'd been just words until he saw the ultrasound, and then it had felt like an avalanche. For a few seconds. And then he'd felt a whole lot more. The love for a baby he hadn't even known he wanted until today.

The wound on his chest started to throb. A bad reminder of his past with Jaycee. He was a long way from forgiving her, but he wouldn't let the past stand in the way of giving their baby the best protection he could.

Grayson finished his call, and for the first time in hours, he looked a little relieved. "That was the hospital. The woman in labor just gave birth to a healthy baby girl. The other two women are fine, too. We're working on getting them all back with their families."

"Good," Jaycee said under her breath, and she repeated it. "But what about the three women and the guards? Any sign of them?"

"Nothing." The frustration returned to Grayson's expression. "But I need you to think. Did you see or hear anything that would give us a clue as to where they would have taken the women?"

"No." And she didn't hesitate, either. "Any time I would go in the house for a checkup, I'd try to look around. Try to figure out who these men were. I don't remember hearing or seeing anything. I'm so sorry," Jaycee added, and her voice cracked.

There was no telling how many nightmarish memories she had of her time as a captive. It sickened Josh to think of all those women and babies being in constant danger for months on end.

Grayson glanced at Jaycee's pregnant belly. Then at Josh. "I gather that you two were once…involved?"

Josh nodded. "The baby's mine."

"You think maybe that's why Jaycee was taken? Maybe so someone would have leverage over you? The baby of two FBI agents is plenty of leverage."

Yeah. It was.

Jaycee made a sound of agreement, too. "But if I was their initial target, they covered it well. I was kidnapped with another woman, and it certainly seemed as if they wanted just her. They only took me because I tried to fight back."

That didn't help the throbbing pain in Josh's chest, either. Of course, he couldn't have expected Jaycee to stand there and do nothing. He wouldn't have.

Grayson released a long, weary breath. "I can get Jaycee's statement tomorrow. Why don't you go ahead and take her to the ranch so she can get some rest?"

Jaycee's eyes widened. "The ranch? With your family?" She shook her head. "That's probably not a good idea."

"I have five brothers," Grayson explained to her. "All in law enforcement. The ranch is safe, or at least it is for now. My dad's a widower, and he's getting married this weekend. There'll be a lot of people in and out for the arrangements and for the ceremony itself. We'll need to add some security when that starts happening."

Grayson didn't mention those armed guards coming back for her, but they all knew it was a strong possibility.

Jaycee was a dangerous loose end, and whoever was running the black-market operation wouldn't want her around to give the cops any details about her captivity.

"Come on," Josh insisted, and he was thankful she didn't argue.

He did a thorough check of the parking lot and the street before he led her outside and to his truck. Josh didn't see anything suspicious, but he hurried anyway and got them on the road toward the ranch.

"I need to remember something," Jaycee murmured. "Anything that'll help us find those women."

Since she'd been held for nearly four months, there were a lot of memories and details to sort through. "Did you ever see the laptop that was recovered from the rubble?"

She stayed quiet a few moments. "Yes, on the kitchen table about two weeks ago. I can't be sure it was the same one, but I remember seeing one there."

Maybe that meant the laptop had been at the house long enough for it to contain something to blow this case wide open.

"What about the checkups you had?" he asked. "Did the same person do them each time?"

"Yes. Caucasian male, about six feet tall, 170 pounds, light brown hair. He always wore a surgical mask, but if he hasn't altered his hair, I think I could pick him out of a photo lineup."

It'd be a bear to sort through all the doctors in the state, but Josh made a mental note to ask the analysts at Quantico to work on it. They might get lucky.

"You know if the baby's a boy or girl," she said.

The out-of-the-blue comment threw him for a moment. But Josh just nodded. "Why? You want to know?"

She shook her head. Groaned softly. "This seems crazy, huh? Me pregnant with your baby."

Yeah, it did. Of course, when they'd made the baby, it was before the shooting, when they were still on good terms. They weren't on good terms now, but like the flashbacks he'd been having, Josh was going to have to put that aside, too.

"I'm scared of you," Jaycee went on. "Scared you'll try to fight me for custody or something."

Again, the comment threw him, and he wasn't sure it was a good thing to have that possibility out in the open like this. Especially since he had plenty of other things to work out in his head.

"I want to be part of the baby's life," he settled for saying. It was a safe response. And an honest one. He might want more than just a *part,* and while he didn't say that aloud, it seemed as if Jaycee picked up on it.

She swallowed hard. "And that's what scares me. You have a normal life. Good roots and a law-abiding family. I don't have any of that."

She didn't. Both her parents had served hard time for an assortment of crimes, and he'd heard that Jaycee had been brought up in foster care. His parents had divorced when he was a kid, and his mother had left, but it wasn't the same. So yeah, by her standards he did have a normal life.

Well, except he was suffering from PTSD and might never recover. That wouldn't look good on a custody challenge if that was what he decided to do.

He took the final turn to the ranch, and Jaycee got an immediate glimpse of his "normal" life. There were now six houses on the grounds, assorted barns, outbuildings and miles and miles of pasture for the horses and cattle raised on the ranch.

"Five of my cousins had houses built after they got married and started families of their own," he explained.

"My other cousin, Mason, lives in the main house with his wife and dad."

"The one who's getting married this weekend."

"That's right. Boone Ryland. He's marrying a former deputy, Melissa Garza. She retired recently, and that's how I got the job."

Jaycee made an idle *uh-huh* sound, but her attention wasn't on anything he'd pointed out, but rather the children in the fenced playground on the side of the main house.

"There's so many of them," she whispered. "It looks like a day care."

It did. "They're all kin. Last count, my cousins have nine offspring, and Mason and his wife have one on the way."

And at the moment it seemed that all nine were out playing while a few of their moms watched.

Josh slowed when he reached the playground. The moms all waved. One of the kids, Kimmie, who was four years old, saw him and blew him a kiss.

"The little red-haired girl seems to like you," Jaycee mumbled.

She did. Though Josh couldn't understand why. He'd never been comfortable around kids, and they seemed to be uncomfortable around him. All except for Kimmie. That gave him a little hope that his own child might feel the same way.

He drove past the playground to the back part of the east pasture to a weathered-looking barn and pulled to a stop in front of it.

"You live *here?*" Jaycee asked, sounding skeptical and surprised.

Another dose of his version of normal. "The top floor's been converted into an apartment. But if you like, I can get you a guest room in the main house."

She glanced back in the direction of the children and their moms. Then the barn. "Your place will be fine."

Josh bit back a smile. Barely. That'd been his reaction when he'd first returned home. "The kids grow on you," he confessed.

At least that's what he'd heard anyway.

He led her up the side stairs to the studio-style apartment. Even though the barn was isolated, it still had all the conveniences of a real house.

Jaycee paused in the doorway, her gaze moving over the room. But there wasn't much to see. Other than the bathroom, it was just one big open space, with the modest kitchen and sitting area on one side and his bed on the other. There were clothes scattered on the floor. Dishes in the sink. Just the way he'd left it when he'd gone to work earlier.

"You haven't been sleeping well," she commented. Jaycee tipped her head to the unmade bed. The covers were in a tangled heap. His prescription pain meds were on the nightstand.

"Sometimes," Josh settled for saying.

He went in, too, shutting the door behind them, and he tossed his keys onto the kitchen counter before he set the security alarm. A first for him since the ranch had always felt so safe, but nothing felt safe enough now.

"A security system in a barn?" she murmured.

"Yeah. Mason had it installed a few years ago after some intruders managed to get onto the grounds. Most of the buildings have security."

That put some renewed fear on her face.

"It's all right," he assured her. "It was nothing recent. Nothing to be concerned about."

But of course, they were both still concerned.

Jaycee inched across the room to the huge bay window

at the far end of the room. It was late afternoon, and the butter-colored sun hit her just right to spotlight her.

Josh felt that punch of heat.

A punch he definitely didn't want to feel but, like the other things going on in his head today, he couldn't seem to push this one aside.

"Should we try to clear the air?" Jaycee asked with her back to him.

"No." And he didn't have to think about it. No way did he want to discuss the shooting with her. Besides, they were well past the air-clearing stage.

She turned, met his gaze. "Then at least let me say I'm sorry."

He didn't want to hear it, but it would have been petty to blast her for an apology that he couldn't accept. Josh was still trying to figure out what to say when she crinkled her nose and slid her hand over her belly.

"Are you okay?" he quickly asked.

"It's just the baby kicking."

It didn't seem to be a painful experience, and she certainly didn't ask Josh to share it. Instead, she went to the bed and started fixing the covers.

"I think I'll take a nap, if you don't mind," she said.

"Don't mind at all." And he went to the bed to help her straighten the sheets. To say this was an awkward moment was a huge understatement. Beds and Jaycee were never a good idea, even when it was the only option they had.

Thankfully, he had an immediate distraction. His phone made a soft dinging sound to indicate he had a text. Josh pulled it from his pocket and saw Grayson's name on the screen.

This probably wasn't good news. And it wasn't short and sweet, either. It had an attachment. Grayson started by saying the reason he didn't call was because he hadn't wanted to wake Jaycee in case she was sleeping.

But there was a lot more than that in the message.

"You know the name Bryson Hillard?" Josh asked, reading through it.

Jaycee repeated the name, shook her head. "Never heard of him. Why?"

"The tech found his name on the laptop they recovered from the house."

Another headshake. "Who is he?"

"A wealthy San Antonio businessman. No criminal record. Grayson plans to bring him in for questioning first thing in the morning."

"I want to be there," she insisted.

Josh didn't try to talk her out of it. Heck, he wanted to be there, too. Because this was personal now. The idiot responsible had put his unborn child and countless others in danger, and if this Bryson Hillard had anything to do with it, Josh wanted to know. And *confront* him.

He scrolled through the rest of the email, and the reading came to a jarring halt when he saw the last sentence.

Hell.

He repeated the mental profanity when he opened the attachment.

"Once I take a nap," Jaycee said, obviously not noticing his change of expression, "I'll make some calls and find another place to stay."

Josh finished reading the message before he went to the window and closed the blinds.

When he turned around, Jaycee was waiting, her mouth slightly open, and she had a white-knuckle grip on the bed post. "What's wrong? What happened?"

Josh debated how much he should tell her and decided she had to know the truth. "You can't leave," Josh told her.

"You'll have to stay here for the night, because those missing guards are looking for you. They left you a message nailed to the door of your old apartment."

He walked closer and held up his phone for her to see the message that one of the deputies had photographed.

Jaycee's gaze darted over the words, and she pressed her trembling fingers to her mouth. "Oh, God."

Chapter Six

The images kept coming at Jaycee in the nightmare. Images of the explosion. Of their escape and the armed guards.

Especially of the women who hadn't been lucky enough to get away.

When she could take no more of those brutal images, Jaycee forced herself to wake up, and she jackknifed to a sitting position.

And nearly smacked right into Josh.

He wasn't in the sleeping bag on the floor, which was the last place she'd seen him before she dozed off. He was there right next to the bed, leaning over her. His hands were lifted as if he were about to give her a hug. But the look in his eyes was pure concern.

"I was about to wake you," he said. "You were having a bad dream."

Yes, and it'd been a doozy, no doubt spurred on by the message the guards had nailed to the apartment door. Just two little sentences, but it was the stuff of nightmares and a serious guilt trip.

Agent Finney, you sealed those women's fates when you escaped. Thanks to you, they'll all soon be dead.

It shouldn't have surprised her that the kidnappers had addressed her as Agent Finney. She'd already learned that they knew who she was. It was the other part of the message that had caused the tightness in her chest. And the nightmares.

Thanks to you, they'll all soon be dead.

She had no doubt that these men would kill in retaliation, but she prayed they wouldn't harm the women until they'd delivered their babies. That would give Josh and her some time to find and rescue them.

"Any sign of the men or the hostages?" she asked, and Jaycee held her breath, waiting for Josh's answer. She didn't dare ask if any bodies had been found, because she wasn't sure she could take the answer.

"None." Josh put down his hands but didn't move off the bed. He stayed right there, looming over her.

And he was naked.

Jaycee did a double take.

Okay, not naked. Just shirtless.

She had a good view of not just those toned abs and pecs but also the scar. It was several inches long and slashed across his otherwise perfect body. Even though it was well healed, she figured the ashy white line would never go away.

The memory of it certainly wouldn't.

"Sorry," he mumbled, following her gaze. "I was changing when I heard you call out my name."

She had? Jaycee didn't remember saying his name, but Josh had certainly been in the nightmare. This time, instead of getting her and the three other women to the truck, he'd been lying in a pool of blood.

Yes, definitely a nightmare.

She didn't want to be the reason that he took another bullet, but it had come too close to happening yesterday.

Too bad she couldn't distance him from all of this, but she knew what his response would be if she even tried.

No way.

And she couldn't blame him. If their situations had been reversed, she would have wanted to keep him close, too. To protect him from those note-leaving guards who seemed to enjoy tormenting them.

"You're sure you're okay?" he asked, examining her eyes, then her face.

His attention dropped lower, and that was when she realized the bulky T-shirt that he'd lent her had fallen off her shoulder to expose a lot of her left breast. And there was a lot more to her breasts these days, since the pregnancy had made them fuller.

Jaycee quickly fixed the shirt situation, and it was her turn to mumble that she was sorry. Not that Josh would have found her attractive anyway, what with her pregnant belly just beneath those fuller breasts.

But she immediately rethought that.

There was indeed some heat in his cool blue eyes. Of course, there'd always been heat between them. That wasn't their problem. Their problem was the scar on his chest, and since she was responsible for that, it would always stand between them.

"Yeah," he muttered as if he knew exactly what she was thinking. And he got up, went to the kitchen area and poured himself some coffee.

"Does it still hurt?" Jaycee asked. "The scar," she clarified when he gave her a puzzled look.

"Sometimes. There was some muscle damage." And with that tiny bit of info, he turned away. Everything in his body language indicated that the subject was off-limits.

Jaycee huffed, looked at the alarm clock on the nightstand. It was 7:00 a.m.

Good grief. Where had the time gone?

She'd fallen asleep shortly after eight, which meant she'd really racked up some serious snoozing time. Of course, this was the first morning in months that she hadn't woken up as a captive.

Well, a real captive.

She certainly wasn't a free woman, not as long as those men were at large. She'd essentially have to stay in hiding until they were caught. Or do something to catch them herself. Jaycee was leaning toward the latter, but she wasn't sure how to go about that.

"I talked to your supervisor a little while ago," Josh went on. "He officially put you on a leave of absence so we'd have time to sort this out. The FBI will assist with the investigation any way they can."

"That's good." After the danger was over, she'd have a job waiting for her. One less thing to worry about.

"Grayson's wife brought over some clothes and toiletries earlier," Josh said, tipping his head to a small suitcase next to the door.

Jaycee hadn't heard their visitor or Josh up and moving around, and that unnerved her. She had to be more vigilant. Had to do more to keep herself safe.

Starting with finding another place to stay.

She'd need to make some calls once she had washed up and changed. And Jaycee didn't want to think about how Josh would react to her decision. Of course, he might be a little relieved. Having her under the same roof couldn't be any easier for him than it was for her.

She got up, took the suitcase with the clothes and headed to the bathroom to shower and change into a loose yellow cotton maternity dress. In fact, all the clothes were maternity, but that shouldn't have surprised her, either. Not with all the children she'd seen running around the ranch.

Josh was on the house phone when she came out of the bathroom. He quickly ended the call, but he'd no sooner done that when his cell rang. The sound shot through the room and caused her to gasp.

Get a grip.

She wasn't the gasping type, and what she needed to settle her nerves was her gun and her badge. A little bit of normalcy might go a long way toward helping her get through the rest of this day.

"It's Grayson," Josh said, and he hit the speaker function on his phone. "Please tell me you have good news," he said to his cousin.

"Some. Two of the women, Marita and Blanca, will be headed back home today. They're sisters, and they said their family is very poor, and their father basically sold them to a man who said he wanted them to work as maids. Instead, he took them to the baby farm where they were inseminated."

Josh's grip tightened on his coffee cup. His mouth tightened, too. "Do the women know the fathers of their babies?"

"No. But they agreed to have an amniocentesis. That's a procedure to test the amniotic fluid, and it'll give us the DNA of the father. Or fathers, whatever the case might be. If he's in the system, we could get a match."

It was another long shot, but better than nothing. Besides, someone who would force women into surrogacy probably did have a police record.

"The other woman will be able to leave the hospital tomorrow," Grayson went on. "Her ex fathered her child, so no need to do DNA tests. She was hiding from the guy. Had a restraining order on him, but he kept finding her and assaulting her. So she moved to San Antonio and was living under an alias when she was kidnapped and taken to the baby farm."

"She won't be going back to the ex, will she?" Jaycee asked.

"No. We're relocating her to a different city."

Good. If she'd been through anything like Jaycee had, then being rescued shouldn't take her from the frying pan and into the fire.

"So she and the baby are okay?" Josh asked.

"Fine. The woman didn't have a scratch on her."

Somewhat of a miracle considering their escape, and it was a dose of good news that Jaycee needed. However, she could hear a "bad news" hesitation in Grayson's voice.

"Did the men leave me another message?" she came out and asked.

"Not that we've found." He paused. "But we did find something else. The tech was able to recover some of the data on the laptop's hard drive. A lot more than just Bryson Hillard's name. It appears there are more baby farms. Maybe dozens of them scattered throughout the state."

Oh, mercy.

It sickened her to think of all those women and their babies in danger.

"According to some emails on the hard drive," Grayson continued, "the people behind this kidnapped pregnant women who wouldn't be immediately missed. Homeless women, runaway teens or those without families."

Like her.

Judging from what Jaycee had found out the night before, her supervisor had simply thought that she'd gone off the deep end because of Josh's shooting and had taken a long leave of absence. She had gone off the deep end. But that hadn't been the reason for her disappearance.

"How many women are we talking about?" Josh asked.

"Dozens at least. Not all came from Texas. Some were illegal immigrants or those on the run from the law, and some appear to have been forced into becoming surrogates like Marita and Blanca."

Josh muttered some profanity. "And there were no missing persons reports filed on any of these women?"

"A few, but not enough for any law enforcement agency to connect the dots."

Jaycee huffed, but she knew that unless there was a pattern, the FBI wouldn't have picked up on it. "What about the people paying for the babies? Any info about them on the hard drive?"

Grayson made a sound of frustration. "They're all listed by case numbers with no personal details. We can try to match the numbers with adoptions filed during that time, but I'm betting the people who paid for these babies didn't file papers."

Jaycee was betting the same thing. She took a deep breath before she asked the next question. "Were the birth mothers murdered?"

"Don't know yet. We don't have identities on the women. Well, with the exception of you and the ones who were rescued yesterday."

She immediately thought of something. "What about the woman who was kidnapped the same time as me? She was at the Hawthorne Medical Center in San Antonio, so there should be a record of her name on the appointment schedule."

"I'll check and see what I can find," Grayson assured her. "But since these people stole your badge, it's possible you were their primary target all along."

That sent a chill right through her. Heaven knows what these monsters had planned to do with her baby. And with her. But she figured they hadn't had anything good in mind. Maybe they'd wanted to use the baby to force her into doing something illegal.

Maybe Josh, too.

Her baby could have become the ultimate bargaining tool, since there were a lot of things that two FBI agents could cover up or overlook in criminal investigations.

"We'll keep digging," Grayson added, and he ended the call.

Jaycee didn't even try to hide her frustration. "That wasn't the way I'd wanted to start the morning," she mumbled.

"No," Josh quietly agreed. "But at least we have a possible lead. If we get a DNA match from Blanca's and Marita's babies, then we can interrogate the birth father. Or fathers. They could help us find the person who honchoed this mess."

Yes, it was a good lead, but it didn't seem nearly enough considering all the lives that were at stake.

"Coffee?" he asked, raising his cup.

Jaycee shook her head because the smell made her a little queasy. "But I wouldn't say no to some toast or milk. Or a doughnut." She wasn't hungry, but she should eat something for the sake of the baby.

His left eyebrow lifted. "A doughnut?"

"Yeah, I've been craving them in between the bouts of morning sickness."

But her suddenly jittery stomach wasn't a result of morning sickness. Probably more nerves than anything else. After all, Grayson had just told them some disturbing things.

Plus there was Josh.

Yet something else disturbing in a totally different way. She was in a very confined space with a shirtless man whom she'd always found attractive. His jeans didn't help, either.

They were snug in all the right places.

And despite the fact that she was five months' pregnant and coming down from a horrible ordeal, she felt the heat trickle through her.

Their gazes met.

Held.

And Josh gave a heavy sigh before he turned around and put two pieces of bread in the toaster. He also crossed the room, grabbed a shirt from the closet and put it on. It still didn't help. Jaycee had a much too vivid memory of how he looked without it.

"Sorry, no doughnuts," he said. "If it'd make you more comfortable, I repeat my offer—you can move to one of the guest rooms in the main house."

"With all those people? No thanks. I can call some friends." If she still had any, that is.

Josh stared at her. "FBI friends?"

Jaycee shrugged. Actually, she didn't have a lot of friends in the FBI because she often worked alone and undercover for long stretches. That didn't give her a lot of socializing time. Ironically, before the shooting, Josh had been her closest friend, and she doubted he'd now classify her as such.

"Look, you've already done so much," she said, "and I don't want to keep imposing on you."

"It's not an imposition." His gaze dropped to her stomach. "And I'd rather be the one protecting you."

A burst of air left her mouth. Not quite a laugh. "I'm a trained agent just like you. The kidnappers took my gun, but if you give me another one, I'll be pretty good at protecting myself."

Oh, no. He got that mule-headed look. The one that let her know he wasn't going to back down on this.

"You're a *pregnant* trained agent." Even though the toast popped up, Josh ignored it and walked closer to her. "I know this isn't what you want to hear, but that baby changes everything."

Jaycee wanted to be mule headed, too. Mercy, did she want that. But he was right. The pregnancy did change things. She'd fought her way out of plenty of bad situations, but fighting wasn't much of an option now because it'd put the baby at risk.

"No one will protect you like I will," Josh added, and he jammed his thumb against his chest.

The moment seemed to freeze, and she thought he was about to move toward her. To pull her into his arms. Jaycee wasn't stupid and knew it wouldn't be for a steamy kiss that her body seemed to want.

Bad.

But Josh looked to be on the verge of giving her something else she needed. A good old-fashioned hug.

It didn't happen, though, because his phone rang again, and the moment was gone. He drew in a hard breath and stabbed the button to put the call on speaker.

"Josh," she heard Grayson say. "I think Jaycee and you should get down here to the sheriff's office right away. Our suspect, Bryson Hillard, just walked in. He's got a lawyer with him, and he says he'll talk if he can speak to one of the former hostages."

In other words, *her.*

Jaycee pulled her breath. Waited.

It didn't take long for Grayson to continue. "Bryson says he knows who's running the baby farms."

Chapter Seven

"You recognize either of them?" Grayson asked Josh and Jaycee.

Josh looked through the one-way mirror and into the interview room of the Silver Creek sheriff's office where Bryson Hillard and his attorney, Valerie DeSilva, were seated. Both appeared to be in their mid-forties. Both wore nondescript business clothes. Bryson had salt-and-pepper hair, conservative but expensively cut. Nothing much conservative about Valerie's hair. It was flame red, short and choppy—the style of a much younger woman.

"Never seen them before," Josh answered.

Jaycee shook her head and echoed the same, her attention returning to the background report on the two that Grayson had given them when they'd first arrived at the sheriff's office. They were all anxious to hear whatever information Bryson had, but Josh knew that Grayson needed to be armed with info so he could convince the man to talk without Jaycee's help.

Just in case this was some kind of ruse to get to her.

Josh certainly couldn't rule it out, especially since the guards knew who she was and also knew that she was in protective custody in Silver Creek. They'd left that threatening note, and if they'd been that brassy, Josh figured they wouldn't hesitate to send someone right into the sheriff's office so they could launch another kidnapping attempt.

There was just one problem with that theory.

Neither Bryson nor Valerie looked capable of kidnapping unless they had help, and lots of it. Of course, those three missing guards would be plenty of help, and if he was looking at the faces of the people in charge of the baby farms, Bryson and Valerie could have those guards waiting nearby.

Josh was in such deep thought and way too much on edge that he nearly reached for his gun when he spotted the movement out of the corner of his eye. But it wasn't a threat. It was one of the other deputies. She had a cup of coffee in one hand and was balancing a large box of doughnuts in the other.

"I'm Bree," she said to Jaycee, and she slid the doughnut box on the table. "Married to Grayson's youngest brother, Kade."

Jaycee nodded. "I know the name. He's an FBI agent."

Josh couldn't help but notice that while Jaycee sounded polite, she was eyeing that box.

"Want some?" Bree asked, obviously noticing, too. "Josh sent me a text asking me to pick up a dozen."

"Thanks, both of you." And the moment Bree stepped away, Jaycee grabbed one of the doughnuts and took a huge bite. "Mercy," she mumbled. "That's really good."

And she made a sound of pleasure that had both Grayson and Josh looking at her.

"I'll eat something healthier later," she added.

That wasn't his concern. It was the dab of sugar at the corner of her mouth. Without thinking, Josh reached out, wiped it away and then licked the sugar off his thumb.

He should have given that some thought.

Because even though it'd been an innocent gesture, it sure didn't seem like it.

"All right," Grayson said, rubbing the back of his neck. "I'm going in there to see if he'll spill something. So far, no luck. He keeps insisting that he wants to talk to one of the former hostages."

Grayson left, and Josh continued to read the backgrounds while trying to forget about the sugar-licking episode. Jaycee had a look, too, and continued eating.

"Bryson owns a successful investment company," she pointed out. "Plenty of money to put a baby farm operation together."

Josh tapped Valerie's page. "Ditto for her. She's a prominent attorney. Once served on the city council."

Hardly the profile of someone who would be involved with black-market babies. Still, he'd seen stranger things. And Valerie definitely had the cash to front such a business.

Josh looked up from the pages to see Grayson walking into the interview room. "I'm sorry, but I can't get one of the former hostages here," Grayson explained, sounding very believable.

But Bryson glanced in the mirror. Scowled.

"I doubt that," Bryson grumbled. "You appear to be a resourceful man, but obviously you haven't understood me. I'll only talk to one of the hostages. I need answers to some questions before I'll tell you what I know."

Jaycee huffed. "He's not buying it." She turned to leave. No doubt to go in to the interview room.

Josh caught her arm to stop her. Dropped his gaze to her stomach. "There's a reason you're craving doughnuts, and it's the same reason you should stay put."

She huffed again and turned around to face him. "Look,

we both know I have to do this," she argued. She crammed the rest of the doughnut in her mouth, licked her fingers.

And his body tightened.

Hell. Not now.

What the heck was wrong with him? He was acting like a teenager.

"Are you listening to me?" Jaycee asked.

"Not really."

That answer got her huffing again, but it was the honest truth. He wasn't listening in part because his body was acting crazy, but another part was because he knew what Jaycee was going to say, and he was pretty sure that he wasn't going to like it.

Her hands went on her hips, and the breath she blew out carried her scent. Or rather the sugary sweet scent, thanks to her doughnutfest.

"Both Grayson and you will be in there with me," she argued. "Besides, they were checked for weapons, right?"

They had been. That didn't mean this couldn't get ugly. Jaycee had already been through way too much, and he hated putting her through more. And an interrogation would definitely qualify as *more*.

She lifted his chin. Made eye contact with him. "This could save those women's lives. Heck, it could save *our* lives. Because if we manage to close down the baby farms and arrest those guards, then the danger will be over."

Josh had known this was a battle he was going to lose from the moment he started it, but he'd had to try. A lot was at stake here, and he just wanted to make sure he was thinking straight. He still wasn't certain he was, but he didn't see a lot of options here. They needed Bryson to talk, and he clearly wouldn't start doing that until he laid eyes on Jaycee.

Josh had to make certain that was the only thing Bryson laid on her.

"Don't make me regret this," Josh mumbled.

The relief on her face was instant. Followed by a quick smile. In midsmile she dropped a kiss on his mouth.

Then froze.

"Sorry," Jaycee immediately said. And she winced. "I just got caught up in the moment because I've never won an argument with you. Or maybe it's the sugar high from the doughnut."

Yeah, Josh knew a little about being sorry. The kiss had been hardly more than a peck, but he'd felt it, all right. It must have made him even more stupid, because he started to think about what it would be like to kiss her for real.

Not a peck.

A real kiss.

Even if the past had been settled between them—and it wasn't—he darn sure shouldn't be kissing someone in his protective custody. It was the fastest way to get them both killed.

"Sorry," Josh repeated, and he pulled way back from her. "We've been saying that a lot to each other."

She nodded, and he caught another whiff of her sweet breath when she murmured an agreement. "I think the 'I'm sorrys' are just getting started, though."

He wasn't stupid. Not about this anyway. He figured that applied to many things. The attraction. Her pigheaded views of how to run an investigation. Her views, period. Jaycee and he always seemed to be butting heads, and he was making it worse with this stupid ache he had for her.

Though he hadn't gone through with the kiss, Jaycee must have sensed what he'd been thinking of doing.

"Yeah." She pressed her lips together a moment, and

even though the simple gesture wasn't meant to tease, it made his body tighten again.

And beg.

"It's all right," she added. "I know this attraction doesn't mean anything."

It didn't.

Well, nothing other than he was playing with fire and losing focus. Something that always seemed to happen when he was around Jaycee.

He quickly got that focus back. Josh fired off a text to Grayson to let him know they were about to come in the interview room. Just in case Grayson had any objection. But his cousin only gave a weary nod. Grayson clearly wasn't making any headway with Bryson.

Hoping this wasn't as big a mistake as he figured it was, Josh stayed ahead of Jaycee when they went into the room, but Bryson looked right past Josh. The man barely gave him a glance and then turned to stare at Jaycee.

"I need your help," Bryson said to her, and he slipped his hand inside his jacket, causing both Grayson and Josh to reach for their guns.

Bryson's hand froze for a moment. "It's just a picture," he explained. But Josh and Grayson kept their hands on their guns until Bryson did indeed pull a photograph from his pocket. He held it up for them to see.

"Do you recognize her?" Bryson asked, his attention back on Jaycee. "Was she one of the women being held captive with you at the baby farm?"

Now, that was a question Josh hadn't seen coming. He looked at the photo.

Grayson and Jaycee did, too.

It was a glammed-up shot of a woman in her early thirties, with dark auburn hair that tumbled onto her shoulders. She was wearing a flimsy negligee and a come-hither expression. It was the kind of photo that a woman gave to her lover.

"I don't think she was there," Jaycee said. "Who is she?"

"Sierra DeSilva," Valerie supplied. "My sister."

"She's missing?" Grayson asked.

Valerie lifted her shoulder, and her forehead bunched up. "She could be. Sierra isn't the most responsible person. She often disappears for months at a time. Usually when she has a rich boyfriend who'll cater to her whims." She made a sound of disgust. "And after she's run through all his money, she comes to me looking for more. But this time, she hasn't come back."

Josh intended to do a background check on this Sierra, but first he wanted more information. "Sierra's pregnant?"

"Yes," Bryson and Valerie said in unison. "She should be just about ready to deliver," Bryson added. "And it's my child she's carrying."

"You can't be sure of that," Valerie mumbled.

"I can be," Bryson fired back. That wasn't an affectionate look he was giving Valerie. Or even a civil one. Odd since this woman was his attorney. "I had Sierra take an amnio, and the test proved the child was mine."

"If she didn't have the results faked." Valerie huffed. "You were only with her for a few months. You don't know how manipulative Sierra can be."

Bryson's face reddened, but he didn't challenge that. So maybe Sierra was running some kind of scam and this had nothing to do with the illegal adoptions or baby farms.

Jaycee had another look at the photo. "I remember the faces of the dozen or so women I saw come and go while I was there. But Sierra's face isn't familiar. What makes you think she was one of the captives?"

"This." Bryson reached into his pocket again, but this

time he took out a piece of paper. He put it on the table next to the photo. "It's a ransom demand."

That got Josh's complete attention. To the best of his knowledge, there'd been no demands for any of the other pregnant captives.

None of them touched the letter, but Grayson, Jaycee and Josh leaned closer to have a better look. It was a typed single page, and it had Bryson's name at the top.

"'If you want to see your newborn baby,'" Josh read aloud, "'it'll cost you two hundred grand. Will be in touch tonight with the drop-off details. Don't go to the cops or the deal's off.'"

"I found it on my car windshield yesterday morning," Bryson explained, "but no one's contacted me yet."

Maybe because the operation had been busted the day before when Jaycee and the others had gotten out.

"Is it possible that Sierra was one of the women in the house?" Josh asked Jaycee.

She continued to study the picture. "Maybe. If so, she changed her hair color. All three women in the house were brunettes." Jaycee drew in a weary breath. "But honestly, I didn't get a good look at their faces. The only times that I was in the house were for my weekly checkups, and they didn't let me talk to the other women."

Valerie stood, shoving back the chair so fast that it made a shrill scraping noise on the floor. "I can't sit here and pretend that Sierra's a victim. Because she'd *never* be a victim."

Clearly, Valerie didn't have a high opinion of her sister. Josh needed to run that check on both women ASAP, because something about this didn't feel right.

"You think Sierra's behind the ransom demand?" Grayson asked.

"I do," Valerie said at the same moment Bryson said, "I'm not so sure."

"Bryson's not sure because he wants that to be his child," Valerie snapped. "Because he wants an heir." She pointed at Bryson. "Tell them what Sierra pulled when you broke things off with her. *Tell them,*" she repeated when he didn't answer right away.

Bryson twisted the button on his shirt cuff before he answered. "Sierra and I used to, well, record ourselves when we had sex. She said it was a turn-on. Anyway, after I broke things off with her, she threatened to release the sex tapes if I didn't pay her fifty thousand dollars."

This woman sounded like a real winner. "You paid her?" Josh asked.

"No. I hired someone to break into her place and steal the recordings." His expression turned into a cold glare. "And I'm not apologizing for it, either. My reputation would have been ruined if she'd released them."

"Bryson's married," Valerie supplied. "In name only, but he's married to Elise Wells."

Josh had known the name before he'd ever read Bryson's bio. Bryson's estranged wife wasn't just rich, Elise had powerful friends. Politicians and community business leaders. And yeah, she wouldn't have wanted her husband's sex tapes leaked.

"Any chance your wife had anything to do with the ransom demand?" Grayson wanted to know. "It could be her way of getting back at you."

"Elise isn't involved in this," Bryson said without hesitation.

"But maybe Sierra is," Valerie said the moment Bryson finished. She looked Grayson right in the eyes. "It's possible Sierra's the one who was in charge of that baby farm."

Jaycee and Josh exchanged glances. "Any proof of that?" Josh pressed.

"Only her past behavior. I figure Sierra was plenty angry when she didn't get the blackmail money from Bryson. That's about the time she drained the rest of her trust fund, and I think she did it to set up this operation."

Josh looked at Bryson to see what he thought of this, but the man certainly didn't deny it.

"Find Sierra and the baby," Bryson said, standing. "If she's guilty, put her in jail, but the child is mine."

Grayson stepped in front of the man before he could leave. "If you get another ransom demand, I want to know about it."

Bryson stared at him, the muscles stirring in his jaw, and he finally nodded. "Just don't do anything to endanger that baby."

Bryson left both the photo and the ransom demand on the table and walked out. Valerie started after him, but then stopped right in front of Jaycee.

"If Sierra contacts you for any reason, don't believe a word she says." And with that not-so-sisterly warning, Valerie left, too.

"I'll bag the ransom letter," Grayson said the moment she was gone. "Doubt we'll get anything from it, though, since it was in Bryson's pocket."

Josh agreed, but it was still something that should be done. Grayson left to get the evidence bag, but Jaycee and he stayed put, staring at the photo.

"This baby seems awfully important to Bryson," she commented.

Yeah, and Bryson hadn't talked about his love for the child, so maybe something else was going on. Josh fired off a text to his cousin, FBI agent Kade Ryland, and asked him to do some digging into Bryson's background and marriage.

"So Bryson could be a suspect," Jaycee concluded. "What exactly was there about him in the laptop recovered from the baby farm?"

"No mention of a ransom demand or a connection to a possible captive, that's for sure. It appeared to be some kind of payment to Bryson."

"Payment *to* him?" she questioned.

"Or it could be a falsified payment to make him look guilty. Grayson didn't want to bring it up yet until we know exactly what it is. We didn't want to give Bryson time to come up with some kind of explanation before we spring it on him. If he lies, then we'll have cause to arrest him."

She made a sound to indicate she was giving that some thought. "Any way to match it to money deposited into his account?"

"Accounts," Josh corrected. "The man has dozens of them. We got the court order to look at them, but it's going to take a while to go through all of them."

And that was time that Josh didn't want to spend with Jaycee standing around the sheriff's office. Yes, they had three lawmen in the place, but he preferred her at the ranch where someone couldn't just come walking in the door.

Like those three guards who'd escaped.

Josh motioned for her to follow him down the hall and toward the back exit where he'd parked. "I need to apologize," he said, keeping his voice low so they wouldn't be overheard.

She didn't ask the reason for the latest apology, which meant she knew he was talking about that near kiss. Jaycee only nodded. "Our bodies are having a hard time remembering we're enemies."

Not good. One of them should be sane about this. And

besides, they weren't enemies. He was just having a hard time forgiving her.

The baby was helping with that.

Hard to be angry at the woman carrying his child.

"Call me if you find out anything," Josh told Grayson, and Jaycee and he headed out.

As he'd done on the trip in, Josh checked the parking lot and Main Street to see if there was anyone or anything suspicious, but it looked like a normal weekday in Silver Creek. Still, he hurried to get Jaycee into the truck, and then drove away. However, he'd gone less than a half mile when his phone rang.

It was Grayson. And that meant something big had probably come up for him to call so soon. Even though it could be something neither of them wanted to hear, he decided to put the call on speaker.

"I just talked to Nate," Grayson said the moment Josh answered.

"That's Grayson's brother," Josh explained to Jaycee. "Nate's a lieutenant with the San Antonio P.D."

"Yeah. And he had some info on Bryson," Grayson continued. "Get this—talk around town is that Bryson needs an heir to collect the rest of his family fortune, and his wife is infertile."

"Well, that explains why Bryson wanted the baby." Josh shook his head. "But it doesn't explain his relationship with Sierra. Certainly, someone with his bank accounts could have found someone more reliable to give birth to his child."

"You'd think," Grayson agreed. "Nate's checking into the possibility that Bryson hired Sierra as a surrogate. Maybe one connected to the black-market baby operation."

"And that's why Bryson's name would have been in the

laptop," Jaycee concluded. "However, it doesn't explain why someone at the baby farm would be paying Bryson."

Josh was about to agree, but something caught his attention. A dark blue van. He'd noticed it and four other vehicles trickling by on Main Street when he'd pulled out of the parking lot.

Now it was two cars behind him.

"Is something wrong?" Jaycee said, obviously noticing his glances in the rearview mirror. She turned in the seat to look, too.

"It's probably nothing." Josh took the turn toward the ranch. The car immediately behind him went straight, but the van turned.

So maybe it was really something.

"I need you to run a license plate." And Josh relayed the numbers to Grayson.

Waited.

He tried to give Jaycee a reassuring look, but was certain he failed. After everything she'd been through, he doubted a mere look was going to reassure her of anything anyway. Her breathing had already kicked up, and the pulse was jumping on her throat.

"Where are you?" Grayson said several moments later.

"Just outside of town, about ten miles from the ranch. Why?"

"I'm sending someone your way now, and I'll alert everyone at the ranch." Grayson's words were rushed together. "Because the license plate is fake."

Chapter Eight

"Fake," Jaycee repeated under her breath.

Not just switched plates, but ones that someone had created with bogus numbers so the cops couldn't identify who owned the vehicle. She doubted it was a coincidence that a van with fake plates would just happen to be heading toward the Ryland ranch at the same time as Josh and her.

"Slide down lower in the seat," Josh instructed.

She did, but Jaycee also opened the glove compartment and took out the Colt revolver. Beside her, Josh drew his weapon, too. That didn't help steady her nerves, but Jaycee knew it was necessary.

"I can't turn around," he told her. "The road's too narrow."

Yes, and he'd have to slow down to even attempt it. Right now, the van was keeping a safe distance behind them, and maybe it'd stay like that all the way to the ranch.

Jaycee lifted her head just enough to look in the side mirror so she could try to see who was in the van. The windows were heavily tinted, but she waited until the sunlight speared through some clouds. She could only see shadows, but that was enough.

"There are two people in the front seat," she said. Of course, there could be others in the back.

Sweet heaven.

Were these the guards who'd escaped?

If so, they'd likely come either to kidnap her and take her back to a baby farm or kill her because they didn't want her using any info she might have learned about them. Either way, she'd put Josh right in the middle of this.

And he might not be ready for it.

Josh was suffering from PTSD. She was sure of that. But Jaycee had no idea how that would affect them if they came under a full attack with someone actually shooting at them at close range. Heck, she had no idea how it would affect *her.* She wasn't the agent she used to be, and the baby had to come first. She had to protect her child, and that meant protecting herself.

"The turn's just ahead," Josh pointed out. "We're about five miles from the ranch now."

Five miles might as well be a million if the people in that van were out to attack them. Still, with each passing second, they got closer to the ranch where there would be backup. Plus, Grayson had someone on the way coming from the opposite direction. Both measures might be needed.

Without warning, the van sped up, the tires squealing on the asphalt. And it would have crashed right into them if Josh hadn't sped up, too. Josh cursed and corrected the steering wheel to keep them in their lane.

The van sped up again.

Josh couldn't go any farther to the right because there was a deep ditch filled with water from the spring rains. The tires would just bog up and make them sitting ducks. The only option they had was to continue ahead and hope they made it to the ranch before things went from bad to worse.

"Stay down," Josh reminded her.

Just as the van moved into the oncoming lane.

Jaycee dropped down even farther, but she shifted the gun into position so she could shoot if necessary.

Her heart slammed against her ribs when the van was dead even with them. The side window had a dark tint. Too dark for her to see inside. She braced herself for the passenger to lower the window so he could shoot into the truck.

But he didn't.

The van sped ahead of them, as if it was just passing them, and then it moved back into the right lane.

Jaycee blew out the breath that she'd been holding and glanced at Josh. He had a fierce grip on both the steering wheel and his gun, and his attention was still pinned to the van.

"Call Grayson," Josh instructed, giving her his phone.

"Are you two all right?" Grayson asked the moment he answered.

"So far." She put the call on speaker.

The van remained at a steady speed ahead of them, and even though it was menacing because of those bogus plates, this could turn out to be nothing. Maybe someone with criminal intentions that didn't involve them or just some kind of mix-up with the plates at the DMV.

And Jaycee desperately wanted to believe that.

"Mason's on the way from town," Grayson continued. "Dade's on the way from the ranch. Both should be there soon."

She didn't know who Dade was, but she figured it was another Ryland brother, since there were six of them and they were all lawmen. Jaycee ended the call with Grayson and felt the minutes and the miles click off in her head.

Nothing happened.

But that didn't last long.

Just ahead, she saw the flash of brake lights on the van. It slowed, and Josh followed suit, slowing, too. And then the driver of the van slammed on his brakes, turning the vehicle until it was sideways on the road.

Directly in front of them.

Josh cursed, hit his brakes as well and gave the steering wheel a hard turn to the right. They went into a skid.

It felt as if everything was moving in slow motion. But it was fast, too. It all happened in the blink of an eye. Josh's truck kept moving closer and closer, and Jaycee braced herself for the collision that would crush Josh against the side of the van.

But somehow, Josh managed to stop the truck just inches from the other vehicle.

Jaycee didn't have time to feel any relief.

The new position put them window to window with the van. It would be the perfect time for anyone inside to start shooting. Josh couldn't drive to the left, right or straight ahead. But he threw his truck into Reverse and slammed his foot on the accelerator, speeding away from the vehicle.

Now the van window came down, and she caught a glimpse of the armed man inside, who was wearing a mask. He lifted his gun. Aimed.

Not at her.

But at Josh.

However, Josh ducked to the side just as the bullet slammed into the windshield. The blast tore a gaping hole in the glass. But even over the roar of the blast, she heard a welcome sound.

Sirens.

They were coming from the direction of town, which meant Mason was nearly there. She prayed he got there in time to stop this attack.

The driver of the van no doubt heard the sirens, too. He turned the vehicle and came right at them. No shots. But while Josh continued to drive in Reverse, he took aim through the hole in his windshield, and he fired. Not once but three times. The noise was deafening, and when Jaycee felt the baby kicking, she put her hands over her stomach to try to muffle the sounds.

Jaycee heard the squeal of brakes and glanced over the dash to see the van come to a stop. There were holes in their windshield, too, so maybe Josh had managed to hit the driver.

But she rethought that.

This part of the road was wider, and the van turned around right in the middle, clipping the ditch. The left tires barely missed going into the boggy water. And the moment the driver had the vehicle facing away from the truck, he put the pedal to the metal.

No!

They were getting away.

IT TOOK EVERYTHING inside Josh not to go after those men in the van. They'd clearly tried to kill him, and in doing so, they had endangered Jaycee and the baby. He wanted to beat both of them to a pulp for doing that and then arrest them so he could force the answers out of them about the location of those missing women and the baby farms.

But going after them would put Jaycee at further risk.

Josh had no choice but to stop his truck and ease onto the narrow shoulder. The first thing he did was look at Jaycee to make sure she was okay. She was pale and shaking, her hands still covering her stomach, but she was unharmed.

Well, physically anyway.

This would be another set of images to add to the nightmares she was already having.

Josh looked in his rearview mirror and saw Mason approaching in the cruiser. The blue lights were whirling, and the noise got louder until he came to a stop beside the truck.

"There are at least two of them," Josh relayed. He tipped his head to the windshield. "They're obviously armed."

"Grayson's right behind me. Get Jaycee back to the ranch," Mason said, and he took off after the van.

Josh figured if anyone could catch those men, it'd be Mason, and since he couldn't help his cousin, he threw his truck into gear and started driving.

"You think that man who fired at us was one of the escaped guards?" Josh asked.

Jaycee nodded, brushed some of the pellets of safety glass off her lap and sat up. "Hard to tell, but I'm betting it was."

Yeah, he would bet that, too. Except maybe if this operation was as big as the laptop files led them to believe, then there was no telling how many guards there were.

And how many more attacks there would be.

"These guys seem hell-bent on getting you back. But why?" Josh pressed, though he didn't expect Jaycee to have the answer.

"It can't be something as simple as they don't want me spilling anything about their operation. If it was just that, why aim at you? Why not just kill me?"

The thought of that turned his stomach. But it was a valid question. The guards had likely wanted him out of the picture so they could take Jaycee alive, force her to be a captive again and then steal the baby once she'd delivered.

Josh was trying to deal with that thought when he saw Dade just ahead. His cousin was in his own truck, but it had a portable siren attached, and he slowed as Josh's truck approached him.

"Mason's in pursuit, going west of the farm road," Josh explained to Dade.

"I'm headed there now." And that was the only thing Dade took the time to say before his truck went racing after his brother.

Jaycee gently rubbed her hands over her stomach. It was a soothing motion, but it didn't seem to be working. She looked ready to lose it.

"Maybe the person running the baby farms has a buyer for my baby. Maybe that's why they want me alive." Her voice quivered over the last words.

And Josh's stomach turned again.

He hated the thought of someone using his baby to make money—especially money from a buyer who had heaven knows what in mind when it came to adopting a child. That was why he had to stop these guys, and maybe his Ryland cousins would be able to do that.

Before he even got to the cattle gate at the ranch, he saw the armed hands guarding the road. They waved him through and then closed the gate. Of course, someone could still cut through the miles and miles of pasture, but the ranch hands were out there, too. And more were surrounding the main house.

No kids on the playground today. Thank God they were all tucked safely inside.

Josh drove straight to his barn apartment where there was another armed ranch hand nearby, and got Jaycee up the steps as fast as he could.

And the waiting began.

Neither of them sat down. Too many nerves for that. Jaycee started to pace, and Josh just leaned his back against the door and tried not to lose hope. His cousins had to find these men so the threats would stop.

Her pacing continued for several minutes, but then she jerked to a stop, and her gaze flew across the room toward him. "I didn't even think to ask. But did all of this cause you to have flashbacks?"

It had. Some bad ones, too. But Jaycee had enough demons to battle without adding to the mix.

"I'm okay," he settled for saying. Not quite a lie. Not quite the truth, either. Josh tipped his head to her hands that were still on her belly. "What about you? You need to see a doctor?"

"No," she answered the second he finished the question. "But I think the noise from the shots bothered the baby. It's kicking a lot."

That sent a jolt of concern through him. Josh hadn't even considered something like that. He took out his phone. "I'll call the doctor."

"No," Jaycee repeated, and she made it across the room to him before he could press the numbers. "It's all right, really. The baby's already settling down." And she took his hand and put it on her stomach.

Josh felt a jolt of a different kind. Soft thumps against his hand. For such a small thing, it sure packed an emotional punch. That was his baby in there, moving around and maybe scared from the gunshots.

As he'd seen Jaycee do, he rubbed his hand over the movements. Then he realized what he was doing. It wasn't just his baby he was feeling.

But also Jaycee.

He lifted his head. Met her gaze. There was no fear in her eyes this time, but there was some kind of connection between them because of the baby.

Or maybe it was something else.

After studying her, he was leaning toward the something else.

Jaycee's mouth parted; her breath was slow and warm. Like the look she suddenly got in her eyes. And he caught her scent. Not the sweat and fear from the attack. But something feminine and fiery hot.

Okay, that last one was probably his imagination.

Or wishful thinking.

Because he was suddenly having some fiery-hot thoughts about her.

He could blame it on the adrenaline, but Josh was suddenly in the mood to make another huge mistake. And he dived right in. He slid his hand around the back of her neck and pulled her to him. In the same motion, he put his mouth to hers for a kiss that shouldn't be happening.

He expected Jaycee to push him away. To remind him they shouldn't be doing this.

She didn't.

Jaycee made a sound. A soft moan of pleasure, and she slipped her arms around his neck. Worse, she kissed him right back.

Part of this had to be the shot of fear they'd just had from the attack and all that touching he'd done on her stomach. But he was pretty sure the bulk of the kiss was just about the fire that'd always been between them. Josh made that fire a whole lot worse by deepening the kiss.

Jaycee did her own share of deepening, and she eased her body against him. Because of her pregnant belly, it wasn't possible for them to get as close as he wanted. But, man, did they try. And what had started out as a stupid, really good kiss ended with a bad ache inside him.

She pulled back. Their eyes met again. And he saw the urgent need there for just a split second before they went at each other again. This kiss was deeper and hotter than the first. As if they were starved for each other.

Maybe they were.

Josh hadn't been with a woman since Jaycee. Not much time for that while recovering from a gunshot wound and jump-starting his life. He doubted Jaycee had been with anyone, either. So, maybe it was just because they needed someone. *Anyone.*

And Josh wished he could believe that.

It would be so much easier than feeling all this fire. This ache. This confusion.

Because it was wrong to kiss Jaycee like this if he couldn't forgive her, and he wasn't certain he was ready to do that.

Josh also got that bad feeling in the back of his head. The one that whispered he might never be able to forgive her. He pulled back. But stayed close.

Her face was flushed, and her breath was ragged. She was looking at him as if they'd lost their minds.

A distinct possibility.

Especially on his part.

"Don't," she said, easing back. "I don't want you to say you're sorry unless you truly are."

Since Josh had no idea if that *truly* applied to him, he just kept his mouth shut and tried to talk himself out of kissing her again.

Yeah, talk about zero willpower.

It took him a few seconds to realize the ringing sound wasn't in his head. It was his phone. Good grief. With everything going on, the last thing he should be doing was kissing Jaycee, since it was a serious distraction. Among other things.

Still cursing himself, Josh took out the phone expecting to see one of his cousin's names. But it was the 911 dispatcher.

"Josh Ryland," he answered, wondering what the heck had gone wrong now.

"Deputy Ryland," the man said, "someone just called

and said it was an emergency, that she needed to speak to you right away. She sounded desperate—"

"Who is it?" Josh asked.

"She won't give me her name, but I can transfer the call to you. You can talk to her yourself." And the seconds crawled by until Josh heard the woman.

"Deputy Ryland?" the woman didn't wait for him to confirm it. "You have to help me. Please."

"Who is this?" he demanded. Jaycee moved closer to the phone so she could hear.

"It's Sierra DeSilva."

Well, he hadn't expected to hear from her. Especially not like this. "I just had a chat with your sister and your ex-lover, Bryson. Did one of them contact you?"

"No. I haven't seen either of them in weeks." She made a hoarse-sounding sob. "I was kidnapped and taken to some kind of place where they're holding pregnant women."

Everything inside Josh went still. "A baby farm?"

"Yes," Sierra jumped to say. "And I just escaped. Please, Deputy Ryland, come and get me. Because if they find me, they'll kill me."

Chapter Nine

Jaycee was back to pacing again. This time at the Silver Creek sheriff's office while she waited for Josh and the other deputies to return with Sierra. Josh had insisted she not go with Grayson, Dade and him to collect the woman.

Because it could be a trap.

So instead Josh had taken her to the sheriff's office, where she was being guarded by yet two more of his cousins. Gage and Bree. According to what Josh had told her, both had once worked for the Justice Department and had loads of training.

And they were a vigilant pair.

Even though Jaycee couldn't see her from the office doorway, Bree was posted at the rear exit, armed and ready for a possible attack. Gage was at the front door. They'd given Jaycee strict orders to stay away from the windows.

Which she'd done.

She wanted Sierra rescued safe and sound. If the woman truly needed rescuing, that was. But Jaycee didn't want to be part of the rescue if it meant putting her own baby at further risk.

If Sierra contacts you for any reason, don't believe a word she says, Valerie had warned them.

But the problem with that was Jaycee didn't know if they could trust Valerie, either. This could be a case of bad blood between siblings, and maybe Sierra was innocent in all of this.

Maybe.

Or this could be some kind of hoax meant to draw out Josh for another attempt to kill him.

She looked up at the clock on the wall again. Frowned. Not even a minute had passed since she'd last checked, and since she couldn't tamp down all this pressure-cooker energy inside her, she just kept pacing.

It'd only been forty minutes since Josh and the others had left to get Sierra at an abandoned gas station just outside of town. That wasn't nearly enough time to start worrying that something had gone wrong.

But Jaycee worried anyway.

She blamed that in part on that stupid kiss. It'd been wonderful, no doubt about it, but that didn't make it right. Josh still had to deal with his feelings for her. Added to that, they needed to focus on the case. However, that wasn't even the best reason to ban all future kissing.

It was because she was falling for him.

Of course, she'd had a thing for Josh since she'd first met him several years ago, but that kiss had reminded her that the *thing* could be a whole lot more. She needed to nip that idiotic notion in the bud and not weave some stupid fantasy of them getting together to be a family.

Besides, she didn't want a family. She'd had one of those once, and it hadn't worked out so well.

She only wanted for her baby to be safe.

The bell jangled over the front door and Jaycee peered out from the office. She saw Grayson come in. Then Dade, who had his arm looped around a pale-skinned woman with flaming red hair.

Sierra, no doubt.

The woman was indeed pregnant and had her hands splayed over her stomach.

As good as it was to see that Sierra had been rescued, Jaycee didn't stop holding her breath until Josh walked in. Her heart did a flip-flop. And she cursed it. Because she figured her heart shouldn't continue to have a say in this.

It'd rarely made good decisions in the past.

Josh snagged her gaze for just a second and she could see the relief in his eyes. Relief no doubt because there'd been no repeat attacks while he was gone. They all moved toward Grayson's office, but Gage kept his position at the door, probably to make sure Sierra and the others hadn't been followed.

"You have to find her," Sierra said, her breath ragged.

"Her?" Jaycee asked.

"The woman who escaped with me. I don't know her name, but we both sneaked out of the house when the guard was asleep."

"Any sign of this woman?" Jaycee asked.

Josh shook his head. "Sierra said they got separated in the woods."

"We did," Sierra verified, frantically bobbing her head. "And this woman isn't well. In fact, I think she's crazy. Doesn't surprise me after being held in that horrible place. Anyway, she was rambling, saying things that didn't make sense."

Yes, it would be easy to lose your mind while being held captive, and Jaycee hated the thought of this woman wandering around in the woods.

"We'll find her," Josh insisted, and the other Rylands voiced some kind of agreement.

"We'll keep Sierra here for a little while," Grayson explained to Jaycee. "There were two suspicious vehicles with out-of-state plates in the parking lot at the hospital, so I thought it'd be safer to bring her here."

That got Jaycee's heart pounding. Those armed guards could be in the vehicles. They could come to the sheriff's office and stage another attack to kill Josh.

Josh must have seen the worry in her eyes because he ran his hand over Jaycee's arm. "It's okay. Mason and the other deputy are checking out the vehicles now."

"It's someone looking for me," Sierra concluded, her voice filled with nerves.

No one in the room disputed that.

Jaycee and Josh moved back so Dade could ease Sierra onto the small leather sofa in Grayson's office. Dade got her a bottle of water, then excused himself, saying he needed to go help Mason and the deputy deal with those vehicles.

Sierra had a hefty sip of water before the tears came spilling down her cheeks. "I can't believe I got away from them. They'll come for me," she added in a broken whisper.

"Where were you when you escaped?" Jaycee asked.

Sierra looked at her as if she hadn't noticed her before in the room despite Jaycee asking her a question earlier. "I'm not sure. I've already told the sheriff that it was about a mile or so from the gas station. I stole a phone before I got away, but there wasn't any service until I actually got to the gas station."

"There are a lot of dead spots for cell phones out there," Grayson added. "But we've called the Texas Rangers so they can comb the area."

"They have to find it," Sierra said. "There are other women being held captive."

It sickened Jaycee to hear that, but if Sierra was telling the truth, those women stood a good chance of being rescued tonight.

"Your sister came in earlier," Josh tossed out there. "And Bryson."

At the mention of those names, Sierra's tears dried up and her mouth tightened. "Let me guess. They had all sorts of lies to tell about me." Not exactly a question.

Josh lifted his shoulder. "Bryson said you tried to blackmail him over some sex tapes."

Sierra didn't blush, didn't even dodge his intense lawman's stare. "I simply asked him to pay me for the tapes. Did he also tell you that he broke into my place to get them?"

Josh nodded. "If you want to file charges against him, I'll put you in contact with someone at SAPD."

"That's water under the bridge." Sierra got that distressed look again as if she might start crying. "I'm the victim here. Not my money-grubbing sister and my ex-boyfriend. In fact, you should look at both of them, because either of them could be behind these baby farms."

Great. The sisters had now accused each other of running this heinous business. "You have any proof that they're responsible?" Jaycee pressed.

Sierra quickly nodded. "I do. I have some of Valerie's bank records at my apartment. They prove that she was withdrawing huge sums of money from her trust fund."

Grayson and Josh exchanged glances. "How'd you get these records?" Grayson asked.

Now Sierra's gaze darted away. "I saw them in her office and copied them, all right? I knew she was up to no good, and I wanted some proof."

So she'd stolen them. And tried to use a sex tape to extort money from her former lover. Sierra definitely had some credibility issues, but at least she didn't seem to be dodging their questions.

"Does your sister need money or something?" Josh

pressed. "I ask because I'm just wondering why you'd think she would do this."

"Money, definitely," Sierra said. "Yes, she's got plenty of it, but she'd love to have much more. With Valerie it's always more, more, more, and she doesn't care who she steps on to get it."

Obviously, they needed to take a hard look at Valerie's financials. Of course, this could all be lies. Or not. Sierra certainly seemed shaken, but Jaycee had to admit that it could all be an act.

Sierra gave a weary sigh. "I know it's hard to think this about one's own sister, but I believe Valerie could have had me kidnapped so she could sell my baby to Bryson."

Interesting.

Jaycee couldn't completely dismiss that theory. From everything she'd seen, Bryson would indeed pay a huge ransom to get his heir. Of course, Bryson himself could be behind this, too. He could have had Sierra kidnapped to ensure that he got his hands on the baby.

So now they had three suspects.

Sierra, Bryson and Valerie.

Jaycee didn't have a gut feeling about any of them except that she didn't intend to trust any of them.

"Can someone call Bryson and tell him I've been rescued?" Sierra asked.

The request was a surprise, considering that minutes earlier she'd accused him of telling lies about her.

"I can call him," Grayson finally said, though he sounded as suspicious as Jaycee felt. "Anything specific you want me to tell him?"

"Yes. Tell him if he cares about this baby at all, he'll get his butt down here to Silver Creek right away or he'll never see his child." But Sierra waved that off and sniffled again. "It's just the nerves talking."

Sierra paused, gathered her breath. "Bryson cut me to the core when I told him I was pregnant. I wanted him to divorce his cold fish of a wife and marry me. But he refused."

Of course he did. His rich wife gave him the standing in the community that he wanted. But what about that standing once everyone learned he'd cheated on his wife and gotten another woman pregnant? He might collect his inheritance but could lose everything else.

Grayson's phone rang, and he glanced at the screen. "It's Mason," he told them, and answered it. "What'd you find out about those suspicious vehicles?"

Jaycee couldn't hear what Mason said, but the call was short. Grayson ended it and looked at Sierra. "False alarm on the vehicles. Some kids on a class trip got food poisoning, and this was the nearest hospital. Come on. I'll take you to see the doctor."

Sierra didn't argue. She wobbled a little when she stood and touched her hand to her head. "Someone please call Bryson and tell him what I've been through."

"I will," Josh assured her.

"Tell him to come to the hospital," Sierra added. "I need to see him."

Josh just nodded, and they watched as Grayson took her by the arm and led her back out to the squad car.

"You believe her?" Jaycee asked.

Josh shrugged. "I believe she's a gold digger, and that means I automatically distrust her."

Yes, so did she. Besides, Sierra was giving off mixed signals about Bryson. In one breath she was bad-mouthing him, and in the next she wanted to see him. Of course, she could have wanted to see him just to try to get money out of him. Still, that seemed a strange reaction considering the ordeal she'd just been through.

Josh located Bryson's contact number in Grayson's files, and he made the call. "No answer," he muttered after letting it ring a half dozen times, and he left a message for the man to contact him ASAP.

"What about Valerie's financials?" Jaycee asked.

Josh nodded, and he fired off a text. This time to his cousin Kade Ryland, who was an FBI agent. He asked not just for info on Valerie but for a search warrant for Sierra's apartment.

"The warrant shouldn't be hard to get," Josh said to her when he finished texting. "We can tie it to her kidnapping and the baby farm investigation."

"Good. And during the search maybe they'll run across those bank statements that Sierra said she had. If not, I figure Sierra would gladly hand them over since they seem to implicate her sister of some wrongdoing. Or not," Jaycee quickly added.

"Yeah. This could be just a bad case of sibling rivalry."

He checked the time and tipped his head to the door. "Ready to get out of here? I can have Gage or Bree escort us back to the ranch."

Jaycee hated to tie up so much manpower just to protect her and now Sierra. However, after what'd happened on their last drive to the ranch, she welcomed the extra security.

"Let me get everything ready," Josh said, but he didn't even make it a step before his phone rang.

Jaycee expected it to be Bryson returning his call, but she saw *emergency dispatcher* on the screen.

"Deputy Ryland," Josh answered. And since he didn't put the call on speaker, Jaycee moved close enough to hear. She prayed this wasn't yet more bad news.

"There's another woman trying to contact you," the dispatcher told Josh. "She says her name is Miranda Culley and that it's important. Could be some kind of prank—"

"I'll talk to her," Josh interrupted. "You know her?" he mouthed to Jaycee.

But she had to shake her head.

"Deputy Ryland?" the woman said the moment Josh answered. "I heard them say your name so that's why I asked for you." Her breath was gusting and her words rushed together. "I knew it was safe to call you. Because I figure if they want you dead, then you're not working for them."

"Who wants me dead?" Josh asked.

"The guards." A sob tore from her throat. "Four months ago I was kidnapped. And I gave birth to my baby yesterday. The guards took her. I don't know where. But they were going to kill me, and I managed to escape. I can't look for my baby on my own. I need your help."

Oh, mercy. This didn't sound good at all.

"Escaped from where?" Josh pressed.

"A ranch out in the middle of nowhere. I need your help, please," she repeated. "And I need you to find my baby and arrest the person who did this to us."

The muscles in his jaw turned to iron. "You know who the person is?"

"I know." The woman made another ragged sound.

And the line went dead.

Chapter Ten

"Miranda?" Josh repeated, though he knew it was useless. The call had ended, and he didn't know if the woman had done that herself or if someone else was responsible for the disconnection.

Josh immediately phoned back the dispatcher. "What's the number Miranda Culley was calling from?"

"It's from a prepaid cell phone."

Josh groaned. There was no way to trace that, but it did make him wonder where she'd gotten the burner. Maybe like Sierra, she'd stolen it from one of the guards.

"If she calls back, put her straight through to me," Josh instructed.

"You know her?" Josh asked Jaycee when he ended the call with the dispatcher.

"No." Jaycee shook her head and moved to Grayson's laptop. "I'll check NCIC."

The National Crime Information Center was a database for missing persons. It was a good start, but it'd be even better if Miranda called back and told them where the heck she was.

And if she gave them the name of the person responsible.

They needed that info from Miranda so they could make

an arrest and put an end to not just the baby farms but the attacks, as well.

"She's missing, all right," Jaycee confirmed several moments later. "Miranda Ann Culley is twenty-eight, single and worked as a waitress in Kerrville. No immediate family, but her boss reported her missing two months ago."

"No mention of the father of her baby?"

Another head shake and more clicks on the computer keyboard. "She does have a record, though. Busted for drugs six years ago. Nothing since."

So she'd cleaned herself up. Maybe. Or maybe she just hadn't gotten caught. And that led Josh to something else he had to consider. "This could be a setup to lure us out into the open."

Jaycee met his gaze from over the top of the computer. "Sierra wasn't a setup." She paused, groaned softly. "I don't want it to be a setup. If she was held captive like I was, then I want her rescued."

Survivor's guilt. Something Josh recognized because he felt it himself. His partner, Ben, had died, and he hadn't. It didn't matter that he'd had no say in the matter as to who had lived and who had died. Jaycee hadn't had a say in her captivity and rescue, either.

But the guilt was still there.

"I want all of them rescued," Jaycee added. Her voice trembled, and she cursed. "Damn hormones."

He suspected the hormones weren't nearly as much to blame as the guilt and Jaycee's need to get justice for all the women who'd been taken. Josh went to her, knowing it was a mistake to get this close when the emotions were sky-high. It was also a mistake to put his arms around her.

But he did it anyway.

"When you're nice to me, it only makes it harder," Jaycee mumbled.

He eased back, looked at her and his eyebrow lifted, questioning that.

"If you're angry with me," she said, her voice barely a whisper now, "then I can forget about that night we spent together."

His eyebrow lifted higher.

"All right, so maybe I can't forget it entirely," Jaycee amended. "But I can focus on the anger and nothing else."

Nothing else as in the heat.

It'd been the overwhelming need for each other that had sent them racing to bed five months earlier. No finesse. No foreplay. Just the fire that had given them no choice. Well, no choice that they'd wanted to take anyway. At the time, Josh hadn't thought there'd be huge consequences, like a pregnancy.

He had definitely been wrong about that.

"You want me to yell at you?" he joked. And it surprised him that he could make light of something like that. Two days ago, he would have shut her out with his anger and his words.

The kisses had changed everything.

And he added to the change by kissing her again.

Oh, man. He was in big trouble here.

There was no way he should feel what he was feeling. It wasn't right. Logical. Or any other label he could put on it. But did that stop him?

Nope.

He just kissed her as if the world around them wasn't a giant powder keg that could explode at any moment. Josh might have kept kissing Jaycee for hours if he hadn't felt the movement. The soft thuds against his stomach.

"The baby's kicking," Jaycee whispered, her mouth still on his.

Josh slid his hand between them and over the kicks. It

felt like a rodeo going on in there, and he chuckled before he realized he was even going to do it.

Jaycee pulled back, looking a little stunned. "I've never heard you laugh before."

Josh was about to say that was impossible, but it had been a while since he'd let himself feel anything close to laughter.

More survivor's guilt.

His dead partner, Ben, couldn't laugh anymore. Couldn't live. So Josh had shut down, too. The problem was that he didn't know how to start back up again. How to forget that Jaycee had been responsible for that attack.

How to forgive.

And it was that reminder that had him pulling away from her. "Sorry."

He could have added more—exactly what, he didn't know—but his phone rang again. Josh snatched it up, hoping to see the 911 operator with Miranda's return call, but it was Grayson.

"We've got a problem," Grayson said the second that Josh answered.

Josh groaned and put the call on speaker so he wouldn't have to repeat the bad news to Jaycee.

"Sierra sneaked out of the hospital," Grayson added. "She told us she had to go to the bathroom, but she's gone. She left a note on the mirror saying that she wasn't sure she could trust us, that she thought one of us would hand her back over to the kidnappers."

Josh cursed. This wasn't just frustrating, it was downright dangerous for Sierra and her baby. Didn't Sierra realize that?

"I doubt she'll come to the sheriff's office," Josh said. "You have someone out looking for her?"

"Yeah, and I'm about to join them. Just thought you should know that Valerie and Bryson are headed your way."

Really? He didn't need this now. "Why?"

"I contacted Bryson just as Sierra wanted, and he said he was on the way. Just called him back though to say she'd left, but Valerie and he were already en route. Bryson insisted on going to the sheriff's office to wait for any news about Sierra."

Of course he would. He wanted to get his hands on that baby, and Sierra was due any time now.

"If Jaycee's holding up all right," Grayson said, "then you two stay put awhile longer with Gage and Bree."

"Will do." But the words had no sooner left Josh's mouth when he heard the jangle of the front doorbell. He also heard Valerie's and Bryson's voices before he even glanced out of the office and into the reception area.

"How could you possibly let her get away?" Bryson demanded of Gage, who'd been standing guard.

"You're looking at the wrong guy," Gage drawled, and then proceeded to frisk them, despite protests from the two. "They aren't armed," he relayed to Josh.

With his gun still drawn, Gage stepped just outside the door and looked around. No doubt to see if the pair had been followed or if they had brought any hired guns with them.

"No one *let* Sierra get away," Josh informed Bryson. "She lied to the sheriff so she could slip out of the hospital." Something he was sure Grayson had already told the man.

"Someone let her sneak out," Bryson argued. "She should have been watched the entire time."

"She wasn't under arrest," Josh fired back. But clearly she'd been a flight risk, something none of them had picked up on. Everything Sierra had said led Josh to believe that she wanted to be rescued. And maybe she still did. She just didn't trust them to do the rescuing.

"Oh, God," Bryson mumbled. He touched his fingers to his mouth. "What if those kidnappers took her again and made it look as if she'd left on her own?"

Josh couldn't totally discount that, but it wasn't adding up to another kidnapping. Grayson would have told him if there'd been any sign of a struggle or if Sierra had called out for help. Neither of those things had happened.

Valerie frowned. "My sister's clever, and if she'd wanted to leave, no one would have stopped her. She would have found a way." Valerie's attention went to Jaycee when she stepped into the hall. "Good, I'm glad you're here. It saves me from tracking you down."

"What do you want?" Jaycee asked, and her tone matched both Valerie's and Bryson's—unfriendly.

"You must remember something about your time as a captive. A name, a face. A place. Anything that would help us get to the bottom of this and find out who might have taken my sister."

Jaycee shook her head. "I've told Josh and the sheriff everything I remember, and it's nothing that would help find Sierra." She looked at Josh, lowered her voice to a whisper. "I think it's time to ask him about what the tech found on the laptop."

Josh stayed quiet a moment, then nodded. "Care to explain why your name was found on a computer recovered from the baby farm?" Josh came right out and asked the man.

"Probably because Sierra told them he was the rich father of her baby," Valerie said before Bryson could answer. "And she would have done that so they could force Bryson to pay up after she delivered."

Bryson huffed. What he didn't do was look surprised at

the revelation that he had a connection to the baby farm. He came out of the reception area and into the hall, but he stopped several yards away. "I just want to find Sierra before she has the baby and does something stupid like try to sell it."

"From everything you've told me about her, Sierra will offer the baby to you first," Josh reminded him. "I don't think you have to worry about her going to a stranger." Unless Bryson didn't pay up, that is. Or maybe Bryson was concerned that someone would pay more than he was willing to.

"What if these guards don't give her a choice?" Bryson pressed.

"Then I'm sure you'll hear about it." Because he was pretty sure the bottom line here was still all about the money. "What I don't understand is why the computer record showed that someone from the baby farm had sent you money."

Now Bryson had a reaction. "Impossible!" he howled. "There's no way I'd accept money from snakes like that. Besides, I don't need money."

On the surface, that was true. "Maybe it was a way of taking care of Sierra. The person running the baby farm could have paid you when you turned Sierra over to them. That way she couldn't run, and if the baby turned out to be yours, then you could always buy it and not have to deal with Sierra."

"That's despicable." Bryson's eyes narrowed. "And if you repeat idiotic lies like that, you'll be facing a lawsuit for defamation."

Valerie caught on to her client to keep him from going closer to Josh. "I'm sure we'll get all of this sorted out once we find my sister."

Josh wasn't so sure of that. Sierra hadn't been able to

give them much info that would lead them back to the person running the baby farm.

Both Bryson and Valerie started throwing questions at him again. Questions about how he intended to find Sierra and what he'd do with her once she was back in protective custody. Josh had no intention of giving them info like that, and besides, he wanted both of them out of there.

"My advice is for both of you to go back to your homes in case Sierra turns up at one of them."

Valerie and Bryson stopped their string of questions, and Valerie whispered something to Bryson that Josh didn't catch because his phone rang again.

Finally. It was the emergency dispatcher.

"I have to take this call," Josh said to their visitors.

He didn't wait for the two to respond. Jaycee and he stepped back into Grayson's office and Josh closed the door before he hit the answer button.

"It's that woman, Miranda Culley, again," the dispatcher said, and put the call through.

"Are you all right?" Josh immediately asked with the call on speaker.

"I had to hang up because I thought I heard footsteps coming toward me. I had to move. I'd stolen one of the guard's phones, and I was worried they'd be able to trace it somehow."

Again, she'd dodged his question. That didn't make Josh trust her, but he was still hoping she had critical information that could make Jaycee and countless others finally feel safe.

"You need to tell me where you are and who's responsible for the baby farm," Josh demanded.

"I will, but first I want to speak to Agent Jaycee Finney."

Everything inside Josh went still. Jaycee had already

said she didn't know the woman, so why did Miranda know her name?

"Why her?" Josh pressed when Miranda didn't continue.

"Because I heard the guards talking about her, too. They want her baby, but she escaped. I think that means I can trust her, that she isn't working for those guards."

"You can trust me," Jaycee said despite Josh shaking his head for her to stay quiet. He didn't want her involved in this any more than she already was.

"The guards hate you," Miranda said a moment later. "They hate Deputy Ryland, too. That's why I called him. Please tell me that you won't try to kill me when we meet."

Josh had to fight to make sure he didn't snap at her, but the woman was testing his patience. "I have no intention of killing you. I want to help. Just tell me where you are."

Silence.

For a long time.

So long that Josh checked and made sure the call hadn't been disconnected. It hadn't been.

"All right," Miranda finally said. It sounded as if she'd just had a long debate with herself. "There's an old cemetery on Martin Road. You know the place?"

"Yeah." It wasn't that far from the Ryland ranch. "Are you there now?"

"No, but I'll meet you and Jaycee there in two hours."

"Jaycee isn't coming," Josh said before the woman even finished.

Thankfully, Jaycee didn't argue with him, though that was an arguing look she had in her eyes.

"If Jaycee doesn't come, there'll be no meeting," Miranda insisted.

"You'd better come up with a different plan, then," Josh fired back.

There was another snail-crawling silence, and Josh hoped at the end of this one, Miranda would show some common sense. It wouldn't be smart for Jaycee to be out there meeting a captive when the guards were looking to kidnap or do heaven knows what to her again.

"If Jaycee isn't with you," Miranda finally said, "you won't even see me. Because if she's there, I know it won't be some kind of trap."

Josh muttered some profanity. "Then tell me who's behind the baby farms." Yeah, he wanted to rescue Miranda—if she truly needed rescuing, that is—but he didn't want to do that at Jaycee and the baby's expense.

"The only way I'll tell you that is when I'm face-to-face with you and Jaycee. If you want to know the truth, then I'll see you both in two hours."

And with that, Miranda hung up.

"You're not going," Josh said to Jaycee before she could launch into that argument he could still see brewing.

"Hey, get away from there," Gage called out.

Josh threw open the door to see what had caused Gage to say that, but Bryson and Valerie were no longer in the hall. They were right outside the office door.

And judging from their thunderstruck expressions, they'd heard every word about the meeting with Miranda.

Chapter Eleven

"The call wasn't about Sierra," Josh snarled at Bryson and Valerie. "And it's time for both of you to leave."

Jaycee agreed. Josh and she needed to make plans for that meeting with Miranda, and she didn't want to do that with Bryson and Valerie lurking around.

But neither moved despite the fact that Gage was charging right at them.

"You found another hostage," Bryson mumbled. "And this woman knows who took her and the others." He latched on to Josh's arm. "I have to go with you to that meeting. I have to find out who's responsible, because these people might have taken Sierra again."

"No," Gage argued. "What you have to do is leave now. And if you don't, I'll arrest you on the spot."

"You can't do that," Valerie fired back. "This woman might be able to tell us about Sierra."

Gage didn't say another word. He just took out his handcuffs and put Bryson against the wall. Bryson didn't go willingly, and he started to curse. When the man struggled to get away, Gage used his forearm to slam him harder against the wall.

"Stop this!" Valerie yelled.

But Gage didn't stop. Neither did Josh. He also grabbed

some cuffs from the shelf in Grayson's office and went after Valerie.

"Okay, we're leaving," she snapped, holding up her hands in a back-off gesture. "But this isn't over."

Gage didn't stop cuffing Bryson until Josh gave the nod, and when Bryson whirled around to face Josh and her, there was pure venom in his eyes.

"Like Valerie said, this isn't over," Bryson repeated through clenched teeth. "And if you think it is, you're dead wrong."

A chill went through Jaycee. "As far as I'm concerned, your business is finished here," Gage fired back.

The staring match lasted just a few long moments, but Valerie and Bryson finally got moving toward the front door—while they tossed out some profanity. However, Bryson gave them one last glare from over his shoulder. Gage glared back, and he shut and locked the door behind them.

"I'm betting they'll try to follow us to the meeting," Jaycee said.

"Us?" Josh challenged.

Jaycee groaned. Josh was going to give her a hassle about going.

"You heard what Miranda said. She'll only talk to both of us." And because it was important, Jaycee stepped in front of Josh and forced him to look at her so he could hopefully see the determination on her face.

But he only dropped his gaze to her stomach. Josh didn't have to say a word. That little glance was her reminder that going to the meeting could put the baby in danger.

"I'm not stupid. I know it's risky, but together we could minimize the risks and still find Miranda." Hopefully, she'd be safe and ready to spill everything about who was behind the baby farms.

Josh shook his head. "Minimizing the risks still means there'll be risks."

"Heck, it's a risk with me just being here. Or anywhere. The sooner we get answers, the sooner the risks will disappear."

She hoped.

But Jaycee had to admit that an operation like this might have many heads.

Nevertheless, it would feel good to get one of those heads off the street and in jail. And besides, one arrest could lead them to another. Then all of them could come toppling down until they got to the idiot who had orchestrated this operation.

Josh drew in a weary breath and sat down on the edge of the desk. Jaycee thought he was beginning to bend just a little, and she was about to propose a plan, but before she could utter a word of it, Josh's phone rang.

"It's Kade," he said, glancing at the screen.

Kade, his cousin in the FBI. Jaycee really hoped this wasn't bad news and that it'd be a short and sweet conversation, because Josh and she had a lot of details to work out. That included her convincing him that she had to be part of that meeting.

"I've found some interesting stuff on Bryson Hillard," Kade said when Josh answered. "Thought you'd like to know right away."

"I do," Josh assured him, and he checked the time. "Just make it fast. Jaycee and I have a lot on our plate right now." It was still an hour and forty-five minutes until the meeting with Miranda, which didn't give them much time to get ready.

Or for her to convince Josh why she should go.

"We ran the financials on Bryson," Kade started. "No red flags, but we got one from a criminal informant. A reliable one, too. He says Bryson has some gambling debts and he owes money to the wrong people. And that those wrong people are sucking huge weekly payments from him to cover the loan."

Jaycee had to mentally repeat that. "But Bryson's rich," she pointed out.

"Yeah," Kade agreed. "But his wife controls most of the money. It's hers, not his, and she's not keen on shelling out cash for her husband's gambling debts. She gave him his annual allowance at the first of the year. A quarter of a million. But it appears he's already gone through the bulk of that."

Wow, that certainly hadn't come up in any of their conversations, and it got the wheels turning in her head. Especially after she remembered his steely glare and the threat he'd issued just minutes earlier.

"If he's not getting the money from his wife to pay off the gambling debts," Josh asked, "then where's it coming from?"

"Not sure," Kade quickly answered. "He's not pulling it from any of his private accounts. Not enough money in them for that. Of course, he could have some account that he's managed to keep hidden."

That was possible, of course. If he was illegally gambling, then he could have some other illegal way to earn some income.

"What if Bryson is the one who set up the baby farms? He could have used what was left of his yearly allowance to hire the guards and such." Jaycee was thinking out loud now, and she wasn't sure all the facts would add up when she was done.

But sadly, it did make some sense.

Desperate people did desperate things, and he could have gotten the idea for the operation after Sierra told him she was pregnant. By kidnapping her, he could contain Sierra and eventually get the child he needed as an heir, all the while kidnapping other pregnant women.

"He could be paying off the debts with the money he gets from selling the babies," Jaycee added. Which could amount to tens of thousands of dollars.

Both Kade and Josh stayed quiet for several moments, and then Josh nodded. "That would explain why Sierra was taken captive. She was trying to force him to pay for his own baby. This way, he could maybe milk the money from Valerie or even his wife with the promise he'll pay her back when he collects the rest of his inheritance."

And if that was true, then it made Bryson a criminal of the worst sort. He was endangering babies and birth mothers—including his own child—for personal gain.

"There's more," Kade said, bringing their attention back to him. "I found a red flag on Valerie's accounts, too. Her sister was right about all those withdrawals. When the dust settles over there, you'll probably want to bring her in and ask her about them."

She really didn't want to have another encounter with Valerie, but now that Kade had verified what Sierra had said, Valerie needed to be interrogated. Jaycee would indeed want to hear what the woman had to say about her finances.

"Were the withdrawals enough to pay for the setup of the baby farms?" Josh asked.

"Could have been. Hard to say just how much an operation like that would need. The rent was very low on the ranch where Jaycee was held. Of course, the name of the lease turned out to be bogus."

Of course. "Is there anything in the lease agreement that could give us the person's real identity? Like a signature maybe, or an address?"

"Nothing. The agreement was done over the phone and the documents then faxed to the owner. The renter's name is Harold Wesson, and there was a fake credit check set up for him prior to the rental agreement. That's disappeared now."

Someone had covered their tracks. Still, the person in charge had hired a lot of people. Guards, nannies and even doctors. All of that couldn't be cheap. And the pay had to have been high enough to keep all these employees quiet. There's no way these people could have worked on a baby farm and not realized they were doing something illegal.

"The guards where I was held were thugs," Jaycee told him. "I'm betting they all had criminal records. There was nothing in the rubble to link back to one of them?"

"Nothing," Kade verified. "The explosion took care of that."

And that was no doubt the reason the explosive devices had been set. Heaven knows how long they'd been in place. Probably the entire time she'd been held captive. The guards had always threatened that things were rigged to explode, but she'd never seen any proof of it.

"What about the vehicles that were at the baby farm?" Josh asked. "I know they were destroyed in the blast, but were you able to get any of the vehicle identification numbers?"

"Just two, and the first led us back to this alias, Harold Wesson. The truck was a cash purchase, and the seller wasn't able to give us much of a description. The second one was a vehicle that'd been reported stolen six months ago."

Jaycee wanted to scream, but she was too tired to waste that kind of energy. It was just so frustrating that this snake hadn't left more evidence behind.

"What kind of gut feeling do you have about Bryson

and Valerie?" Kade asked. "Any chance they could have funded this together?"

"Yes," Josh and she said in unison.

"They're too chummy if you ask me," Josh continued. "And I don't trust them. Sierra included."

"Glad you agree, because I need search warrants on both Bryson and Valerie to do any further digging."

And that reminded Jaycee of something else that was on their to-do list. "What about the search warrant for Sierra's place?"

"We finally got a signature on it, and agents are on the way over there now to execute it. By the way, any sign of her?"

"None so far, but Grayson and a couple of others are out looking," Josh answered.

If Sierra was truly innocent in all of this, Jaycee hoped Grayson found her before those guards did.

"Gotta go," Josh told his cousin. "Let me know if anything turns up in the search at Sierra's place." He paused. "And I'll let you know if anything comes of the meeting I'm about to have with someone claiming to be an escapee from one of the baby farms."

Now it was Kade's turn to pause. "You need some backup?"

Jaycee released the breath she'd been holding. Kade could have just threatened to nix the meeting, claiming that this was a federal matter now. Technically, it was. But his offer was the opposite of nixing it.

"I wouldn't say no to backup," Josh answered.

"When and where's the meeting?" Kade asked.

Josh rattled off the details, his gaze coming back to her again. "This woman says if Jaycee doesn't show up, then neither will she."

Kade cursed. "I'm guessing you're more than a little hesitant about that, and Jaycee wants to do it?"

Boy, did he hit the nail on the head.

"Yeah," Josh finally said.

"Okay," Kade continued. "There's an agent in the area taking one last look at the baby farm that was blown up. I'll get him over to the cemetery right now to secure the perimeter, and I'll meet him there. If we see anything suspicious, you can get Jaycee out of there fast."

"Thanks." Josh ended the call and snapped toward her. "The way I see it, I've got three choices. With Grayson and the others tied up with finding Sierra, I could leave you here with Gage and Bree. Take you back to the ranch. Or Gage and Bree can come with us and guard you during the meeting."

"You know which option I want. And it's the only one that's going to get us answers from Miranda."

He stood there, jaw muscles stirring and his forehead bunched up. "I don't want to regret this," he said under his breath.

"Neither do I." She touched his arm, rubbed gently, hoping it would soothe him. "But I also don't want any other women held captive if I can do anything to stop it."

The muscles kept stirring, and she wondered if he was thinking about another rogue investigation. The one that'd nearly gotten him killed before she'd been taken captive.

She wanted to tell him that it wouldn't happen again, but any reassurance she could give him would only be wishful thinking on her part. Jaycee only knew this was something she had to do.

Without saying anything, Josh went to the front of the building. She couldn't hear what he told Gage, but it prompted Gage to make a call. Then Gage went back to talk to Bree.

"They're coming with us," Josh informed her. "Another deputy will be here soon to cover the office." He took her by the shoulders and met her eye to eye. "I only want Miranda to get a glimpse of you. You won't get out of the vehicle. And you won't take any unnecessary chances. Agreed?"

She nodded.

Josh still didn't jump to say she could go, but he surprised her when he leaned in, popped a kiss on her cheek.

"Take one of the guns," he instructed.

Jaycee did. A Glock and some extra ammo. She prayed they wouldn't need it, but they might not just run into Miranda at the cemetery. The guards could be there, too.

It didn't take long for another deputy to arrive, and Josh, Bree, Gage and she got into an SUV parked behind the sheriff's office. By her estimations, they weren't supposed to meet Miranda for at least another hour, but maybe the woman would arrive early so they could learn the truth, put Miranda in protective custody and get the heck out of there.

With Josh behind the wheel, they drove out of town. And all of them kept watch. She didn't see any signs of Valerie and Bryson. Nor the guards. She hoped it stayed that way.

The sun was blinding. Already too hot considering it was still spring, and despite the AC running, Jaycee felt the beads of sweat pop out on her forehead. Nerves, maybe. She wasn't having second thoughts about doing this, but she was afraid. Not just for her baby, but for everyone involved in this tangled mess.

Josh's phone rang, and without taking his eyes off the road, he pressed the answer button. A moment later, she heard Kade's voice.

"We're in place," Kade said. "I'm on the east side of the cemetery. Agent Seth Calder's on the west. I can see the road, and he's got a good view of the woods that aren't that far away."

"Any sign of a woman we're supposed to meet?" Josh asked.

"No sign of anyone right now, and I'm using thermal-imaging binoculars so I'll be able to see her or anyone else if they come from the woods. I'll let you know when or if she gets here."

"Thanks, we're about five minutes out." Josh ended the call and met her gaze in the mirror. "If she doesn't show soon, we're leaving. I don't want to sit out here in the open for too long."

Maybe Miranda would call. Because Jaycee didn't want to be sitting ducks, either.

Josh took a turn onto a rural road, then another, and she saw the cemetery just ahead.

"Mercy," Jaycee mumbled, "why the heck would Miranda pick this place?"

It wasn't the pristine church cemetery that Jaycee had expected. In fact, there was no church at all. No buildings. Just some bleached headstones on a weed-infested hill. There were a few large oaks dotting the area and thicker woods farther away, but even they looked dark and sinister. Like the setting for a horror movie.

No vehicles in sight. Of course, there were likely trails nearby where she could have hidden a car. Maybe Miranda had stolen a vehicle along with the phone she'd used to call them.

Or maybe this was all a ruse.

Josh didn't drive all the way up the hill. He pulled onto the narrow shoulder about thirty yards from the cemetery, and both Gage and he took out binoculars. Bree turned in the seat to keep a watch on the road behind them, so Jaycee took the right side. There were some trees in that area, too.

An ideal place for armed guards to hide.

But Jaycee was hoping Kade would be able to pinpoint anyone before the person got in a position to shoot at them.

"Nothing," Josh said several moments later, and Gage echoed an agreement.

Josh's phone rang, the sound knifing through the SUV and through her. "It's that woman again," the emergency dispatcher said, and he put Miranda's call through.

"They're after me," Miranda blurted out. Her words ran together, and she seemed out of breath. "Did you send them to kill me?"

"I didn't send anyone. But there are two FBI agents by the cemetery. They won't hurt you."

"These guys aren't agents, and they're definitely trying to kill me."

Oh, God. Miranda was in trouble. She thought of Valerie and Bryson outside the office door, listening to the conversation. Had one or both of them alerted the guards?

If so, they were no doubt connected to the baby farms.

"Who's after you and where are you?" Josh demanded.

"The guards. They're chasing me." And that's all Miranda said for several moments. "I'm near the cemetery, but the meeting is off. If I go out there now, they'll kill me."

The last word had no sooner left her mouth when the sound of a shot cracked through the air.

Chapter Twelve

Josh didn't have to tell Jaycee to get down. She was already headed that way before he glanced back at her. Like the rest of them, though, she kept her gun ready.

His phone rang again, and when Josh saw Kade's name on the screen, he answered it right away. "Do you see Miranda?" Josh asked.

"No. But I just picked up someone on the thermal scan. A person in the woods directly ahead of me. He or she appears to be running."

"You see just one person?" Josh pressed. "Because she says someone's chasing her."

"If they are, I'm not seeing them yet."

That didn't mean they weren't there. Josh knew there were ways to fool a thermal scan, including special clothing or simply hiding behind a pile of rocks that had been warmed by the sun. Still, Miranda had made it seem as if the guards were right on her heels.

Another shot.

It had come from the woods, but he couldn't pinpoint it beyond that.

"I need to go after her," Josh told the others. "I can't leave her out there to die."

"No." Jaycee took hold of his shoulder to stop him from opening the door.

"It's my job," he reminded her, and he eased her hand away. "I'll be back." He glanced at Gage and Bree. "Make sure Jaycee stays put."

But he figured she wouldn't go out there. Too risky for the baby. Josh knew it was risky for him, too, so he texted Kade for an update.

See the attackers? Josh asked, and he didn't have to wait long for an answer.

Whoever's out there, the person just went down to the ground. They're not moving.

Mercy. That meant Miranda could have been shot.

I'm going closer to check on her now, Kade texted a moment later.

I'll be coming in right behind you. And Josh started up the hill.

He soon caught sight of Kade and the other agent. They were moving toward the woods. Josh kept low. Kept his gun ready. And he followed them, cutting across the cemetery. Just ahead, a few yards into the woods, Kade stopped, stooped down and touched something while the other agent stood watch.

Hell. Had Kade found blood?

Josh hurried, running now, and he saw Kade take out his phone. "I'm calling an ambulance. She's alive."

Thank God.

But Josh did a double take when he saw the woman on the ground. Not Miranda.

But Sierra.

She was moaning and had a cut on her head, and blood was trickling down to her eyebrow. It didn't look serious, but a blow to the head was never good—especially since she was pregnant.

"What happened to you?" Josh asked, kneeling down beside her. He also continued to keep watch around them. "Why are you out here?"

"I was supposed to meet Miranda." Her words were barely a whisper and slurred. She moaned again. "She called and asked me to meet her here, but there were men with guns. Those guards," she added, and the tears rolled down her cheeks.

"There's no sign of them now," Josh told her.

But that didn't mean they weren't close by. He hoped it didn't take long for the ambulance to get there because he didn't want Sierra or Jaycee in the middle of another gunfight. And as long as those guards were in the area, a gunfight was likely.

Josh was about to ask Sierra why she'd run away from the hospital, but she lifted her hand. She had something clutched between her fingers.

A small piece of torn paper.

"Miranda was going to give me the address of the baby farm," Sierra continued. "And the person who's in charge. She tried to hand me the note, but then the guards came and we had to get away from them. I lost sight of her."

Using just the tips of his index and middle fingers, Josh eased the paper from her fingers. The ink was smeared, maybe from the perspiration on Sierra's hand, but he could just make out a name.

Valerie.

Oh, man.

Did she have something to do with this?

Josh wasn't sure how reliable Miranda was, but since Valerie was already a suspect and had those suspicious cash withdrawals from her bank accounts, this moved her to the top of his suspect list.

There was something else on the paper, but the writing was smeared and Josh couldn't read it. He needed to have it analyzed.

"We'll wait with her for the ambulance to arrive," Kade offered. "Why don't you go ahead, take the note and get Jaycee out of here?"

It was a generous offer, and Josh took him up on it. "Thanks. But keep an eye on her. The last time she was at the hospital, she ran."

Though he doubted Sierra would pull that stunt again. The head injury had clearly shaken her.

Josh went back to the SUV, where Jaycee, Gage and Bree had a dozen questions, but he didn't have many answers. "It was Sierra out there." He rummaged through the SUV and found an evidence bag for the piece of paper.

Bree and Gage just looked ready for more questions, but Jaycee leaned across the seat and hugged him when he got behind the wheel. It surprised him a little.

All right, it surprised him a lot.

Those walls he'd built between them were crumbling fast. No doubt because she was the mother of his child. And Josh was having a hard time figuring out how to stop it from being anything more.

That hug sure didn't help.

"Thank God you're all right," she whispered. "How's Sierra?"

"I think she'll be fine, but Kade called an ambulance." He started the engine and got them out of there in case the guards made a return appearance, and he passed his phone to Jaycee. "Scroll through the numbers and call Valerie."

Her eyes widened. "Why? You think she had something to do with this?"

"Maybe." And he waited until Jaycee had the woman on the line before he said anything else. "Who did you tell about the meeting with the woman who escaped?" Josh asked Valerie.

"I don't know what you mean. I didn't tell anyone."

"Well, someone did, and because of the snitch, your sister was attacked."

"Oh, my God. Is she all right?"

"No." That was stretching the truth, but he didn't want to give Valerie any reassurances. "When we found her, she was clutching a piece of a note that the escaped woman had given her. The note had your name on it. Care to tell me why?"

Valerie's gasp came through loud and clear, but whether it was genuine or not was anyone's guess. "I have no idea." She muttered something Josh didn't catch. "I handle adoptions sometimes, but I swear none of them have any connection to this black-market operation."

"Then why did you withdraw a small fortune right about the time this operation started up?" And he didn't bother to make that sound civil. By God, he wanted answers, and he wanted them now.

"Withdrawals?" Valerie repeated. "I took money out, yes, but not for anything illegal. My law partner had some huge medical bills that his insurance didn't cover, and I gave him a couple of loans, that's all."

"I want proof of that. Get down to the Silver Creek sheriff's office so I can take your statement, and bring copies of your bank records with you. While you're at it, I want proof of these loans. Medical records, statements, whatever you have that could possibly convince me you're not guilty."

"Of course I'll come. But I won't be treated like a criminal."

"You will be if you are one," Josh fired back. "Be there in one hour."

"Wait," Valerie said when Josh was about to hit the

end-call button. "What about my sister? Is Sierra on the way to the hospital?"

"Yeah. In an ambulance, and she'll have FBI escort. In other words, if Sierra says she doesn't want to see you, then you're not getting close to her." Josh punched the end-call button.

"You believe she's telling the truth about the withdrawals?" Gage asked.

But Josh just shook his head. It would be so much easier if Valerie was guilty. Then they could arrest her and maybe dangle a plea bargain in front of her so she'd give them details of the entire baby farm operation. But so far, everything had been circumstantial.

What they needed was proof.

Or a confession.

Now, that was something he could maybe make happen if he pressed Sierra hard enough. And he intended to press her *hard.*

Josh met Jaycee's gaze in the rearview mirror. The nerves were still there, right at the surface. And he silently cursed what this was doing to her. Too bad there wasn't much he could do about it. The danger just kept coming no matter how hard he tried to keep her safe.

He drove back to the sheriff's office, grabbed the evidence bag and hurried Jaycee inside. However, they hadn't even made it to his office before his phone rang. Hell. He couldn't deal with any more bad news right now, but it was his cousin Nate.

"You okay?" Nate asked the moment that Josh answered. "Just got off the phone with Kade and he told me what was going on."

"I've been better."

Jaycee took the evidence bag from him. Ready to examine that note again. So despite everything, she was clearly still an FBI agent looking for the truth.

"I just got a report back on the search at Sierra DeSilva's apartment," Nate continued. "The place had been trashed, and I'm pretty sure a lot of stuff was removed before we got there. Including her computer and the copies of those bank records that were supposedly there."

Great.

"There's more," Nate went on. "I'm sending you a photo of it now."

Judging from Nate's tone, this wouldn't be good, either, so Josh tried to brace himself. The photo loaded slowly, but pretty soon he saw the words that'd been scrawled on what appeared to be her bedroom wall.

Talk and you die.

"It was written with her lipstick," Nate explained. "I'll have the place processed for fibers, prints—anything—and I'll call if we find anything else."

Josh mumbled a thanks, ended the call and took a deep breath. Jaycee was right there, and pulled a bottle of water from the fridge. She opened it, had a sip and then passed it to him. It wasn't a shot of whiskey, but it'd have to do.

"Today, I really hated the job," Jaycee said. "I didn't like you going out there after those shots had been fired."

He lifted his shoulder, had some more water. "You hugged me."

"Yes." She dodged his gaze. "Sorry about that. It was another 'getting caught up in the moment' reaction."

So that was all there was to it. Relief that he hadn't been shot or killed. Funny, it'd felt like more. Good thing it wasn't.

At least he thought it was a good thing.

Josh had a dozen things to do before Valerie showed, but he wanted to take just a minute to test his "good thing it wasn't" theory. He reached out, put his hand around the back of Jaycee's neck and eased her to him.

He kissed her.

Jaycee made a little sound of surprise but didn't pull away. She kissed him right back.

The taste of her slammed through him, and his senses went into overdrive. The feel of her in his arms. Her breasts against his chest. The sound of surprise that melted into one of pleasure.

He pulled back. Wasn't easy. But he forced himself to do it so he could assess things. Now, that was easy. He'd made another mistake, because using a kiss to test a theory was playing with a giant ball of fire.

"Sorry," he murmured.

"You're sure about being sorry?" No gaze dodging this time. She was staring at him.

No, he wasn't, and that was what made him truly sorry. Or maybe just stupid. "This has to stop. Agreed?" he asked, but there would be only one right answer.

And Jaycee gave it to him. She nodded. However, she stared at him a moment as if trying to figure out if stopping was something they could genuinely do.

Maybe they couldn't.

"Pretend if you have to," he added.

Another nod. "I can pretend."

Not exactly the hands-off declaration they should be making, but it would do for now.

Cursing under his breath, Josh forced his mind back where it should be—on work. He put on a pair of plastic gloves and took the torn note from the evidence bag so he could have a better look. Soon, he'd need to send it to the lab, but first he wanted to see if he could make out the rest of what it said.

"That's definitely Valerie's name," Jaycee said, pointing to the top line. Her finger accidentally brushed against his arm, and she backed away.

Far away.

Obviously, she had this pretense thing down pat. Well, except for the slight throat clearing she made. And the glance she gave him. Josh ignored both. He ignored everything except the evidence in front of him.

"Of course, she might say it refers to another Valerie," he added.

If so, it wouldn't do her any good. Because she was tied to this case through her sister. What he needed, though, was more than just something to tie her to the case. He needed proof that she was guilty. Josh studied the lines below Valerie's name.

"I think it says William," Jaycee said. Without touching the paper or him, she scrolled her finger above the word below Valerie's name, tracing the scrawled letters.

Josh nodded. He could see it. But who the heck was William? That name hadn't come up in the investigation.

Yet.

He turned the paper at a slightly different angle and put his attention on the next two words. The last one was four letters, all lowercase.

"Road?" Josh mumbled. He tried other possibilities, but that was the only one he could think of that worked. And that led him to the middle word.

"William Casey Road," he said. "It's about ten miles outside of town."

He hurried to his computer so he could access land records. It took him several moments to work through the passwords and get to the right page. Thankfully, there weren't a lot of people living on William Casey Road because it was mainly ranch and farmland. And one name in particular snagged his attention.

Bingo.

"Last year Bryson bought an abandoned ranch on William Casey Road."

"If you ask me, Bryson doesn't look like the ranching type."

No. He didn't. And even though a lot of people were buying ranch land as an investment because of its rock-bottom prices, Bryson could be using it for something else.

Like a baby farm.

He took out his phone and called Grayson. Thankfully his cousin answered on the first ring. "We might have a lead. Bryson owns a ranch at 623 William Casey Road. Can you get someone out there right away to check on the place?"

"Dade and I'll go. Mason and Kade can stay at the hospital with Sierra."

"How's she doing?" And Josh hated that he hadn't already checked on her.

"She's with the doctor now. And don't worry. We'll cover all exits just in case she decides to jackrabbit again."

Good. Because he needed to interrogate Sierra again, too.

"I'll let you know if we find anything at Bryson's place," Grayson assured him, and ended the call.

"Speaking of Bryson, where do you think he is?" Jaycee asked.

He hoped the man was at the baby farm so Grayson could arrest him on the spot and close the place down. Josh didn't intend to give Bryson a heads-up about Grayson's visit, but he did want to check on the man to see what he had to say about this latest attack on Sierra. Josh was betting that Valerie had already contacted him and spilled everything she'd learned.

Josh punched in Bryson's number. Waited. It rang so long that Josh was about to hang up, but he finally answered.

Except it wasn't Bryson.

"Deputy Ryland," a woman answered. She sounded frantic. "I'm Bryson's secretary. He left in a hurry and didn't take his phone. Oh, God. Please tell me you can stop him."

Josh pulled back his shoulders. "Stop him? Why would I need to stop him?"

"Because he intends to hurt her. He was so angry. I've never seen him like that before. He drove out of here like a crazy man."

"Slow down," Josh insisted. "Where was Bryson going?"

"To the Silver Creek hospital. He heard that Sierra would be there. Please, Deputy Ryland, go after him. Because as angry as Bryson is, I'm afraid he'll kill her."

Chapter Thirteen

Jaycee could hear the shouts when they stepped into the emergency room of the Silver Creek hospital. And there was no mistaking that the person doing the shouting was none other than Bryson.

Josh and she followed the noise and found him outside one of the E.R. examining rooms. He was demanding to go inside, but Mason had blocked his way. Considering that Mason looked like an ornery vampire who was about to rip off Bryson's head, Jaycee was surprised the man was continuing his tirade.

"I will see her!" Bryson shouted. "Sierra, get out here now!"

That was apparently all Mason intended to put up with because he caught on to Bryson's shoulder and slammed the man face-first against the wall. Bryson sputtered out a cough but seemed too stunned to do anything but cooperate. Mason cuffed him and then spun him back around.

"You yell one more time," Mason warned him, his voice dark and dangerous, "and I *will* make you hush."

Finally, Bryson shut up, but the moment he spotted Josh and her approaching, he apparently decided to plead his case to them.

"Sierra's in there, and I have to talk to her now." Bryson

kept his voice at a normal level, probably because Mason was still in his face.

"Sierra's been through an ordeal," Jaycee reminded him. "I think she needs to see the doctor more than she needs to talk to you."

Bryson snarled something she didn't catch, and he turned back to Mason. "Take off the cuffs."

Mason didn't jump to answer that. "You planning to do more yelling?"

"No," Bryson said through clenched teeth.

Mason kept staring at the man, and his stare was a lot worse than Bryson's glare. "What about it, Josh?" Mason asked without looking at his cousin. "You want the cuffs on or off when you talk to this loudmouthed dirt wad?"

Josh eyed Bryson for several seconds. "Off for now, but if he raises his voice again or tries to go in that room with Sierra, then I'll cuff and arrest him."

Clearly, that didn't please Bryson, but he kept his mouth shut when Mason took off the cuffs. Mason shot Bryson another warning glare, then sank down in one of the waiting room chairs and stretched out his legs.

"You know what Sierra did?" Bryson asked them, but he didn't wait for an answer. "She tried to blackmail me again. She sent me a letter this time, demanding a half million dollars for my own baby."

A letter? Now, that was a surprise. Jaycee couldn't figure out when the woman had had time to do that, considering she'd been on the run.

Josh walked closer, positioning himself between Bryson and the examining room door. "Did you know that someone clubbed her on her forehead?"

"No." Bryson's breath caught as if he was genuinely surprised, and if he was acting, it was good. "I thought she was faking an injury so she wouldn't have to deal with me."

Well, Jaycee couldn't rule that out. "It seems odd, though, that she'd make a demand for all that money and then try to dodge you."

"She knew I'd be furious."

"Yeah," Josh agreed. "But getting clubbed on the head isn't my first choice of ways to avoid a man's fury."

Bryson opened his mouth, closed it and then cursed. "How badly is she hurt?"

"We're not sure," Josh answered. "In fact, we're not sure of a lot of things right now. We were supposed to meet another woman in an area just outside of town, and Sierra showed up instead."

What Josh didn't mention was the note and the ranch property that was hopefully being checked out as they spoke. While she was hoping, Jaycee added that Grayson and his brother would find enough evidence for them to make an arrest in connection with the baby farms. It didn't matter if it was Bryson, Valerie or even Sierra, Jaycee just wanted this person off the streets and behind bars.

"Any idea why Sierra was at that meeting?" Josh asked.

Bryson immediately shook his head. "None. The only thing I know about Sierra is that she's up to her old tricks. But I won't be blackmailed. If I had that kind of money, I wouldn't be paying it to her."

"But what about your *heir?*" Jaycee purposely used that term instead of baby.

"I'll challenge her for custody. I already have the test to establish paternity, and it shouldn't be hard to prove her an unfit mother."

That was the pot calling the kettle black, because in her opinion Bryson was an unfit father.

Unlike Josh.

Jaycee hated that the thought popped into her head, but she couldn't shut it out. Josh was a good man, but it was also clear that he had a huge interest in this baby she was carrying. Maybe Josh would pull a Bryson and challenge her for custody, too.

If he did, he could win.

She didn't have family support like Josh did, and she was the daughter of not one but two convicted felons. Her time in foster care wouldn't help, either, because she'd been pretty much labeled a juvenile delinquent. Hardly a good track record for a mother fighting for custody of her child.

"What's the matter?" she heard Josh ask.

It took her a moment to realize he was looking at her because she'd made a soft moaning sound at the prospect of losing her child to him.

"Nothing," she mumbled and tried to get her mind back on Bryson. But Josh obviously didn't believe her, because he took her by the shoulders and had her lean against the wall. He studied her eyes.

"Come on," Josh insisted. "I'll take you to the cafeteria and get you something to eat."

She wasn't hungry. Hard to be hungry with the threat of those armed guards looming over them, but Jaycee figured it would do the baby some good if she ate something. Her mealtimes had been regimented when she was being held at the baby farm, but her life had been so chaotic since Josh had rescued her.

"What about Valerie?" she asked. "Shouldn't we get back to the sheriff's office?"

"Gage can handle the interview," Josh insisted. "While we're here, I want you to get checked out by a doctor. Just to make sure everything's okay." A muscle flickered in his jaw. "There's no telling what those guards did to you."

Jaycee was certain they hadn't done anything to harm the baby—especially since a healthy baby had been all they'd wanted. Still, an exam wouldn't hurt.

Josh looked back at Mason and motioned for him to watch Bryson again, and he led her down a corridor. He'd only made it a few steps when he got a text.

"Not more bad news?" she asked when he looked at the screen.

He shook his head but then lifted his shoulder. "The text was from Melissa Garza, the woman who's marrying my uncle this weekend. She wanted us to know that the decorators are at the ranch now."

That could be bad. *Very* bad. "These people were screened for security?"

"Sure, but it's a big crew, so it's possible for someone to slip through." He glanced at her, probably trying to reassure her with that look. "Everyone's being checked for weapons, and when we get back, I'll make sure to turn on the security system in the apartment."

Jaycee tried not to overreact to something as simple as arming a security system. Hard not to do, though, because Josh was right. It was possible for those guards to make it onto the ranch, and if they couldn't stop them, she at least wanted to be alerted if one of them tried to break in while Josh and she were sleeping.

The cafeteria wasn't far, just a few doors away, and Jaycee got a sandwich and some milk. Josh got a chili dog, loaded, and some soggy-looking fries. He didn't waste any time before he started wolfing it down.

"Now, will you tell me what's wrong?" he asked.

Apparently, she no longer had the poker face that'd made her a decent undercover agent.

"The baby. Our baby," she clarified. "And custody. I know you said you only wanted to be part of the baby's life, but I'm worried that maybe you would change your mind when you gave it some more thought."

He stopped in midbite, staring at her from over the top

of that dripping chili dog. "Are you planning to challenge me to get full custody?"

She nearly choked on the sandwich. "No. But I figured you'd challenge me."

He dragged a fry through the chili, popped it in his mouth. "Right. Because I'm such good father material."

"But you are." He knew that.

Right?

Obviously not, judging from the flat look he gave her.

"I'm a mess," he continued, sounding disgusted with himself. "And let's not forget that my own mother left when I was a kid. Bad divorce," he added in a mumble. "My father was, well, absent after that despite being around. Grayson's the closest thing I ever had to a dad."

Jaycee was glad she had the sandwich because it gave her something to do. She nibbled on it while she tried to process what Josh had just told her. "I didn't know."

"Well, yeah, I don't share that with a lot of people." He paused, ate another fry. "Will you use that against me when you try to get full custody?"

"No." And she stretched that out a few syllables. "Remember, my parents did hard time for aggravated armed robbery and an assortment of other felonies. Plenty of people would argue that their criminal history makes me an unsuitable parent."

Great. Now she was handing him ammunition to use against her. Not that any of it had been a surprise, but it probably wasn't a good idea to remind him of it now. She didn't have time to talk her way out of the hole she'd just dug because Josh's phone rang.

"It's Mason," he let her know right before he answered it. He didn't put the call on speaker, probably because other diners were close by, and Jaycee couldn't hear what Mason said even when she leaned across the table.

"Sierra's water broke," Josh told her when he finished the call. "Her contractions are coming nonstop, and the doctor doesn't think it'll be long before she has the baby. They just moved her to Labor and Delivery, so Mason's heading over there, too, to make sure Bryson stays away."

That was good, but the timing of the labor perhaps wasn't so good. "Maybe the trauma of what happened in the woods caused her contractions to start."

But Josh just shrugged. "Mason had a quick word with the doctor. He said the cut on Sierra's head was superficial, hardly more than a scratch. It didn't even need stitches."

Jaycee didn't have to give that much thought. "You think she did it herself?"

Another shrug, and he continued to eat. "I think Sierra's capable of just about anything. And while I don't like the idea of Bryson trying to confront her at a time like this, I'd be pissed, too, if she tried to blackmail me like that."

Jaycee silently agreed, and she cringed at the thought of Bryson raising the child. Maybe just having an heir would be enough for him to collect the rest of his inheritance, and that way he wouldn't need to have an active part in his son's or daughter's life. Of course, Sierra wouldn't exactly qualify for mother of the year, either.

Josh finished his fries and hot dog and took out his phone again. "I'm calling Grayson to see if he made it out to Bryson's property. After that, I need to find out how the interrogation is going with Valerie, and then I can see about getting you examined. Then I can take you to the ranch so you can have a nap."

The married-to-the-badge part of her wanted to insist that they stay at the sheriff's office to deal with anything else that might come up. But she was exhausted. In need of a nap.

And craving doughnuts.

She looked back at the display cases, but didn't see any in the cafeteria. "You think there's a place nearby where I can get a doughnut?"

"We can hit the drive-through on the way home," Josh murmured right before Grayson came on the line. Again, she couldn't hear what he was saying, but it caused Josh's forehead to bunch up.

Please, no more bad news. Jaycee had already had her fill of that today. Besides, she really was tired. At the baby farm, she'd slept most of the day. When she wasn't figuring out how to escape. But since Josh had rescued her, there hadn't been time in between attacks for her to get much rest.

"They didn't find anything at the ranch," Josh said after he ended the call. He stood. "No sign that anyone had been there recently, but they'll keep looking."

It would have been nice to find something incriminating, but maybe there was still a chance for that. "What if it's to be a future site for a baby farm?"

Josh nodded. "Grayson's putting up a hidden surveillance camera on the porch of the abandoned house. It's motion activated, so if anyone goes out there, we'll know about it."

And she wouldn't be surprised to see Valerie, Bryson or those missing guards making that visit. Or even Sierra once she'd had her baby and then recovered. That meant they might have to wait awhile for any possible answers they might get there.

As they turned toward the exit, Jaycee saw a woman making a beeline for them. She was tall and rail thin, and had choppy blond hair. Even though the woman wasn't armed and didn't appear to be a threat, Josh still stepped between her and Jaycee.

"Deputy Josh Ryland," the woman said, extending her hand for him to shake.

"Who are you?" Josh snapped. He darn sure didn't shake her hand.

"I'm Miranda Culley. And I understand you and Agent Finney have been looking for me."

Chapter Fourteen

Josh just stared at their visitor. He didn't recognize her, but he sure as heck recognized her name. His gaze dropped to the woman's stomach.

Flat.

Definitely not pregnant.

And that wasn't the only thing that snagged his attention. Miranda was wearing what appeared to be a waitress uniform. She definitely didn't look like someone who'd just escaped armed guards and a baby farm.

"Did you recently have a baby?" Josh asked.

"No." She didn't exactly seem comfortable with the question, and she cleared her throat. "I've never been pregnant. Nor have I actually been missing."

"But no one at your job knew where you were," Jaycee pointed out.

"Because I was having some trouble with my boss hitting on me. I didn't leave because I was pregnant. I left because I wanted to get away from him. So I certainly wasn't going to tell him where I was going."

Josh shook his head. "What about the calls you made to me through the emergency dispatcher?"

"I didn't make the calls, either." Miranda paused, swallowed hard. "Look, I'm not sure what's going on, Deputy Ryland, but a friend from the diner where I used to work emailed me and told me you were trying to find me because of those calls. That's when I realized someone must have been impersonating me. My name's not that common. I don't think there's another Miranda Culley in the state."

He searched her eyes and body language for any sign she was lying, but he saw nothing other than a confused, frightened woman. Still, he took out his phone and pressed the record function.

"I need a sample of your voice," Josh explained. "So it can be compared to the 911 recordings."

She didn't refuse. In fact, she moved closer to the phone. "Am I in danger?" Miranda asked.

Josh couldn't swear to her that she wasn't, because he didn't know what was going on either. "Has anyone been following you? Had any hang-up calls?"

She shook her head to both. "Not that I know of."

"Someone could have just used your name," he explained. He kept the recorder on, hoping to get a decent sample of her voice along with some answers. "Maybe because the person knew we'd check and find that missing persons report your boss filed on you."

And it wouldn't have been hard to find such a report, since they were often posted on the internet.

"Do you have any idea who would have done something like impersonate you?" Josh pressed.

"None. Like I said, I was having trouble with my boss, but I don't think he'd do this just to find me. Would he?"

Probably not, since it would mean he would have gotten access to information about the baby farm and then involved himself in a high-profile investigation. Pretty risky when it would have been easier just to try to worm the info from someone who knew Miranda.

"You have any friends you can stay with until this is over?" he asked.

"Yes. My boyfriend."

"Then go to him and call me at the Silver Creek sheriff's office if anyone suspicious contacts you." Josh turned off the recorder.

The woman gave a shaky nod, thanked him and hurried out. Josh watched her leave and wanted to curse. He'd thought Miranda would be a solid lead, someone who could give him information about the owner of the baby farms, but she seemed to be just another dead end.

"Why would someone have impersonated her?" Jaycee questioned.

Josh had been asking himself the same thing, and he had a theory. One that Jaycee wasn't going to like. "To draw us out into the open. If one of our suspects had asked for a meeting, we might have said no. But it's hard to say no to a woman who's running for her life and claiming we're the only people she can trust."

Jaycee made a sound to indicate she was thinking about that, and then she groaned softly. "But something must have gone wrong at the cemetery. Maybe because the FBI agents showed up. Or maybe because Sierra did."

Either was possible, but Josh had a way of checking who'd set up that meeting. Well, maybe. He took out his phone to make another call. In case someone was following Miranda, it probably wasn't a good idea for Jaycee and him to hang around the hospital. Her checkup would have to wait a little while longer.

"Sawyer," he said when his brother came on the line. "I need some 911 tapes analyzed."

Josh gave Sawyer the date and approximate times of the possible imposter's calls and sent him the recording of Miranda's voice. If the woman wasn't lying about having made those calls—and Josh didn't think she was—then maybe they'd soon know who did make them.

Josh finished talking with Sawyer and made another call—to Gage at the sheriff's office. He asked his cousin to come to the hospital so he'd have some backup and extra security when he left with Jaycee. Gage assured him that he was on the way, and it wouldn't take him long to get there since the sheriff's office was just up the street.

However, Jaycee and he had just made it out of the cafeteria when his phone rang again, and this time it was Mason's name on the screen.

"Sierra had the baby," Mason said. "A girl. According to the doc, both of them are healthy."

That was good news, but that *good* wasn't coming through in Mason's voice. "Anything wrong?"

"Yeah. Sierra's already insisting she wants to leave the hospital, that she doesn't feel safe here. You got grounds to arrest her, because that might be the only way I get her to stay put?"

"No grounds." Josh huffed. Though he wished he did have reason to arrest her—or anybody else. "But I'm sure the doctor's not going to let her go."

"You'd think, but the way Sierra's driving everybody crazy with her fussing and carrying on, the doc might call her a taxi. You're sure she could be in danger?"

"No," Josh had to admit. "I'm not sure of much of anything right now."

"Then, hell, I might call her a taxi," Mason growled, and ended the call.

Josh was pretty sure his cousin was joking about that last part, but with Mason, you never knew.

"Should we go see Sierra?" Jaycee asked. "And try to talk her into staying put?"

"No. I doubt we can talk her into anything. Since she's not a witness, we can't force her to accept police protection. Besides, she might just want to get away from Bryson."

After all, the man had accused Sierra of trying to blackmail him. And maybe she had. Maybe she was ready to cut her losses and run. Or she could just want to get out of there before they found the proof to make that arrest.

Josh led Jaycee through the corridors, back through the emergency room and to the exit. The doors were glass, so he could see the parking lot, and he took a moment to look around, to make sure there weren't any suspicious people or vehicles out there. No one was milling around. But there were about a dozen vehicles parked in the same area as Josh.

He spotted Gage.

His cousin was sitting in his own truck, parked next to Josh. Gage stepped from his vehicle, had a look around, as well. "Don't see anyone," he called out to Josh.

"Move fast," Josh instructed Jaycee, and he led her out the doors and toward his truck. Before he could get her inside, Josh heard a sound he damn sure didn't want to hear.

Someone fired a shot.

JAYCEE PRAYED THAT the noise was a car backfiring.

No such luck.

A bullet blasted through the air and into the front of Josh's truck. At the same time, the fear and adrenaline slammed into her. And Josh shoved her forward to the side of the nearest vehicle, and then pushed her to the ground.

He drew his weapon and got ready to fire.

But there wasn't another shot.

"Stay inside!" Josh shouted to a woman who was about to come out through the exit doors. Thankfully, the woman did and ran back into the hospital.

With his gaze firing all around, Josh lifted his head a little. Jaycee couldn't see a thing because Josh was literally right in front of her, and the only thing she could hear was the May breeze and her pulse hammering.

"See anything?" Gage called out. She hoped he'd taken cover, as well.

"Nothing," Josh answered.

But just as he spoke, another shot came, smashing into the ground directly in front of them. Josh pushed her back and took aim.

"He's on the roof," Josh shouted to Gage.

Oh, mercy. Definitely not a good spot, since the shooter would be able to see them while having good cover from any shots coming his way. Besides, Josh and Gage couldn't just start randomly firing because someone inside the hospital could be hurt.

"Move back," Josh instructed.

He stayed in front of her as Jaycee scrambled to get behind the rear of the car. It meant the shooter likely wouldn't be able to see her, but he would certainly be able to see Josh.

The next bullet proved that.

It came straight toward Josh, tearing across the concrete and scattering debris right at them. Jaycee caught on to his arm, pulled him back with her.

Gage returned fire. A single shot. But Jaycee couldn't tell where it went.

"It's me. Don't shoot," she heard Gage say a split second before he dived behind the car with them. "He's behind the big AC unit on the left. I got just a glimpse of him when he came out to fire."

Jaycee hadn't gotten a glimpse, but she was betting this was one of the armed guards who'd escaped. "Is he alone?"

Gage shook his head. "Not sure. I only saw one, but there could be others. Plenty of places to hide up there."

Yes, and any other backup that came to assist them

could be walking right into an ambush. Of course, the same could be said for anyone who was coming in to assist the shooter. Gage and Josh would see anyone trying to cut through the parking lot. On this side anyway.

"Anyone have a gun I can use?" Jaycee asked.

Josh took his from his boot holster but then shot her a warning glare. "That doesn't mean I want you up and shooting. Stay down."

She would. For the baby's sake. But she wanted the gun just in case this went from bad to worse. She figured Josh and Gage would do everything within their power to protect her, but if something happened and they got separated, then she wanted to be able to fight back.

Gage's phone buzzed, just a split second before there was another shot.

"It's Mason," Gage relayed and then answered the call. "He's on the roof. Make sure no one leaves the hospital. Tell Grayson to keep his distance, too. But try to get someone on the back side of that roof so you can stop this fool." He hung up and shoved the phone back into his pocket.

"This guy's being careful about his shots," Josh mumbled.

Yes, he was. Single shots that'd come darn close to Josh, but if the guy was heavily armed—and Jaycee figured he was—then he could be firing nonstop into the car until he ripped it to pieces.

And killed them.

But he wasn't doing that.

Why?

Only one answer came to mind. Because this wasn't a murder attempt, but rather a kidnapping. And that linked it right back to the baby farm.

Jaycee turned to check behind her. She was on the ground, but she could see beneath some of the other vehicles, and she saw something she definitely hadn't wanted to see.

"Someone's crouched behind that dark green truck," she whispered. She had to repeat it, though, because the guy on the roof fired at them again, and Josh didn't hear her.

Josh whirled around, lowered himself to the concrete, looked around. And cursed. "It could be someone just trying to get out of the path of those bullets."

However, he didn't sound very convinced of that. Neither was Jaycee. Especially when the person moved and darted behind another vehicle. One that was closer to Josh, Gage and her.

He was moving in for the kill. Well, the kill for Gage and Josh. She was betting the guy would try to eliminate them so he'd have less of a fight taking her.

But he was wrong about that.

Jaycee wouldn't give up without a hard fight, because her baby's life depended on it.

"Watch the guy on the roof," Josh told Gage, and he went even lower to the ground until he was practically on his belly. He took aim.

Fired.

Judging from the sound, the bullet zinged off some metal, but she couldn't tell what it hit. Definitely not the person lurking there, because he returned fire almost immediately.

And so did the guy on the roof.

Cursing, Josh crawled over her, protecting her and the baby with his body, and he fired at the shooter behind them. Gage took a shot at the one of the roof.

Both gunmen fired back.

And that meant Josh, Gage and she were caught in the middle.

This was exactly what Josh had no doubt wanted to

avoid, but here they were in a bad situation where he was having to put his life on the line to keep her safe.

The shots kept coming at them, pelting the ground and slamming into the vehicles. Jaycee wanted to fight back. To stop this. But she couldn't risk getting up. Because if these goons managed to kidnap her, they'd kill Josh and Gage.

Probably kill her, too, once they had what they wanted from her.

Jaycee wasn't sure exactly what they did indeed want, but if it was the baby, they weren't going to get it.

The shooters kept firing. Gage and Josh fired, too, but not as much. No doubt trying to conserve ammunition.

Gage's phone buzzed again, and without taking his attention from the guy on the roof, he took out his phone and slid it her way. She saw Grayson's name on the screen and answered it.

"We're pinned down," she let him know.

"Stay put. Tell Josh and Gage to get down, too. Mason's got everyone behind cover inside the hospital, and Dade, Bree and I are coming in."

"Grayson says for us all to get down," she relayed.

Josh and Gage both dropped down. Gage on the ground next to her, and Josh still on top of her.

They didn't have to wait long before Jaycee heard another shot. It hadn't come from the roof or behind them. This one had been fired to their right. And the shots didn't stop. They just kept shooting until she saw the man behind the car scramble to get away.

"He's on the run!" she heard Grayson shout. Jaycee also heard the sound of running footsteps. Not just one set but several.

There was another shot from the roof. Just one. She waited, holding her breath and praying that none of Josh's family had been hit. But if it'd happened, Grayson had been spared. He hurried toward them.

"Stay where you are," Grayson warned them. "Dade and I are going after the guy on the roof. Bree's blocking the back exit now in case he tries to get out that way."

This time Josh didn't listen.

"Watch Jaycee," he told Gage. "I'm going after the other gunman."

Chapter Fifteen

The shooters had gotten away.

That thought kept going through Josh's head like a broken record, and it didn't play any better than the first time he'd heard it.

He wasn't sure how that had happened, not with Gage and the others helping. But somehow the guys had managed to give them the slip, which meant they were still there.

Ready for another attack.

This one had been well planned, and obviously the two shooters had worked out solid escape routes before the attack had even started. Josh figured the one on the roof had gone through a ventilation duct to get inside the hospital, where he'd just blended in until he could walk out. It didn't help that neither Gage, Jaycee nor he could give accurate descriptions of the guys.

The other one Josh had been after had likely had a vehicle parked nearby. Again, he'd blended in with the rest of the traffic on Main Street.

Too bad the escape plans had worked.

But why had they tried to kidnap Jaycee again?

And there was no doubt in his mind that this had been a kidnapping attempt. The guy on the roof was supposed to take Josh out. Gage, too. Leaving the one in the parking lot to kidnap Jaycee. Obviously, they wanted her bad, or else they wouldn't have staged an attack in broad daylight.

Was it the baby they wanted?

Or was it Jaycee so they could eliminate her in case she'd seen something at the baby farm that she could use to make an arrest?

Josh didn't have answers for that and probably wouldn't until he managed to catch one of those guards and question him. And he would catch one. Too bad that might not happen before there was another attack.

That went through his head like a broken record, too.

At least he'd managed to get the doctor out to the ranch to examine Jaycee. From what the doc had been able to tell, everything was fine with both the baby and her. Josh needed to make sure things stayed that way.

He lay on the bed, stared up at the ceiling and listened to the sound of the shower running. Jaycee had been in there for a long time, but then she no doubt had a lot of tense muscles that needed relaxing. He wished he could say it was the end of the tension-causing events, but he couldn't.

This was just getting started.

He'd already verified that the woman who'd come to the hospital cafeteria was indeed Miranda Culley, and that she'd never been held captive at a baby farm and had not made those 911 calls to set up the meeting at the cemetery. So why had someone impersonated her?

To lure him out when he tried to rescue her?

Maybe.

But the lure hadn't worked because no one pretending to be Miranda had shown up. Still, Jaycee and he had gone out to that cemetery, and he might have been shot if he hadn't had plenty of backup with him. Jaycee could have been hurt, too, with a botched kidnapping.

Heck, they'd come close to being shot again today.

Josh touched the scar on his chest. It wasn't hurting much tonight. Probably because he'd had plenty of other things to occupy his mind.

Like keeping Jaycee safe.

He had to do a better job of that, but all the measures seemed temporary at this point. Especially now with the decorating crew for the wedding on the grounds.

Soon the caterers would arrive, too, and then the day after tomorrow, the guests. It was one wedding that Josh couldn't attend. No way. Not with several hundred guests expected, and he couldn't very well ask his uncle Boone to postpone it. That was why Josh had already called his brother about making arrangements for a safe house.

If he couldn't catch those armed guards and shut down the baby farms, then Jaycee and he would be joined at the hip, well, forever. A safe house and this apartment were going to get pretty darn small if things weren't settled soon.

His phone rang, something it'd been doing a lot since they'd arrived back at the ranch. Just calls to let him know that all their attempts to find those guards had failed. This time, he saw Grayson's name on the screen.

"Thought you'd like to know that Sierra left the hospital with her baby about an hour ago," Grayson said. "Mason tried to stop her. The doctor, too, but she wouldn't stay."

And that made her stupid. "Does she know about the latest shooting?"

"She knows. Still didn't change her mind. Before she left, Bryson made a fuss about seeing the baby," Grayson went on. "I finally had a nurse let him see her through the nursery window. He took one look at the baby, cursed a blue streak and said she wasn't his, that she didn't look like him. He stormed off, mumbling something about demanding another paternity test."

"Valerie did say that Sierra could have had the results of the first test faked." Of course, Valerie could have said that to shift suspicion from herself onto her.

"She repeated that to Bryson. Valerie was with him when he saw the baby."

Another case of being joined at the hip. That closeness between two of their suspects bothered Josh, but he wasn't sure what to make of it. Maybe it was something as simple as Valerie being his attorney. After the shooting today, however, he wasn't about to take anything at face value.

"What did Sierra have to say about Bryson and her sister's reactions?" Josh asked.

"Not much. She insists the child is Bryson's and says to prove it she'll have as many tests as he wants."

That didn't sound like the offer of a guilty woman. Unless Sierra figured she could fake those results, too. Of course, it could have been all talk, because Sierra had left the hospital for some reason. Maybe because she was afraid for her life or maybe just because she was afraid of what Bryson might do to her if he found out she was lying about the baby's paternity.

The bathroom door opened, and Jaycee stepped out. She was wearing a stark-white loaner bathrobe, and her face was flushed, no doubt from the warm steamy water. For just a split second Josh got an image of her standing in the shower.

Naked.

His imagination was a little too good in that area, because he felt the heat coil through his entire body. Of course, it didn't help that he had the real thing standing right in front of him and looking far better than a scared pregnant woman should look.

"Call me if anything comes up," he said to Grayson

when he managed to stop himself from being tongue-tied. He ended the call and sat up.

"No, you should stay there." Jaycee motioned for him to remain on the bed. "I'd imagine your back is sore from sleeping on the floor."

Well, it didn't feel good, but because of that heat coursing through him, it was best if he didn't stay on the bed. At the moment it wasn't a safe place to be. Because there was one stupid part of his body that might try to talk Jaycee into joining him there.

"Sierra left the hospital." He got off the bed, the mattress creaking a little. Stood. Faced her. "She took the baby with her."

Jaycee blew out a long breath. "I feel sorry for that child. Especially if Bryson is the father. The idea of him getting custody makes me a little ill."

Even though this was a serious discussion, she glanced at him. Then at the bed. She fidgeted with the tie on the terry-cloth robe, though it didn't look as if it needed any kind of adjustment.

Well, except for that V opening that went practically to her breasts.

The garment wasn't meant to be provocative, but it was on Jaycee. Her breasts looked ready to spill right out of there, and sadly, that stupid part of his body was hoping they did.

Just to give his head and his mouth something else to do, he tipped his head to the kitchen area. "Bessie, the cook, sent us over some beef stew with one of the ranch hands. It's in the microwave."

The stew didn't get much of a reaction, but her eyes widened when her attention went to the table and the plate of doughnuts covered with plastic wrap.

"I told Bessie about your doughnut craving," Josh explained, "and she fixed those for you, too. She said I'm to tell you though that they're not as good as the ones you'd get from the café in town."

The place they'd intended to stop before someone had tried to kill them.

That had certainly put a hold on the doughnut plans. Instead, Josh had rushed Jaycee back to the ranch, literally locked them inside and set the security system.

Jaycee gave a sheepish smile. "I'll have just one and then some stew." She crossed the room and dived into the plate of doughnuts.

"I swear, I ate healthy while I was a captive." She made that sound of pleasure again after she'd had a bite.

The sound that reminded Josh of sex, the bed and other things that he shouldn't be reminded of right now. Man, he really needed to get a grip.

But that didn't happen.

His eyes went wandering, and when Jaycee lifted the doughnut to take another bite, her robe shifted, and he got a glimpse of her breasts.

No bra.

No gown.

Unless she had on panties, she was butt naked beneath the robe. His body didn't let him forget that, either.

"Sorry," she mumbled.

He looked to see what she meant. She'd noticed him gawking at her, all right. She fixed the robe to cover her breasts but then licked the sugar off her fingers.

Yeah, he was definitely toast.

He wasn't sure why she was having this effect on him now. Maybe it was because he was pushing through the rest of the adrenaline crash. Or if he was truthful with himself, Jaycee had always had this effect on him.

Well, before the shooting that nearly killed him anyway.

Josh had been able to use that incident to keep the heat at bay, but he was failing miserably at it right now.

"Sorry," she mumbled again. And yep, she'd noticed that he was practically drooling over her.

He muttered some profanity and moved away from her. "I think I'll go ahead and grab a shower." An ice-cold one to chill him down. Maybe two of them.

But she stood and blocked his path.

A really bad idea.

The last thing he needed right now was to be close to her. Even if that was exactly what he wanted.

"I don't want this to be an issue between us." She licked her lips this time, no doubt searching for any stray sugar bits left over from the doughnut, and she was driving him crazy in the process. "The attraction was always there. *Always,*" she repeated when he gave her a flat look.

Yeah, it had been.

And it still was.

It took Josh several seconds to repeat the bad stuff that'd gone on between them. Several more seconds to drill it into his brain that while he did forgive her, crossing the line with her now could be dangerous.

Did that stop him?

Nope.

With the sane part of him yelling for him to stop, he reached out, sliding his hand right into that robe, and he found exactly what his body was looking for.

A warm, soft, naked woman who could burn him to ash.

Even though she'd been the one to stop him from leaving the room, Jaycee suddenly got that deer-caught-in-headlights look. "Uh, you're sure about this?"

At least that was what Josh thought she said. He couldn't be certain because he kissed her before she finished talking. Still, he caught the gist of what she meant. Like him,

Jaycee knew the timing for this sucked. And not just the timing—everything about this was wrong, wrong, wrong.

That didn't stop him, either.

He just kept kissing her. Kept sliding his hand deeper into the robe until he was cupping her breast. He swiped his thumb over her nipple and got a very good reaction.

Or bad, depending on perspective.

From his insane body's perspective, it was the right reaction. She moaned, that little silky sound of pleasure, and she melted against him.

She tasted sweet, like the sugary doughnut, but it was mixed with something else. Something dark and forbidden.

Which she was.

But that only made the kiss hotter. It only made him want her more.

He shoved open the robe. He'd been right about the naked part. Not a stitch of clothes, and he broke the kiss just long enough to look at her.

Yeah, he'd also been right about the burning-to-ash part.

Before he could talk himself out of it, he backed her against the counter. He didn't think beyond the moment of pleasuring her. Pleasuring himself by touching her. And his hand was already sliding between her legs when he got a quick slap back to reality.

The baby.

Or rather her pregnant belly.

He shook his head, hoping to clear it. Didn't work. And he opened his mouth to ask a question that he shouldn't ask.

Was it okay for them to be doing this?

Of course, the answer was *no.* It wasn't okay, but since his body wasn't going to listen to that, he needed to know if it was physically okay for them to be doing this.

He got his answer fast.

Jaycee kissed him, pulling him right back to her. "There's no reason to stop because of the baby. It's okay for pregnant women to have sex."

There went his out. Because there were only two things that could have stopped him from jumping off this cliff—Jaycee saying no or her telling him she couldn't continue because of the baby. But clearly she didn't want an out, either.

And Josh didn't give her one.

He shoved open her robe and dropped some kisses on her neck. Then her breasts, which were full and warm and smelled sweet like the rest of her. Each touch of his mouth caused her to make those silky sounds of pleasure.

So Josh kept going.

Kept kissing until the fire was burning too hot inside him. He was pretty sure it was burning inside her, too, because she kept fighting to get closer.

"The bed," Jaycee managed to say. She pulled him up, kissing his mouth and maneuvering him in that direction.

She had the right idea about the bed, but it was taking way too long to get there. Everything was taking too long. Because his body kept hammering home that he needed her *now.*

Without breaking the kiss, Josh scooped her up, took her across the room and eased her onto the bed. He reminded himself to stay gentle.

But Jaycee didn't help with that, either.

The moment her back touched the mattress, she hooked her arm around his neck and pulled him on top of her. He kept most of his weight on his forearms, but Jaycee took full advantage of the gap between their bodies, and she unbuttoned his shirt. It involved a lot of touching, and when she shucked it off him, her clever hands went to his bare chest.

Stomach.

And lower.

To the front of his jeans.

Oh, man. Josh hadn't thought the fire inside could get any hotter, but he'd been wrong. That did it. When he got his eyes uncrossed, he stood just long enough the rid himself of his boots and jeans. He would have gotten to his boxers next, but Jaycee reared up to help him.

More eye crossing.

Either she wasn't very good at taking off a man's underwear or else she wanted to torture him. Josh didn't have time to decide which because she pulled him back onto the bed with her.

"Let's finish this," she insisted.

He did. Josh eased into her, and he had to bite back some profanity because she felt that good. That slick heat only made him need her more.

And that need was yelling for him to finish her *now*.

Part of him wished he could savor this moment, but that part of him lost the battle fast. Jaycee saw to that. She wrapped her arms and legs around him, pushing him deeper inside her. And faster. Until she could take no more.

The climax rippled through her body, and Josh watched the pleasure of her release spread across her face. She touched her tongue to her top lip. Closed her eyes.

Whispered his name.

Josh didn't even try to speak. Didn't try to hold on for one last moment of pleasure.

He just let himself fall.

Chapter Sixteen

Jaycee just wanted to lie there in bed and enjoy every bit of this moment.

But Josh obviously had different plans.

He eased off her as if she was delicate crystal that might shatter beneath him, and he dropped on his back beside her. His breathing was still heavy, the pulse jumping on his throat, but because he was staring up at the ceiling, she could no longer look into his eyes.

Which was just as well.

Right before he'd moved, Jaycee had caught a glimpse of his "what the heck have I done?" expression. She'd expected it, of course. Because part of her felt the same way.

Probably not for the same reason as Josh, however.

What she'd told him was true—she always had been attracted to him. That's why she'd fallen so easily into bed with him five months ago. However, deeper down, it had felt like more than a mere attraction.

And that scared the heck out of her.

Josh had told her that he hadn't considered himself father material because of his parents' messy divorce when he was a kid. Well, she didn't consider herself relationship material because of messy parents, either.

Yet here she was. In bed with Josh again. Complicating both their lives.

Still, she didn't regret it.

Even if she should.

He groaned. Not quite as bad as the groan he'd made five months ago when he had learned she was in part responsible for his partner's death and his own injury. She turned to him, ready to apologize—just to get it out of the way—but he leaned over and dropped a kiss on her mouth.

"I moved back to Silver Creek because I thought it'd be safer," he grumbled. "Ironic, huh?"

She thought about that a moment. "Are you talking about me, the baby or the gun-slinging guards?"

He turned his head, snagged her gaze. "Definitely not the baby." And he planted another kiss on her belly. "The guards, for sure. You, well, you're dangerous in your own way."

Jaycee cringed and pushed aside the memories of his shooting. Playtime was apparently over. Reality and their painful pasts were back. She pulled the sides of the robe over her naked body and started to get up.

She didn't make it far.

Josh pulled her right back down with him.

"I wasn't talking about the shooting five months ago," he clarified. He slipped his arm beneath her and brought her closer to him. "It's hard for me to concentrate around you."

She looked down his body at the part of him that'd been very hard just minutes earlier, and she smiled. Yes, it was stupid. She didn't have much to smile about, except this was the most relaxed and satisfied her body had felt in five months.

Since the last time Josh and she had been together.

Jaycee levered herself up a little so she could make eye contact with him. She wanted him to see the determined look on her face when she gave him an out that he obviously wanted. He'd certainly wanted one five months ago.

"This doesn't have to mean anything," she said. *There.* It was the perfect out.

Except she didn't get quite the reaction she'd thought she would from him. Josh frowned. "I was about to ask you to marry me."

She sucked in her breath so fast that Jaycee got choked on it. Jaycee couldn't even repeat what he'd said, much less answer it. "You've lost your mind," she managed to say after several moments.

"Probably. But neither of us had the chance to be raised by two parents. We could give that to her...our child."

Jaycee froze again. Josh was really throwing the surprises at her tonight.

"It's a girl?" she asked.

But he didn't confirm or deny it. "You said you didn't want to know."

"I said I didn't want to know right then, when I was ready to jump out of my skin. I don't feel that way now."

He only shook his head and gave her a naughty-boy smile. "Just consider it a slip of the tongue. Now, back to my proposal—"

"My answer's no," Jaycee interrupted.

That brought him to a sitting position, and every trace of his smile vanished. "No?"

"No," she repeated. She sat up, too, and looked him straight in the eyes. "We can both raise our daughter, or our son," Jaycee amended, "and we can do that without being married."

"How? With me here and you over in San Antonio? I know it's not that far, but sooner or later you'll want to go back to work."

Yes, and she'd thought Josh would do the same. "Does that mean you're staying here in Silver Creek?"

"Possibly. Probably," he amended several seconds later. "The deputy job feels right, you know. So does being around family."

No, she didn't know, and her silence must have told Josh that he'd hit a nerve. "You love your job as an agent," he added.

"Do I?" She hadn't intended to say that aloud, but with it out there, she just continued to bare her soul that she probably should keep covered. "I always thought I had to work twice as hard to prove myself."

"Because of your parents," he finished for her. "But you love it?" And that time it was a question.

"Parts of it. Like finding justice for people who might not get it any other way." That was what she'd always believed, but she slid her hand over her stomach.

The baby had changed everything.

It had changed *her*.

Jaycee couldn't see herself kissing her baby goodbye each morning while she went out and dodged bullets for the rest of the day.

When had this happened? When had she turned into something she'd always believed she wouldn't become? A soon-to-be mother. One who'd just minutes earlier offered Josh joint custody. Apparently, a good round of sex had caused her to have a dull brain, because she hadn't even made up her mind about that.

"I'll look for a different job," she finally said. "Maybe one here in town so that distance wouldn't be a problem."

"Marriage might make things easier."

"Or harder," she argued. Jaycee huffed. "The sex will only take us so far if we stay under the same roof. Sooner or later, we'd have to deal with the issues that drove us apart five months ago."

He stared at her. Didn't dispute that. Nor did he verbally withdraw his proposal.

However, Jaycee could see the withdrawal in his eyes.

She could see the pain, too, and she was responsible for a lot of that. Since she doubted he wanted to discuss that pain, she brought up the other bombshell he'd dropped.

"So is it a boy or a girl?" she asked.

He opened his mouth, and Jaycee thought she might finally get an answer to her question.

But she didn't.

His phone rang, and after she saw Grayson's name on the screen, she knew it was a call he'd have to take. Thankfully, he put it on speaker so she could hear.

"The blood tests on Sierra's baby just came back," Grayson started, "and Bryson's not the father."

Jaycee shook her head. "They can determine that from blood tests?"

"They can if they know the blood types of the parents. Sierra's is type A, and Bryson's type O. That means the baby has to be either A or O to be their child, but the baby's type B. The baby had to have gotten that blood type from her biological father."

And that was something they might never find out. Well, unless Sierra could figure out how to use it to her advantage. "So Sierra faked the amnio test results?"

"Looks that way, and Bryson's not going to be too happy about it."

"He knows?" Josh asked.

"Not yet. I'm calling him next. I'll let you know how it goes."

"Bryson's going to be furious," Jaycee mumbled, but she was thankful that the man wouldn't get custody of the child. Still, she wasn't sure the baby would fare much better with Sierra. Or even the real birth father.

And speaking of babies, that reminded Jaycee of what Josh and she had been discussing before Grayson's call. The sex of their own baby.

"I want to know," Jaycee insisted. But again, no answer.

The lights went out, plunging them into total darkness.

JOSH WENT STILL for several seconds. And listened. Waiting for the power to come back on.

It didn't.

It wasn't unusual for the electricity to go off during storms, but there was no storm outside. Not the kind created by Mother Nature anyway.

He got up from the bed and dressed. Fast. Jaycee did the same, and he hurried to the window to look out. The main house was dark, too, and so were the exterior security lights and Grayson's house. So not just a power outage at his place but what appeared to be the entire ranch.

His phone rang, and he reached for both it and his gun. "Grayson," he answered after seeing his name on the screen. "What's going on?"

"Not sure, but Gage and I are heading out to check on it now. Stay with Jaycee. The security system will kick over to battery power so we should know if someone breaches the fence or the houses."

Including his apartment, since it was on the same security grid.

Josh hated to put his cousins in possible harm's way again, but protecting Jaycee had to be his priority, so he'd definitely stay put.

And keep watch.

Jaycee did the same on the other side of the window after she took his gun from the top of his fridge.

"I don't see anyone. Do you?" she asked.

No more heat in her voice. Just fear that caused her words to tremble a little. Something he hated to hear because lately fear had been there way too often.

He shook his head. Kept watching. And not just the area in front of the barn. Josh watched the sides, too.

Of course, he had one big blind spot because there were no windows at the back of his apartment. If anyone did come in from the pasture or the back road, he wouldn't be able to see them until they got to the exterior stairs that led up to his place.

He saw some movement near the main house. Ranch hands, probably. They didn't head his way but fanned out, staying close to the house. No doubt looking for anyone who might be a threat. Too bad there were plenty who could fall into that threat category since there was still a decorating crew on the grounds.

Jaycee was breathing through her mouth now, her breath fogging up the glass. Thanks to the moonlight, he could see her face. Could see the terror there and the death grip she had on the gun.

Josh was about to reassure her that it was probably nothing.

But he saw *something.*

Or at least he thought he did.

"What's wrong?" she asked, her gaze frantically searching the grounds below.

Josh didn't answer. He focused all his attention near the stairs where he thought he'd spotted some kind of movement, but no one was there. At least no one in his line of sight.

However, there were plenty of places for someone to hide.

He kept watching. Kept waiting. And he cursed the

stress that Jaycee had to be feeling by now. If it was only partially as high as his, then it was too much. Not just for her but for the baby.

Just when he thought he could release the breath that he'd been holding, Josh saw it again. The shadow at the base of the stairs. He hoped it was just the moonlight playing tricks with his eyes and the wooden railing.

No such luck.

The shadow moved again.

And he saw that it was a man dressed all in black. He also got a glimpse of the gun he was holding.

One of the guards from the baby farm, no doubt.

"Move away from the window," Josh ordered Jaycee. "And get on the floor."

While she hurried to do that, Josh took out his phone to call Grayson, but the man in black starting running up the stairs.

He wasn't alone.

There were two others following him.

"Get under the bed," Josh told Jaycee. No time to do much else.

He could hear the footsteps thundering on the stairs, and he pivoted and took aim at the door.

Just as one of the men kicked it in.

There was the cracking sound of the wood, and the door slamming into the wall. Then the security system. Not a blare yet, but a steady beeping sound to give him time to punch in the code to stop the alarm from going off. Josh wouldn't do that. He wanted the alarm. Wanted everyone on the ranch alerted that he had an intruder.

Josh held his fire, waiting for them to step inside.

But that didn't happen.

Through the frantic beeps of the security system, he

heard another sound of something metal hitting the floor. Unfortunately, this sound was familiar.

A tear-gas canister.

Not just one of them but three.

It didn't take long, just a few seconds, for the milky-white gas to start billowing through the room. And to reach Jaycee and him. They started coughing, and Josh's eyes burned like fire. He couldn't see, and he couldn't risk shooting because he didn't want to hit Jaycee.

The alarm came. Full blast. The sound vibrated through the room and through his head.

Josh ran to Jaycee, groping to find her in the darkness. He tried to shield her with his body, but he couldn't stay standing. The coughing and burning took over, and he couldn't catch his breath. He had no choice but to drop to his knees.

He heard movement to his right. Tried to take aim at the dark figures moving through the cloud of gas. He got just a glimpse of one of them wearing a mask.

Before the guy bashed the butt of a rifle against Josh's head.

The pain exploded through him, and even though he tried to fight back, he dropped like deadweight onto the floor.

Jaycee made a sound. A strangled scream that he heard even over the piercing alarm. Josh tried to get up. To fight back so he could protect her. But another blow to his head put him right back down on the floor.

A shot blasted through the room, causing his fear to snowball out of control. "Jaycee?" he managed to say.

But she didn't answer.

Oh, God.

Had she been shot? Or was she the one who'd done the firing?

Josh couldn't tell, but he heard another clanging sound and got a glimpse of a gun falling to the floor next to him. He couldn't be sure, but he thought it was the same gun that Jaycee had been carrying.

"No!" Jaycee said through the coughing and wheezing. And she just kept repeating it.

One of the mask-wearing men scooped her up, giving Josh a hard kick to the chest in the process. Another jolt of pain, but despite the searing pain and the tear gas, he didn't stay down. He fought to get up and stumbled across the room toward the still-open door.

He had to get to her.

Had to stop these men and save her.

Though it seemed to take an eternity, Josh made it to the doorway. And he took aim. But the men had already made it all the way down the stairs and were heading toward the rear of the barn.

"Stop!" Josh yelled. He knew they wouldn't listen, but he hoped to alert some of the ranch hands. There were several already running his way.

He was dizzy, still fighting to breathe and see, but Josh got down the stairs. Running as fast as he could. But he heard two more sounds that he didn't want to hear.

Jaycee's scream.

And the engine of a vehicle starting up.

There were several vehicles parked back there for the ranch hands to use, but he doubted any ranch hand was behind the wheel. No.

It was one of the guards.

Josh took aim, praying he'd be able to shoot out the tires. But the truck didn't come his way. He caught just a glimpse of the bloodred taillights as the truck sped across the pasture.

With Jaycee inside.

Chapter Seventeen

Jaycee fought as if her life depended on it.

Because it did.

Her life, the baby's and Josh's were all hanging in the balance. She'd seen the way the goon had kicked Josh and bashed him with a gun. Jaycee prayed he wasn't hurt. Or worse. And while she was praying, she added one for her to get away from these monsters.

It wasn't working.

No matter how hard she fought or how loud she screamed, it didn't help. The hulking scumbags just held on to her and shoved her into a truck a split second before it sped away. They peeled off their gas masks, tossing them on the truck floor, but it was hard to see their faces because they were covered in camouflage paint.

She kept blinking her eyes, trying to focus even though they were still stinging and watery from the tear gas. But she finally got just a glimpse of Josh in the side mirror. He was running toward her like a madman, and he had his gun aimed but didn't shoot.

Couldn't.

Because he wouldn't risk hitting her.

Her heart went to her stomach as the truck drove away and Josh disappeared from sight. This couldn't be happening. She couldn't go through this again.

She tried to push aside the fear and the dread and concentrate on what she could do. Not much with three armed goons squeezed into the truck with her. It was a two-seater vehicle, and one of the guys was in the back, a gun pointed at her head. She was on the front seat sandwiched between the other two.

Jaycee reached between the driver and her, hoping to snag a weapon he had in his pocket, but the other two jerks stopped her before her hand even made it to the man. The one on her right cursed her, calling her a bad name, and he grabbed the seat belt and buckled her up.

"Who are you and what do you want?" she demanded, and Jaycee hoped she sounded like an FBI agent and not a terrified pregnant woman.

None of them answered. In fact, the two in the front seat didn't even spare her a glance. The driver had his attention on the rocky dirt road, and the one in the passenger's seat was looking in the side mirror. No doubt looking for whoever would follow them.

And someone would follow.

Josh, no doubt, and she prayed he didn't get himself killed while trying to rescue her again.

The goon in the passenger seat didn't take his eyes off the side mirror, but he made a call. Because he sheltered his hand over the phone, Jaycee couldn't see the numbers that he pressed in, and she didn't hear who answered over the noise of her heartbeat crashing in her ears. However, she did hear his single-sentence response.

"We have her."

So none of these three were in charge. They were just minions for the person who was no doubt responsible for the baby farms.

Jaycee couldn't go back there.

She looked around the cab of the truck for anything she

could use as a weapon. The discarded gas masks were on the floor, and if she could grab one she could wallop one of them with it. Of course, the other two would just stop her attack.

Or they might crash.

A crash *might* get her free of them, but it was a huge risk to take.

So what could she do to get away from them?

Normally, she'd try negotiation, but Jaycee seriously doubted that would work with these three. No. They were on a mission to take her to someone who would do heaven knows what with her baby and her.

She had a very short list of things she could try to get herself out of this mess. And next up was some old-fashioned deception. She clutched her stomach and moaned as loudly as she could.

"The baby," she yelled. "Oh, God. The baby! I think I'm miscarrying."

Just as she'd hoped, that got their attention. The two in the front seat exchanged concerned glances, and the goon on her right took out his phone to make another call.

"She's making a fuss about the baby," he said to the person on the other end of the line. "I'm pretty sure she's faking it, but better get the doctor out there just in case."

Jaycee wished she could reach through the line and crush the person her captor was talking to, because he or she had almost certainly orchestrated all of this. She seriously doubted she'd get to see the culprit though because this dirtbag was a coward, letting the hired muscle do the kidnapping.

The guy put his phone away again. And he cursed. For a moment Jaycee thought she was the reason for the renewed profanity, but she followed his gaze to the side mirror.

There were headlights behind them in the distance.

It was an SUV, and it looked like the one that'd been parked behind the barn.

Josh.

Maybe he'd brought a family full of backup with him.

She kept up the moaning and arched her back so that her elbows jabbed into the men on each side of her. They didn't seem to notice, and the one in the backseat swiveled around and took aim. Not at her but at the person trying to rescue her. There was a small slide window that was open so the idiot goons would likely have a good shot.

Jaycee needed to do something about that.

She upped the volume on her moaning and levered herself up even higher when she pretended to have a contraction. In the same motion, Jaycee threw back her hand, knocking into the arm of the man in the rear seat. Now he cursed her and raised his left hand as if he might slap her.

"Keep your eyes on the SUV behind us," the driver snarled.

Even in the dim light, she saw the anger flash in the guard's eyes, but he turned back around and pointed his gun again.

Now Jaycee cursed.

She'd failed.

And worse, the guy fired a shot at the SUV. Not one shot but two. She couldn't tell if he'd hit anything, but she prayed Josh and anyone else inside were all right.

The truck bobbled over a rough patch of road, and the driver had to give the wheel a sharp turn to the left to stop them from going into the ditch. Behind him, the other vehicle gained some ground. Probably because the driver was familiar with every inch of this road and the guard wasn't. Her captor practically had to slam on his brakes when they reached a sharp turn.

Jaycee saw another of those sharp curves ahead, and

she held her breath, waiting for the driver to slow down so he could safely take the turn. Anything she did at this point was a huge risk, but so was just sitting there while the idiot behind her continued to pop off shots at the SUV.

Shots that could hit Josh.

When the driver slowed as much as she figured he'd slow for the curve, Jaycee drew back her elbow and rammed it as hard as she could into his ribs.

He howled in pain.

The other one in the passenger's seat reached for her, but she grabbed a gas mask and bashed first him, then the other. More howling. And the truck did more than just bobble. It went into a skid.

From the corner of her eye, she saw the guy in the back turn his gun on her, and her heart went into overdrive. He was going to shoot her.

But he didn't get a chance to fire.

The truck skidded right off the road, hurling them over some rocks and shrubs. Jaycee's head hit the ceiling, and the guards and she bobbled around like rag dolls.

Ahead she saw the tree, but there was nothing she could do except shelter her stomach with her hands.

They plowed right into a sprawling oak.

JOSH'S BREATH VANISHED when he saw the truck leave the road. He figured the driver had lost control, but then he could see some kind of struggle going on in the cab.

Hell.

If Jaycee was hurt, every one of those men would pay for it.

Josh pulled his SUV to a stop and barreled out. Grayson and a ranch hand weren't too far behind him, but he didn't want to wait for them. He had to make sure Jaycee was all right.

His head was still pounding. So was the pain in his chest where the kidnapper had kicked him. But Josh fought through the pain, jumped the ditch and ran full speed toward the collision.

The truck was wrecked, no doubt about that, and there was steam spewing from the hood, which was now smashed against the tree.

The driver's door flew open, and the man practically spilled out. He was armed, but he didn't take the time to turn around and aim at Josh. He just raced behind a big clump of rocks and dropped to the ground.

Not good.

Josh ducked, darted behind a tree. The passenger's side door opened, too, and he braced himself to see scumbags number two and three.

However, it was Jaycee who crawled out.

Not easily. She climbed over one of the men, who appeared to be only partly conscious. He was moaning and cursing at the same time, but Jaycee managed to get by him. The moment her feet touched the ground, she ran toward him.

Josh caught her in his arms and pulled her behind the tree with him. He didn't kiss her. Didn't want to take his attention off that truck and the kidnappers, but he was beyond thankful that she hadn't been hurt.

"You're okay," he managed to say at the same time that Jaycee said it to him.

"I was wearing a seat belt," she added. "They weren't."

Thank heaven for that, and Josh added a wish that the trio was hurt too badly to put up much of a fight.

His wish didn't come true.

A bullet smashed right into the tree, just inches from where Jaycee and he were standing. Josh pushed her against the rough bark, protecting her as best he could with his body, and he glanced out to see what was going on.

Scumbag number one had been the person to fire the shot. Scumbags two and three were climbing out on the driver's side. Away from Jaycee and him.

Which meant Josh didn't have a good shot at any of them.

Three guns to one weren't good odds. Especially when all three of them opened fire. The shots blasted into the tree.

"Give me your backup weapon from your boot holster," Jaycee insisted.

But Josh had to shake his head. "I don't have it." Because he'd literally had to throw on his clothes after the power had been cut.

"How about a knife, anything?" she pressed.

There was no knife or anything else he could give to Jaycee. Only himself. And that had to be enough, because he wasn't willing to deal with the alternative of her being taken captive again.

Josh looked behind him and saw truck lights slash through the darkness. His backup was on the way, but it was dangerous for Grayson to drive straight into a hail of bullets. He handed Jaycee his phone.

"Text Grayson." He had to yell over the noise from the shots so she could hear him. "Let him know where we are and that he needs to stay back until they stop shooting."

Josh wanted backup now, but it'd be suicide for Grayson to come driving into this.

Jaycee sent the text and shoved his phone back into his pocket. Josh fired off a single shot at the gunmen just so they'd know he was armed and so they wouldn't try to come closer.

Just up the narrow dirt road, Grayson stopped his truck,

but he kept the headlights on. It was a like a beacon for the kidnappers because they sent some of the shots in that direction. Josh hoped his cousin and the ranch hand stayed down. Sooner or later these idiots were going to run out of ammunition.

He hoped.

Then Josh could make his move. He wasn't sure exactly what his move would be, but he needed to get Jaycee far away from these men who'd kidnapped her.

It'd been a brazen attack. The kind that only dangerous criminals would attempt, and he had to do everything humanly possible to make sure they didn't get their hands back on her.

His phone dinged, indicating he had a text message, and Josh motioned for Jaycee to read it. "Grayson says he's going to create a diversion. His brothers are closing off the other end of the road."

So the kidnappers would be trapped. That was good. He wanted them trapped and caught, but Josh wasn't so sure about this diversion.

"What diversion?" he asked Jaycee. But she didn't have time to answer.

"Put down your weapons!" Grayson shouted.

Of course, the men didn't listen. That only caused them to fire more shots in Grayson's direction. Josh wondered if this was a ploy to make them use up the ammunition even faster, but then he saw Grayson's truck.

It was creeping along, headed not toward Jaycee and him but right toward the clump of rocks that the men were using for cover.

Not a bad diversion.

Josh put his mouth against Jaycee's ear. "When the truck gets between us and the men, we move."

She gave a shaky nod. Actually, everything about her

was shaky, and he hoped she hadn't lied about being okay. It seemed to take an eternity for the truck to reach them, and the gunmen cursed it and kept shooting. When it gave Jaycee and him the best possible cover, he caught on to her hand and got her moving.

They'd only made it a few steps before the shots came right at them.

Chapter Eighteen

Jaycee kept as low as she could and kept running.

Thanks to Josh.

He had hold of her arm, and he didn't let go despite the bullets kicking up dirt and rocks all around them. He pulled her onto the other side of a dirt embankment, and they dropped to the ground.

There were more shots.

But not all were coming from the kidnappers.

Some were coming from the direction of the dirt road where she'd last seen Grayson and another man. A ranch hand, most likely. Jaycee had caught only a glimpse of them before their truck had started moving their way. Now that truck had run into the clump of rocks where the kidnappers had taken cover.

At least one of the men was hurt. She'd gotten a glimpse of the blood on his face before she had crawled over him and escaped. Jaycee hoped his wounds were bad enough that he couldn't return fire and also so that his comrades would want to get him out of there fast and to a hospital. They would have to stop shooting to do that, and then maybe Grayson and Josh could move in to arrest them.

The shots kept coming, but they weren't aimed directly at her. Most of the shots were going to the left, the bullets tearing through the dirt and scattering the debris everywhere, including her eyes. She was still feeling the effects of the tear gas, and the debris and the darkness didn't help.

That thought froze in her head.

Not the debris. But the tear gas.

Oh, mercy. Could that have harmed the baby?

She slid her hand over her stomach and prayed that it hadn't, but it made the situation even more urgent. She, too, needed to get to a hospital. Of course, these men would try to stop that from happening. Clearly, this was still a kidnapping attempt.

And she still didn't know why.

Was it because she was an FBI agent and they wanted to find out what she'd learned? Or did they only want the baby? Jaycee hoped she found out soon because that answer might give her some clues as to who was behind this.

Josh was already practically on top of her. Sheltering and protecting her. And as before, he put his mouth right against her ear.

"The ranch road curves and continues over there," he said, tipping his head to a heavily treed area on the right. "If we can get there, someone can pick us up and get us out of here."

Jaycee was all for that, though moving would mean leaving cover. For a few seconds anyway.

"Send Grayson another text," Josh added. "See if he can create another diversion and tell him we're going to move to the road away from the shooters. Have him get someone out there if he can."

Her hands were shaking like crazy, but Jaycee managed to write the text. And the waiting began. The kidnappers kept shooting, but from what she could tell, they weren't moving in for the kill.

Why not?

She shook her head, glad that it wasn't happening but wondering what the heck they were waiting for.

Or who.

Maybe their boss hadn't given them an out—they weren't to come back unless they had her.

Josh's phone dinged, and she saw the response text from Grayson. Will do.

Grayson didn't give details, but a moment later, she saw the plan in action. A hot pink flare shot into the night sky like fireworks. But not just into the sky. Several of the flares came shooting like rockets right at the kidnappers.

Josh didn't wait to see what would happen. He got them moving again away from the embankment and to those trees. It took a few seconds, just enough time for them to reach cover, before the shots came their way again.

The second diversion had worked.

Well, for Josh and her anyway.

With the new position, she was able to see the shooter, and two were firing at Grayson. The other, at Josh and her.

So much for hoping that one guy was injured too badly to fire.

All three men looked fit and ready to kill. And they were sending most of their shots at Grayson. She hoped he'd taken cover before shooting off those flares.

"Let's go," Josh said over the deafening noise, and that was the only warning Jaycee got before he moved them to another tree. Then another.

Each step was a huge risk because the shots kept coming—not directly at her but at Josh and the others. Even when one of the men stopped to reload, his partners picked up the slack and just continued firing.

Josh and she worked their way through the trees, and she tried to position herself so the men wouldn't be able to shoot him. But Josh would have no part in that. He just shoved her right back behind him and continued their trek to the road.

So did one of the kidnappers.

The bulky one who'd driven the truck moved out from behind the rocks and came after them.

That sent her heart crashing against her ribs, but it didn't slow them down. Even when the guy fired into the tree they were using for cover, Josh just kept them moving toward the road.

It seemed to take an eternity before Jaycee finally saw the dirt road just ahead.

She also saw the kidnapper behind them.

Josh did, too. He leaned out, sent a bullet the man's way, but the guy just briefly ducked out of sight. The snake used the same trees for cover that Josh and she had.

"Wait," Josh said to her, and he stopped several yards from the road.

It was much darker in this area because the towering trees on both sides blocked most of the moonlight. Her eyes had already adjusted to the darkness, but she could hardly see anything.

Certainly no headlights from a rescue vehicle.

"We'll follow the road until someone from the ranch gets here," Josh explained.

Jaycee had no idea how long it would take for a vehicle to circle back around to this point, but she prayed it wouldn't take long.

Josh got them moving again. Not on the road itself but along the side of it. Probably so they could still use the trees for cover if things got worse.

Without the gunshots blasting nearby, she could hear the kidnapper clomping his way through the woods. She couldn't tell how far away he was, but he was close.

Too close.

Once the rescue car arrived, he might be able to kill Josh and anyone else who got in his way.

The road made another of those sharp curves, and Josh slowed when they made it around the curve and came out onto a straight stretch.

"Hell," she heard him mumble, and he pulled her to the ground.

It took Jaycee a moment to figure out why he'd done that.

And then she saw it.

The car.

No headlights, and it was black, blending right into the murky darkness.

The driver's-side door opened, and she held her breath. Hoping it was someone from the ranch there to rescue them. But her heart went to her knees when she saw the camouflage clothes.

Identical to those the other kidnappers were wearing.

Josh fired at the man.

Just as the man fired at them.

JOSH PULLED JAYCEE back down again. Not a second too soon. Because his shot missed the guy, and the bullet that came their way slammed into the tree just above their heads.

Or rather *his* head.

The scumbags didn't seem to be aiming for Jaycee. That was the good news. The bad news was the bullets were still coming damn close, and she could be hit.

Three more shots came his way. Plus one from the guy following them from behind.

Jaycee and he were trapped in the middle.

The flashbacks came, of course. And Josh cursed them.

He didn't have time for this, but they came anyway. Images of another shooting.

Of his partner lying dead in a pool of blood.

Of the shots slamming into Josh's chest.

He pushed them aside and hoped he could keep them at bay. Jaycee's life might depend on that.

"This is over," the one by the car said. He'd taken cover behind the door, and it was too dark for Josh to tell if he was alone or if anyone was inside.

He was betting someone was in there.

Maybe the scumbags' boss.

But Josh figured Jaycee and he wouldn't get that lucky. So far, he'd sucked in the luck department.

"If you want to live," the guy added, "you'll put down your gun now."

Josh was pretty sure that wasn't the way to stay alive. Without his gun, the men would just have an easier time killing him and kidnapping Jaycee.

He looked around, trying to find someplace that Jaycee and he could use for cover. Preferably something to his right so he could keep an eye on the two armed men and anyone who might be in that car.

Josh finally spotted something.

A fallen tree that'd just missed hitting the road. It was huge, the trunk at least two feet thick, and it was only about four yards away. If they could get to that, it would give him a better position to take out at least one of the gunmen.

But they could just gun him down before he got a chance to do that.

He considered another plan. One that he hated because it would test his theory that they didn't want Jaycee dead. Only him.

"What are you thinking?" she asked, following his gaze to that tree trunk.

He could no longer see her face as well as he had by the embankment, but he could hear the terror in her voice. Yes, she was a trained agent, but she didn't have a gun, and she was no doubt worried about the baby. And also worried about what would happen if those men got their hands on her.

"What?" she pressed. "I'll do whatever it takes to get us out of here."

He believed her, but she still wasn't going to like what he had in mind. Hell, he didn't like it much, either. However, it might keep Jaycee alive. Of course, he didn't want her kept alive just so she could be kidnapped.

"Text Grayson again," Josh whispered to her. "See if he can get someone to the back road where we are. Tell him we're near the big fallen tree."

She nodded, her fingers flying over the buttons on his phone, and he heard the little sound to indicate the text had been sent.

Now the waiting began.

It was eerily quiet. No one was shooting at them, and he didn't know how long the pair would just hang around until they closed in on them.

"You heard that part about me telling you to drop your gun," the guy by the car said. Then he said something over his shoulder.

To the person inside the car.

So he did have help. Help that would no doubt spring to life the moment they had Josh in their kill zone.

And that was about to happen soon.

The guy behind them was moving closer. Getting into position so he could shoot and not hit Jaycee. Only Josh.

"What happens if I put down my gun?" Josh asked. He didn't really want an answer. He knew. But he needed a little time for Grayson to answer.

The guy said something over his shoulder again and stayed crouched behind the car door, making it next to impossible to shoot him. "Put down your gun and we'll talk."

Right. Just talk. Josh figured there was no chance of that happening.

"Jaycee's right next to me," Josh reminded them. "If you shoot me, you could hurt her. Or worse."

It wasn't easy saying that, and it felt as if someone had clamped a big meaty fist around his heart. Still, he'd say or do anything to keep her alive, and he was bargaining on the armed pair feeling the same way.

Finally, he heard the soft dinging sound to indicate they had an answer to the text. "Grayson said the road's blocked by another vehicle, but Gage is coming to us on foot."

Good. Well, good about Gage. The other vehicle bothered him a lot. He hoped like the devil that there weren't more armed men inside.

"I want you to move over there," Josh told her, tipping his head to the tree trunk. "Move fast. Then get down and stay put."

She shook her head. "But what about you? Where will you be?"

Now here was the part she wouldn't like. "I'm staying here. I want to take out at least one of these idiots."

She pulled in her breath. Stared at him. "But if I move away, they'll shoot you."

Yeah. No way to sugarcoat that. "I'm a good shot," Josh reminded her. It was true. But he wasn't good enough to take out two men standing at different locations at the same time.

Though he couldn't see her eyes, he could feel the argument coming on, and he wanted to nip it in the bud. "You have to think of the baby."

Josh hadn't wanted to play the baby card, but he figured that was the only chance he had of getting her to agree to this plan.

"Just do it," he pressed. "It won't be long before Gage is here to help."

At least he hoped that was true.

"We can wait for Gage," she insisted.

But they couldn't. They were already on borrowed time, and the scumbag behind them was closing in. Inch by inch. Soon, he'd be close enough to pick Josh off.

And that would leave Jaycee unarmed and unprotected.

Josh brushed a kiss on her lips. "Please, just do it."

"Time's up," the kidnapper said.

It was. The guy behind him was in position, and Josh could see him ready to take aim.

"Go now!" Josh ordered Jaycee.

Maybe it was the sheer volume of his voice, but she finally moved. She scrambled toward the tree trunk, and Josh pivoted and took aim at the guy behind him.

He fired, a double tap of the trigger.

And hit him.

Josh didn't watch to see if he fell. If the guy wasn't dead, he at least wouldn't be able to return fire anyway. From the corner of his eye, he saw Jaycee drop to the other side of the tree truck.

Out of the line of fire.

However, Josh wasn't.

The gunman by the car pulled the trigger, and the bullet slammed right into Josh.

Chapter Nineteen

This was the repeat of a nightmare that Jaycee had already had way too often. Josh being shot and her being the reason for it. Now here it was again, playing out in the dark woods. But it wasn't a nightmare.

It was real.

So was the bullet that'd hit Josh.

Jaycee didn't think. She needed only to get to him to make sure he was alive. She ran to him, slinging her arm around him to steady him, but Josh only tried to push her behind him.

"You're hurt," she told him, just in case he was in shock and hadn't realized it.

But no shock. He glared at her and stepped in front of her. "You should have stayed behind the tree trunk," Josh said through clenched teeth.

"You've been shot," she repeated.

"I'm okay."

He darn sure didn't look okay. Jaycee saw the gaping tear on his shirtsleeve and his arm. The blood looked black and shiny in the darkness and was already seeping through the fabric.

"What the deputy's trying to tell you," the gunman calmly said, "is that I gave him a superficial wound to draw you out. I kept him alive so you'd cooperate."

Oh, mercy.

Jaycee had been too crazy with worry to consider that. And it'd worked.

Well, it'd gotten her out from cover anyway, but she couldn't just let his goon kill Josh and kidnap her.

"Now, Deputy, drop your gun, or the next shot goes into her. It won't kill her, but it'll put her in enough pain to make you wish you'd cooperated."

She looked back at Josh. Didn't see surrender in his eyes. She saw only determination to end this. But he dropped his gun. It fell on the ground just a few inches from her feet.

Jaycee glanced around the woods, but didn't see Gage or anyone else who could help them. She hoped he was nearby and hearing all of this so he could maybe ambush the gunman. After all, this goon was just one man, and Josh had killed the other one who'd been behind them.

Of course, there could be others in the car.

Her stomach knotted.

Because there might be more than one other kidnapper. With all their attempts to kidnap her, Jaycee wouldn't be surprised if the whole car was filled with guards ready to haul her off to a baby farm.

"So what now?" Jaycee demanded from the kidnapper. She hiked up her chin and tried to sound a lot tougher and stronger than she felt.

"We wait for a few minutes until the road is clear so we can leave."

She prayed that didn't mean one of the guards had found Gage, but she figured if they'd set up a plan like this, then they would have brought enough reinforcements.

"In the meantime, the deputy puts down his gun, steps aside and you come with us," the gunman continued. "If you don't make a fuss, the deputy lives."

She swallowed hard. Jaycee didn't believe him for one second. No way would he allow Josh to live, because they'd both seen his face. Still, she wanted to do something—anything—to save Josh.

But what?

There were a lot of options here, and she couldn't count on Gage and the others arriving in time.

"I'll come with you if you bring Josh, too," she blurted out.

Her offer wasn't well received.

Josh cursed. "What the hell do you think you're doing?"

The goon just stared at her as if she'd lost her mind. "If this is some kind of trick," he said, "it's a dangerous one."

Maybe, but Josh and she stood a better chance of surviving if they were together in the car, preferably with her in front of him so the goon couldn't shoot him again.

She couldn't be sure, but she thought the kidnapper smiled. "Admirable, trying to save your boyfriend, but it won't work if he doesn't cooperate." He turned his head slightly and mumbled something. To the person in the car no doubt. "Okay. Time to move."

Neither Jaycee nor Josh budged. "Whatever your buyer's paying for the baby, I'll double it," Josh fired back.

If the offer surprised the man, he didn't show any signs of it. And he definitely didn't step out from cover. "Oh, you'll get the chance to do that when the baby's born and if you're still alive then."

So this was about selling the baby and maybe didn't have anything to do with her being an FBI agent. And if the man was telling the truth, they did indeed have a buyer.

A thought that sickened her.

Someone was out there and wanted to buy her baby as if it were cattle.

"The being alive part is up to you," the man said to

Josh. "It's simple. Cooperate now and you live. Don't cooperate and you die."

"Let's walk toward the car," she whispered to Josh.

However, it went against all her FBI training to actually get in the car. Because the stats were that once these goons had control over Josh and her, things would only get worse. But there were a lot of steps between the car and them.

Those steps could be their chance to escape.

Escape how exactly, she didn't know, but it was clear this goon wasn't going to give them much more time.

Jaycee took the first of those steps but then stopped when she heard the sound.

Gunfire.

Not behind them where Josh had shot the kidnapper and where she'd last seen Grayson. This was coming from their right. Where Gage would likely be.

Again, the kidnapper didn't seem surprised. Nor did he even glance in that direction. He kept his attention pinned to Josh and her, and he aimed his gun at Jaycee.

"Move now, Deputy, or I shoot her in the arm just like I did you. I'm pretty sure blood loss wouldn't be good for that baby she's carrying."

Jaycee took another step and Josh followed. Putting him closer to his gun that he'd dropped on the ground. If she dived to the side, maybe Josh could get his gun and get off a shot. It wouldn't be an easy one with the moron crouched behind the door, but it might be the only chance they had.

The gunshots stopped, and she said another prayer. That Gage had won that round. It was impossible to tell because the kidnapper didn't have a reaction to that, either. He simply used his gun to motion for her to keep moving.

One more step.

Josh, too. And he stopped.

His boot was right next to the gun.

"Drop now," Josh whispered to her.

Jaycee was about to do that to give Josh a chance to take out the kidnapper, but she froze when she heard the sound to her right. The person was walking straight toward them.

Not Gage.

However, it was someone Jaycee recognized.

And the person was pointing a gun right at Josh.

SIERRA.

Josh wasn't sure who would be on the other end of that gun, but he'd figured it would be Bryson. Or Valerie. He hadn't expected Sierra, since it'd been less than twenty-four hours since she'd given birth to her daughter.

This was hardly the place for a new mother.

Or a mother-to-be.

He had to get Jaycee out of there, but how? It was hard to think with the pain stabbing in his arm. Yeah, it was just a flesh wound, but that didn't stop it from hurting like crazy and dulling his mind.

Sierra kept the gun on Josh, and after blowing out a weary, tired breath, she opened the back door of the car and sank down on the seat, facing outward and with her feet still on the ground. She did not look like a happy camper when she glanced over at the kidnapper.

Correction: her minion.

It was clear who was in charge here, and Sierra was definitely the boss.

"You just couldn't get this done yourself, huh?" she snarled at the guy. "Made me walk all the way over here from the other car. You know how hard it is to push out a kid?" She didn't wait for an answer. "Damn hard, and I expect you to pick up the slack while I'm recovering."

"What do you want me to do, boss?" the man jumped to ask.

"Well, now we have to wait, don't we? No doubt thanks to one of his badge-wearing cousins." She shot Josh a glare. "Someone disabled the vehicle we used to block the road so no one else could drive in and get to me. I'm guessing it was a Ryland lawman who did that."

That was Josh's guess, too, and he was glad one of them had managed to do that.

"You shot the person?" Jaycee asked, her voice trembling now. It was exactly what Josh had planned to ask.

"Of course. I killed him." Sierra added a taunting smile.

Josh didn't put much stock in the answer or the smile. "Liar. If you'd killed him, you wouldn't be worried about being ambushed right now. You wouldn't be cowering in the car."

That put some venom in her eyes that even the darkness couldn't hide. "If you think you're going to goad me into standing out in the open, think again, cowboy. I'm not stupid, and just because I took care of one Ryland, that doesn't mean there aren't others out and about."

There were. Or at least there should be. By now, Grayson would have alerted the entire family, and they'd be combing the woods looking for Jaycee and him.

"Of course, the fires we set will keep them occupied for a while," Sierra added a heartbeat later.

"What fires?" Josh lifted his head, hoping this was yet another lie, but then he silently cursed. Because he did indeed smell some smoke.

What the hell had she done now?

"We set a few fires in the barns and near the houses," she happily explained. "They were on timers, so you probably didn't get a glimpse of them before you came running out to save Jaycee."

He hadn't, but Josh didn't think she was lying about this. "If you hurt my family, you're a dead woman."

Sierra laughed, a short burst of laughter that had no humor in it. "You Rylands breed like rabbits," she added in a grumble. "Too bad you're not all women because you'd make nice additions to my little cottage industry."

So that's what she was calling it. "Cottage industry is tame sounding for what's really multiple felonies," Josh accused her. "How many people have you murdered, Sierra?"

"Enough that you should be worried about me holding this gun on you," she continued, sounding pleased with herself now. "All I want to do is finish this up and get a good night's sleep. And that'll happen. Once that car's out of the way, we're leaving."

Josh figured it wouldn't be easy to move a car on such a narrow road. No place to put it because of the trees and the ditches. Sierra's plan to keep anyone else from using the road had backfired. He hoped the rest of her plan did, too.

"What'd you do with your baby?" Jaycee asked. "Did you sell her, too?"

If Sierra was insulted by that, she didn't show it. She just lifted her shoulder in a careless shrug. "She's with the nanny, along with some other soon-to-be mothers. She's all tucked away safe and sound, waiting for Bryson to pay through the nose if he wants an heir as much as he claims he does."

So her daughter was likely at a baby farm. Too bad Sierra hadn't spilled the location, but he might be able to get that out of her if she kept talking.

"But Bryson's not the father of your baby," Josh tossed out there. "Blood tests prove it."

Again, she just shrugged. "Blood tests, like everything else, can be faked. Bryson wants to believe this child is his. Or maybe it's not even that. Maybe he just wants an heir and doesn't care about the test results."

Sad, but true. Bryson was all about the money. Still,

the man had seemed plenty upset that Sierra was trying to extort money from him.

"Bryson got himself into a bad fix," Sierra went on. "He owes money to the wrong people. Loan sharks. So what did he do? He borrowed more money from even worse people to pay his debts. I figure right about now, he'll do anything to get an heir so he can claim his inheritance."

"I'm guessing you'll be more than willing to take some of that inheritance from him," Jaycee muttered, sarcasm dripping from her voice.

"Seems only fair that I get half." In Sierra's warped, money-hungry mind, that probably did seem fair.

Josh's phone buzzed, but it was in Jaycee's pocket so he couldn't see it.

"Uh-uh," Sierra warned Jaycee when she reached for it. "Keep your hands where I can see them." She glanced over her shoulder. "Find out what the hell's taking so long with that car. I want out of here now."

Josh got a glimpse of the person she was speaking to. Not Bryson or Valerie, but Josh was pretty sure it was one of the guards who'd escaped from the baby farm raid. The one who'd shoved Jaycee into the barn. The man took out a phone and made a call.

Jaycee adjusted her position just a little and just enough so that she was no longer in the way of him getting his gun. Now all he needed was some kind of distraction. Too bad he couldn't let Grayson know that. But then, Grayson might be too occupied with the fires to do much of anything right now.

"Quit moving," Sierra snapped. "You're making me antsy with that fidgeting."

"What about your sister and Bryson?" Jaycee asked, obviously not addressing the moving issue. Which she did again. Just a fraction to the side. So that she wouldn't be in Josh's line of fire. "Are they in on this with you?"

"Please, I don't need help running this operation. Bryson's an idiot, and Valerie's too busy bad-mouthing me to help me. However, my sister did fund the start-up of my business."

"With or without her knowledge?" Jaycee fired back.

"Without," Sierra readily admitted. "Valerie wouldn't knowingly help me do anything that would get me ahead in life."

Well, that was something at least, and Josh thought Sierra was telling the truth. About this anyway. "How did you milk the money from her?" Josh asked. "Did you just come out and steal it?"

There it was again. That flash of anger in her eyes. Maybe Sierra didn't like being called a common thief. Well, she was a thief, all right, but not of the common variety. It'd taken a lot of money and brains to put together an operation like this.

"I didn't steal it," Sierra snapped. "I cut a deal with one of her longtime employees. Someone she trusted but who was in desperate need of cash. He lied to Valerie, saying he needed lots of cash for medical treatments. I had the medical records faked, and the employee and I split the money."

That explained the withdrawals from Valerie's bank account. It didn't, however, explain plenty of other things about the baby farms. Josh wanted those answers, but he wanted to get them with Sierra handcuffed and on her way to jail.

"About five more minutes," her hired gun relayed to Sierra when he got off the phone.

Josh saw the man's guns then. All three were armed with multiple weapons, and that wasn't good odds for him. Still, he had to do something, and five minutes wasn't much time. His best shot was probably when one of them got behind the wheel. Of course, by then they'd be trying to force Jaycee into the car.

"Come on," Sierra said, her voice taunting again. She looked at Jaycee. "You don't want to ask me why you were kidnapped?"

"I figured you'd tell me when you were ready." Jaycee sounded about as happy with this conversation as Josh was. He hoped he could use every bit of info Sierra was gushing about to put the woman away for life. Of course, for that to happen, Jaycee and he had to get out of there alive.

"Guess I'm ready." Sierra smiled. "I have a buyer who can't father his own children, but he had a very interesting shopping list when it came to baby characteristics. Your eye and hair color but with some criminal DNA so he could train the kid to follow in his footsteps. Perfect match. You might wear a badge, Agent Finney, but your mama and daddy were lifers in prison. That appealed to him."

Jaycee made a soft moan. It was torture listening to this and imagining their precious baby being handed over to a slimeball criminal.

"And what about Miranda Culley?" Josh asked. He didn't really want to know, but he had to stop Sierra from talking about his baby. Because if she said one more word about it, he might just pick up his gun and risk being shot so he could put some bullets in her.

"The woman didn't even know about what was going on. I picked her name from the missing persons registry on the internet. Figured she'd be the perfect front to lure you to the cemetery so I could take Jaycee."

"But you failed." Josh took pleasure in reminding her of that.

"Yes, that time I did because doofus here got the car bogged down on a dirt road." She tipped her head to the man behind the door and motioned for him to get behind the wheel. "I didn't want the Ryland clan combing the woods and maybe coming up on that car, so I faked the injury. It hurt like hell, too."

Sierra touched the spot on her forehead, smiled at Josh when her gaze dropped to his arm. Then his chest. "But you know a little about hurt and pain, don't you, Deputy Ryland? Just how bad are those flashbacks from your PTSD?"

Suddenly, they weren't bad at all.

In fact, Josh's head was pretty damn clear. Especially now that one of the minions had his back to him.

"Get down," Josh warned Jaycee, and in the same breath, he snatched up his gun.

Josh was the first to pull the trigger.

THE SHOTS BLASTED through the air, punctuated by Sierra's screams and sounds of pain, and Jaycee had no choice but to dive for cover. Unarmed, she couldn't help Josh, but she could hope and pray that they both got out of the path of those bullets.

Jaycee got behind the tree trunk again, and when she looked in the direction of the car, the driver was slumped on the ground. Josh had taken cover, too. Well, of sorts. He was behind a small tree that didn't fully protect his body.

"You bastard!" Sierra yelled. "You'll pay for that." And she snatched the gun from the guard who was on the back-seat with her.

She fired, despite the fact the man was trying to get the gun back.

Jaycee's breath stalled in her throat, and she started praying again. It must have worked, because Sierra's shot didn't come anywhere near close to Josh. Of course, any shot fired right now could hit one of Josh's cousins. She figured there were plenty of them in the woods and maybe on the road trying to figure a way to stop this.

"Give me the gun," the man in the car said. Not an order because he was obviously talking to his boss, but he was clearly pleading with her.

Sierra ignored him. Cursing, she fired again.

So did Josh.

Sierra missed. Josh didn't.

Josh's shot slammed into Sierra's shoulder and she screamed again. Cursed him, too. What she didn't do was let go of the gun despite the blood that was seeping through her blouse. However, the man pulled her all the way inside the car and shut the door.

"We need Sierra to keep alive," Josh called out.

Yes, they did. Because she was the only person who could tell them the extent of the baby farms. They didn't even know how many there were and where they were located, and they could pressure Sierra to help them save the women and their babies.

With the door closed and both Sierra and one gunman still alive, Josh stayed down but maneuvered himself closer to the car.

Jaycee had lost count of how many bullets Josh had left. He had his Glock, which meant he'd started with twenty-two bullets. Not a lot considering the gunfight they'd been in since the kidnappers had dragged her away from Josh's place.

Sierra was still cursing and howling in pain, but Jaycee saw some movement in the car.

No.

The remaining guard was climbing over the seat to get behind the wheel. If that happened, they might escape. Jaycee didn't want Josh or his family to take any more risks, but she didn't want Sierra getting away, either.

Josh moved closer at the same time the car engine started. The driver rolled forward, pushing the dead gunman out of the way. If he managed to get the door shut, Josh wouldn't be able to fire inside. Not with that bulletproof glass in the way.

"Jaycee, watch out!" someone yelled.

It took her a moment to realize that it wasn't Josh, but rather Grayson. She turned around and didn't see Grayson, but she saw something that put her heart right in her throat.

The armed man running toward her.

He lifted his gun, aiming not at her but at Josh. Josh turned, too, his gaze snagging the guy, and he dropped to the ground.

And Josh and the guard fired at the same time.

Jaycee was afraid to look. Terrified that the bullet might have killed Josh.

But he was fine.

Unfortunately, so was the other guy, and he fired another shot as he ducked behind one of the trees. She was beyond thankful that Josh hadn't been shot again, but that didn't stop the car from moving.

Sierra was getting away.

"Everyone get down!" she heard Gage yell.

She dropped all the way to the ground and prayed that Josh and Grayson did the same. A split second later, the shots started. Not coming from the side of the car where they were but from the other side.

Gage, no doubt.

He just started shooting, and unlike Josh, it didn't sound as if he'd run out of ammo. The bullets pelted against the glass, and judging from Sierra's screams, some of them got through.

She saw Josh lift his head, take aim, and he shot out the

two tires on their side. The car bobbed to a stop, the flat rubber unable to get enough traction on the dirt.

Jaycee blew out a quick breath of relief. But there was no relief when she saw both car doors fly open. Sierra and her henchmen didn't get out of the vehicle, but still using the protective glass in the car, they took aim.

The man aimed at Josh.

Sierra, at Jaycee.

The shots tore into the fallen tree, chipping away huge chunks of the wood. Jaycee saw Josh dive back to the ground, and she could hear shots from the direction where she'd last heard Grayson. The only armed one who wasn't firing was Gage, and she soon caught sight of him.

He was on the other side of the car.

And he joined the gunfire. This time at much closer range, and even though Jaycee couldn't see it, she figured his shots had to be chipping away at the glass.

"Stop!" Sierra yelled. "We're surrendering."

Gage, Grayson and Josh all stopped, and eerie silence settled over the road and woods.

Jaycee couldn't believe Sierra would surrender, but maybe she was smart enough to realize it was the only way she was going to make it out alive. So she could then escape. No way would a woman like Sierra go to jail, and unfortunately, she had plenty of henchmen in place to make sure that didn't happen.

The gunman stepped from the car slowly, dropping his weapon on the ground and lifting his hands in the air. The seconds crawled by, all of them waiting for Sierra to do the same.

But she didn't.

Screaming like someone crazy, Sierra came out, a gun in each hand, and she started shooting.

"You're a dead woman, Jaycee!" she yelled, and she took aim at Jaycee's head.

However, Sierra never got a chance to pull the trigger. Josh's shots saw to that. This time, he didn't aim for her arm. He couldn't because he had to stop her from killing Jaycee. When the bullet hit her chest, Sierra froze, her eyes wide with shock.

Then, nothing.

Her guns slid from her hands, and she crumpled onto the ground.

Jaycee and Josh started running toward the woman at the same time. Josh got there first and touched his fingers to Sierra's neck.

"Call an ambulance," Josh yelled. "She's alive."

Chapter Twenty

Josh tried not to wince or react when the nurse stitched up his arm. Jaycee was no doubt already feeling enough stress without his bad reaction adding to it. With the eagle-eyed way she was watching him, it would definitely add stress if she thought he was in pain.

"You sure you're okay?" Jaycee asked, and it was something she'd asked a lot on the drive to the Silver Creek hospital and since they'd arrived.

Yeah, despite the throbbing from the gunshot wound and the stitches, he was fine, even better now that the doctor had said Jaycee was all right. Josh hadn't let the doctor check him out until he knew all was well with her and the baby.

Sierra was a different matter.

She'd been alive when the ambulance had finally managed to get into that remote part of the ranch, and she was now in surgery. However, Dr. Mickelson had warned them that while Sierra's chances looked good, she still might not survive.

And Josh blamed himself for that.

He'd had no choice but to shoot her, or Sierra would have gunned down Jaycee. Josh had tried not to go for a kill shot, but that had been hard to do, especially since Sierra hadn't been standing still. Instead, the woman had let the rage take over and had been trying to get into a better position to end Jaycee's life.

Now he could only hope for the best.

In this case, the best was for Sierra to stay alive at least long enough to lead them to the baby farms and her own daughter. Josh was hoping and praying they could get that info by some other means, but it was sad but true that Sierra might be their only chance at doing that.

The nurse finally finished with him, and Josh stood, pulling down his sleeve so that Jaycee wouldn't have to see the stitches. Of course, that meant she could see the blood on his shirt.

She saw it, all right.

Tears welled in her eyes, and she pulled him into a gentle hug. "I'm so sorry."

Jaycee made it sound as if all of this was her fault. It wasn't. She'd been a victim, and if Sierra and her minions had had their way, Jaycee would have soon been a dead victim. After she'd delivered the baby who would be sold to some slimeball criminal, that was.

Sierra's heart had to be as black as night to have made an arrangement like that.

"Don't let it eat away at you," Jaycee whispered, as if she knew exactly what he was thinking. It was spooky just how often they were on the same wavelength.

Josh brushed a kiss on her cheek. Didn't dare risk more. His body was one big giant nerve right now, and if he really kissed her, he might not stop. Because right now, having Jaycee in his arms melted away the pain. The memories.

And even the nightmare that'd just happened.

As she'd said, he wouldn't let it eat away at him, but that was because he had Jaycee there to remind him that there was another side of life. A good one that didn't involve kidnappers and baby farms.

Josh kept his arm around Jaycee's waist as they left the examining room and went back into the waiting area. In this case, it was aptly named since there were two people waiting for them.

Grayson and Valerie.

The person missing was his brother, Sawyer, who'd been there earlier, not long after Josh and the others had arrived.

Valerie immediately got to her feet. "How's Sierra?"

Josh had to shake his head. "She's still in surgery." And she might be there for a while. That was a best-case scenario because it would mean she was not only still alive but also that the damage was being repaired. "The doctor expects her to live."

Valerie's legs buckled, and she dropped back down into the chair. "Good. I know you don't think much of her, but she's still my sister."

Josh could understand that. In part. He would be devastated if something happened to his brother. But then, Sawyer wasn't an insane criminal who'd wrecked heaven knows how many lives for the sake of money.

Grayson stood, blowing out a long, weary breath, and he studied both Jaycee and Josh. "Are you two really okay?"

Josh waited for Jaycee to nod before he added one of his own. He figured it'd be a while, though, before it was actually the truth, since both of them had come damn close to dying tonight, and they could thank Sierra and her henchmen for that.

Josh tipped his head to the empty seat where he'd last seen his brother. "Where's Sawyer?"

"Out looking for the baby farm and Sierra's daughter. Gage found two recent addresses on the GPS in the car Sierra was using."

That was the best news Josh had heard all day. Well,

other than hearing from the doctor that Jaycee and the baby were okay. "Sawyer and Gage are checking them out now," Grayson added.

"Not alone?" Jaycee immediately said.

Grayson shook his head. "Kade and some other FBI agents went with them." He glanced down at the phone in his hand. "I'm hoping for a call from them any minute."

Josh hoped that call would be good news. He was sick and tired of hearing mostly bad stuff when it came to this. Plus, if this turned out to be the locations of the baby farms, they wouldn't need to wait for Sierra to come out of surgery and then recovery. They could go in and rescue the captives.

"When Sierra's baby is found," Valerie said, getting to her feet again, "I'll take her." She stopped, sucked in a quick breath. Blinked back tears, too. "She's my niece, and I love her. I swear, I'd do my best to take care of her."

She sounded sincere enough, and heck, maybe she was. Josh had been dealing with scum for so long that it was hard to see the good in people.

"When the baby's found," Josh started. And he used *when* instead of *if* because he refused to believe the little girl would just disappear in this baby farm maze. "We'll get it all sorted out. You're the next of kin so you'll have a big say in what happens to her."

Valerie gave a shaky nod and sank back down onto the chair. "And when Sierra recovers from her injuries, she'll be going to jail."

For a long, long time. They were all thinking it, but none of them said it aloud. Judging from Sierra's behavior tonight, she had likely even committed murder, and that could get her the death penalty.

Ironic that she would survive a gunshot only to face

that. But Josh had no sympathy for the woman who'd destroyed and tried to destroy so many lives.

Including his and Jaycee's.

"You should take Jaycee back to the ranch," Grayson suggested. "Not to your place but mine or the main house. It'll take a while to clear out the smell of the tear gas in your apartment."

Yeah, it would, but thankfully that was the only damage. Josh had been worried about the fires that Sierra had claimed had been set. And a few had been. But Grayson had already told him that the ranch hands had easily contained them, and there'd been no real damage. Sierra had only meant the fires to be a distraction.

They'd worked, in part.

The fires had tied up some of his cousins and the ranch hands. But that hadn't stopped Gage, Grayson, Jaycee and him from stopping Sierra.

"Did you figure out how the kidnappers got on the ranch?" Jaycee asked.

Grayson lifted his shoulder. "Probably came in with the wedding decorators. Dad tried to check everyone's IDs, but there were a lot of people coming and going. He thinks they might have sneaked in one of the vans that were bringing in supplies."

"This wasn't his fault," Jaycee said. "Sierra was determined to kidnap me. Sooner or later, she would have found a way to get to me."

It was the truth, and it hurt Josh far more than a gunshot wound. No matter what precautions they'd taken, Sierra and her goons had figured out a way around them. But that was over now. Sierra and her hired guns would go to jail for the rest of their lives.

"I'll call you with any updates," Grayson added, and he handed Josh the keys to his truck. "Dade and Bree are waiting outside to go with you."

"Oh, God," Jaycee mumbled, and he knew why she'd said that.

Because the danger maybe wasn't over.

That was the reason Grayson had arranged for Bree and Dade to ride with them. They were protection that they might end up needing. Again.

"It'll be okay," Josh whispered to her, and he got her moving toward the exit. "Soon we'll put all of this behind us, and you can focus on having a healthy baby."

That was his wish list anyway. Now he had to make it happen.

However, Jaycee stopped and faced him. "It will be okay," she said, surprising him.

After everything that'd just happened, he expected at least a little bit of gloom and doom, but she slid her hand over her stomach. And kissed him.

"You saved my life tonight. Multiple times. Thank you for that," she said.

You're welcome didn't seem nearly heartfelt enough. "You saved me a couple of times, too."

She nodded, and Josh leaned in for another kiss, but she pressed her hand over his mouth. "I'm just going to say this fast. Like ripping off a bandage. I'm in love with you, and I know that's not the right thing to say. That it puts a lot of pressure on you—"

Josh moved her hand away and kissed her. It wasn't to shut her up.

Okay, that was part of it.

He just figured the best way to shut her up was to remind her of this heat that was between them.

And it was a reminder, all right.

He kissed her until air became a serious issue, and they had to break away to catch their breaths.

"I tell you I love you, and that's how you react?" Jaycee frowned, shook her head. "Wait, that didn't come out right. What I meant—"

He kissed her again. "I know what you meant," he whispered against her mouth. "You want to know how I feel about that? Well, I don't feel pressured, that's for sure, and it was the absolute right thing to say. Because I'm in love with you, too."

Until that moment he hadn't known for sure, but it was true. He was crazy, head over heels in love with Jaycee. He wasn't sure when or where it'd happened, but he was certain of his feelings for her.

She smiled. Then it faded, and she got another of those concerned looks in her eyes. "But what about the past?"

"It's the past," he quickly let her know, and he put his hand on her stomach. "Seems best for us to focus on the future now."

Despite everything he'd just told her, her concerned look went up a significant notch. "You're not in love with me just because of the baby?"

"No." And that was yet something else he knew with absolute certainty.

Josh would have proved that with another kiss, but he heard Grayson's phone ring, and both Jaycee and he turned back around to see if this was good news.

Or if they truly did need protection driving to the ranch.

"Gage," Grayson said.

Josh couldn't hear a word Gage said, and he couldn't tell from Grayson's expression, either. All he could do was stand there and wait to find out what was going on.

And take care of some much-needed personal stuff.

"Marry me," he whispered to Jaycee.

She didn't move. Didn't respond. She certainly didn't jump into his arms and say yes. And that meant he'd blown this big-time. He should have guessed after her reaction to his last marriage proposal. Of course, that one hadn't been the real deal.

This one was.

"I'm not asking you to marry me because of the baby," he quickly clarified. "Though that's a nice bonus. But the reason I proposed is because I'm in love with you and I want to spend the rest of my life with you."

Jaycee still didn't move, but tears welled in her eyes, and she made a little gasping sound.

"Oh, man." Josh groaned. "Now I've made you cry."

"For the best of reasons," she said.

Her voice was all warmth and breath now, and there was no more concern in her expression. She put her arms around him and kissed him until Josh was feeling all warm and breathy, too.

Actually, he was wishing he could haul her off to bed. And he figured soon he could make that happen.

"Yes," she whispered.

Because he was caught up in the kiss, it took him a moment to realize that was the best thing Jaycee could have said to him.

"Yes?" he clarified and hoped like the devil that he hadn't misunderstood.

He hadn't. Her slow smile and quick nod proved that. So did their next kiss, and it went on a little longer than planned because he heard Grayson clear his throat.

"Sounds as if congratulations are in order," Grayson said, smiling. "Well, I can give you two something else to celebrate. You, too," he said to Valerie. "They found both of the baby farms, and Sierra's daughter was at one of them."

While that sounded good, Josh immediately thought of the guards who'd escaped with those women. "Did Gage say if there were any injuries or escapees?"

"Doesn't appear to be. There were four women at the first place. Three more at the second, and those women are the ones who were taken from the farm where Jaycee had been held."

"And they're okay?" Jaycee asked.

Grayson nodded. "Everyone is okay, and the guards have been arrested."

Jaycee made a sound of sheer relief and landed in his arms again.

"Are the guards talking?" Josh asked. Because they might need info from them to find any other baby farms that Sierra had set up.

"One's talking, and that's all it takes. We'll cut a deal with him so he can testify against the others. And against Sierra. He's already told Kade that he'll spill any- and everything."

That was definitely a huge reason to celebrate. Of course, the guard might not know the full extent of Sierra's operation, but Josh wasn't going to borrow trouble. What the guard didn't know they could probably piece together with the other evidence they'd find at the baby farm locations.

Plus, there was Sierra.

When she came out of surgery, she might be willing to give information to take the death penalty off the table. Sierra was the sort of woman who'd do all sorts of bargaining to stay alive, and that in turn could save anyone else who was unlucky enough to have been kidnapped and held.

"I'll wait here until Sierra's out of surgery," Grayson added. "When she wakes up, I'll let you know."

Josh thanked him and got Jaycee moving toward the door again. It seemed odd, stepping outside without worrying if someone was going to try to kidnap or kill them. It felt like a new lease on life.

Which it was.

He was in love with Jaycee, and she was in love with him. Yeah, definitely a new lease.

"So how will this work?" she asked, looping her arm around his waist. "Will we live at the ranch after we're married?"

"I'd like that. But if there are too many bad memories—"

"There are good memories, too," she interrupted. "Like before the kidnappers came."

Yeah, making love to Jaycee was indeed a good memory, and he hoped to create a lot more memories just like that one. In bed and out.

"Don't know if your place will be big enough, though, when the baby comes," she continued.

"So we can build a place like Grayson's. There's plenty of land, and it might be fun to see our baby playing with all the cousins."

"Our baby," she repeated and stopped again. "So when we build this house, what color are we painting the nursery?"

"Green," he teased. "It's my favorite color."

She gave him a playful jab in the stomach. "Pink or blue?"

"Both."

Jaycee blinked. And Josh laughed. “Blue this time. But I’m hoping next time, we can go for pink.”

Josh kissed that smile right off Jaycee’s mouth, scooped her up and started for home.

Oh, yeah, there’d definitely be a next time.

* * * * *

Don’t miss USA TODAY *bestselling author Delores Fossen’s next book in her miniseries* THE LAWMEN OF SILVER CREEK RANCH. *Look for SAWYER next month.*

He lifted one eyebrow. "Is that what you think this is all about? Protection? Securing a witness?"

The pulse in her wrist ticked up several notches. Could he feel it? "I'm the only witness you have right now."

He chuckled in the back of his throat, and the low sound sent a line of tingles racing down to her toes.

"The SFPD is not in the bodyguarding business. We're not going to put you in the Witness Protection Program. Everything I've done for you has been off the books and off the clock."

She twisted her own napkin in her lap as she tilted her head back to take in his imposing figure. "Why'd you do it?"

"Do you have to ask?"

THE BRIDGE

BY
CAROL ERICSON

Published in Great Britain 2014
by Mills & Boon, an imprint of Harlequin (UK) Limited,
Eton House, 18-24 Paradise Road, Richmond, Surrey, TW9 1SR

ISBN: 978 0 263 91354 5

46-0414

Harlequin (UK) Limited's policy is to use papers that are natural, renewable and recyclable products and made from wood grown in sustainable forests. The logging and manufacturing processes conform to the legal environmental regulations of the country of origin.

Printed and bound in Spain
by Blackprint CPI, Barcelona

Carol Ericson lives with her husband and two sons in Southern California, home of state-of-the-art cosmetic surgery, wild freeway chases, palm trees bending in the Santa Ana winds and a million amazing stories. These stories, along with hordes of virile men and feisty women, clamor for release from Carol's head. It makes for some interesting headaches until she sets them free to fulfill their destinies and her readers' fantasies. To find out more about Carol, her books and her strange headaches, please visit her website, www.carolericson.com, "where romance flirts with danger."

For Elise
and childhood imaginations
that run wild.

Chapter One

He wanted to kill her.

"Elise."

The whispered name floated along the fog, mingled with it, surrounded her.

Her eyes ached with the effort of trying to peer through the milky white wisps that blanketed the San Francisco Bay shoreline, but if she couldn't see him, he couldn't see her.

And she planned to keep it that way.

A foghorn bellowed in the night, and she took advantage of the sound to make another move toward the waves lapping against the rocky shore. If she had to, she'd wriggle right into the frigid waters of the bay.

She flattened herself against the sand, and the grains stuck to her lip gloss. It now seemed ages ago when she'd leaned over the brightly lit vanity at the club applying it.

"Elise, come out, come out wherever you are."

His voice caused a new layer of goose bumps to form over the ones she already had from the cold, damp air. Her fingers curled around the scrubby plant to her right as if she could yank it out of the sand and use it as a weapon.

If he caught her, she wouldn't allow him to drag her back to his car. She'd fight and die here if she had to.

The water splashed and her tormenter cursed. He must've stepped into the bay. And he didn't like it.

She drove her chin into the sand to prop up her head and peered into the wall of fog. The lights on the north tower of the Golden Gate Bridge winked at her. The occasional humming of a car crossing the bridge joined with the lapping of the water as the only sounds she could hear over the drumbeat of her heart.

And his voice when he chose to speak, a harsh whisper, all traces of the refined English accent he'd affected outside the club gone.

What a fool she'd been to trust him.

Another footfall, too close for comfort. She held her breath. If he tripped over her, she'd have to run, find another place to hide in plain sight. Or at least it would be plain sight if the fog lifted.

The damp cover made her feel as if they were the only two people in this hazy world where you couldn't see your hand two inches in front of your face.

Who would break first? The fog? Her? Or the maniac trying to kill her? Because she knew he wanted to kill her. She could hear the promise in his voice.

"Elise?"

She wanted to scream at him to stop using her name in those familiar tones—as if they were old friends. Instead of predator and prey.

She didn't scream. She pressed her lips together, and the sand worked its way into her mouth. She ground it between her teeth, anger shoving the fear aside for a moment.

If this guy thought she'd give up, he'd picked the wrong target. The Durans of Montana were nobody's victims.

A breeze skittered across the bay, and debris tickled her face. White strands of fog swirled past her, and for the first time since she'd hurled herself from the trunk of her captor's car, she could see the shapes of scrubby plants emerge from the mist.

She swallowed a sob. When she'd least expected or wanted it, the cursed San Francisco fog was rolling out to sea.

A low chuckle seemed to come at her from all directions. He knew it, too.

Time to make a move.

Elise pinned her arms to her sides and propelled herself into a roll. Once she had the momentum, the rest was easy as she hit a slight decline to the water.

Arm. Back. Arm. Chest. Around and around she rolled. She squeezed her eyes shut and scooped in a breath of air. Her preparations didn't make the impact any easier.

When she hit the icy bay, she gasped, pulling in a breath and a mouthful of salty water with it. She choked it out and ducked her head beneath the small waves.

The bay accepted her in a chilly embrace, and she clawed her way along the rocky floor. Fearing the swift current, she didn't want to swim away from the shoreline, but the water might just be enough to hide her from the lunatic trying to kill her.

She popped up her head and dragged in another breath. The wind whipped around her, blowing her wet hair against her cheeks.

The fog dissipated even more, and she could make out the form of a man loping back and forth, swinging something at the ground.

She took a deep breath and went under again. The current tugged at her dress, inviting her into the bay. She resisted, scrabbling against the rocks. The current snatched her shoes anyway.

She scraped her knees on the bay floor and lifted her face to the surface, taking a sip of air. The figure on land seemed farther away. Would he be able to see her head in the water? Would he come after her?

She submerged her head again and managed a breaststroke and a scissor kick to propel herself farther from the man combing the shore.

She'd have to get out of the water soon or she'd die from hypothermia. As if to drive this truth home, her teeth began to chatter and she lost the tips of her fingers to numbness.

Once more she poked her head up from the water. The steel buttress of the bridge was visible in front of her. Maybe she could clamber on top of it to escape the cold fingers of the bay.

She twisted her head around. The man had disappeared from view. A seagull shrieked above, cutting through the rumbling of a car engine.

Elise whipped her head around. An orange service truck trundled along the road fronting the shore, its amber light on the roof revolving.

Elise screamed for the first time since her ordeal began. She clambered from the water, her dress clinging to her legs. She bunched the skirt of the dress around her waist and waded from the bay.

"Help! Stop!"

The occupants of the truck couldn't have heard her, but the truck pulled to the side of the road anyway. A door swung open.

Her frozen limbs buckled beneath her, but she willed them to support her. She rose to her feet and screamed again, waving her arms above her head. "Help! I'm in the water!"

The white oval of a face turned toward her.

Elise pumped her legs, hoping they were obeying her command to run. She tried to scream again, but her jaw locked as a shower of chills cascaded through her body.

The man in the orange jumpsuit started jogging toward her, and another orange jumpsuit joined him.

Her bare feet slogged through the sand and she kept tripping over the bushes dotting the shore, but she continued to move forward.

By the time she and the service workers met, her body was shivering convulsively.

"Oh, my God, Brock. I think we've got a jumper."

She shook her head back and forth. *Really? Would a jumper be able to swim to shore and run toward help?*

Brock joined his buddy, shrugging out of his orange jacket. "I already called 9-1-1. It's gonna be okay, lady."

He wrapped his jacket around her, and she began to sink to the ground. He caught her under the arms. "Stay with us. The ambulance should be here soon."

"How did you do it? How did you survive the jump?"

She licked the salt from her lips and worked her jaw. "I didn't jump from the bridge."

Brock tugged the coat around her tighter. "Then what the hell were you doing out there?"

As sirens wailed in the distance, she blew out a breath and closed her eyes. "Escaping a killer."

HER TOES TINGLED and she took another sip of the hot tea. When the ambulance got her to the emergency room, the nurses had stripped off her soggy dress and wrapped her in warm blankets. They'd tucked her into this bed and piled an electric blanket on top of her as well as wedged some heat packs under her arms and behind her neck.

When she could sit up, they'd brought her a cup of tea. Now Elise inhaled the lemon-scented steam from the cup and tried to relax her limbs.

Someone yanked back the curtain that separated her bed from the other beds in the emergency room. A doctor approached her with a small tablet computer clutched under his arm.

He clicked his tongue. "It's clear you're not a jumper since you don't have any injuries that would indicate you'd just hit the water at seventy-five miles per hour from a height of two hundred and twenty feet."

Elise slurped the hot tea and rolled it on her tongue before swallowing. "I told Brock and the other city worker I didn't jump. Didn't they believe me?"

"The first report was of a jumper, but the EMT said you were attacked."

She wrapped her hands around the cup as her ordeal knocked her over the head all over again. "I went into the water to avoid him."

"Boyfriend? Husband?"

Elise's jaw dropped. Everyone sure liked making assumptions. "A killer. A stranger. He abducted me from the street. I escaped."

The doctor nodded as if this was his second guess all along. "Based on the EMT's report of his conversation with you, the police are on their way."

"Here?"

"They want to question you immediately. Once you're warmed up, you're free to go." He tapped the tablet screen. "The nurse indicated you have a bump on the back of your head, too."

"He hit me, maybe with the cast he had on his arm."

"Says here you're not showing any signs of concussion and the skin on your scalp didn't break. How's the head feeling?"

"My head is the least of my worries right now."

The doctor snapped the computer shut. "You're lucky. A few more minutes in that water and you'd be dead. It was a crazy thing to do."

"A few more minutes with that maniac and I'd be dead. I figured the water gave me a better chance."

The doctor lifted his shoulders in his white coat and stepped beyond the curtain to practice his feeble bedside manner on another emergency-room patient.

Beneath her warm blankets, Elise shivered at the memory of the man stalking her. Would the police be able to find him based on her description? And how accurate was that description? The man she'd helped outside the club had spoken to her with an English accent. That accent had disappeared when he'd been searching for her on the sand. How much of his appearance was phony, too? The beard? The mustache?

"Knock, knock. Ms. Duran?"

A male voice called from outside the curtain.

"That's me."

The man brushed aside the curtain and pulled it closed behind him. "I'm Detective Brody. How are you feeling, Ms. Duran?"

"Elise. You can call me Elise. I feel…warm." And it wasn't because a fine specimen of manhood had just emerged from curtain number three. At least she didn't think it was.

"That's good after what you've been through." He pointed to the plastic chair by the wall. "May I?"

"Sure. Of course." It beat craning her neck to look up at all six feet something of him.

"They're keeping you warm enough?" He tipped his chin at the space heater glowing in the corner.

She nodded, although she wondered if she'd ever feel warm again.

Detective Brody dragged the chair to her bed and slipped out of his suit jacket. He hung it over the back of the chair, smoothing the expensive-looking material.

Hunching forward, he withdrew a notepad and pen from the pocket of his crisp white shirt.

"The EMT reported that you were out in the bay trying to escape from someone. Tell me what happened from the beginning, Elise."

His dark eyes zeroed in on her face, making her feel as if she were the only woman in the world. She shook her head. He was a policeman and she was a victim—she *was* the only woman in the world for him right now.

She took a deep breath. "I was coming out of a club on Geary Street at two in the morning—the Speakeasy. Do you know it?"

"Private club, right? Stays open past two."

"My friend got invitations from a member."

"Was your friend with you at—" he glanced at his notepad "—one-fifty?"

"I was alone. I left her inside the club."

"Had you been drinking?"

His tone got sharper and the muscles in his handsome face got tighter. She was glad she wouldn't have to disappoint him.

"One drink's my limit, and I'd had that at around eleven o'clock when we first got there."

His spiky dark lashes dropped over his eyes briefly, and Elise knew she'd just passed some test.

"How were you getting home?"

"Taxi. There's no parking in that neighborhood. I had the bartender call me a taxi, and I went outside to wait for it."

"What happened next?"

Goose bumps rippled across her arms, and she pulled the blanket up to her chin. "I saw a man standing beside a car. The trunk of the car was open."

"Did he see you? Speak to you right away?"

"I'm sure he saw me, although we didn't make eye contact. He must've seen me come out of the club, but by the time I looked at him he was bending over the open trunk."

"What kind of car? Make? Model?"

Was he serious? "I'm not sure. It was a small, dark car, old."

"Then what? Did he talk to you?"

Elise licked her lips, and she could still taste the salt from the bay. "He seemed to be struggling with something. Then he poked his head around the open trunk and asked me if I could give him a hand."

"Did you?"

"I guess I shouldn't have." She knotted her fingers, studying his face for signs he thought she was an idiot. She didn't see any.

"I walked toward him, and that's when I noticed his arm."

Detective Brody's dark brows shot up. "His arm?"

"It was in a cast."

The pen dropped from the detective's fingers and rolled under the bed. He ducked to retrieve it. When he straightened in his chair, his handsome face was flushed.

He cleared his throat. "The man's arm was in a cast?"

"A full cast almost up to his shoulder, like he had a broken arm. When he asked me for help, I…I didn't think anything of it. I wasn't suspicious, and he looked…"

"He looked what? What did he look like?"

She shrugged and the blanket slipped from one bare shoulder. "Normal. He looked normal—blond hair, kind of on the long side, jeans. Normal."

"We'll get to the rest of the description in a minute. So, what did you help him with?"

"A box." She folded her arms across her stomach, where knots were forming and tightening. "There was a box on the ground that he was trying to get into his trunk."

"And you helped him with the box?" His hand froze,

poised over his notepad, where he'd been scribbling her every word since retrieving the pen.

"I didn't get the chance." She clutched her arms, digging her nails into her skin. "When I bent over the box, he hit me on the back of the head."

Detective Brody jumped from the chair, knocking it to the floor.

"What's wrong?" His sudden movement had caused her to jerk forward, and the blanket fell from her shoulders.

"A man with a cast asked you for help and then bashed your head in. Did he stuff you in the trunk?"

"Yes, yes. Has this happened before?"

Closing his eyes, he stuffed the notepad in the pocket of his shirt. His lips barely moved as he mumbled, "A long time ago."

"What? A long time ago? Last year?" She hadn't heard about any crazed killers in the news lately. Were the cops trying to hide a serial killer from tourists?

He righted the chair, brushed off his jacket and dropped onto the hard plastic. Pinching the bridge of his nose, he said, "How'd you get out of the trunk? How'd you get away?"

Did he plan to let her know whether or not somebody was running around San Francisco abducting women?

"M-my dress must've gotten caught in the trunk when he closed it. I came to, and there was a light in the trunk."

"Wouldn't there have been some indicator on the dash that the trunk was open, alerting him?"

"I told you. It was an older car. Maybe there was no indicator. Maybe there was and he didn't notice it."

"You pushed open the trunk and jumped out?"

"Not right away. When I woke up, I was a little groggy and a lot terrified. The car was going fast, too. I waited until he slowed down. Once he did—" she pushed her hands against the air "—I shoved open the trunk and rolled out."

"Ouch."

"It beat the alternative."

"But he heard you." He dipped into his pocket and retrieved his notepad again.

"Yeah, the trunk lid sprang up, so he would've seen it. After I hit the ground and rolled, I jumped up and started running toward the shoreline, running into the fog."

"You had a couple of things going for you tonight—the dress getting caught and the heavy fog."

"I could barely see the lights on the bridge, and we were right there."

"The bridge?" A muscle ticked in the corner of his mouth.

"The Golden Gate. He was driving down that road along the strip of shoreline at the base of the bridge, or close enough to the base before you pull into the parking lot there."

"I know it." He tapped the end of the pen against his thumbnail in a nervous gesture. "You've described the car. What about the man? Did you get a good look at him?"

"He had shaggy blond hair." She skimmed her hand on the top of her shoulder. "Long. He had a full beard and mustache."

"Height and weight?"

"I have no idea. He was kind of stooped over when I joined him at the car. He could've been short, but I think he was probably medium height because he was bent over. I think he only straightened up when he was behind me."

"And was he a thin guy? Big?"

"Seemed heavyset, but he was wearing a jacket so it was hard to tell."

"Other clothing?"

"Jeans, dark shirt, that bulky gray jacket." She snapped

her fingers. "Wait. He was wearing a jacket with elastic at the sleeves and had both sleeves pushed up. That's how I saw the cast. And on the other arm, the one not in the cast, he had a tattoo."

"Perfect. What was it?"

"It was a bird, a bird with wings spread open."

The detective lifted his gaze from his notepad and drilled her with his dark eyes.

A chill zigzagged down her spine. Had she hit on something? He must know this killer. This *had* happened before.

He unbuttoned the left cuff of his pressed white shirt and pushed it up. "Do you know what kind of bird it was?"

"No—dark colors. It was hard to see. I just noticed the bird's wings."

Then he extended his forearm toward her. "Was it like this?"

A tattoo of a dark blue bird spreading his wings, his claws rising from a flame, decorated the detective's forearm.

Elise clapped a hand over her mouth and jerked back against the bed. "Exactly like that."

Chapter Two

The tattoo on Sean's arm tingled and burned. Some killer had the same tattoo? And why this killer? The M.O. of someone luring women to his car by feigning an injury and then hitting them on the head was all too familiar to him.

Familiar and painful.

Now he'd gone and scared the color out of the victim—Elise, who was shrinking against her pillow, her face as white as the sheets. He'd already startled her when he jumped from his chair, knocking it over. No need for both of them to be freaking out right now.

Sean scooped in a breath and shook down his sleeve. "Similar to that, huh?"

"Similar? Exactly the same."

Her blue eyes took up half her face, and she eyed him like a trapped animal.

He should've never shown her his tattoo. He'd completely misplaced his professional demeanor during this interview. A bird with spread wings—lots of tattoos like that out there.

"I doubt it's exactly the same, Ms. Duran."

"Elise."

"Elise." At least she still wanted him to use her first name. "You said it was dark. A bird is a bird."

She chewed her lip and then relaxed her shoulders. "Can I see it again?"

He hadn't buttoned his cuff, so he shoved the sleeve up his arm again and rotated his forearm.

She leaned forward and her blond hair tickled the inside of his elbow. She smelled salty—not at all what he expected from this blue-eyed blonde with the peaches-and-cream skin.

She wrinkled her nose. "I guess it could've been different. He had a bird tattoo. You have a bird tattoo."

He smoothed down his sleeve and buttoned the cuff. "I'm glad we got that out of the way. I wanted to show you mine to see if it would prompt any more detail."

Actually, he hadn't been thinking at all. What did it matter if he and a killer both had a tattoo of a bird on their arms? Unless someone was trying to pin something on him.

Just as someone pinned something on Dad.

"I…I really didn't mean to imply that I thought it was you out there." She twisted her damp hair into a rope over her shoulder. "The similarity just startled me. You have to admit it's a coincidence."

Despite the warmth of the space, he slid into his jacket. "Yeah, a coincidence. A lot of people have tattoos today, but that detail might make it easier to find this guy."

"I hope so. I'm not his first, am I?"

"I can't say for sure, Elise." He tucked his notepad into his jacket pocket. "Is the hospital releasing you soon?"

"The nurse is coming back to check my temperature. If it's at a safe level, I'm free to go."

"It's almost morning. How are you getting home?"

"Taxi." She hit her forehead with the heel of her hand. "My purse. It must've fallen on the ground outside the club."

"Or he took it."

She widened her baby blues, which seemed to get even bluer. "My license is in there, my phone, my credit card."

He has her address and her contacts and God knows what else.

"If he tries to use the card, we can track him."

"He knows my address now. I got away. I can give a description of him." Her hands clawed at the sheets.

He resisted the urge to take one of those small fists in his hand. "Maybe he left the purse at the scene. We'll call the club to see if anyone found it. We're going to canvass outside the club anyway, see if he left any evidence, question the employees."

Still clutching the sheets, she said, "I'm sure he has my purse. He called my name wh-when I was hiding from him. I never told him my name."

A nurse peeked around the curtain and tiptoed to the bed in the small space. "Excuse me, Detective. I need to take her temperature."

Sean scooted his chair back to give her room, and the nurse leaned over Elise, pinching a thermometer between her fingers and wheeling the machine on the stand closer to the bed.

"I'm just going to put this under your tongue and we'll see how you're doing." The nurse made a tsking noise. "They could've done a better job drying your hair."

Elise twirled a damp lock around her finger and shrugged.

The nurse peered at the thermometer. "You're good to go. How do you feel? How's the head?"

"I'm warm, I'm dry and my head hasn't hurt since the last ibuprofen I took."

"Then I'll bring your clothes and have the doctor sign your release. I'm sorry we have to kick you out of the emergency room. You should see your own doctor as soon as possible for a once-over."

"I will, thanks."

When the nurse left, Elise clasped her hands in her lap, looking…lost.

Sean cleared his throat. "Since you don't have your purse, can I give you a lift home? Unless you want to call a friend."

Or a boyfriend? Husband? Surely this woman had someone in her life, someone to keep her safe.

"I'll take the ride, if you don't mind. My best friend is the one I went to the club with. I doubt she's going to be up at this time of the morning. I doubt she's going to be home."

"I'm assuming you lost your keys, too. How are you going to get into your place?"

"I hide a set outside."

"Not a great idea." He started to shake a finger at her, and then snatched it back. She didn't need one of his lectures on safety.

Color rushed into her pale cheeks as she dropped her gaze to her folded hands. "I guess it wasn't a great idea to approach this guy at two in the morning on a deserted street, either."

"Don't beat yourself up, Elise. He's clever. Why would you think he'd be a danger with a cast on?"

He's not the first killer to use this ploy, and he won't be the last. He had to remember that, too. The M.O. wasn't unique, just as bird tattoos weren't unique.

"I should've known. My friend, Courtney, would've known. Street smarts she'd call it."

"Is Courtney the one who stayed at the club past two and may not be home this morning?" He raised one eyebrow.

"Yeah." A smiled hovered on lips.

"Doesn't sound too street smart to me."

"Here are your clothes." The nurse had a plastic bag hanging from her wrist and a black dress dangling from her fingers. "We did our best to dry them, but I think the dress is ruined."

"Oh, well. Small price to pay." Elise took the dress from the nurse and shook it out.

Sean pushed up from the plastic chair. "I'll be in the waiting room."

It didn't take long for Elise to get dressed. After he'd circled the waiting room twice and inspected and rejected the vending machine in the corner, Elise shuffled into the waiting room, hospital slippers on her feet and a snug black dress hugging her curves.

She crossed her bare arms, and Sean strode across the room, shrugging out of his jacket. "Can't the hospital loan you a blanket for the trip home?"

"I think the nurse expected someone to pick me up and bring a change of clothes."

He draped his jacket around her shoulders. "Do you want me to call someone for you?"

"It's too early in the morning to call anyone."

"Family?"

"None here."

"Boyfriend?"

"Nonexistent."

At least he'd gotten that out of the way. He pulled the jacket tight under her chin. It was as if her assailant had known she was alone. Maybe this wasn't a random attack.

He pointed to her feet. "Can you walk in those things?"

"If I don't pick up my feet, they're surprisingly comfortable. My shoes have been swept out to sea by now."

Sean had parked his unmarked car in the small driveway in front of the emergency room entrance. He guided Elise to the car with a hand on the small of her back. Comfortable or not, it looked as if she could trip over those slippers at any minute.

He opened the front passenger door for her and she

ducked in the car, tugging at her short dress. Had it shrunk after her dip in the bay? The black, sparkly material barely covered her assets—not that he minded.

He cranked on the heater after cranking on the engine. "Are you warm enough?"

"I'm fine." She wiggled her toes and tapped on the window. "Maybe we'll get some clear weather today."

"That fog saved you last night, or rather earlier this morning."

"It did." She pinned her hands, completely covered by the sleeves of his jacket, between her bouncing knees.

"Where to?" He rolled away from the curb, looking over his left shoulder.

"Sunset District. I live in a house—the owner has the upstairs and I get the downstairs. It was divided into two apartments."

"Okay, just give me directions as we get closer." He scratched his chin. He didn't want to keep bringing up the attack, but that's why he was here, wasn't it?

"We need you at the station sometime today to work with a sketch artist. Even if the guy was wearing a disguise, maybe we can get down the shape of his face or some other distinguishing characteristic."

"Like the tattoo."

The pulse in his throat jumped. "Yeah, like the tattoo."

"Do you mind if we stop on the way for a coffee or something hot? Just a takeout."

"Sorry." He drummed the steering wheel with his thumbs. "I should've thought of that. You probably still need something warm to drink."

As he swung into a U-turn, Elise said, "Hot chocolate."

"Hot chocolate it is."

"With whipped cream."

"Of course."

She bit her lip. "I suppose I should learn to like coffee like a grown-up, but there's something so comforting about hot chocolate."

"After the experience you had, you deserve comfort." And protection. And whipped cream.

"I don't have to go in like this, do I?" She yanked at the hem of her dress, which had hitched up around her thighs.

"I'm parking right out front. You can wait in the car."

"One of the perks of riding with a cop."

He parked the car illegally at the curb and hopped out. Even though the sun was rising on the busy street and people bustled in and out of the busy coffeehouse, Sean kept his focus on his car and Elise's profile through the window.

She must've been terrified coming to in that trunk. Despite her soft, feminine appearance, she had to be made of steel to have waded into the San Francisco Bay to avoid her captor.

Holding a cup of hot chocolate in one hand and a coffee in the other, he nudged open the door and strode toward the car. Before he reached the door, Elise hopped out and took both cups from him.

"Which is which?"

"Yours is on the right."

She bent over into the car to secure his coffee in the cup holder. As she did so, her skimpy dress slid up dangerously high.

She backed out of the car, one hand flattening the dress against her thighs. When she straightened up, she rolled her eyes. "This dress was a lot longer when I started out last night."

"I believe you." He rubbed her arms as if to erase her goose bumps. "You shouldn't be out here without my jacket, anyway."

"I couldn't figure out how to roll down the window. Must be locked." She licked her lips and gave a little shiver—more like a wiggle.

It was the sexiest combination of moves ever aimed at him, and she didn't even mean it—didn't mean it as a come-on anyway.

"Get back in the car and wrap your hands around that hot chocolate. I asked for extra whipped cream."

She scurried around to the other side of the car and huddled in his jacket again, one hand darting out to grab her cup.

She slurped a sip through the lid and closed her eyes. "Perfect."

"Are you up for a few more questions?"

Her slim fingers tightened around the cup, but she nodded. "Absolutely."

"Have you been having trouble with anyone? Gotten into any arguments? Coworkers? Neighbors?"

She snorted. "You think someone put out a hit on me?"

"Just covering all bases, Elise. What kind of work do you do?"

"I'm a teacher, a kindergarten teacher."

Her students must love her sweet sincerity. You couldn't fool kids that age.

"No trouble at the school?"

"Everyone's great, no politics on the playground."

"What about your landlord?"

"Oscar? He travels a lot. We get along great. I pay my rent on time and don't have any wild parties. He's my friend's brother. That's how I met her, Courtney."

"Ex-boyfriends? Ex-husbands?"

She sipped her cocoa—too long.

"No." She sucked in a breath. "It's beautiful."

"What?" He jerked his head to the side.

"The bridge. I've been here for almost a year now, and it always takes my breath away when I get an unexpected view of it."

Sean grunted.

"They thought I was a jumper, you know."

He gripped the steering wheel. "Who?"

"The city workers who discovered me. They thought I'd jumped from the bridge. How crazy is that?"

Sean's eye twitched and he dug his knuckles into his eye to stop it. "Crazy. Chances are you wouldn't be walking out of the water if you had."

"I know there have been a few survivors, but I don't think they swam to shore on their own." She snuggled deeper into his jacket. "What would make someone do that?"

Sean lifted his tight shoulders. "Only they know. Right or left?"

She blinked her eyes. "Keep going straight, and then make a right at the next signal."

"So, no bad blood between you and anyone?"

"No. I…I don't like to fight—typically."

Except for her life.

She guided him the rest of the way to her house, and he parked on the street. Single-family homes lined the block, but he could tell several of them were conversions.

She shrugged off his jacket and shoved her feet into the paper slippers. "Thank you, Detective Brody. Will you call me to let me know what time to come down to the station? If you give me something to write on, I'll jot down my home phone number. I guess my cell is gone."

Did she really think he'd drop her curbside while some lunatic had her purse, her address and her keys?

"I'll walk you up."

She thrust her arms into the sleeves of his jacket and scrambled from the car, holding on to her cup.

She led him to the side of the house and through a gate onto a brick walkway. Holding up her finger, she dipped beside a planter. She raked through the dirt and pulled out a key.

He'd seen better hiding places, but at least she hadn't stashed the key beneath the welcome mat.

She puckered her lips and blew on the key before inserting it into the dead bolt. It clicked.

The key scraped when she pulled it out of the lock, and Sean's stomach knotted with the sound. He cinched her wrist as she reached for the doorknob.

"Wait. Me first."

Her gaze darted to the door and back to his face. She dipped her chin and stumbled back.

He withdrew his weapon from his shoulder holster and edged open the door. Coiling his muscles, he stepped into Elise's house.

The rising sun filtered through the slats of her blinds, throwing a vertical pattern across the deep blue carpet on the floor. A low light glowed beneath a whimsical lampshade painted with flowering vines. Colorful children's books littered a coffee table in the shape of a piece of driftwood.

Sean eased out a slow breath and took another step into the inviting room. "Everything look okay in here?"

She peered around his body, nudging his arm with her head. "Looks fine to me."

Something scratched at the sliding glass door, and Elise grabbed his biceps, digging her nails into the material of his shirt. She released a noisy sigh along with his arm and pointed to the door. "My mangy friend is looking for a handout."

A gray-and-white-striped cat pawed at the door again, flicked his tail and walked away.

"How many rooms?"

"This one." She waved an arm in front of her. "You can see the kitchen, and then there are two bedrooms and a bathroom down the hall. That door leads to the garage."

"That would be a good place to start." Sean swung

open the door to the garage. A little hybrid crouched in the center of the garage floor and well-ordered shelves surrounded it. A washer and dryer were tucked in a corner. Not many places to hide here. He took a look under the car for the heck of it.

"Let's have a look in the bedrooms just to be on the safe side."

"I'm all for safe."

She led the way down the short hallway, and Sean tried really hard to drag his gaze away from her swaying hips and the dress that seemed to be shrinking by the minute.

The doors to both bedrooms yawned open, and after a cursory look at the rooms and in the closets, Elise assured him all was well.

She traipsed down the hall to the bathroom at the end, calling over her shoulder. "It's a good thing I have a small house."

She tripped to a stop at the bathroom door and gasped. "Oh!"

With his heart thudding, Sean took two giant steps to join her. The room tilted and he slammed a hand against the doorjamb to stop the spinning.

Elise hooked a finger through his belt loop. "Wh-what does it mean?"

Sean's eyes burned as he read the words on the bathroom mirror in red lipstick: *Here we go again, Brody.*

"I don't know what it means."

Sean ran the back of his hand across his mouth.

Oh, but he did. He knew exactly what it meant.

Chapter Three

Elise's gaze edged from the lipstick words on her mirror to the cop's reflection. *Brody*—that was his name. Why had someone scrawled it on her bathroom mirror along with a cryptic message?

She loosened her hold on his belt loop and crept closer to the vanity. Wedging her hands on the tile, she leaned toward the words on the glass.

"Don't touch anything."

"Oops!" She snatched her hands off the vanity. "Do you think he left fingerprints?"

"Maybe."

The color had returned to Detective Brody's face, but his expression remained hard and tight, alert. The tension vibrating from his body wrapped her in its coils, creating an ache in her shoulders.

She coughed. "It's him, isn't it? The man who abducted me."

"He has, or at least had, your purse and your driver's license. He found your house and used your key to get inside."

His matter-of-fact words socked her in the gut. She sank to the edge of the tub and folded over to pin her forehead onto her knees.

Detective Brody crouched beside her, curling one warm

hand around her bare calf. "You need to get your locks changed and get out of here for now."

Poor small-town girl lost in the big city. Everyone back home had predicted she wouldn't last six months here. She'd doubled that and would continue to prove them wrong.

Hot anger cascaded through her body, and she curled her hands into fists. She jerked her head up and pushed the hair out of her face. Time to take control of this situation.

She hadn't been Ty's victim back in Montana, and she didn't plan to be anyone's victim here in San Francisco despite what her family feared. It started with answers. It started with Brody.

She planted a finger on Detective Brody's granitelike chest. "Why is this guy communicating with you? How does he even know you're on this case?"

He blinked, his spiky lashes and dark eyes momentarily distracting her from her purpose.

Her finger drilled farther into his starched shirt. "I want some straight answers. Is this guy a serial killer? Has he been communicating with you?"

Brody shifted away from the accusatory finger and rose to his feet, smoothing imaginary wrinkles from his gray slacks. "The only serial killer we have at work right now in the city is a guy killing transients. You're hardly his typical victim."

She ground her teeth together. "I'm nobody's victim. I got away, remember?"

"I do." He raised his eyebrows.

She didn't expect him to understand the vehemence behind her words, and she didn't care what he thought about it. "So, why is this guy sending you messages via my bathroom mirror? How did he know you'd be here, in my house?"

"A lot of serial killers follow other cases." He shoved his

hands in his pockets and lifted his shoulders. "I've been a homicide detective in the city for several years. My name's been in the papers a few times. He obviously knows who I am and correctly figured I'd be working this case."

Her gaze slid to his forearm, where the sleeve of his shirt hid the bird tattoo. Then she looked into his dark eyes, shuttered and secretive. Weren't the criminals supposed to be the ones with the secrets, not the cops?

"And he knew you'd be here?"

"Maybe not, but he assumed you'd tell the cops about his little message." He pulled a cell phone from his pocket. "I'm going to call this in, get a tech down here to dust for fingerprints."

His expression and tone told her she'd get nothing more out of him. She smacked her hand against the doorjamb. "And I'm going to get my locks changed."

"You're going to stay here, in this house?"

She wedged her hands on her hips. "Where would I go? I'm a kindergarten teacher, not an heiress like London Breck. I can't afford to camp out in a hotel until you catch this guy… *If* you catch this guy."

"How about staying with a friend?"

"Indefinitely?" She jerked her thumb at the ceiling. "I have Oscar."

"Oscar?"

"Oscar Chu, my landlord." She formed a gun with her fingers and pointed at him. "I also have my .22."

"You have a gun?"

"It's in my closet and it's unloaded, but yeah I have a gun and I know how to use it." A smile pulled at one side of his mouth, and Elise narrowed her eyes. "You find it funny that I have a handgun? I can assure you it's all legal."

"I find it…awesome." He tilted his phone toward her. "Get someone out here to change your locks then, and I'll get a tech to dust for fingerprints in case this guy got even more careless than writing a message on a mirror."

She tiptoed down the hallway and ducked into her office to retrieve her laptop to look up locksmiths in the area.

"After you call the locksmith, why don't you check around to see if anything is missing? I'll take a look at your doors and windows."

She tapped her computer and called out, "My laptop's still here, and I don't think you're going to find any signs of a break-in. It's pretty apparent he used my key to get in."

"Look around anyway."

She pulled open a drawer in her dining nook where she kept a camera and her MP3 player. Both were undisturbed. "I don't think he was interested in stealing anything, just game playing."

"Obviously, he used your key. I'm not checking your doors and windows to see how he got in."

She returned to the bathroom door with the laptop tucked under one arm. "What for then?"

Brody balanced on the edge of her tub and peered at the small frosted window above it. "I'm just making sure he didn't rig something so he can get back in once you change the locks."

She shivered and hugged the computer to her chest. "I'm glad someone's mind works that way."

"Keep looking. Maybe he left something behind." He jumped from the tub, surprisingly light on his feet for a big guy.

She settled the laptop on the kitchen table and did a search for locksmiths. She placed a call to one who worked weekends and made emergency calls.

While Brody continued checking the doors and windows, Elise rifled through her drawers and closets. She didn't find anything amiss, but the thought of that maniac in her house gave her pause every once in a while, and she had to close her eyes to catch her breath.

She had no intention of telling her folks back home about this. She could picture the pinched faces and I-told-you-so's already. They didn't need to know. Of course, there'd be no hiding it if she wound up dead.

A figure moved across her window, and she gasped and crossed her hands over her heart. She crept closer and let out a long breath when she saw Brody poking around the plants by the sliding glass door.

She rapped on the glass, and he looked up. He'd tossed his tie over his shoulder and rolled up his shirt sleeves, his tattoo peeking from the cuff.

She wouldn't mind seeing that sight out her window every morning.

She unlocked the window and shoved up the sash. Pressing her nose to the mesh screen, she called out, "Find anything weird?"

He thrust one arm into the tangle of flowers and withdrew a blue ball of glass. He cradled it in his hands, lifting it as if in offering. "Just this. What is it?"

Her face warmed, but he probably couldn't see her heightened color through the screen. "It's just some decoration."

The woman at the psychic shop in The Haight had told her it would ward off evil. Guess the killer with the fake English accent hadn't come through the backyard.

Someone knocked on the front door.

"That's either your guy or my locksmith."

"Don't answer it yet. Wait for me."

She slammed the window shut and rubbed her fingers together to brush away the dust.

Detective Brody stepped through the sliding glass door from the patio and strode to the front of the house. Leaning forward, he placed his eye at the peephole. "That's my guy."

He swung open the door. "You're fast, Jacoby."

"So are you." The short, powerfully built man hoisted a black bag off his shoulder. "You haven't even written your report yet and you're working the case."

Detective Brody pointed down her hallway. "The man who abducted Ms. Duran made his way back to her place and left a message on the mirror." He gestured to Elise. "This is Elise Duran, the vic—the woman who got away."

His words caused a warm glow in her tummy. A man who listened.

"I'm Dan Jacoby, fingerprint tech extraordinaire." They shook hands and he squeezed her fingertips as if trying to get a read on her pads. "You're one brave lady."

"Nice to meet you, and I did what anyone would do to get away." She waved a hand behind her. "Do you want to see the mirror first?"

"After you."

Jacoby followed her so closely, she tugged on the hem of her skirt. She really needed to put on some clothes.

Elise led the two men to her bathroom and pushed the door wide, not that the small space could accommodate all three of them. Side by side, the shoulders of the two men could practically span the room.

Jacoby whistled through his teeth. "You failed to mention he'd left the message for you, Brody."

"Yeah, one of these megalomaniacs seeking attention. He's not happy just committing murder. He wants to make sure everyone knows how smart he is."

"The joys of being a homicide detective. These nut jobs know your names, follow your careers." Jacoby dropped his bag on the tile floor. "Give me my fingerprints and anonymity."

While Jacoby unzipped the bag, Brody tugged on her

arm. “Let’s give him some room to work, unless you want to watch.”

She backed out of the bathroom. “That’s okay. I’ll wait for my locksmith.”

She didn’t know if it was Jacoby’s muscles or personality, but his presence overpowered the bathroom.

A few minutes later, there was a knock on the door.

Again, Brody went to it first and peered through the peephole. He opened the door a crack. “Yeah?”

“Someone called for a locksmith.” The locksmith held out a card between two fingers.

Brody plucked it from his grip and showed it to Elise.

She nodded. “That’s the company I called.”

Brody widened the door, and the locksmith stamped his feet on the mat outside.

“Show me what you need.”

“All locks with a key, changed.” Elise twisted the doorknob. “Starting with this one, as well as the dead bolt. There’s an interior door to the garage, too. Same key.”

“Can you show me some ID?” He eyed Detective Brody. “You’re not the only careful ones around here. We have to look up the title to the house and verify the owner.”

Elise twisted her fingers. “I’m not the owner. The owner lives upstairs and he’s not home.”

The locksmith squinted at a piece of paper in his hands. “Who’s the owner?”

“Oscar Chu.”

“Yep. That’s what I have here.”

“I can give you his cell. He’ll vouch for me.”

Detective Brody stepped between her and the locksmith, whipping out his badge. “I’ll vouch for her. I’m Detective Sean Brody, and Ms. Duran needs her locks changed for security reasons.”

The locksmith scratched his jaw as he eyed the badge. “If you say so.”

Elise pressed her lips together as she led the locksmith to the door leading to the garage. While she felt grateful that Detective Brody had intervened and smoothed the way for her to get her locks changed, his take-charge attitude on her behalf left a sour taste in her mouth. She'd had her fill of it from her father and brothers.

Shaking her head, she rolled back her shoulders. This situation bore little resemblance to the way the male members of her family had tried to control her life. This was a matter of life and death, not marriage and betrayal.

And here she thought she'd gotten over the "all men are scum" stage.

She tapped the garage door. "Just match the dead bolts and door handle locks for the garage and the front door, and give me two keys—three. I'd better give one to Oscar."

"You got it." The locksmith dropped to his knees, his toolbox clinking and clanking as he set it on the floor next to him.

Elise wandered back to the bathroom, where Detective Brody was parked against the door jamb. "Anything interesting?"

Jacoby looked up, running a hand over his shaved head. "Nope. Looks like one set of prints, and I'm assuming they're yours. Do you live alone?"

"Yes." And that was all she had to say on the subject. She slid a glance at Brody, who was intently watching the tech's work. She hadn't brought a date back to her house since moving to San Francisco.

She didn't trust these smooth-talking city boys much. If she couldn't read a boy she'd known all her life back home in Montana, what chance did she have figuring out some metrosexual urban dweller?

Since Brody seemed consumed with interest in what Jacoby was doing, Elise took the opportunity to assess the detective—not the metrosexual type at all, although he had the clothes. After a year of hanging out with Courtney, she'd learned to recognize an expensive suit when she saw one. The drape of Brody's suit screamed custom-tailored, but the fine material and precise cut couldn't mask the naked power of the man.

He practically hummed with purpose and strength—a man's man her brothers would call him. If her brothers approved of him, that might be reason enough to steer clear, but Brody didn't possess any of the cockiness and good old boyness that characterized her brothers and Ty.

Steer clear? She'd let her imagination get way ahead of her. She didn't have to steer clear of or move in on Detective Brody. He was a cop investigating a crime—a crime aimed at her. Heck, he could be married for all she knew. A surreptitious inventory of his left hand suggested otherwise.

Jacoby tossed the last of his implements in his bag, and Elise jumped.

Detective Brody made a half turn and cupped her elbow. "Still nervous? Even when the locksmith changes the locks, you don't have to stay here. You don't have anything to prove—to me."

Elise swallowed. Had she been so transparent? "Is the SFPD going to foot the bill for my room at the Fairmont?"

"Uh, no."

"Then it looks like I'm digging in here."

"Before I take a look at the doors and windows, press your index finger on the pad and then roll it onto this card." Jacoby held out a small white ink pad cupped in his palm and a card pinched between the fingers of his other hand. "Just want to have your fingerprints on file to compare with these."

She plucked the pad from his hand and pressed her finger against the smooth ink. "I'm a teacher. My fingerprints are already on file."

"That helps. And teachers are the best. My mom was a teacher." Smiling, he put the card on the vanity, and she rolled her finger from right to left.

Jacoby tucked the pad and card in a side pocket of his bag and then patted it. "All set. I'm just going to take a quick look at the front door."

They watched his work for several more minutes and then Detective Brody hovered over the locksmith, asking a million questions.

Elise smirked. The guy probably couldn't wait to finish up this job.

Jacoby came in from the patio and hoisted his bag over his broad shoulder. "Nothing much of anything."

"Thanks, Dan. Send me your findings, and I'll include them in my report."

When he reached the door, Jacoby turned. "I'm glad you're okay. This could be the work of a serial killer. Your attack could be linked to that woman's body we found dumped near the Presidio."

Elise whipped her head around toward Detective Brody. "I thought you said there'd been nothing matching this M.O.?"

He shot a dark look at Jacoby, who shrugged. "We know very little about that murder. It could be related to the transient killings."

"That woman had a bump on the back of her head, too. He could've hit her and stuffed her in a trunk before he did…other things."

A frisson of fear tickled her spine, but Elise preferred to concentrate on the anger boiling her blood. "It sure sounds like it could be related. Why is the SFPD hiding these murders? Women have a right to know if they're being hunted down in the streets."

"Stop." Detective Brody crossed his two index fingers, one over the other. "You've both made a lot of leaps here.

We're not hiding anything. That murder had a couple of columns in the paper. Maybe you skipped the front page that day."

Elise sucked in her bottom lip. She didn't even get the newspaper. She got most of her news from the internet, and she had to admit she didn't search for murder stories.

"Miss?" The locksmith poked his head around the corner of the hallway. "The garage door's done. I'm going to start on the front door."

"Perfect." Elise opened the door for Jacoby. "I suppose you're not going to find anything from the evidence you collected. He wouldn't go to all the trouble of letting himself into my house to scrawl messages and then leave a nice set of his fingerprints."

"You're probably right, but I'll let Sean here know if I find anything out of the ordinary. He's the man."

He swung his bag from one shoulder to the other and saluted as he walked to the sidewalk.

Elise stepped away from the door, leaving it open for the locksmith. "What now?"

"I'll wait for him to finish with your locks, and then I have to go back to the station to write up my report."

"Do you want to tell me about that other woman? The one dumped by the Presidio?"

"Not really. You don't want to hear the gory details."

"How do you know?" Tugging at the hem of her dress, she sat on the arm of the couch. "I'm tougher than I look, you know."

"I have no doubt about that. Anyone who can escape a killer by wading into the San Francisco Bay is hard as nails."

"I would've done anything to escape him." She folded her arms across her chest. "So why do you think I can't handle the details of a murder?"

He rubbed his eye with his knuckle. "Because it's ugly

and sordid. Why invite that into your world when it doesn't have to be there? There are some images that you can never erase from you mind."

She gripped her upper arms, digging her nails into her flesh. He should know. Maybe she *didn't* want to hear the particulars.

Voices at the door had Elise raising her eyebrows at Brody. He headed across the room first, blocking her view.

The locksmith rose. "This guy's looking for Ms. Duran. Says he found her stuff."

Elise's steps quickened. "Really? My purse?"

A man dressed in running shorts and a sweaty T-shirt held up her small black bag from last night. "I found this on the street, a few blocks up. I looked inside, found your license and knew the address was back this way."

She moved forward, hands extended. "Thank you."

"Wait." Brody handed her a white handkerchief. "In case he left prints."

As she poked around in the purse, Brody asked, "What time did you find it?"

"Just now. Maybe five minutes ago." The runner was already backing down the porch.

"Can I get your name and address?"

"Hey, man, I didn't steal the purse."

Brody held up a hand with his badge cupped in the palm. "I'm not accusing you of anything, just in case we have further questions."

Hopping from one foot to the other, the man gave Brody his name and address and then took off at a sprint.

The locksmith pointed his drill at the runner's retreating form. "Nervous, huh?"

Brody took her arm and steered her back to the kitchen. "Anything missing?"

"Let's see." She held up her hand and counted off from the first finger. "My money, my keys, my lipstick."

"Your lipstick?" He jerked his thumb over his shoulder toward the bathroom.

"Different shade, but now that makes two of my lipsticks he's stolen."

"Even if he hadn't kept your keys, you would've still had to change your locks since he got a look at your license."

"I know." She slipped her cell phone from the bag. "At least he left me my phone."

She glanced at the display and noticed two text messages blinking. "Do you want something to eat or drink while we're waiting for the locks?"

"Just some water, please."

She placed the phone and handkerchief on the kitchen counter and went to the refrigerator to fill a glass with water from the dispenser. She clinked the glass in front of him and swept her phone from the tile.

She opened the first message, which Courtney had sent earlier this morning. One word—*breakfast?* If Courtney thought she had a lot to tell Elise about last night, Elise definitely had her beat.

She clicked on the next message from an unknown number. Someone had sent her a picture. A wisp of apprehension brushed the back of her neck as she touched the picture to expand it.

The eyes of the girl in the picture mesmerized her, and she felt darkness closing in around her.

Chapter Four

Elise dropped the phone. The corner hit the counter and bounced once before landing facedown. Her body convulsed, and then she began to sway.

"Elise?" He caught her with one arm, supporting her against his chest. He barely felt the pressure from her tiny frame. Was she having some kind of delayed shock or reaction to the hypothermia?

He started to lead her out of the kitchen, but she dug her heels in the floor.

"The phone." The rasp in her voice made it sound as if she were choking.

"Sit first. I'll get the phone in a second." He swept her up in his arms and carried her to the couch. Her dress had hiked up nearly around her waist, exposing an expanse of smooth thigh and a pair of wrinkled black panties.

He settled her on the couch and dragged a colorful afghan across her lap. "What's on the phone?"

He charged back into the kitchen. Had her abductor sent her a message, too? Good. The better to track him down.

Her teeth chattered. "I-it's a p-picture."

Sean snapped on a rubber glove and touched the screen, bringing it to life. He swore at the image—a young woman, bound, her eyes wide and terrified above her gag.

"Do you know her?"

"Wh-what?"

Sean sat beside Elise and wrapped an arm around her shoulder, pressing her close against his body. Gradually, her trembling subsided.

He rubbed her arm. "Do you know the woman in the picture?"

She shook her head, and her hair, still stiff from the salt water, scratched his cheek.

"The number. Do you recognize the telephone number?"

"No." She took a deep breath that caused a shudder to run through her body. "It came up as unknown. He sent that to me, that vile, horrible…" Her words broke off in a sob.

"Shh." He wrapped his other arm around her so that he enfolded her in a hug, and still the ripples coursed through her.

She tilted her head back and stared into his face. "She's in the trunk of a car, isn't she? Just like me."

"It looks like it. He's an idiot. He's allowed his hubris to get the better of him. We're going to blow up this picture, trace the phone number. He's just given us a bunch of evidence we didn't have before."

"And the girl? Do you think she's dead?"

Of course she was dead. "I don't know, Elise. It doesn't look good."

"That could've been me. That *was* me, only he didn't tie me up. Maybe he perfected his technique after I got away."

"We have no idea when this picture was taken. I don't think he went out after you escaped this morning and found another woman."

This morning. Did all this just happen today? She chewed on her bottom lip. "I want it off my phone."

"I know you do." He stuffed the phone in his pocket.

"But right now the picture is evidence, and so is your phone. We need to find that girl."

"Have there been any missing girls reported?"

"Always." He didn't plan to tell Elise about all the sad stories that crossed their desks, all the calls from desperate family members. He traced the edges of her phone with the pads of his fingers. Which family members would claim this one?

"Why did he send that to me?" Elise buried her face in her hands. "I'll never be able to get that image out of my head."

"He's a sadist." And somehow he'd dialed into him. Maybe the killer knew about his past, maybe he didn't, but now they were tied together. That message on the mirror tied them together.

"Ms. Duran, I'm all done with the locks on the front door." The locksmith poked his head around the front door. If he'd heard any of their conversation, he gave no sign.

Elise tried the locks and then settled the bill with him, but it was obvious her mind remained on that picture on her phone.

"He's a serial killer, isn't he? He's a serial killer you don't know about yet. He's just getting started and he wants to play some sick game with you…and now me."

It was a game he knew too well. He gestured around the small house. "Are you going to be okay here? I have to get to the station, turn in your phone and purse."

She glanced over her shoulder toward the hallway. "I have to take a shower."

"Do you want me to wait here? When you're done, I can take you to the station with me and you can look through some mug shots."

"Would you do that?" She was already moving toward the back rooms. "I won't be long."

He waved a hand. "Take your time. I'm going to call in

and report this picture. Maybe they can get a trace started when I give them your phone number."

She ducked into her bedroom and then darted across the hall to the bathroom, clutching a bundle of clothes to her chest.

Sean let out a long breath and collapsed onto Elise's colorful couch. What the hell was going on? Why did the guy who abducted Elise share a similar tattoo with him? Why did he write a message to him on Elise's mirror? This had to be a coincidence.

Serial killers had toyed with homicide detectives way before his father's time, and they'd continue to do so long after Sean's career. When he saw the message, Dan Jacoby hadn't jumped to any conclusions and Dan definitely knew the story of his past.

He was probably overreacting. That's what his brothers would tell him, but as the eldest the burden had weighed most heavily on him. Hell, Judd could barely even remember the old man, couldn't remember the life they'd had before…before everything had been sucked into the bay by a strong, merciless current.

He plowed his fingers through his hair and shifted to the end of the couch. The soft cushions made it tough to sit up straight, so he gave up and slouched against the back of the couch while he made his call.

When he heard the water in the shower shut off, he struggled off the couch and began to pace the small room.

Elise emerged from the bathroom on a cloud of fragrant steam. She'd pulled her blond hair into a ponytail and had replaced her ridiculously small dress with a pair of tight jeans and a beige cable sweater, giving her a blond-on-blond look that made her jaw-droppingly beautiful. He kept his jaw in place.

"Do you still think it's a good idea to stay here on your own?"

"Probably not. I'm going to have to change my cell phone number when I get that new phone." She slid a knotted scarf from the back of a chair. "I don't want any more surprises from this guy."

She headed to the door leading to the garage, and Sean stopped. "You're not coming with me?"

"I think it's easier for me to take my car, so I don't have to bother you for a ride back here."

"It's no bother." Bother? He didn't want to let Elise out of his sight.

She slid her new key in and out of the dead bolt. "I decided I'm going to call my friend Courtney to see if I can crash at her place for a few days. If it's okay with her, I'm going to head over there this afternoon."

"Good idea. Follow me to the station, and you can park in the lot there."

He sat in his idling car until Elise's garage door opened and her little hybrid rolled down the driveway. He kept an eye on his rearview mirror, stopping at every yellow light.

He sure as hell hoped the killer's fascination with Elise came to an end soon. He could bring it to an end sooner rather than later if he caught this guy. Then he could find out why he was sending him personal messages.

He cruised into the station's parking garage with Elise close on his tail. The morning shift had already gone out, depleting the ranks of patrol cars waiting in their slots.

Sean swung into an empty space at the end of the row, and Elise parked next to him.

"We're really in the bowels of the police station here, aren't we?"

"Shh, don't tell anyone we have all this parking down here." He led her to the elevator, and after a short ride, the doors opened onto a corridor bustling with both cops in and out of uniform and civilians.

He nodded at a few people on his way to homicide, trying not to read suspicion in their eyes. He'd have to lose this paranoia if he hoped to catch this guy and help Elise. Because he did want to help Elise.

He pulled out a chair on the other side of his cluttered desk. "Have a seat. I'm taking your phone to the lab, and I'll try to round up a sketch artist. We might have to call one in. Coffee? Water?"

"I'm fine." She folded her hands in her lap, her wide eyes taking in the activity of the room.

Yanking a binder from his drawer, he said, "You can pass the time looking at mug shots."

He left Elise running her finger across the plastic inserts in the binder. He dropped off the phone with instructions to print, blow up and distribute the picture the killer had sent. He put the word out for a sketch artist, and then he stopped by the coffee machine.

By the time he returned to his desk, Elise was halfway through the six-packs of mug shots in the binder he'd left with her.

Flipping a page, she looked up at his approach.

"Any luck?" He dropped into his chair and loosened his tie.

"No." She tapped the book. "Who are these guys, again?"

"Killers, rapists, batterers."

She flinched and jerked her hand back from the page. "Why are they out on the streets?"

"They did the crime and then did their time." His hand tightened around his coffee cup. "I rounded up a sketch artist for you. Do you want to give it a try after you finish looking at those mug shots?"

"Sure, although I don't know how much help I'm going to be. It was dark, and he wore a disguise—I'm positive about that. I should've realized that much facial hair was concealing something."

Elise seemed determined to blame herself and her naïveté for the attack. He couldn't sit back and allow her to browbeat herself.

He pushed away his coffee, and it sloshed over the edge. "The majority of men who have beards and moustaches are not criminals or trying to hide anything. That's not a clue that anyone would've picked up on."

Her face awash in pink, Elise smacked the book of six-packs closed. "None of these guys looks even vaguely familiar to me except one who's the spitting image of my geometry teacher, and I'm probably just projecting because I hated geometry."

A smile tugged at the corner of his mouth. "I doubt your geometry teacher is moonlighting as a criminal in San Francisco from…wherever it is you're from."

"Montana. Is it so obvious I'm not from the city?"

It was to him. She lacked that brittle edge so many urbanites had. But far be it from him to stoke the image she had of herself as the country bumpkin in the big, bad city.

He shrugged. "Not at all. I think you mentioned living here for just a year."

Nodding, she relaxed her shoulders and slumped against the back of the chair.

Sean picked up the receiver of his phone and punched the button for one of the interrogation rooms. Tony Davros, the sketch artist, picked up. "You're already there. You must be ready for the witness."

Sean pushed back his chair as he stood up, dropping the receiver back in the cradle. "Let's see what you can give us on this guy."

Elise followed him to the interrogation room, her head cranking from side to side as they waded through ringing phones, shouts across the room and people crisscrossing the space with papers or files clutched in their hands.

She wrinkled her nose. "It's noisier than a kindergarten classroom in here."

"Probably about the same level of maturity, too." He pushed open the door to the interrogation room and ushered her inside.

Davros stood up and extended his hand. "I'm Tony Davros, Ms. Duran. Wish we were meeting under happier circumstances."

Sean raised one eyebrow in Davros's direction. That's the most words he'd heard from the artist's mouth in almost two years. Davros had even pulled out a chair for Elise.

First Jacoby and now the sketch artist. He got it. Elise's fresh-faced, angelic appearance spurred men on to chivalrous deeds, prompting them to pull out chairs and hand over jackets. Even the typically surly Davros wasn't immune.

"Me, too." She shook Davros's hand and dropped onto the wooden chair. "I'm afraid the man was wearing a disguise—beard, wig, glasses, even a phony accent."

"That's not uncommon." Davros swept his palm across a piece of sketch paper and caressed his pencil. "We'll start with the shape of his face—what you could see of it."

The two of them went back and forth for several minutes, the artist coaxing and praising as his pencil moved swiftly across the page in front of him.

Shoving his hands in his pockets, Sean sauntered to where Davros sat hunched over his sketch pad, the tip of his tongue lodged in the corner of his mouth as he further defined the nose of the suspect.

Sean squinted at the face. Would someone be able to recognize him without the beard and moustache? Davros's job entailed drawing another picture without the facial hair and glasses, perhaps with shorter hair.

"That's close to what I remember." Elise tossed her ponytail over her shoulder as she leaned over the drawing.

A sharp rap at the door interrupted them, and before

Sean could even offer an invitation, it swung open and banged against the wall.

Sergeant Curtis from homicide, his eyes bugging out, thrust his head into the room. "We just got a call from patrol about a dead body, and I think you're going to want to head out there, Brody."

Sean's heart slammed against his rib cage. "And why is that?"

"It's the girl in the picture."

Chapter Five

The blood rushed to Elise's head and she gripped the edge of the table as the room spun. She had a picture of a dead woman on her phone.

He'd killed her. He abducted her, took her picture and murdered her. And he sent that picture to her.

"How do you know it's the same person?" Detective Brody had straightened up to his full height and his body seemed coiled for action. The waves of his tension reverberated off the walls of the small room.

The cop who'd delivered the news gripped the doorknob. "As soon as you forwarded the picture to us, we sent it out to patrol. When the unit discovered the body, they checked the picture. It's a match."

"Do you have any details, Curtis? Cause of death?"

"Not yet, but she didn't drown even though the fishermen found the body at the edge of the bay."

"The bay? Her body was found in the bay?" Detective Brody shot Elise a quick glance.

"Not in the bay, at the edge. Right over that small incline that borders the parking lot for the Golden Gate. That's why we know she didn't drown unless it was recent." His eyes shifted between Elise and the sketch artist, and he cleared his throat. "No bloating."

Elise covered her mouth and clenched her teeth.

Detective Brody stepped in front of her as if to shield her from the other detective's words and the image they'd already created in her head.

"We'll discuss the rest of this on the way."

Sergeant Curtis dipped his head. "Sorry, Ms. Duran. I'll ride with you, Brody."

"Are you going to be okay?" Detective Brody made a half turn toward her.

"I'm fine." Elise held up her hands. "I'm going straight to my friend's house after this."

"How will I reach you? We have to keep your phone."

"I should hope so." She shivered and rubbed her arms. "I'll pick up another phone today and contact you with the new number."

"Make sure you do. And Elise—" he pinned her with his dark gaze "—don't go back to your house."

She drew a cross over her heart. "I promise."

And that's the only thing she'd promise him right now.

Fifteen minutes later Elise sat in her car, her hands clutching the steering wheel. She could do this. She needed to know more, had a right to know more.

She rolled out of the parking garage and hung a left. She knew better than to follow Detective Brody's car. The guy seemed to be on high alert at all times. He'd notice one small hybrid following him to a crime scene.

Besides, she already knew the way. Hadn't her life almost ended in the exact same spot?

When she pulled into the parking lot for the bridge, she didn't have to worry about standing out. The tourist season was in high gear, and a trip to the Golden Gate Bridge was high on everyone's list.

A crowd of people had already formed at the edge of the lot where it led down to the gravel by the water. She stumbled from her car, and a brisk breeze cut her to the bone. She fished a sweater out of her backseat and put it on over her bulky cable knit. You could never have too many layers in San Francisco.

She scrambled from the car and tugged the sweater around her tighter, unrolling the sleeves so they hung over her hands. She shuffled up to the fringes of the crowd.

"What happened?" Elise stood on her tiptoes, not knowing what she hoped she would or wouldn't see.

A man looked over his shoulder. "There's a dead body down there."

The woman standing to her right clicked her tongue. "Is it a jumper?"

That's what the city workers had thought of her. Is that what this killer wanted everyone to believe? No. He wanted to shout his deeds from the rooftops. He wanted the distinction of impressing everyone with his cleverness or he never would've left that note for Brody.

The tall man in front of her snorted. "That's not a jumper this close to the shore. The current's too fast out there."

Elise ducked and shimmied between two of the curious onlookers. She zeroed in on Detective Brody's unmistakable form, his arm raised as if directing traffic.

Someone had covered the body with a sheet, securing the four corners against the wind that snatched at its edges. Frustrated in its efforts to pluck the sheet from the dead body, the wind found another outlet, puffing up the sheet so that it looked like a sail at full speed ahead.

But that girl wasn't going anywhere—ever.

Elise didn't know what she'd hoped to discover out here, but as soon as the other detective had burst into the interrogation room, she knew she had to see the crime scene for herself.

Had the killer intended this little patch of desolate shore as *her* final resting place? She turned her face to the right and gazed at the beach a short distance away where she'd scrambled into the water to save her life.

Had he killed this woman here or was this just his dumping ground?

She asked no one in particular. "Wh-who found her?"

The man with the broad shoulders turned sharply, bumping Elise's arm. "It's a woman? Who told you it was a woman?"

Elise grabbed the ponytail that whipped across her face. "Oh! I don't know. I guess I just assumed..."

The woman beside her grunted, "It's a woman. Count on it. Unless it's some drug hit or something. The cowards always go after the women."

The wail of a siren drew closer, causing the clutch of people to shift and sway.

Would they take her away now? Away from the prying eyes of this nosy group of people?

Elise felt protective toward the woman, and maybe that protectiveness sprang from guilt. Had this woman taken her place?

Detective Brody had pointed out that the killer could've taken that picture at any time. He was right. Chances are the killer hadn't found another victim after two in the morning when Elise had escaped.

Sergeant Curtis crunched across the gravel and faced the crowd. "Did anyone else see anything out here?"

Elise dropped her head and pulled the sweater up to her chin, not that he'd notice her after their brief encounter in the interrogation room.

People murmured and mumbled, but nobody stepped forward with any information.

Undeterred, Sergeant Curtis continued. "If anyone was here earlier, if anyone was taking any pictures, give us a call."

A few people began peeling away from the group as

the cops continued to scour the ground. A coroner's van had pulled up on the gravel, but still nobody made a move to retrieve the body.

They might be here all afternoon.

Elise spun away from the scene, her stomach rolling. Her presence here had served no purpose except to confirm how close her own brush with death had occurred to an actual death.

She reached into her purse for her cell phone before she remembered that her phone was in the possession of the SFPD with a picture of the dead woman below on it.

She meant what she told Brody. She wouldn't return to her house, not yet, especially with Oscar still out of town.

She tapped the arm of the woman next to her. "Can I borrow your phone for a minute? It's a local call."

"Sure." She dipped into the pocket of her sweatpants and pulled out a smartphone.

Elise tapped in Courtney's phone number.

"Hello?" Courtney's voice, low and seductive, purred over the line.

"Court? It's Elise."

"Elise?" The dulcet tones turned to a squeak. "Where are you calling from? I thought for sure you were Derrick from last night when I saw the unknown number."

"You wouldn't believe me if I told you."

"Are you okay? I texted you earlier but you didn't respond."

Elise took several steps away from the rubbernecking crowd, out of everyone's hearing. "All hell broke loose when I left you at the club last night."

Her friend paused for two beats. "Tell me you're okay right now before I have a full-fledged panic attack."

"I'm okay."

Courtney blew out a noisy sigh. "You scared me. What

do you mean all hell broke loose? Where are you and whose phone are you using?"

"After I left the club last night—" Elise closed her eyes and squeezed the phone "—I was attacked."

"Attacked? What are you talking about?"

Her friend's voice screeched over the phone and Elise pulled it away from her ear.

"Someone pretended to need help and when I went to help him, he knocked me on the head and stuffed me into his trunk."

Courtney's breath rasped over the phone. "Elise, you're joking. Tell me you're joking."

"I'm not joking, Courtney. I got away. I'm okay."

"How can you be okay after something like that? Where are you?" She sucked in a breath. "Oh, God, you're not in the hospital, are you?"

"Not anymore."

"Not anymore? Where *are* you? I'm coming to get you."

Elise switched the phone to her other hand and wiped her clammy palm against the seat of her jeans. "I was hoping you'd say that. There's more to the story."

A lot more to the story. She caught sight of Detective Brody's head as he clambered onto a rock, his tie dancing over his shoulder in the breeze.

"I don't need a ride, but I was hoping I could crash at your place for a night or two. Your brother's out of town again, and I don't feel like staying in the house alone."

"Absolutely. Do you have your car?"

"I do. Are you home now? I'll drive over."

"I'm not home. I'm shopping, and I was going to grab some lunch. Why don't you meet me for lunch?"

"I can do that. Where?"

"I'm at Union Square. How about Chinatown?"

"I don't know how I'm ever going to find parking there, but I'll give it a try. Han Ting's?"

"I'll meet you there at around one o'clock. Is that enough time for you?"

Elise agreed to the time and ended the call. She held the phone out to the woman. "Thank you."

"No problem."

"Any progress down there?" Elise stood on her tiptoes, but the scene looked much the same—people searching the ground, heads together conferring, and still the white sheet billowed in the wind.

"No. I'm going to continue my walk over the bridge. I suppose we'll be reading about this one in the newspaper."

"I hope so."

The woman's brow furrowed and Elise felt her cheeks warming. "I…I mean, I hope the cops keep the public informed about crime. Do they ever underreport this kind of stuff? You know, shove it under the carpet to give people a false sense of security and to keep the tourists coming?"

"I suppose." The woman cocked her head. "I read about another murder last month, a young woman. I hope we don't have some serial killer on the loose."

Elise didn't want to dash the stranger's hopes, so she sealed her lips. "I hope not. Anyway, thanks for the phone. Enjoy your walk."

She shoved her hands in the pockets of her sweater and watched the woman cross the parking lot and head toward the bridge's pedestrian walkway.

Elise had ventured across the bridge a few times since moving to the city. Round-trip was a good three-mile walk, and while she could use the exercise to clear her head, she had a lunch date with Courtney—not that she was looking forward to it.

She dreaded revealing the rest of last night's details to Courtney, except for meeting Detective Brody. She wanted her friend's take on the tall, muscular cop and his protective attitude toward her. Was his behavior normal for a homicide detective questioning a witness?

Normal or not, Elise had felt something click between them, or maybe that was just her desperately reaching out for a knight in shining armor. After Ty, she'd begun doubting the existence of those knights.

She dug in her purse for her keys, and then someone touched her shoulder. She spun around, dropping the keys and hugging her purse to her chest.

Sergeant Curtis faced her, his eyes narrowed and his arms across his barrel chest. "What are you doing here, Ms. Duran?"

Her gaze skittered over his shoulder to Detective Brody still clomping around the beach. "I just had to see for myself. That's not against the law, is it? All these other people are here."

"Of course not." He hunched his shoulders until his short neck disappeared completely. "But you're not like all these other people, are you?"

"I'm a curious looky-loo, just like them."

"Don't start doing your own investigating, Ms. Duran." He shook his stubby finger in her face. "Leave it to us. We'll tell you what you need to know."

Bending over, she swiped her keys up from the ground, hoping for a little composure. Sergeant Curtis's paternalistic tone caused a spiral of anger to shoot through her body. Why did men always think they knew what was best for her?

"Maybe I don't want to wait for information. That woman was on my phone. I have a right and a need to know what happened to her."

He took a step back and blinked. "Sorry. Just don't want you putting yourself in any danger."

"I get it." She waved him off and strode to her car, jabbing her thumb on the remote. He'd probably go and tell Detective Brody now.

And what if he did? She didn't owe Detective Brody anything, either.

As she rounded her car, a white square on her windshield caught her attention. She rolled her eyes. Perfect—a parking ticket.

She snatched the object from beneath her wiper, her eyebrows colliding over her nose. This was no ticket envelope. She unfolded the slip of paper and scanned the words.

The blood thundered in her ears as she crushed the paper in her fist, her gaze shifting wildly around the parking lot. Her dry mouth made forming words almost impossible.

She swallowed. She licked her lips. She tried again. She screamed.

"He's here. The killer's here."

Chapter Six

The woman's scream pierced through the air. The sound tore at Sean's insides. He jerked his head up and scanned the parking lot. A few of the vultures who had been circling the crime scene shifted their attention to a lone woman standing beside a car, waving her arms.

Standing beside a blue hybrid.

A long blond ponytail whipping across her face.

What the hell was Elise Duran doing here, and why the hell was she screaming?

The adrenaline pumped through his body, and his legs responded. He shot up the incline to the parking lot and sprinted across the asphalt.

Curtis had beaten him to it, but it didn't look as if he was having any luck getting a coherent response from Elise, still waving her arms around and talking gibberish.

"Elise! What's wrong? What are you doing here?"

She stumbled toward him, holding out a clenched fist, her face white. "He's here. He's here. The killer."

Adrenaline crashed through his body again before the first wave had even subsided, and he grabbed Elise's arms. "Where? Where is he?"

"Here." Her trembling fist prodded his chest. "He left this."

He had to practically pry open her frozen fingers to

get to the crumpled piece of paper she'd balled up in her clenched hand. He smoothed it out against the back of his hand and cursed.

Curtis hunched forward. "What is it, Brody? What's it say?"

"It says, 'Did you come to see my handiwork?'"

Curtis gurgled, his hand hovering over his weapon. "The SOB is here?"

"How long have you been away from your car, Elise? How much time did he have?"

Her head cranked back and forth. "I don't know. I mean, I've been here for about twenty minutes. I didn't notice anyone near my car. He's here. He was here."

"Maybe someone saw him." Sean shielded his eyes and tipped his head back to look at the lampposts. "Are there cameras on this part of the parking lot?"

"Nope. It's like our guy knows this area. No cameras where he dumped the body, either." Sergeant Curtis held out his hand for the note, and Sean extended it between two fingers even though he wanted to rip it to pieces.

Why had Elise come here anyway? He'd been worrying about her all the way to the crime scene, and she'd been right behind him.

"Where's Officer Jackson?"

"He's back at the crime scene, extending the yellow tape. Why?"

"I had him combing through the crowd earlier, asking questions, on the lookout for something just like this."

Elise's eyes popped open. "Really? You suspected the killer might be here?"

"A lot of times they stick around to prolong the thrill."

"That's taking a risk." She hugged herself and hunched farther into the big sweater she'd wrapped around her body.

"Our boy likes taking risks, doesn't he? He used your key to enter your house, sent a picture to your phone."

Her face crumpled. "Sent me *her* picture. Who is she, anyway?"

"We don't know yet." But the killer had sliced off her finger as a keepsake—something Elise didn't need to know.

Curtis held up the note. "Do you want me to put this in an evidence bag and track down Jackson to see if he saw anyone suspicious?"

"Yeah." Sean smacked the roof of Elise's car. "Ask him if he noticed anyone lurking around the parking lot, if he saw anyone near a blue hybrid."

Elise dragged a hand through her hair, loosening strands from her ponytail. "How did he find my car, Detective Brody? How did he know I was here?"

Despite her rigid posture, Elise looked ready to shatter into a million pieces. He tilted his chin toward the stone benches on the walkway to the visitor center. "Let's sit down over here. And you can call me Sean."

She turned and tripped over her own feet.

"Whoa." He took her arm to steady her and kept possession of it as they walked toward a bench.

She sat on the edge and crossed her legs, her head swiveling from side to side. "Do you think he's still here?"

"I think he's long gone. He must have a police scanner or he was watching the area, knew we'd gotten the call and rushed over to see the spectacle." He cleared his throat. "He must've seen you, Elise. Must've recognized you."

She closed her eyes and a breath shuddered through her body. "He knows my car because he saw it in my garage, so he looked for it."

"It must've increased his excitement tenfold to see you here."

She slammed a fist against the back of the bench. "Now I'm even more upset that I came out here. I don't want to give him any more satisfaction."

"Why did you follow us?"

"I didn't exactly follow you." She rubbed her hand, red from the sudden contact with the bench. "Sergeant Curtis had mentioned the location of the body, so I waited until you took off."

"That doesn't answer the question." The strands of her golden hair danced around her face, and his fingers itched to tuck them behind her ears. Instead he folded his arms and drove his fists into his biceps. "Why'd you come out here?"

"Are you seriously asking me that? Why wouldn't I come when I'm so involved?"

He sliced a hand through the air. "That's exactly why you need to stay out of this. Don't tempt this guy. You're the one who got away. Don't keep reminding him of that."

"You're right." She sniffled and pulled a tissue from her purse. "I guess I just had to see for myself. I feel…connected to this woman."

"I understand that, but just let us do our jobs. He's careless, addicted to the thrill. He wants the limelight. We'll bring him down." He touched her shoulder and then buried his hand in his pocket.

There was no doubt Elise needed protection, but she didn't need it from him. Death and darkness dominated his existence. Elise needed life and light and laughter. She needed to get out of this city.

"You're right." She lifted her shoulders and then blew out a sigh. "I just felt compelled to be here."

Sean narrowed his eyes as he turned his attention to the crime scene, where an officer was waving his arms at him. "Looks like they're flagging me down. What are you going to do?"

"I'm meeting my friend for lunch." She tugged at the sleeve of her sweater to reveal a watch. "And I'm going to be late."

"Where are you having lunch?"

She blinked. "Chinatown."

"It's going to be crazy over there. They're having a parade for the Dragon Boat Festival."

"I'm pretty sure my friend doesn't know that. Maybe I'll park elsewhere and hop on the Muni."

"I have a better idea. I'll put a call in to the station there and let them know you're going to park your car in the lot." He slipped the notebook from his pocket and jotted down the intersection for her.

"You can do that?"

"One of the perks of being a cop in the city." He pushed up from the bench and tucked the piece of paper in her hand. "I'll walk you back to your car. Just be aware of your surroundings. Keep an eye on your rearview mirror."

Her eyes widened. "You think he might follow me?"

"I think you need to be careful. Everyone should be aware of their surroundings."

"Especially me."

She clicked her remote, and he opened the car door for her, hanging on the frame. "You're going to get a phone and give me a call so I have the number?"

"I'll do that after lunch, and I have to at least drop by my place to pack a bag and get my school stuff together."

His gut knotted. "You still have to teach."

"One more week of school."

"Like I said, be aware of your surroundings."

She started her engine and snapped on her seat belt. "Thanks, Detective…Sean. Thanks for everything. I'll call when I get that phone."

His gaze trailed after her little car as it scooted out of the parking lot, and the knots in his gut tightened even more.

Of course she had to go to work and see her friends and live her life. He couldn't follow her around the city.

Even though he wanted to.

ELISE GLIDED INTO a parking stall at the Central Division and gave her rearview mirror one last glance. If anyone had followed her here, he'd have to be a ninja. She'd taken so many twists and turns to avoid the areas blocked off for the parade route, she would've noticed someone on her tail taking the exact same route.

She flipped up the mirror cover on the visor and dashed some color across her lips. She needed all the artificial brightening she could handle after that shock at the bridge.

He'd spotted her. Knew her car. Maybe he'd been watching her.

She smacked the visor against the roof of the car. He was too cocky. Detective Brody—Sean—was right. The killer would trip up sooner rather than later with his attitude of invincibility.

"Sean." Just saying his name made her feel more at ease. He'd even secured a parking space for her in the middle of Chinatown on a parade day. Now, there was a man you could count on—not like Ty, filled with secrets, lies and betrayals.

She slipped out of the car and walked down the ramp to the sidewalk. Red and gold banners festooned lampposts and flapped in the breeze. Elise navigated between colorful lawn chairs and blankets lining the sidewalks. She sniffed the air filled with the scents of incense, spices and fried food. A pack of kids jostled her as they ran down the sidewalk clutching flags with red dragons emblazoned upon them. Their grandparents shuffled in their wake, smiling and nodding at Elise.

She ducked into the dark confines of Han Ting and surveyed the packed dining room. She and Courtney would be lucky to find a table.

"Elise!"

Elise peered across the room at Courtney bobbing up from her seat and waving in her direction. She wound through the tables and gave her friend a one-armed hug before sitting down.

"How in the world did you get a table? Did you even know that the Dragon Boat Parade was going on today?"

Courtney flicked her perfectly manicured fingers. "Duh. I grew up in Chinatown, remember? I know what today is."

"And how did you manage to snag a table? It's wall-to-wall people in here."

"My auntie's family owns Han Ting. Technically, she's not my aunt, but her family and my mom's family lived next door to each other in the old neighborhood."

"First a prime parking spot, and then the best table in the house at Han Ting. It pays to know people in high places."

"You got a parking spot?"

"It's a long story." Elise dropped a napkin in her lap and poured herself some tea from the ornate pot.

"Stop stalling and tell me what happened after you left me." Courtney tapped her cup and Elise filled it with the fragrant green tea.

As Elise relayed the details of the frightening episode, Courtney's lipsticked mouth formed a perfect O and she clutched her napkin to her chest.

"Oh, my God, you are so amazing."

"Amazing? I wasn't even thinking straight. I just knew I had to get out of that trunk. I was also mad at myself for falling prey to his broken-arm scam."

Elise held her breath, waiting for Courtney to agree with her. *She* never would've fallen for that ruse.

"Are you kidding?" Courtney dropped her napkin and gulped the rest of her tea. "Anybody would've done the same thing. He had a cast on. Who would go to those lengths?"

"I guess it's not the first time a serial killer has used that method."

"Serial killer?" Courtney covered her mouth when the waiter approached the table. She rattled off their order in Mandarin, and when the waiter left she focused her bright eyes on Elise again.

"How do you know this is a serial killer and not some random nut?"

Elise folded her hands around the warm cup. "Because he killed again."

"How do you know?"

Elise explained how the runner found her purse and phone and how the killer had sent the picture of his next victim. "Then when I was at the police station working with the sketch artist, a call came in that someone had found the woman's body."

"Elise, this is too creepy." She grabbed Elise's wrist, her nails digging into her skin. "You can't stay at the house, especially with Oscar gone."

"That's where you come in, if it's okay."

"Of course it's okay."

The waiter rolled up a cart with enough steaming plates to feed the Hun army. When he transferred all the dishes to the table, Elise dumped a mound of sticky white rice onto her plate.

As Elise ladled three different entrees onto her plate, she wondered whether or not she should tell Courtney about the note on her windshield.

She glanced at her friend dabbing a spot of red sauce at the corner of her mouth with a napkin and decided against it. She'd shocked Courtney enough for one sunny afternoon. She didn't need to hear the rest of the frightening details.

"Do they know how the woman died or how long she'd been there?"

"Change of subject, please. I want to enjoy my lunch."

"You don't have to tell *me* twice." Courtney stabbed a shrimp and shook it at Elise. "Here's a subject change for you—how hot is this Detective Brody who's following you around and scoring you parking places all over the city?"

Elise's face got warmer than the kung pao chicken. "Who said he was hot?"

Courtney snorted. "You did. Every time you mentioned his name and or his heroic deeds, you got all dreamy-eyed."

"That's ridiculous." Elise plucked the shrimp from Courtney's fork and popped it into her mouth.

"Don't forget, I read body language for a living, and you have one of those faces that show all your emotions—must be a Montana thing."

"Okay, I succumb to your superior understanding. Detective Sean Brody is hot—tall, dark and handsome."

Courtney held out her fist for a bump. "Well, all right. That's one silver lining to a very scary night."

"And you? Who's Derrick, and did he ever call you?"

"Derrick is that fine African-American who bought us that second round of drinks."

"Bought *you* a second round. I just had one, remember?"

"Whatever. After you left, we danced the rest of the night."

"He seemed like a nice guy, but kind of a player."

"Okay, not every guy is a player like your Montana cowboy. Look at the luscious Detective Brody. I'll bet he's not a player."

She shrugged. "Doesn't seem like it, but I don't know much about him."

Courtney's phone buzzed, and as she checked the display, a crease formed between her eyebrows. "Client. I need to take this."

"Do you want to take some of this food to go?"

"Sure. Have them pack it up." Courtney scooted back her chair, already punching in her client's number.

She might be a party girl on the surface, but as a therapist Courtney was committed to her clients. She'd drop everything at a moment's notice to see them and talk them through some crisis.

Elise asked for some to-go boxes and was scooping the food into the little white cartons when Courtney returned to the table.

Courtney unhooked her purse from the back of her chair. "I'm so sorry. I'm going to have to run out on you and meet my client at my office—emergency. Can you take the food? You can go straight to my place. I'll give you the key."

She reached for her wallet, but Elise held up her hand. "I'll get lunch. After all, I'm going to be your guest for the next few days."

"Longer if you need it." She waved to an old Chinese woman stationed by the door. "Auntie Lu, come and say hello to my friend."

Elise stood up and exchanged a quick hug with her friend, who then kissed Auntie Lu's pale cheek on her way out of the restaurant.

The old woman placed a hand on Elise's arm. "Sit."

Elise sat down and Auntie Lu arranged herself in the chair across from her.

"Courtney busy girl."

"Courtney is a good friend." Elise pulled some bills from her wallet and dropped them onto the check tray. "How long has your family owned this restaurant?"

"Many years. You going to watch the parade today? Starting soon."

"I am."

Auntie Lu tapped Elise's teacup. "You have leaves. Do you want me to read your tea leaves?"

"Can you do that?"

"Ancient practice." She winked at Elise and slid the cup in front of her, wrapping her gnarled hands with their painted nails and heavy rings around it.

Auntie Lu studied the bottom of the cup, and the smile she'd been wearing faded. Then she pushed the cup away. "Silly."

A wisp of fear trailed across Elise's flesh. "What is it? What did you see in there?"

Auntie Lu spread her crooked fingers. "Nothing. I lost my touch."

She eased from the chair, patted Elise's shoulder and shuffled back to her stool by the door, where she stared onto the street through the window.

Elise tipped the cup and squinted at the residue swimming in the bottom. Then she splashed a little more tea into the cup and gulped it, leaves and all. "That takes care of that fortune."

She dropped her wallet back into her purse, hitched it over her shoulder and hung the plastic bag of food over her wrist. She smiled and nodded at Auntie Lu by the entrance and grabbed the door handle.

Auntie Lu's seemingly frail hand gripped Elise's elbow in a vise. Elise looked into her dark, gleaming eyes.

Auntie Lu whispered, "Be careful."

For a second, Elise thought she'd imagined the entire exchange as Auntie Lu's grip turned into a light squeeze and she smiled and nodded. "Goodbye, Ming Na friend."

Elise knew Ming Na was Courtney's middle name, so she smiled back and pushed out of the suddenly oppressive darkness of the restaurant into the sunshine.

The pedestrian traffic on the sidewalk had doubled since lunch. Elbows and shoulders bumped as people jostled for position on the sidewalk facing the parade route.

Elise threaded through the crowd, looking for a gap

she could squeeze through to get a clear view of the festivities. She darted across the street and then backtracked toward Han Ting.

Spying daylight, she scooted through two people and popped up behind a boy and a girl wiggling with excitement.

The acrobats led the parade, clutching sticks with colorful streamers on the end that created a kaleidoscope of hues as they leaped and tumbled. A float decorated with flowers sailed past, cradling the royal court of Dragon Boat princesses and their queen, all doing the parade wave and smiling.

A few firecrackers popped and the kids in front of her squealed as Elise jumped, clutching her purse.

A Boy Scout troop marched by and the fresh, innocent faces of the kids calmed her nerves.

Nerves? When had she started feeling anxious? The press of people didn't bother her; even after coming from the wide-open spaces of Montana, Elise had reveled in the crowds and excitement of the city.

It must have been the noise from the firecrackers that had set her teeth on edge. Or the warning from Auntie Lu.

Ridiculous. She already knew to be careful after her encounter with a killer. Auntie Lu wasn't telling her something she didn't already have imprinted on her brain, and Auntie Lu probably issued that warning to all young women.

Standing on her tiptoes, Elise clapped loudly and whistled as the winner of the boat race passed by displaying his victorious boat. The kids in front of her covered their ears. She got the attention of her kindergartners by whistling—worked every time.

With each passing parade participant, the people behind her pressed in closer and closer. She leaned back, not wanting to push the children into the street. By now she could barely move, barely turn her head.

The dragon float made its appearance, its head shaggy with crepe paper tilting back and forth to the delight of the crowd, which surged forward. Elise hooked her arms around the kids' shoulders to protect them.

The dragon undulated forward, its body twisting this way and that way. Another round of firecrackers exploded so close Elise could smell the acrid gunpowder.

A sharp pain stabbed her thigh and she lurched forward, knocking the kids off the curb.

"I'm so sorry."

They giggled as she tried to pull them back onto the sidewalk. Elise couldn't even drop her arms to her sides to feel her leg. Someone must've had something sharp in a purse or pocket, or maybe a little kid had jabbed her with some trinket from the knickknack shops that lined the streets.

The last flick of the dragon's tail signaled the end of the parade, and people began to shuffle away, giving everyone a little more breathing room.

"Are you guys okay?" Elise finally had room to bend forward and check on the kids.

They nodded and scampered away.

Elise trailed her hand down the back of her thigh toward the sore spot. The material of her jeans gaped open, and she drew her brows over her nose.

What the heck had gouged her?

Her fingers probed the ripped denim and her skin beneath, and she gasped as they met moisture. She snatched her hand away and brought it in front of her face.

Her stomach lurched and a scream ripped from her throat. The people milling around her backed away, creating a ring of space around her.

She dragged her gaze away from her hand and tried to

focus on the faces swimming before her. Only one face stood out—Auntie Lu's as she hovered in the doorway of her restaurant, her dark eyes sharp amid the lines of age.

Elise swallowed and gasped to no one and everyone. "I've been stabbed."

Chapter Seven

The woman had been stabbed, her throat slit.

Sean massaged his temples. So much blood. Had that been the fate this maniac had intended for Elise?

He pounded his fist on his desk, and the pencils in the holder jumped and rattled. He slid one between his fingers and rat-tatted it on the blotter.

Elise hadn't called him yet with her phone number. He checked his watch. She and her friend had a lot to talk about over lunch, and the Dragon Boat Parade was probably still going on.

He ran his finger over the receiver of his desk phone. He could call Central Station to see if her car was still parked in the lot.

As if by magic, the phone rang beneath his hand, and he wrapped his fingers around the receiver. "Brody, homicide."

"Detective Brody, this is Officer Yin with Central. We have a situation here with one of your witnesses, Elise Duran. She requested that we call you."

"A situation?" Sean's pulse picked up speed.

"Someone stabbed her on the parade route."

The pencil in Sean's other hand snapped. "Is she all right?"

She had to be. She'd asked for him.

"The wound just broke the skin. She's okay, but understandably upset. We've got an ambulance on the scene, but she doesn't want to go the hospital and insisted we call you first."

"Does she need to go the hospital?" Sean had already grabbed his jacket from the back of his chair and swept his keys into his pocket.

Elise needed him.

"My guess is she's going to need stitches."

"Get her in that ambulance and tell her I'll meet her at the hospital. And I'm gonna want your report."

"You got it."

For the second time in as many days, Sean raced to the hospital to see Elise—only this time it was much more personal.

When he got to the emergency room, he found her sitting on an examination table, her legs swinging and hospital paper wrapped around her waist.

She jerked her head up at his approach. "Can you believe this? He got to me. I swear I wasn't followed."

In two steps he was at her side. "Tell me what happened."

"I was standing in a big crowd of people watching the parade. When the dragon float passed by, everyone surged forward. I could barely breathe. I was just trying to keep my balance when I felt a sharp pain in my thigh."

She rolled onto the side of her hip and pointed to a bandage on the back of her leg.

Sean flinched at the spot of blood forming in the center of the white gauze bandage. It was not as if he hadn't seen his share of blood. Hadn't he just left a bloodbath on the shore of the bay? Seeing Elise injured made his blood boil. She'd endured enough already.

How had he gotten to her?

She continued. "When the crowd cleared, I reached

down to feel the sore spot and found sliced jeans and blood instead."

"Did anyone see anything? Notice anybody?"

"Not that I know of." She twisted her lips. "I screamed bloody murder, and I think that scared everyone away. The cops asked around, but nobody noticed anything."

"Cameras in the area?" He knew that some cameras were stationed in Chinatown, but closer to the banks on the edge of the area.

She shrugged and her eyes widened. "How'd he find me, Sean? I'm sure nobody followed me. I kept my eyes glued to that rearview mirror."

"Maybe this was just a random attack. Were there any other reports of violence along the parade route?"

"You don't believe that. I can tell by your voice you don't believe it. You don't have to try to make me feel better."

Oh, but he did. He wanted to run his hands across the smooth skin of her face and brush away all the pain and fear.

"Just trying to look at all possibilities."

A doctor poked her head into the room. "Are you Elise's husband?"

"I'm Detective Brody, SFPD Homicide."

The doctor's brows shot up. "Homicide?"

"We think this attack is related to a murder. Is Elise going to be okay?"

"She'll be fine. We cleaned the wound and I'm going to put in a few stitches. You can wait in the hallway or the waiting room."

"I want him to stay...if he wants to."

"I'm not going anywhere." He shouldn't have made a promise he couldn't keep. He couldn't be Elise's round-the-clock bodyguard and protector—but the wobbly smile she'd just aimed at him made him want to try.

The doctor snapped on a pair of gloves, and the nurse wheeled a cart of instruments next to the cot.

"Lie down on your stomach and we'll get this stitched right up."

The paper on the table crinkled as Elise scooted back and rolled to her stomach.

Sean sat in a plastic chair in the corner while the doctor and nurse went to work. The killer must've followed Elise from the bridge parking lot and she hadn't noticed. That meant he'd been lurking around waiting for her. Someone that bold would make a mistake sooner or later.

And if this guy wanted to continue playing games with him, he'd have the pleasure of bringing him down.

"Try not to get it wet." The doctor was peeling off her gloves. "And you should be fine."

Fifteen minutes later, Sean was escorting Elise out of the hospital. "I'm assuming your car's still parked in Chinatown."

"It's still at the station." She turned and wedged her back against his car. "Why did he do it? Why did he come after me again if he wasn't planning to kill me?"

"I think it's obvious."

"Why didn't he take the opportunity to kill me?"

"In the middle of Chinatown? That would've been a little more noticeable. He sliced your leg in the crowd, knowing you might not register the pain right away or wouldn't immediately identify what had happened. Then he made his getaway."

"But why did he bother? Why take that chance if he wasn't going to finish the job he'd started last night?"

"He's toying with you, Elise. He's sending you the message that he can get to you."

She shrugged off the car and yanked the door open before he could reach for it. "Let him try."

Sean chewed the inside of his cheek as he went around

to the driver's side of his car. He understood Elise's anger, but a healthy dose of fear wasn't necessarily a bad thing.

He started the car. "I didn't ask, but I take it your friend wasn't with you at the time of the attack?"

"She had an emergency with a client—she's a therapist."

"I hope you asked if you could stay at her place."

Elise reached into the side pocket of her purse and dangled a key ring from her finger. "I'm all set, but I have to go back to my place to pack a bag and get my stuff for school."

"Does your friend live closer to you or closer to Chinatown?"

"Closer to Chinatown. Why?"

"How about if I drive you to your place first and then take you to your car at the station?"

"Are you a cop or a chauffeur?"

"Sometimes I ask myself the same question."

She tapped his arm. "No, really, I don't want to put you out."

"No problem." Problem? Sean was reluctant to let her out of his sight. If she thought she'd been looking out for a tail when she'd left the bridge and this guy managed to follow her anyway, he must be good.

Elise's temporary digs had better be secure, or he didn't think he'd be able to leave her. She'd gotten under his skin, not that he hadn't felt protective about witnesses before. That was in his DNA. It was in the Brody DNA.

Something about Elise pushed all his buttons. Her prettiness had a different quality from the rest of the drop-dead-gorgeous women in the city. Her fresh face and quick smile had an irresistible openness—irresistible to him, anyway.

He had to admit that his attraction to her stemmed, in part, to her ignorance about him, about his family. About the dark cloud that hung over his head. Couldn't she see it following him around?

When they got to her house, he stepped in front of her at the door. "Let me check it out first."

He did a quick sweep of the small house, including the bathroom, where the note on the mirror still mocked him. "All clear."

"I figured that."

Crossing his arms, he blocked her entrance into the living room. "Don't let down your guard, Elise. He's out there. He's watching you. He's already proved that."

"You're right." She swept past him. "I just don't like the idea of this guy controlling my life. I don't want anyone controlling my life."

"I get it, but you still need to be careful."

"I know." She banged a few cupboard doors in the kitchen and emerged holding a bowl and a carton of milk. "I'd better leave something for Straycat."

She tucked the milk in the crook of her arm as she slid open the door to the patio. The dish clinked as she set it down on the porch. "Straycat!"

"Does he actually come to that name?"

"No, he's very independent."

"I guess he doesn't want anyone controlling his life, either."

She jerked her head up and studied his face. Then she opened her mouth, snapped it shut and stepped into the room. "I'm going to throw some things in a bag. Would you like something to drink or eat? A banana?"

"Banana?"

"I just bought a bunch and I don't want them to go to waste if I have to leave them for several days."

"I'll take one." He walked into the kitchen and snapped a banana from the bunch. Peeling it, he strolled to Elise's room, where she was pulling clothes from a hanger and stuffing them into a suitcase, and he leaned against the doorjamb.

"How's your leg feeling?"

Without looking up from her task, she replied, "Fine."

"Do you need me to do anything? Check your locks? Leave a lamp on?"

She stood back from the overflowing suitcase, hands on her hips. "You like to help, don't you?"

Heat crawled up his neck and he took a big bite of the banana. Chewing allowed him to avoid the question. He swallowed and shrugged. "I'm a cop. That's what we do."

"Ah, but which came first?" She plunged her hands into the suitcase to flatten the clothes. "Did your desire to help people encourage you to become a cop, or once you became a cop did you just naturally develop that trait?"

He swung the banana peel back and forth. "You know, I never analyzed it. The career runs in the family."

"Really?"

"My brothers are all in law enforcement."

"How many brothers do you have?"

"Three."

"That's a coincidence. I have three brothers, too."

Great. He needed to change this subject. If he spent much more time in Elise's presence, he'd be revealing all his secrets. Secrets better kept to himself.

He backed out of the room, waving the banana peel. "I'm going to toss this."

When he returned to the bedroom, he took up his position at the door. "So, what do your brothers do?"

"Make my life miserable." She leaned on the suitcase with one hand and used the other to yank at the zipper.

Sean took two steps into the room, hunched over and held the suitcase down while she zipped it. "Mine can do that, too."

Still bent over the suitcase, she turned suddenly and her golden hair brushed his arm. "Nice to see a human side to you, Detective."

He didn't move an inch. The ends of her ponytail tickled his arm. The pulse in her throat beat out waves of her floral perfume. Her bright blue eyes sparkled with curiosity and humor.

Time seemed to freeze for a few seconds, and in those few seconds he had an overwhelming urge to take possession of her plump lips. To lose himself in the rush of senses that her presence stirred in him. To find out what it felt like to taste sunshine.

The over-the-top thoughts running through his mind must've shown on his face.

Her eyes widened and her lips parted as she lodged the tip of her tongue in the corner of her mouth.

He didn't need a body language expert to tell him what her response meant. Hell, he *was* a body language expert. If he kissed her now, he'd meet no resistance.

He smacked his palms on the lid of the suitcase and straightened to his full height, feeling as if he were emerging from a spell. "School stuff?"

"What?" Elise blinked her eyes.

"I can take your suitcase out to the car while you get your school materials."

"Oh, yeah. I keep them all together in a bag." She swiveled her head from side to side as if lost in her own house.

Sean hoisted the suitcase from the bed, pulled out the handle and stated the obvious. "I'll take this."

She nodded and scooted past him into the living room to retrieve her school bag.

Sean loaded the suitcase in the car and returned to the house.

Elise dropped her school bag at his feet. "I forgot my shampoo and stuff. I'll dump it in another bag."

She darted for the hallway, and Sean followed. As she plucked items from her medicine chest and a shower caddy,

Sean pointed to the mirror. "Do you want me to clean that up? We got all the evidence we're going to get from it."

"Go ahead. It's your message." She hitched the bag over her shoulder and tilted her head. "Did you ever figure out what it meant?"

"He hasn't contacted me again. Probably just a jab at law enforcement."

He'd figured the guy probably knew his history and was taunting him. Wouldn't be the first time.

"There's a roll of paper towels on the counter and window cleaner under the sink in the kitchen."

The lipstick smeared the mirror as he swept damp paper towels across it. A few more swipes and the words disappeared. If only he could erase them from his mind as easily.

Elise hovered at the bathroom door. "Ready? I have everything."

"Let's go." He crumpled the used paper towels in his hand and dropped them into the kitchen trash and replaced the glass cleaner under the sink.

He loaded her remaining bags in the trunk of his car and took off for what he hoped would be her safe house for a while.

They wended their way through the city streets as the late-afternoon sun streamed through the buildings and glinted off the water that made an occasional appearance when they crested a hill.

Sean pulled into the lot at the Central Station in Chinatown, where Elise's hybrid huddled between two patrol cars. If the killer had followed her here, where had he parked? Spaces were at a premium and he wouldn't have wanted to risk a parking ticket, which could be traced.

Maybe he'd watched from his car as she went into the restaurant and then figured he'd have time to park in a public lot near Union Square and pick up her trail on foot when she'd finished lunch. However he'd done it, the guy was no amateur.

Had he killed before somewhere else and then taken his sick proclivities on the road to terrorize a new city?

He pulled behind Elise's car, leaving the engine running.

She opened the door and placed one foot on the ground. "Aren't you going to transfer my bags from your car to mine?"

"I told you. I'm following you over. I'll bring your bags in for you when we get there."

She rattled off her friend's address. "In case I lose you on the way."

He whistled. "Nice neighborhood."

"Family money. Their parents owned a lot of properties here, including that house where I live."

"Good. That's a safe part of town."

He followed Elise's car. She drove so slowly, there's no way she could lose him—and probably no way she could've avoided being tailed by her stalker, no matter what she believed.

She pulled in front of a modern building, supported by gleaming white pillars. She pointed out her car window at a driveway that sloped down toward a wrought-iron gate.

Sean made a U-turn and parked in front of the condo complex while Elise rolled into the parking garage. He popped the trunk and gathered Elise's two bags over one shoulder and settled her suitcase on its wheels.

"I can take one of those." Elise had appeared on a walkway next to the driveway.

"I got 'em. Lead the way." He followed her up the marble tile steps, and she used her friend's key to open the front door. "Is your friend going to be home?"

"I have no idea."

They went to the second floor and Elise stopped at one

of just three doors on the hallway. She knocked first, listened and then unlocked the door.

The decor of the condo almost blinded him—modern, tasteful and white. He preferred Elise's jumble of colorful styles.

She called out, "Courtney?"

There was an upstairs as well, and Elise stood at the foot of the staircase, her hand resting on the chrome banister.

"I guess she's not home yet."

Sean parked her suitcase in a corner and piled her other two bags on top of it. "I'll stick around until she gets here."

Elise spun around and plopped down on the second step of the staircase. "Did you find out anything about the woman on my phone?"

"Her name's Katie Duncan, twenty-five years old."

"Duncan? That's weird."

"Do you know the name?"

"Duncan, Duran—maybe he's going through the phone book." She snapped her fingers. "What was the name of the other woman? The one found at the Presidio?"

"Carlson."

Her eyes popped. "C, D."

"Are you in the phone book?" Sean's hand tightened on the banister. Of course, he'd noticed the similarity between Elise's and Katie's names, but who used phone books anymore?

"No, I'm not. I suppose it's just a coincidence, but maybe he's looking at some alphabetical list of something."

Pain needled the back of his neck and he clasped it, rolling his head.

"Are you okay?"

"Headache." He dropped to the bottom step and leaned against the wall. "Katie wasn't a teacher, so it's not some alphabetical list of teachers."

"What *did* she do?"

"She was a legal secretary."

"Had she ever been to the Speakeasy, like me?"

"We're looking into it." He leveled a finger at her. "You're becoming a good detective."

"I have a vested interest in seeing Katie's, and maybe the Carlson woman's, killer nailed. I don't want to live in fear. He may not know where I'm staying now, but he knows my name. Who knows what kind of info he can get on me?"

A key scraped in the lock and the front door swung open. Sean jumped to his feet as a young Asian woman stumbled into the entryway loaded down with shopping bags.

She stopped when she saw them and dropped half the bags. "You scared the spit out of me!"

"Sorry." Elise squeezed past him on the stairs and hugged her friend, bags and all. "Courtney, this is Detective Sean Brody. Sean, this is Courtney Chu."

Courtney dropped the rest of her bags and stuck out her hand. "Nice to meet you."

She arched an eyebrow at Elise. "Is he moving in, too?"

"N-no. He, well, he followed me here. There was an incident at the Dragon Boat Parade."

"What?" Courtney gripped Elise's shoulders.

"I was attacked."

Courtney let out a yelp and then herded Elise to her spotless living room and sat her down.

Elise told her the story while Courtney alternately gasped, cursed and covered her mouth with her hand.

"Elise, this is crazy." She turned on Sean, her black hair whipping across her face. "What are you doing to catch this guy?"

"Everything we can." He pulled the sketch Elise had helped create out of his pocket and smoothed out the creases. “Here he is. You didn’t notice him in the club that night, did you? You didn’t notice anyone watching Elise?”

“Look at her.” She jerked her thumb at Elise. “She’s gorgeous. Of course I noticed guys watching her, but not this nut job.”

Sean’s phone buzzed in his pocket and he pulled it out, glancing at the display. “It’s the station. I’m going to take this and then I’ll get out of your way.”

He rose from the chair and wandered into the kitchen as Elise and her friend continued their excited chatter.

“Brody.”

“Brody, it’s Curtis. You’d better get down here.”

Sean’s heart pounded and the blood thudded in his ears. “What’s up?”

“That dead girl we found today? Katie Duncan?”

“Yeah?” With his mouth suddenly gone dry, Sean could barely form the word.

“Her killer sent you a message.”

“What’d it say?” Sean clenched his jaw where a muscle twitched erratically.

“It’s not so much what he said, dude, as what he sent.”

Sean spat out an expletive. “Just tell me.”

“He sent you a finger, Brody. Katie Duncan’s severed finger.”

Chapter Eight

Only half listening to Courtney's exclamations, Elise directed her gaze at Sean clutching his cell phone to his ear. With his back turned toward her, she couldn't see his face but his shoulders had a rigid set and his white knuckles made it look as if he could crush that phone with one hand.

Courtney snapped her fingers. "Earth to Elise."

"Sorry. What were you saying?"

"Never mind." Courtney turned her head to look at Sean. "Not as important as *some* things."

Sean ended the call and took a few steps into the room, his face stern and white. "Duty calls. I gotta go back to the station. Take care of that leg, and don't forget to pick up a phone and give me the number."

"My leg's fine, and I'll get that phone." Elise pushed up from the sofa. "Hold on, I'll see you out."

Courtney waved. "Bye, nice to meet you. Maybe we'll see each other again."

Elise stepped into the hallway with him and pulled the door shut. "Is everything okay?"

He relaxed his jaw enough to speak. "Everything's fine, except we have a diabolical killer loose in the city."

"What was the call about?"

"Murder and mayhem—just an ordinary day on the job. That's my life, Elise, and you don't need to hear about it."

Did he think she couldn't handle reality? She grabbed his arm and his biceps felt like granite. "You can tell me. You don't have to push me away."

He cupped her face in one large hand and stroked his thumb across her cheek. "Yes, I do."

His touch belied his words, and his proximity had her breath coming in short spurts. "But I don't want you to."

The harsh kiss he pressed against her mouth came so suddenly, it took her breath way. Just as quickly it ended and he turned on his heel and disappeared into the stairwell.

Elise put two fingers to her bruised lips and backed into Courtney's condo.

"Sean Brody is one hot detective." Courtney's words sang out amid the banging of cupboard doors and pots and pans.

Closing her eyes, Elise took a deep breath and then turned and joined her friend in the kitchen. "Good-looking guy, but still a cop."

Courtney dropped a package of pasta on the countertop. "Are cops off-limits for some reason?"

"Oh, you know." Elise waved her hand in the air. "Control issues."

"Small price to pay, girl. And I'd say you're the one with control issues. He's obviously interested."

"Why do you say that?" Courtney involuntarily brushed the tips of her fingers against her chin where Sean's stubble had scratched her.

"I'm a therapist, remember? I'm trained to read people, even people as zipped up as Detective Brody."

"Do you think he's zipped up?"

Courtney bit her lip as she filled a pot with water. "He holds himself very still, holds his emotions in check. But, come on. What cop goes out of his way to escort a witness around? Even a cute little girl-next-door like you?"

"I think he's just doing his job and he's thorough." Elise tugged on the ends of Courtney's hair. "How was your client this afternoon?"

"I had to talk her down from a ledge, but she was okay."

"Not literally?"

"An emotional ledge." Courtney presented a bottle of wine to Elise, label out. "I think you need a little vino tonight."

"I think you're right." She took the bottle from Courtney and held out her hand. "Corkscrew."

Elise poured two glasses of wine and sidled next to Courtney at the sink. "Let me make the salad since you're sacrificing your Saturday night to stay in with me, and don't even deny it. Did Derrick ever call?"

"He texted me. We'll probably get together sometime this week. He's out of town this weekend." She stirred the pasta into the bubbling water as steam rose to the ceiling.

They worked side by side in the kitchen for several minutes, and Elise soaked in the normalcy. She had a hard time grasping the events of the past twenty-four hours. She'd been abducted, had escaped and had been attacked again—and she'd met Sean Brody. This time yesterday, she'd been getting ready to go out with Courtney.

As her friend dumped the pasta into a colander in the sink, Elise carried the salad to the table. "Do you mind if I turn on the local evening news?"

"Really? I don't mind but it's the last thing I thought you'd want to watch." Courtney wiped her hands on a dish towel and retrieved the remote from the coffee table in the living room.

They settled at the kitchen table, and the smell of the garlic mingled with the hint of fennel in the sausage to make Elise's mouth water. She took a sip of red wine, lolling it on her tongue before she swallowed.

Then she clicked on the TV and muted the sound. She

kept her eye on the commercials as she stabbed a couple of rigatoni with her fork. "Yummy. You'll have to give me..."

A wind-blown reporter was speaking into a mic, a shot of the Golden Gate Bridge behind him. Elise pointed the remote at the TV and stabbed at the volume button.

"...found this morning by a couple of fishermen." The reporter backed up to the yellow crime tape flapping in the breeze. "Detective? Detective? Ray Lopez, KFGG News. Can you tell us anything about the victim? Does this murder have anything to do with the transient murders in the Tenderloin or that woman found near the Presidio?"

Sean's profile looked carved from stone. He barely moved his lips when he said, "No comment at this time."

"What about the attack on the woman last night? Is this related, Detective?"

"No comment." Sean turned his back on the reporter and bent his head to talk with one of the cops on the scene.

"There you have it, Jan. The police are keeping tight-lipped about this one, but the women of this city want to know. Is it safe to go out at night?"

The anchor and the reporter prattled on for several more seconds before Elise muted the TV again. "I guess my story's already out there."

"Sounds like it." Courtney raised her glass and swirled the contents. "But if those vultures ever get your name, make sure you follow Brody's example. No comment. They'll tear you apart."

"The last thing I need is publicity."

Courtney ran her fingertip along the rim of her glass. "Detective Brody sounds familiar to me. Did he write a book or something? Or maybe he was involved in a big case."

"If so, it was before my time here."

"Brody, Brody." Courtney's brow furrowed. "He must've been in the news."

"Probably. More wine?"

"Sure. It's Saturday night. Why not live it up?"

"You don't have to babysit. My leg feels fine, and I'll probably just go to bed early."

Courtney tossed back the last of her wine and held out her glass to Elise. "No problem. I'm tired from last night anyway. Besides, what did that reporter say? Is it even safe to go out at night?"

Elise took the glass by the stem and padded back to the kitchen, running her tongue along her lower lip. Apparently, it wasn't even safe for her to go out in broad daylight. At least not without the protection of Detective Sean Brody.

And how long could that last?

SEAN STARED AT the severed finger with the blue nail polish nestled in cotton. The package in which it had been delivered had come addressed to SFPD—Homicide. But when the front desk opened the box, they'd found the gruesome souvenir with a note pasted in the lid of the box: *This finger is pointing at you, Brody.*

"What does it mean, Brody?" Captain Williams's dark eyes drilled him. "This along with the note at the escaped victim's house make it clear that this is the same guy—and for some reason he's got it in for you."

"I'm supposed to know why?" Sean closed the lid on the finger and pushed it across the captain's desk. "Has the lab tested the finger yet?"

"Not yet, but who else's could it be?" Captain Williams steepled his own fingers and peered at Sean over the pinnacle. "I don't like this communication business, Brody."

Sean pinched the bridge of his nose. "That makes two of us."

"We took a risk bringing you into homicide, a risk I never regretted for one minute based on your performance."

"Until now?" Sean's fingers curled around the arms of the chair.

"Do you really think this killer would be sending you messages and uh…other gifts if not for your father?"

"Serial killers send messages to homicide detectives. It happens all the time."

Williams snorted. "Happens all the time in movies and TV. You and I both know it's not so common in real life."

"What do you want from me, Captain? I'm not going to hide under a rock. I have a murder and an attempted murder to solve, and if this guy wants to give me clues, so be it. I'll take whatever I can get."

"All right. I just hope some hotshot reporter doesn't start snooping around and dredging up old news. The department doesn't need it."

"Neither do I, sir."

"Now, do your job and—" he waved one hand over the box on his desk "—take this thing with you."

Sean picked up the box and walked out of the captain's office, his back stiff and his chin held high. If just one person mentioned his father, he'd deck 'em.

He strode down the hallway, holding the box in front of him, daring anyone to make a comment. Nobody even seemed to notice what he was holding.

Blowing out a breath, he poked his head into the lab. "I think you guys are waiting for a finger."

Tom Kwan, one of their forensic guys, smirked. "I could go all out with the black humor of that comment, but you already look like you're in a black humor so I'll keep my mouth shut."

"Good idea, Kwan." Sean placed the box on one of the chrome tables. He could exchange gallows humor with the best of them. It blew off steam, made the unbearable bearable. But with Elise out there in danger, it didn't seem right.

"When are we getting the finger, and I don't mean from

the captain." Jacoby had burst through another door and stopped short when he saw Sean. "I guess you heard."

"Heard," Sean flicked the box, "and saw. We've got one twisted individual on our hands. I thought he'd kept the finger as a trophy."

"I'm gonna take the print, but we all know it belongs to Katie. Same blue polish, same missing digit. Elise Duran was one lucky lady."

Kwan tapped his chin. "I wonder if he took the finger before or after he killed her. That's gotta hurt."

"I'll leave you to figure that out. I'm outta here." Sean backed out of the lab with a queasy stomach. Kwan's morbid fascinations had never bothered him before. Before Elise.

That's why you never make it personal, son.

His father's voice rumbled up from Sean's subconscious. Where had that come from? Was it something his father actually said to him?

Jacoby's head popped out of the lab door. "Brody, I meant to tell you, I didn't get any prints from Elise's house other than Elise's."

"Yeah, I guess that's what we figured anyway."

"Her house was clean. Doesn't look like she has anyone over—ever."

Sean raised an eyebrow. "And your point?"

Jacoby shrugged his pumped-up shoulders. "Just thought I'd let you know. In case you want to make a move."

"Why, do you?"

"You're the hotshot detective." Jacoby dove back into the lab to dodge the barb Sean was getting ready to fling at him.

Sean dropped into his chair and shuffled through a few messages at his desk. Nothing from Elise. That didn't mean he couldn't check on her. He should've never kissed her, but it didn't mean he couldn't call her. Did it?

He dug into the pocket of his jacket and pulled out Courtney Chu's business card. She'd scribbled her home phone number on the back.

He ran his thumb along the edge of the card once, twice and then punched in the number. With each successive ring, the knots got tighter in his gut. When he got Courtney's voice mail, the words rasped from his dry throat.

"This is Detective Brody. I'm calling..."

"Hello, Sean? It's Elise."

Her breathy voice capped his growing dread, and he slumped in his chair. "For a minute there, I thought you two had gone out."

"My leg's feeling okay but not that good, and Courtney stayed in with me and cooked dinner."

"Your leg's bothering you? Do you need to go back to the hospital?"

"It's throbbing a bit, but I can handle it with a little ibuprofen."

"Take a lot if you need it."

"Any new developments in the case?"

"Some things I can't share."

"Not even with someone who's intimately involved... with the case?"

Sean hunched over his desk and cupped his hand around the receiver. "I'm sorry about...about what happened in the hallway."

"No apology necessary, but an explanation would be nice."

"An explanation?" Maybe he'd have to rethink his appreciation of her forthrightness. "Don't people do that in Montana?"

"Kiss? Yep, lots of that going on in Montana."

"That's a start. I'm glad you recognized the gesture."

"Don't be obtuse, Sean. You kissed me right after you told me to stay out of your life. And I'm not saying people in Montana don't send conflicting messages with their kisses, because they do. I'm saying I don't."

"Can't I just excuse myself by admitting I'm a caveman? I acted on impulse without thinking."

"But you're not the impulsive type, are you?"

"I can be." Especially looking into a pair of big blue eyes.

"If you're so impulsive, tell me what upset you so much tonight."

He cleared his throat. "It was another message from the killer. That's the game he's playing, but I'm glad he's playing it with me now instead of you."

"Whether we like it or not, I'm involved in this and I appreciate your openness."

After Sean hung up the phone, he stared at it until his eyes ached and grew bleary. He hadn't been open with Elise at all, and he had no intention of inviting her into his misery.

THE FOLLOWING MORNING, a dull pain in Elise's leg woke her up and the fear she kept tamping down in her semiconscious state welled to the surface. Closing her eyes, she massaged her thigh around the stitches and took a couple of deep breaths.

Last night she'd sensed Sean holding back, but she couldn't force him to confide in her. She could get through this with or without Sean Brody. With would be better, a lot better.

She stretched her legs and swung them over the side of the bed. Then she shuffled across the hardwood floor and poked her head out the door of Courtney's spare bedroom. Nothing but silence greeted her.

Determined to earn her keep, she shoved her feet into a pair of flip-flops and made her way down to the kitchen.

She blended some plain yogurt with a few berries, sprinkled some granola on top and added a sliced banana.

She found a couple of stale bagels, dropped them into the toaster oven and began pouring water into the coffeemaker.

"Stop right there." A sleepy-eyed Courtney lounged against the entryway to the kitchen, yawning. "The breakfast looks great, but I'll handle the coffee. You don't even drink the stuff."

Elise backed away from the coffeemaker. "It's all yours. I don't want to mess with your morning elixir."

Courtney brushed past her and grabbed a bag of coffee beans. "You did realize you'd have to grind the beans first, didn't you?"

"Of course." Elise dipped a spoon into the yogurt. "How old are the bagels? I figured we could toast away the staleness."

"They're not that old. I have some cream cheese, too." She pointed to the fridge. "How's your leg feeling?"

"Sore. I took some ibuprofen."

"Are you going to stay home from school tomorrow?"

"No way. We have all kinds of activities planned for the last few days of school. It's the best part of the school year."

Courtney pursed her lips as she flipped the switch for the coffee grinder.

When the grating noise stopped, Elise crossed her arms and said, "What? Why are you looking like a disapproving schoolmarm?"

"Maybe you should just take personal leave for the rest of the school year and get out of Dodge."

"You mean turn and run away with my tail between my legs?"

"You're allowed to be a coward. Nobody expects you to hunt this guy down."

Elise curled her fingers into her upper arms. "He had

his second chance to kill me and he sliced my leg instead. He knows I already gave his description to the police, and he's not worried about it because he was wearing a disguise. There's nothing I can do to him now."

"He doesn't know what you told the police. For all he knows, you could remember more details. You're a threat to him, Elise. And that makes him dangerous."

The ringing phone made them both jump. "Who's calling this time of the morning?"

"It's ten o'clock."

Courtney made a face and answered the phone. "Good morning. Yes, she's right here."

She pressed the receiver against her thigh and whispered. "It's the hunky cop."

"Give it over." Elise rolled her eyes and snapped her fingers for the phone. "Hello?"

"Hi, Elise. It's Sean Brody. How are you doing this morning?"

So much better right at this minute.

"I'm good. Leg's a little sore, but that's stitches for you. Any more news since last night?" She hadn't expected to hear his voice last thing before she went to bed and then first thing this morning. Not that she was complaining.

"Nothing new, although the woman at the Presidio may have been a victim of domestic violence. Seems her boyfriend has disappeared." He coughed. "I'm in front of the building on the street. I was just driving by."

"Do you want to come up?"

"I can't leave the car."

"I'll be right down. Give me a minute."

She ended the call and dashed upstairs with Courtney's questions trailing after her. She pulled on her jeans from yesterday and zipped a sweatshirt over her pajama top.

Breathless, she stopped at the front door. "Sean's downstairs. I'm just going to say hello."

"Is this what they call community policing?" Courtney winked.

With her step lighter than it should be, Elise skipped downstairs and squinted as she hit the sidewalk.

Sean waved out the open window of his Crown Vic, and Elise approached the car on the passenger side.

The passenger window slid down, and she hunched over and thrust her head inside the car, resting her arms on the window frame. She inhaled the masculine scent of the car—new leather and fresh soap.

"Thanks for stopping by."

"I was—" he waved his hand vaguely out the window "—in the area. Are you going to get that phone today?"

"I might as well get a permanent phone instead of a pay-as-you-go. I'm not sure I can ever use that other phone again."

"I don't blame you." He opened his car door. "I need to stretch my legs."

He joined her on the sidewalk and wedged his hip against the car. "One of the detectives stopped by the club yesterday and gave them a sketch. Nobody remembers the guy. We're also reviewing some video from some cameras at the bridge and Chinatown. He's going to trip up, Elise."

She scuffed her toe against the cement. "I agree that he's going to screw up, and I appreciate that you're taking the time to keep me informed. Really."

"I know what's it like to be left out of the loop, and while I can't let you in on everything, I don't want to keep you completely in the dark."

His eyes seemed to be looking beyond her face and he'd escaped to that place where she couldn't reach him.

Out of the corner of her eye, she noticed someone moving quickly toward her on the sidewalk. Sean noticed him at the same time. He snapped to attention and his head jerked up as he pushed off the car.

Elise's mouth dropped open and she stumbled back. This was not happening.

Sean caught her as she tripped, and then spun around in a crouch, his fists raised.

She screamed. "Wait! I know him."

"No kidding. I'm Elise's fiancé."

Chapter Nine

Sean lowered his hands, but his fists remained clenched at his sides. He shot a sideways glance at Elise, whose face sported three different shades of red. But she didn't look afraid. Angry, but not afraid.

"What are you doing here, Ty?"

"What do you think? I'm here to take you home."

"I am home." She twisted her head around to look at Courtney's building. "Sort of."

"You don't belong here. You're coming back with me."

Elise made a cross with her fingers and held them in front of her. "No, I'm not. And stop calling yourself my fiancé. That ended a long time ago."

That last line finally made Sean's shoulders relax. He knew Elise wasn't hiding anything.

Not like him.

"Who is this, Elise, and what's he doing here?"

The man threw back his shoulders and his cold blue eyes raked Sean from head to toe. "Who are you?"

"This is ridiculous. Ty, this is Detective Sean Brody. Sean, this is Ty Russell from back home, and I have no idea what he's doing here or how he found me."

Ty took a step back. "I found out what happened to you, and I'm here to bring you back."

Elise closed her eyes and pressed her fingers to her

temples. "How in the world did you find out and how did you find me here?"

"I have my sources."

Elise raked her hands through her loose hair. "Oh, please. Did you con Courtney somehow? Because we both know what a con artist you are."

The man physically flinched as if Elise had slapped him. Obviously, these two had history but it sure didn't sound as if they were engaged anymore—if they ever were.

"Someone attacked you and broke into your house. You're not safe here." He turned to Sean. "Detective, don't you agree?"

He did agree, but he didn't want Elise going back to Montana with this cowboy—her ex-fiancé. And what did he do to become Elise's ex? Must've been something really stupid.

"I'm…we're doing what we can to keep Elise safe. The choice is hers."

Ty narrowed his eyes as his gaze shifted between him and Elise.

Had his feelings for Elise seeped into his voice? What *were* his feelings for Elise?

"Thank you very much." She stamped her bare foot on the ground. "Go home, Ty—alone. I'm not going with you, now or ever."

Ty's face reddened and his face puffed up as if he was about to explode. Had he been abusive toward Elise?

"Step off." Sean inserted himself between Ty and Elise.

Ty sputtered. "Are you kidding me? Why don't you go get yourself a doughnut and leave me to talk some sense into my fiancée?"

"Thanks, but I don't eat doughnuts." Sean drew his shoulders back. "And Elise already told you she's not engaged to you, so giddyap on back to Wyoming."

Ty's mouth gaped open and he bunched his hands in front of him. "It's Montana."

"Whatever." He dropped his gaze to Ty's white-knuckled fists. "Or I can take you in for disturbing the peace."

Ty jabbed his finger in the air. "I'm not giving up on you, Elise. I'll be here for a few days if you change your mind, and if you don't I'll bring your brothers down here with me to this freak-show city to get you home."

"Buh-bye." Elise curled her fingers into a wave. "Try the sourdough bread bowl with clam chowder on your way out of the freak show."

Ty grunted and stalked off, calling over his shoulder, "I'm staying at some dump in Fisherman's Wharf."

"Good. You can get the bread bowl there." She tossed back her hair and sighed. "I can't believe Courtney called him. It had to be her. I thought she was on my side."

"Maybe she was just worried about you and thought it best that you take a break."

She jerked her thumb at Ty's retreating form. "With that?"

"So, what's the story, if you don't mind my asking?"

She dropped onto the low stone wall in front of Courtney's building. "We *were* engaged. We were high school sweethearts and all that stuff, blah, blah, blah."

"He obviously had the stamp of approval from your brothers since he's considering calling them in as reinforcements."

"Oh, yeah, my parents, too."

"And then you grew up? Changed?" He rested his foot on the wall next to her.

"I wish I could claim that, but I was a coward. All the forces in our world were pushing us together and the flow carried me along in its current even though I had misgivings."

"What finally happened to get you to swim against the tide?"

She pinned her hands between her knees and lifted her shoulders. "He cheated on me."

"What an idiot." What man in his right mind would risk losing this woman? "How'd you find out?"

"My maid of honor told me." She raised her eyes to his. "On my wedding day."

"Ouch."

"I didn't want to believe it, at first, but I guess deep down I knew."

"You called off the wedding."

A grin spread across her face. "Not at first."

"What does that mean? You married him and had it annulled?"

"My maid of honor told me while she was helping me dress for the wedding, while all the guests were arriving or sitting in their seats." She stuck her legs in front of her and tapped her toes together like a naughty schoolgirl. "I figured they got all dressed up for the occasion, I might as well give them a show."

"You called it off during the ceremony?" The corner of his mouth twitched into a smile.

"I did. It was a big story in town, even made the local newspaper—runaway bride."

He threw his head back and laughed. No wonder Ty was so desperate to get her back. He had some face to save.

"I walked down the aisle, smiling into the lying face that waited for me under the trellis, and when I got there I exposed him as a liar and a cheat." She pointed her toes. "Then I kicked off my white satin shoes and ran back up the aisle—alone."

"I've never met anyone who ran out on their wedding. That's impressive."

"It was just like a country music video."

"What did old Ty do after that?"

"Came after me, of course, but I wasn't having any of it. My bags were already packed for the honeymoon that never happened, so I threw them in my car and drove to San Francisco."

"And you've been here ever since?"

"I went home once to get the rest of my stuff."

"That's quite a story." He wiped his eyes. "Why this city?"

"The bridge."

His head shot up. "The Golden Gate Bridge?"

"Is there any other?" She linked her fingers and stretched her arms over her head. "My parents took my brothers and me here on a vacation one year. I was fascinated by that bridge, and when we walked across it and I looked back toward the city and out to Alcatraz, I decided then and there I'd come back."

"And here you are."

"The other night when I was out in the bay scrabbling for my life, I almost felt like the bridge was protecting me, looking over me." She glanced up, a blush flagging her cheeks. "Silly, huh?"

"No."

"Anyway—" she stood up and brushed off the seat of her jeans "—that's my sordid story."

"I knew it took guts to escape from a killer, but it really took guts to run out on your wedding."

Screwing up her face, she shook her head. "Not really. I was a wimp. I didn't want to marry Ty even before I found out he'd cheated. I let myself be railroaded by him, my family and what everyone expected of me."

Sean wedged a knuckle beneath her chin. "You're too hard on yourself."

"I just don't think it's all that admirable to run out on a wedding that should've never taken place to begin with."

The radio crackled from the car, and Sean dropped his hand and stuffed it in his pocket before he could do anything stupid again. "Keep safe and get that phone. I'm off tomorrow, but you have my personal cell. Give me a call when you get your new number."

"Yes, sir." She saluted. "I'll probably get it today if the phone store is open."

He waved and ducked into his car.

Sean kept an eye on Elise in his rearview mirror as she watched his car pull away. She looked small and defenseless against the dark force hanging over her head, but he knew better.

She had a lot of courage and pluck packed into that lithe frame, and she wasn't the kind of woman to back down from a challenge…or a killer.

THE NEXT MORNING, Elise drove across the Bay Bridge to her school in Oakland. If Ty could see the school where she taught her kindergarteners, he'd kidnap her to take her back to Montana.

She'd confronted Courtney and discovered it was her brother, Oscar, who had called Ty. Once he'd discovered where she lived, Ty had made it a point to contact Oscar, befriend him and enlist him as a spy.

She'd have to give Oscar a piece of her mind when he returned from his trip.

Turning onto the school's street, she swerved around a trash can that had tumbled from the sidewalk. She slowed down to glare at a couple of older boys hanging out on the street corner. Her kids had to dodge so much just to get to school.

She pulled into the parking lot, dragged her bag from the back and hitched it over her shoulder.

One of the second-grade teachers held the door open for her. "How was your weekend?"

"Not long enough." Elise slipped past the other teacher and headed down the hallway to her classroom. She had no intention of telling anyone at her school about her terrifying brush with a serial killer.

The students hadn't filtered in yet. They lined up outside until the bell rang, and the teachers in the lower grades always escorted their pupils into the school.

Elise unlocked the door to her classroom and bumped it open with her hip. She breathed in the smell of crayons, books and stale bread—all hallmarks of a kindergarten classroom.

"Ready for the last week of school?" Lydia Cummings, one of the other kindergarten teachers, poked her head in the room.

"I don't know." Elise's gaze scanned the colorful artwork tacked up on the walls and the fledgling lima bean plants growing in the windows, finally resting on the big, red number four she'd written on the whiteboard to indicate the number of days left in the school year. "I always miss them over the summer until I get the new batch in the fall."

"Spoken like a true kindergarten teacher." Lydia gave her a misty smile. "We're really lucky you came to us this year."

"I feel exactly the same way." Elise pulled a new book and a deflated beach ball out of her bag and dropped them on her desk before leaving to collect her students.

She tugged her sweater around her body and held it closed with folded arms as she walked onto the playground shrouded in a gray mist indistinguishable from the blacktop. Kids scurried between the white lines to get in place before the bell rang.

She approached the line for her classroom, which resembled a worm, wriggling this way and that.

Three of her students chanted in unison, "Good morning, Miss Duran."

"Good morning." She put on her brightest smile.

A small boy darted from the line and wrapped his arms around her legs in a kindergarten hug.

She patted his back. "Good morning, Eli."

This is what she'd miss over the summer, this pure, honest affection—no deceit, no subterfuge.

The bell blared over the playground, and the older kids shuffled off to their classes, bumping each other and snickering at private jokes. Elise clapped her hands. "Here we go."

The line of squiggling children wended its way through the double doors down the hallway to the kindergarten rooms.

The kids sensed their impending freedom in four days. Restlessness bubbled throughout the classroom, and Elise had to raise her voice and rap on her desktop more than once to get her students back on task.

Her gaze wandered to the big clock on the wall several times. The antsy kids were having an effect on her. Finally the bell rang for recess and lunch. Elise escorted her kids to the playground and then headed for the teachers' lounge to grab some lunch. The kinder teachers rotated lunchtime duty every day, two of them helping the aides and two enjoying the luxury of lunch in the staff room.

Elise popped the lid of a plastic container of Courtney's leftover pasta and shoved it into the microwave. She turned toward Viola, the other teacher on break. "Are you headed to Alabama right after school ends or later in the summer?"

"Leaving next week." Viola kicked off her shoes and propped her feet up on the chair across from her. "I'm enjoying the cool weather while I can, although I'm kind of looking forward to getting out of the city."

"Really?" The microwave beeped and Elise removed her container and carried it to the table next to Viola's.

"You were dreading the thought of heat and humidity and extended family just a few weeks ago."

Viola wiggled her toes and glanced up from her smartphone. "That's before we had a killer on the loose."

Elise's hand jerked and the steam burned her wrist. She dropped the lid. "Y-you mean that woman found by the bay?"

"She's not the only one."

"She's not?" Elise's throat tightened. Had there been another murder? Sean hadn't mentioned anything on the phone last night when she'd called him with her new number. Had they finally tied the woman at the Presidio to this killer?

Viola shook her head. "Not yet, but there was another one that got away."

"When was that?" Viola must be referring to her attack. The SFPD had been trying to keep Elise's encounter out of the press, just as they were trying to keep particular aspects of Katie's murder a secret, despite that reporter's best efforts. They had to do that. Sean had to keep certain secrets.

"Not sure. Friday night. No details on that one, but the police suspect it was the same guy who murdered the other one." Viola hunched her shoulders and dropped her phone. "I hate it when stuff like this happens."

"Me, too."

The phone on the lunchroom wall rang, and they both jumped. Elise shoved back from the table and grabbed the receiver. "Lunchroom."

"Elise, is that you?"

"Yep."

"I got a call in the front office for you. He's still on the line, so I'm going to transfer him over."

Elise swallowed. "Okay."

"Go ahead, sir."

"Did you change your phone number because of me?"

She heaved out a sigh and rolled her eyes at Viola. "No, Ty. I had to get a new phone and a new number. Why don't you just go home?"

"I've been doing a little investigating of that Detective Brody. You're not going to like…"

"What I don't like is you harassing me. For the millionth time, I'm not going home with you—now or ever. Give it up and move on. It's been over a year. Don't call me again." She slammed the receiver home.

"Girl, is that the ex-fiancé?"

"He came all the way here to take me home. What's he going to do, kidnap me?"

She shook her head. "Men. They don't want you unless they can't have you."

They finished lunch discussing more pleasant topics, such as the end-of-the-school-year party. Elise hadn't felt like telling Viola that Ty had come here to rescue her from a killer. That she was the one who got away. She didn't want to be the object of anyone's pity or amazement or projected fear.

The door to the teachers' lounge burst open and Mrs. McKinney, the senior kindergarten teacher, charged through clutching Eli's arm.

Eli turned his round eyes on Elise, his mouth a matching circle.

Elise jumped up. She didn't like Mrs. McKinney's disciplinary methods with the kids, and Eli looked scared out of his wits. "What's going on?"

"This young man was disobeying school rules on the playground."

"But he told me. He gave me…"

"Silence, young man."

Elise crossed the room and took Eli's hand, pulling him

away from Mrs. McKinney's clutches. "What happened, Eli?"

Mrs. McKinney butted in. "I spotted Eli on the far side of the playground on the grass by the gate. He's not supposed to be outside of the kindergarten play area."

Elise squeezed Eli's hand. "You need to stay on our playground, Eli. Miss Ellen and Mrs. Dory can't watch you way over there."

"That's not all, Miss Duran." Mrs. McKinney thrust out her formidable bosom. "Eli was talking to a stranger at the fence."

Elise tapped Eli's brown cheek with her finger. "You're not supposed to talk to strangers, Eli. Promise Mrs. McKinney you won't do that again."

Eli dropped his gaze and scuffed the toe of his Converse sneakers against the linoleum floor, shoving his hand in the front pocket of his jeans. "I promise."

She smiled. "That's better. Are you satisfied, Mrs. McKinney? I don't think Eli needs to go to Principal Yarborough."

Mrs. McKinney huffed. "I suppose not, but we can't have these kids wandering around the playground and talking to strangers."

"Okay. That's settled, then. You can walk to the line with me, Eli." She held out her hand and wiggled her fingers.

He buried his hand deeper in his pocket and jutted out his lower lip. "But he gave me something."

"Candy?" Mrs. McKinney snapped her head around. "Did he give you candy, Eli? Hand it over."

"N-no." His big brown eyes met Elise's. "He gave me something for you, Miss Duran."

Elise's stomach dropped and she grabbed on to the back of the chair. "What do you mean, Eli? The stranger you were talking to at the gate gave you something to give to me?"

"Yes." He bobbed his head up and down.

Viola cleared her throat and whispered, "Maybe it was your crazy ex."

Maybe it was Sean. "Was he a police officer?"

"Yes, Miss Duran." He slid a sideways glance at Mrs. McKinney that tried to put her in her place.

Elise's pulse quickened. It must've been Sean checking up on her, but he should've just come into her classroom. He should know better than to bother the children.

"What did he give you?" Mrs. McKinney's eyes narrowed.

Eli dragged his hand out of his pocket, a crumpled piece of white paper in his fist. "Here. He gave me this."

Viola raised her brows and shook her finger at Elise. "Why is a cop coming to school and sending you notes?"

Elise's cheeks warmed as she flipped open the folded piece of paper. The words swam before her eyes, and the blood in her veins turned to ice water.

"What does it say, Elise?" Viola took a step forward.

Elise raised her eyes from the note and blinked, bringing Viola's face, lined with worry, into focus. Then she glanced down at Eli, his usually sweet face contorted by fear.

She dropped to her knees in front of him and tweaked his nose. "Thank you for bringing the note to me, Eli. But promise me you'll never talk to a stranger like that again."

"I promise, Miss Duran." His lower lip trembled. "I-is the note bad?"

"This?" She waved it in the air. "Not at all. Mrs. McKinney's going to take you back outside to play, but stay in the kinder yard."

A tremulous smile wobbled across his face. "Yes, Miss Duran."

Mrs. McKinney shot her a worried look. "Let's go, young man. I heard you're the only kindergartner who can hop on one foot all the way across the blacktop, and I want to see that before the bell rings."

Elise mouthed *thank you* over Eli's head and transferred his grimy little hand from hers to Mrs. McKinney's.

When the door closed behind them, Viola spun around. "What is in that note?"

Elise took a deep breath and read aloud. "'One plus one equal 187. Six plus twelve equal 187. Thirty-seven plus forty-nine plus 122 plus twenty-eight equal 187. 187 for you.'"

Viola cocked her head and plucked the note from Elise's fingers.

Elise rubbed her damp hands against her skirt and swallowed. "I have no idea what it means, but it's probably related to something that happened this past weekend."

"Elise, you know my husband's a cop with the Oakland P.D."

"Yeah, I know that, but I'm sort of already working with the SFPD on this."

Viola shook her head. "It's not that, but I know what 187 means in cop-speak, anyway."

"What does it mean?"

"Murder."

Chapter Ten

"Why is he doing this?" Elise sat on a table strewn with colorful wooden blocks, one leg crossed over the other, kicking back and forth.

"For fun. For attention. He's a sick SOB. The rules don't apply to him."

Sean paced in front of her. The Oakland P.D. had already been out to question the boy and get a description, which had been useless—a white man with a baseball cap and sunglasses is all Eli could give them. Oh, yeah, and the stranger had a badge.

That last bit of information had punched him in the gut—not as if any Tom, Dick or Harry couldn't get a fake badge to fool a kid.

The teachers on playground duty hadn't been much more helpful than Eli. Mrs. McKinney had seen him from a distance. The stranger must've seen her barreling toward him because before she'd made it halfway across the field, he'd hightailed it out of there. He'd completed his business anyway. He'd given Eli the note to give to Elise.

Why was he harassing Elise? It wasn't good enough for him to taunt the lead detective on the case?

"How did he know where I taught? Do you think the kids are safe?"

Sean stopped pacing and flicked the leaf of a plant

growing in the well of an egg carton. "He had your purse, your wallet, your phone. He probably figured out the name of your school from something in your purse."

"My paycheck stub." She hit her forehead with the heel of her hand. "I had picked it up from the mailbox that night and crammed it into my bag."

"That made it easy for him."

"And the kids?" She hopped from the table and took up the pacing where he'd left off. "Do you think he'll do anything to the kids? I couldn't stand it if something happened to any one of them."

She covered her face with her hands and choked out a sob.

Despite his better judgment, he readied himself to go to her, to comfort her, but she looked up at him with dry eyes and a tight mouth.

"If he so much as touches one of these kids, I'll take care of him myself. I still have my .22 at home."

Her ferocity called to him even more than her pain. On his way to her side, he tripped over one of the little plastic chairs, which tipped over and bounced once before he caught it.

He righted it and then put an arm around Elise's rigid shoulders. "He's not interested in those kids, but the Oakland P.D. is going to have a patrol car here during school hours for the rest of the week. Doesn't hurt that one of the officer's wives works here."

"Viola Crouch. She teaches kinder with me. She's the one who told me what '187' meant." She shivered beneath his arm. "If he knows that and has a badge, maybe he's a cop."

Sean dropped his arm and turned away. "A lot of people know that 187 is the penal code for homicide, especially if they follow crimes, and anyone can pick up a fake badge."

"I'm sorry." She touched his back. "I didn't mean to

insult you or your profession, but it does happen, doesn't it? I read somewhere that a few arsonists actually become firefighters or arson investigators."

"It happens." What was happening to his cool, calm demeanor? He'd always prided himself on his poker face, and now he was allowing all kinds of emotions to spill over for this woman to read. Or could she just see through his barriers easily?

"I suppose there won't be any fingerprints on the note or the gate since Eli said the man was wearing gloves, not to mention Eli handled the note and Viola and I touched it, as well."

"He's arrogant, but he's not stupid. He's not going to get caught over a set of fingerprints. The Oakland cops looked anyway and they'll let us know."

"What do you think those numbers mean, other than the 187?"

"I don't know, but we'll find out. These guys aren't as clever as they think they are." Sean traced his fingers along the edges of the blocks. "It's getting late. Why don't you get out of here?"

"Three more days." She strolled to the whiteboard and erased the number four, grabbed a red marker and wrote *three* in its place. Then she changed the date in the upper-right corner of the board for tomorrow.

Sean focused on the date and approached the whiteboard, his muscles tense. "It's June twelfth tomorrow."

"Our last day is the..." She dropped the marker and spun around. "It's six, twelve tomorrow."

"One plus one equals 187, and six plus twelve equals 187."

"He's going to kill again tomorrow. One plus one?"

"Maybe he's going to kill more than one person."

Elise put her hands over her eyes as if she could block

out the truth. "Why is he telling me? I don't want to know this."

This time he did take her in his arms—hard. He pulled her against his chest and wrapped his arms around her body. She stiffened for a second. He knew she wanted to stand on her own, but then she melted against him, her arms curling around his waist.

The trembling of her body subsided, and Sean stroked her silky hair.

Sighing, she tipped back her head. "I guess I am involved in your work, whether you like it or not. He's sending messages to both of us now."

"I definitely don't like it, but this does have a weird silver lining."

Her eyes widened, and he felt her heart pick up speed.

Did she think he was going to admit having her in his arms was the silver lining? Not even that could make it okay that she'd become the obsession of some serial killer.

"Since he's communicating with you, he's not going to want to hurt you. For whatever reason, he wants to brag to you, keep you in his sick loop. For now, that's keeping you safe."

She dropped her head in a sharp nod and pulled away from him. "I guess that's something."

He'd disappointed her, and he immediately wanted to make it up to her. "I'm going to follow you back to your friend's place."

"That's not necessary." She hoisted her school bag over one shoulder and her purse over the other. "Didn't you just say I was safe as long as he was still communicating with me?"

"*Safe* is a relative term. What are your plans for dinner?" He flicked off the lights of her classroom and stepped into the hallway as she pulled the door shut and locked it.

"Food." She spun away from her classroom door, and

her low heels clicked on the floor as Sean tried to keep up with her.

She unlocked her car door and he stepped in front of her to open it for her. "Is Courtney going to be home?"

"I'm not sure." She opened the back door of her car and tossed her bag inside. "She sometimes sees clients late so they can come in after work."

That's all he needed to hear. He didn't want to leave her on her own. "I'll be right on your tail just to make sure you get back to her place safely."

Elise wheeled out of the parking lot and Sean followed her through the rough neighborhood. It didn't surprise him that she taught the kids in this area, and they needed a teacher like Elise—strong and fearless and willing to go up against a killer for them.

He tailed her across the Bay Bridge, and that other bridge invaded his thoughts. Why had this killer chosen to dump his victim in view of the Golden Gate? Was it a nod to those other murders so many years ago? The murders that impacted his life, formed him, shaped him?

He rubbed his knuckles across his tattoo—a Phoenix that symbolized his rise from the ashes of his early life. A life that threatened to stake its claim over him with these recent murders.

Twenty minutes later, he turned onto Courtney's street and watched Elise's taillights disappear into the underground parking garage. He pulled to the curb and exited his vehicle. He waited by the building's entrance until Elise peeked out the window, cupping her hand around her face. The electronic lock clicked and he pulled open the door.

"That's not a bad commute for you to your own place, either."

"It's a lot better when I leave school at my regular time. You know, the days I'm not involved in a police investigation."

He jerked his thumb toward the garage. “Is Courtney home yet?”

“No.”

“Do you want to share some dinner with me?”

“Dinner?” She folded her arms across her chest and gripped the straps of her bags.

“My stomach was growling all the way over, so I ordered some Italian to be delivered here.” He spread his hands. “It would be a lot better if I could eat my dinner here and share it with you instead of hauling it home to eat by myself.”

She hunched her shoulders. “Is that allowed? Are you still working?”

“I thought I told you. I have the day off today. Can’t you tell?” He plucked at his T-shirt. “I think I’m allowed to eat where I want on my day off.”

A small red car squealed to a stop at the curb.

“I think that’s your dinner now.” She pointed out the door as the driver climbed out of his car and popped his trunk.

“*Our* dinner. A little ravioli, eggplant parmigiana, chopped salad, garlic bread.”

“Is there enough for two?”

“I ordered for two. Even if I didn’t, you don’t look like you could make much of a dent in a pile of ravioli.”

She snorted. “You’d be surprised.” She stepped around him and pushed the door wide, gesturing to the driver. “Get that food up here.”

The kid stumbled, his eyes darting from Sean to Elise.

Sean laughed. “It’s okay. She’s harmless, just hungry.”

The delivery boy thrust the box, piled with white paper bags, toward Sean.

Sean dug into his pocket for some bills and paid the kid. “Lead the way.”

By the time they got to Courtney's door, the smell of garlic filled the hallway.

Elise stepped into the condo and pulled him in after her. "Quick, before Courtney's neighbors riot. They're a snooty bunch."

He placed the bags on the granite countertop of the kitchen's center island. "Restroom?"

She pointed to a door across from the staircase.

By the time he returned, she'd pulled plates, bowls and silverware from the cupboards and drawers.

He lifted the foil tins from the bags and removed their covers. Steam rose from the dishes, and Sean's mouth watered.

Elise scooped up the salad and dropped it into the two bowls with her head tilted to one side. "You actually laughed down there."

He tore a piece of garlic bread from the loaf and bit into it, a warm trickle of butter running down his chin. He blotted his face with a napkin while he chewed. "I do occasionally laugh. I am human."

And despite the circumstances, he felt more human than he had in a long time. Despite the death all around him, more alive.

"Well, I like it." She popped the lid off a plastic container full of salad dressing and held it above one of the salad bowls. "Do you want me to do the honors, or do you prefer to put your own dressing on?"

"Dump it on there." He pulled another piece of bread from the loaf and held it to her lips. "You gotta try this."

She ducked her head and sank her teeth into the spongy part of the bread, soaked with garlic butter, which dribbled out of the corner of her mouth. Raising her eyes to the ceiling, she murmured, "Mmm."

"You have—" he dabbed the corner of a napkin on her luscious lips "—a little bit of butter right there."

"Charming. That's almost as bad as having spinach between your teeth."

"Blame it on the bread." He picked up the salad bowls and walked to a round table next to the sliding glass doors that led to a balcony that overlooked the city.

Elise followed him with the pasta and bread. "Do you want something to drink? I'm sure Courtney has some wine around here."

"Just water."

"Oh, are you not allowed to drink even a little when you're driving?"

He reached for the silverware and arranged it on the two placemats. "As long as I'm not working it's okay, just like anyone if I stay under the legal limit. But I usually never drink and drive. I'm fine with water. Don't let me stop you."

"I told you the other night I'm not much of a drinker." She wrinkled her nose. "It's a good thing, too, because I may not have regained consciousness so fast in that trunk."

It always came back to that. The laughter, the food, the sexual tension between them—none of it mattered, none of it would've been possible if some maniac hadn't stuffed Elise in the trunk of his car.

But Sean would do his best to make it normal, and for the remainder of the meal he tried to do just that.

He held up a spoon full of pasta. "More ravioli?"

Elise pushed her chair away from the table and patted her flat tummy. "I'm stuffed. I had pasta for dinner last night and for lunch today, too. With all that carb loading, I could probably run a marathon tomorrow."

"Sorry, I could've ordered Chinese."

"Had it for lunch yesterday."

"Greek?" He lifted one eyebrow.

"I don't think I've ever had Greek food." She dabbed

at a crumb of bread with her fingertip and sucked it into her mouth.

"We'll have to remedy that sometime. There's a great little place in North Beach, right smack in the middle of all the Italian places." The words came out automatically as if this were a regular date with a regular woman.

There was nothing regular about this date—or Elise Duran.

She stood up abruptly and grabbed the rim of her plate with both hands. "Are you still eating, or can I take your plate?"

He handed her the plate. "You can take it, but I'll do the cleanup since I sort of invited myself over."

"We'll both do it. I'll wrap up the food. If you can rinse the dishes, I'll stick them in the dishwasher."

"Deal." He gathered the silverware and glasses and followed her to the kitchen. He ran the warm water and swiped a dish sponge across the streaks of tomato sauce and bits of cheese stuck to the plates.

Elise replaced the lids on the food containers and glanced over her shoulder. "You're pretty good at that for a single guy, or maybe that's why you *are* so good at it since you have to fend for yourself in the kitchen."

"Believe me, I got a lot of practice growing up."

"Ah, was your mom one of those liberated women who believed in teaching her sons how to do housework? Sounds like my kinda woman."

He ducked his head to scrub at a stubborn piece of cheese. "My mom was…ill. My brothers and I did most of the work around the house."

"Oh, I'm sorry. That must've been tough on your dad, too."

Why the hell had he brought up his childhood? A voice in the back of his head chided. *You're the one who wanted this to be a regular date.*

"My dad..."

"Who opened an Italian eatery in my place and forgot to tell me?"

Courtney burst through the front door to save the day. She waved a hand in front of her nose. "I can smell that garlic all the way down the hallway. The homeowners' association is going to bring it up in their next meeting and give me a lecture."

She dropped a laptop case and a leather briefcase in the corner of the room and spun around. "Oh, hello."

Sean lifted a soapy hand. "Hope you don't mind me barging in."

Courtney's dark eyes darted from his face to Elise's. "Nope. How was your day, Elise? Those little monsters still running you ragged?"

"My kids are not little monsters. How about you? Busy day?"

"I saw a new client today. Those first sessions are always a little rough." Courtney checked her phone and then connected it to her charger on the counter.

"Do you want some food before I finish wrapping it up?" Elise held up one of the containers.

"That's okay." Courtney pointed to her bags. "I picked up a sandwich in my building before I left, but I will have a glass of wine while you tell me what happened today that a cop has to follow you home and eat dinner with you."

Elise sighed and stood on her tiptoes to reach for a bottle of wine in the cupboard. "If you insist."

She opened the bottle and splashed a quantity of the ruby liquid in the glass. When she carried it to her friend, Sean joined them at the table.

Courtney sipped her wine as Elise told her what had happened at her school.

When she finished, Courtney threw back the rest of

her wine and held out her glass for a refill. "That's creepy, Elise. How did he know where you taught?"

Elise reached behind her for the bottle. "I had a pay stub in my purse. He probably got it from there. He may have even seen something on my phone. Heck, maybe he even did a search for me on the internet. It's not like he doesn't already know my name and address."

Courtney turned to Sean. "What do those numbers mean?"

He slumped in the chair and stretched his legs in front of him. "The penal code for murder is 187. We figured the one plus one means two murders or two people. The six and twelve might mean tomorrow's date."

Courtney had covered her mouth with her hand, and it slid to her throat. "What about the other numbers?"

"Don't know yet. I sent the note to the station, and one of the detectives is working on deciphering it."

"Do you think there's going to be another murder tomorrow?"

"If so, I hope the other numbers tell us where."

"Who, what, when, where and how." Elise took a sip of Courtney's wine and puckered her lips. "Is that obnoxious journalist still bothering you?"

"What are you implying? Do you think he's involved somehow?"

"Seems awfully anxious to get some big scoop."

"That's his job. It doesn't mean he's a killer."

Courtney snapped her fingers. "I know that guy. Ray Lopez, right? I've seen him on the local news. He's a big mouth, but he's entertaining in a tabloid kinda way."

"Yeah, that's him. You've seen him do other stories?" Elise asked.

"He has that half-hour show after the news. I heard his promo today, and he's going to feature Katie Duncan's murder."

"Great." Sean rolled his eyes. He just hoped none of the officers had talked to Lopez and revealed any of the details they wanted to keep hidden from the public—like the severed finger.

"In fact—" Courtney rose from the table and stepped down into the living room, where she swept the remote from the coffee table "—I think he's on right now."

A commercial blared from the TV and Courtney tossed the remote on the couch. "I'm going to soak in the tub and scrub off my clients' troubles. I'm sure I'll see you later, Detective Brody."

"Sean, and sorry again for intruding on your space."

She waved a manicured hand. "Any…friend of Elise's is welcome as long as she's staying here."

Sean turned back to the TV just as Lopez's program began. As Courtney promised, Lopez jumped right into Katie Duncan's murder and connected it to Elise's escape the night before, although he didn't mention Elise's name on the air.

Lopez stared into the camera. "The autopsy report on Katie isn't finished yet, but preliminary reports suggest she received a blow to the head before she was sliced."

"You didn't tell me that." Elise crossed her arms and perched on the arm of the couch.

"Didn't think I had to. We knew her murder was connected to your assailant."

The next shot featured Lopez stationed in front of the Speakeasy, and Elise's grip on her upper arms tightened.

"In the attack in front of this club, the killer pretended to be injured with a cast on his arm, and then used the plaster cast to viciously hit the victim over the head. This incapacitated her, and he was able to stuff her into the trunk of his vehicle."

Lopez went on to describe the vehicle and show Elise's composite sketch.

"We can turn this off." Sean reached for the remote, but Elise snatched it up first.

"Wait. I want to watch the rest."

As the half-hour show drew to a close, Lopez was back in the studio. "The interesting thing about these murders is that this city has seen something like this before."

Sean's eye twitched and he tightened his jaw. He wanted to punch his fist through the TV as Lopez continued blabbing.

"Almost twenty years ago, another serial killer in the city used the same M.O. He feigned an injury to lure in his victims, knocked them out and then cut them to ribbons."

Elise murmured something that Sean couldn't hear over the pounding in his head.

"That serial killer murdered five women but was never caught. And the strangest thing about that old case and this new one?" He paused for dramatic effect. "The killer twenty years ago was communicating with SFPD Homicide Detective Joseph Brody, and the current killer is communicating with Brody's son, SFPD Homicide Detective Sean Brody."

Elise gasped. "Sean?"

And then there it was. A picture of a young officer with dark hair and brooding eyes.

Not satisfied, Lopez continued in his awed voice. "The story gets even more bizarre. Detective Joseph Brody was actually suspected of being the murderer, and the killings stopped after Brody threw himself from the Golden Gate Bridge."

Chapter Eleven

The remote fell from Elise's hands, and she flinched as it hit the table. "Sean?"

Without turning to face her, he leaned sideways and grabbed the remote control, the muscles in his forearm corded and tense.

The TV went silent although Ray Lopez was still moving his lips.

"I-is all that true, what he said about your father?" She licked her lips, and her gaze dropped to his tattoo. What else had he been keeping from her?

He placed the remote on the coffee table with a click, put his hands on his knees and pushed up from the couch. He took one turn around the room and then stopped in front of her.

"It's not true." He dragged a hand through his hair. "It is true."

She searched his face, the muscle ticking in his jaw, the deep grooves on each side of his mouth. "Just tell me the truth, Sean. I want to know the truth."

"My father was a homicide detective, and there was a string of murders—similar to Katie Duncan's but not exactly."

"Like Lopez said, the M.O. was the same? The killer used some fake infirmity to trick his victims?"

"Yes." He ran the back of his hand across his mouth. "Faked an injury to catch the victims off guard."

"The killer communicated with your father?"

"He did, but I told you before, that's not so uncommon."

She folded her hands in front of her, twisting her fingers. "What about the other part? Was your father really suspected of being the killer?"

Sean slammed his fist into his palm. "That's a lie. My father never killed anyone."

"Except himself."

Sean's face blanched, and his lips tightened. "At the height of the investigation, someone witnessed a man jumping from the bridge and items belonging to my father were found there. The Coast Guard never found his body."

"I'm sorry." The words bubbled to her lips. How could she be angry with him for withholding the truth from her when such pain filled his eyes?

Squeezing those eyes shut, he pinched the bridge of his nose. "Because of his suicide and because the killing stopped afterward, the department suspected him, but nobody was ever able to prove anything—not even that he committed suicide."

"You don't believe he killed himself even though his stuff was left on the bridge?"

"I don't think he would've done that to us. We got nothing. His life insurance wouldn't pay out and neither would the department."

"Sean." She reached out and trailed her fingers down his arm. When they skimmed over his tattoo, she snatched her hand back.

"What about the rest of it? Was there any proof that he was the killer?"

Sean plowed a hand through his hair again. "There was plaster of Paris in his patrol car. But would he really be stupid enough to leave that in his patrol car? Someone planted it."

"You think someone was setting him up for the murders?"

"Absolutely. There's no way...my father could never be capable of anything like that."

Of course he'd say that about his father. He'd been a boy. How could he know for sure?

"Why would someone set him up? Who?"

"You don't think I've gone through this in my mind a million times? I can only guess, but I think it was probably the real killer. He taunted my father and then set him up so he could get away with murder."

"The murders stopped when your father...killed himself?"

"Exactly." Sean smacked a hand on the counter. "That was the whole point. It got the killer off the hook."

"And then he just stopped killing? Isn't it unusual for a serial killer to stop on his own?"

"It's not typical, but it does happen. Besides, how do we know he didn't move to some other big city to continue his spree?"

She held out her hand. "Wait a minute. So you think a serial killer made contact with your dad and when your dad starting closing in, the killer started planting evidence implicating your father? When your father jumped, the killer packed up and started plying his trade somewhere else to escape?"

Sean nodded as he clenched his hands into fists.

"Why would your father commit suicide? Was the evidence against him that strong?"

"I don't know. That's the hardest piece of this puzzle for me to figure out. My dad—he wasn't one to run from a fight. If he was innocent, and I know he was, he would've stood up to his accusers. He would've proved his innocence."

Elise edged through the space between them, vibrating with tension, with a slow, cautious gait. She placed her hand on Sean's tight arm. "But he didn't do that, Sean."

Raw emotion flashed across his face, twisting his features into a mask of pain.

Trailing her fingers across his tense jawline, she whispered, "I'm sorry."

His chest heaved and he caught her hand in his warm grip. "I can't figure out why he did it, Elise. I know he's no killer, but I guess he was a coward."

"You were a child, Sean." She squeezed his hand. "You can't know what demons he faced. You can't get into someone's head like that."

His lips twisted and he raised his eyes to the ceiling. "Courtney thinks she can."

"And maybe if your father had been able to see a good therapist like Courtney, she could've gotten inside his head."

Sean's eyes widened and he brought her hand to his lips and kissed her knuckles. "You've just given me a great idea."

With the impression of his lips still burning her skin, Elise smiled. "Do you want me to get Courtney down here so she can shrink your head?"

"No, thanks." He dropped her hand and took a turn around the room. "I went through my father's files when I started working with the department, and I noticed that he'd been referred to a psychologist specializing in law enforcement issues. The referral had been made when the killer started communicating with him, before he became a suspect in the killings."

"Did he go?"

"I don't know. I didn't follow up on it."

Missing his touch, she crossed her arms and pulled out a chair from the kitchen table. “Courtney would be the first one to tell you about client confidentiality. You can’t go barging into a therapist’s office asking about his or her patients.”

“Even after twenty years? Even if the patient is dead?” He parked himself on the arm of Courtney’s white brocade couch.

“I don’t know how long confidentiality lasts. What are you hoping to find?”

“Answers, Elise. I need answers, especially because I’m afraid the whole thing is happening again.”

“Was the therapist’s name in your father’s file?”

Sean scratched his chin. “No, but the department uses the same ones, so I’m sure I’ll be able to find out whom we were using back then. Plus, I have my sources in the department.”

“Would the powers that be allow you to reopen your father’s case?”

He snorted. “Not likely. They’d rather forget about it. I’m sure there were plenty in the department who didn’t want to hire me in the first place. If I start making trouble, that faction will use that as justification.”

“But you still have sources?”

“Yeah. One of the most powerful people in the department.”

“Chief Stoddard?”

“Chief Marie.” He winked.

“Who’s Chief Marie?”

“Marie Giardano. She keeps our records.”

“Ah, friends in high places.”

“She worked there when my father did, and she knew both of my parents. She never believed he was the Phone Book Killer, either.”

She raised her eyebrows at the name. "I'm assuming he picked his victims out of the phone book?"

"In alphabetical order, starting with the letter D."

Gasping, Elise clutched her throat. "Just like Duran and Duncan."

"You see why it looks like déjà vu to me?"

"Sean—" she reached out and traced her fingertips along the wings of his tattoo "—do you think your ink has anything to do with it?"

He shivered beneath her touch. "Of course I thought about it. That's why I freaked out in a totally unprofessional manner when you told me about your attacker's tattoo."

"Do you think he's some kind of copycat?" She covered her mouth with her hands. "Is that what the message on my mirror was all about?" She cinched his arm. "Is someone going to start trying to pin these murders on you?"

"I can't say the thought didn't cross my mind."

"Why didn't you tell me all this before?"

He placed his hands on her shoulders, wedging his thumbs against her collarbones. "I didn't want to drag you into all of this, Elise. It's ancient history to most people, but it haunts me every day, every day I catch a glimpse of the bridge."

Her heart ached for this man and the burden he carried. Her issues with her family and Ty seemed trivial compared with Sean Brody's family legacy.

She encircled his wrists with her fingers. "I am involved, Sean, and it's not ancient history to me. It's my story, right now. And I want to help you in any way I can."

His dark eyes burned into hers, and she didn't look away. She didn't ever want to look away. She wanted to get lost in the depths of his soul and bring light to his darkness.

When his lips touched hers, they scorched her with

their heat and passion. She sagged against his chest, and he wrapped one arm around her waist.

He deepened the kiss and she drank him in, getting drunk on the sensations that swirled through her body. Who needed wine? She had Sean Brody.

Courtney yelped from the top of the stairs, and they jumped apart.

She called down. "This new client is going to be a pain. First session today, and he's already calling me after hours."

Elise rolled her eyes at Sean. "Is it an emergency?"

"He thinks so, but I talked him down from the ledge, so to speak." Courtney stopped on the staircase, clutching her phone in her hand. "Oh, I'm sorry. I didn't realize you were still here, Sean."

He held up his hand. "I'm on my way out."

"Don't let me scare you away." She drew a circle around her face, which was caked with green paste. "When this comes off, I'm more beautiful than ever."

Elise slipped her arm through his. "I'll walk you out. Thanks for dinner."

"My pleasure." He brushed a loose strand of hair from her cheek. "I hope you're feeling better after today's events."

"I feel fine, but it'll be nice having the Oakland P.D. patrolling the school this week."

"And your leg?"

"Stiff and sore, but it could be worse, right?"

"You're tough, kid."

"It's like you said before. He's going to make a mistake soon."

He cupped her face with one hand and brushed his lips against hers. "I just don't want you getting burned."

As she watched him walk down the hallway to the elevator, she murmured, "Too late for that, Sean Brody. Too late for that."

Chapter Twelve

Sean hunched over the counter, studied Marie's lined face and gave her his best smile. "I know where the boxes are, Marie."

She tapped a pen on top of the log book. "You should. You've practically worn a path in the linoleum back there over the years."

He plucked the pen from her fingers, the long red fingernails at odds with her age-spotted skin, and slid the log book toward him.

Marie snatched it away. "You don't need to sign in, Sean."

He lifted one eyebrow. "Since when?"

"Since the brass has been snooping through the books."

His pulse jumped. "Looking for what?"

"Your guess is as good as mine." She raised her plump shoulders. "I just don't think they need to see your name written in ink checking out your dad's case files again. Especially now."

He leaned in closer, his breath fogging the glass in the window. "What are you hearing?"

"I'm hearing a killer has you on speed dial."

"And?" He licked his lips.

"Just that."

Sean dropped the pen. "Maybe I don't need to look through the boxes again."

"Be my guest. I won't remember that you were here. My memory is notoriously bad on Tuesdays."

"Even Tuesdays twenty years ago?"

"Mmm, back then I had trouble with Saturdays." She put her finger on the side of her prominent nose. "What am I supposed to recall about twenty years in the past besides the fact that I had cleavage that could cause whiplash?"

"You still got it, Marie."

"You Brody boys are all charmers." She tapped on the glass with one of her long nails. "Tell me what you need."

Sean folded his hands on top of the log book, pressing his thumbs together. "Who did the department use for therapy in those days? You know, for officer-involved shootings, alcoholism, the works."

She laughed, a sharp bark that filled the small front office of the records room. "I thought you were going to test me, Brody."

"You remember without even looking?"

"The department used only one guy in those days, and we had him for eighteen years. Dr. James Patrick. He retired just seven years ago. That's who your dad would've seen."

"Did he see him?"

Marie looked both ways. "I don't know, but I do know they made the recommendation. Usually when the department makes the recommendation, you'd better follow through or it could be your job."

"It wound up being his life."

Marie reached through the space under the window and patted Sean's arm. "He must've had a good reason to do that, Sean, leaving you and your brothers and Joanne. Someone or something drove him to it, and I don't believe for one minute it was guilt over any murders."

"I appreciate that, Marie."

She coughed her smoker's cough. "If you appreciate it so much, why don't you send those good-looking brothers of yours over here to visit an old lady?"

"I'll get right on it—after I solve this case."

"Which case, Sean?"

He slapped the log book. "You're a lifesaver, Marie."

He jogged up two flights of stairs and paused at the fire door, pulling out his phone. He typed in a quick text to Elise, and she responded immediately that everything was fine.

Blowing out a long breath, he pulled open the door and crossed the hall to the homicide division. When he got to his desk, he shoved Curtis off the edge. "Go sit on your own desk."

Curtis waved a piece of paper in the air. "You wouldn't say that if you knew what I had in my hand."

"A first-class ticket to paradise? 'Cuz that's what I need about now." *Two* first-class tickets to paradise.

"Almost as good." He slapped the paper on Sean's desk. "Patterson ran the numbers from the note through a few computer programs and came up with coordinates."

"Coordinates for a location?"

"Exactly."

"Don't just stand there with that annoying grin on your face. Where's the location?"

"Golden Gate Bridge."

Sean swore and dropped into his chair. "Not possible. He's not going to commit a murder at the bridge—too many cameras."

"He dumped a body there."

"He was obviously aware of the cameras." Sean kicked his feet onto his desk and crossed his arms behind his head. "He kept out of their range. He's not going to kill at the bridge."

Curtis tugged on his ear. "Then why put down those coordinates in the message? If you're right, he told us he was going to kill two people on today's date. Makes sense he'd tell us where."

"He's toying with us. Don't expect logic from him or any real clues to his actions."

"You know more about that than I do." Curtis parked his cup on the blotter on Sean's desk and put a finger to his lips. "Did you catch Lopez's report on TV last night?"

"What of it?" Sean smiled through clenched teeth.

Curtis blinked and glanced over his shoulder. "The brass doesn't want the detective to become the story."

"Duh. Tell me something I don't already know."

"I'm just telling you to watch your back, bro." Curtis scurried off, his hands wrapped around his third mug of coffee for the day.

With the blood pounding against his temples, Sean tapped his keyboard to bring his computer to life. That was the second warning that he'd been issued this morning by well-meaning friends. How many not-so-well-meaning friends were out there spreading rumors and gossip?

When the search engine glowed brightly from the computer screen, Sean typed in the name Marie had given him earlier. He swiveled the monitor to the left, dragging it closer to the edge of the desk. If the brass could see what he was doing right now, they wouldn't be too thrilled about this, either.

It would be easier to use the police database to look up Dr. Patrick, but Sean didn't want to leave any kind of trail of his activities. He'd have to get his info like everyone else. A few papers Dr. Patrick had written about post-traumatic stress disorder popped up in the results, as well his attendance at a charitable organization's fund-raiser several years ago, but Sean couldn't get a line on a current location or phone number. Maybe he'd moved after his retirement.

His phone buzzed and his heart skipped a beat when he saw Elise's name on the display. "Everything okay?"

"Besides the fact that two of my students decided it was a good idea to color off the paper and onto the desktop, everything's good. Any news about that third set of numbers?"

"Longitude and latitude coordinates for the Golden Gate Bridge."

Elise sucked in some air. "That's the *where.*"

"It could've been if it were any other location, but the bridge? He can't think he's going to get away with murder on the bridge with the cameras up there."

"You have a point, but he avoided the cameras before when he dumped Katie's body."

"I think he's just messing with us…me."

"He seems to know your past, for sure." She coughed as the sound of kids floated over the line. "Did you get the name of the therapist?"

"Dr. James Patrick." He tapped his screen as if she could see it. "Just doing a search on him now but not having much luck. I could do better if I used my department resources and connections, but I don't want to go there right now."

She paused. "The department wouldn't be happy about you digging around in this stuff?"

He lowered his voice. "Apparently, they're already ticked off about Ray Lopez's report last night on the news."

"That's not your fault. You didn't ask him to dredge up ancient history."

The passion in her voice made his lip twitch—as if she were advocating for one of her kindergarteners. It had been a long time since he'd had an advocate.

"I can't change the past. Lopez has a right to delve into any story he wants. That's his job."

"I don't like reporters, never have."

"Is that because they made the runaway bride a three-day wonder back in Deer Loop, Montana?"

"It was longer than three days—must've been a slow week for news."

"Isn't every week a slow week for news in Deer Loop?"

She laughed and the noise over the line grew louder. "The bell just rang. I have to go back to class. Talk to you later?"

"Sure. Stay safe."

"You, too."

Sean held the phone to his ear a minute longer, listening to silence. It felt good to have someone in his corner—not that his brothers weren't. But they were younger when tragedy struck the family. It hadn't impacted them as much as him, and he'd wanted it that way.

After Mom had descended into a haze of booze and prescription drugs, he'd taken it upon himself to shield and protect his younger brothers.

Now, apparently, Elise had taken it upon herself to protect him. Not that there was much she could do, but yeah, it felt good.

He didn't want to start getting used to it.

ELISE SLASHED A red crayon across the neon green construction paper. "I will owe you big-time if you can find him for me."

Courtney tsked over the phone, but Elise could hear the click of her keyboard. "He's the cop. He can't get this info on his own?"

"He's doing this as a private citizen and doesn't want to use the department's resources." Elise held her breath as Courtney hummed across the line.

"Found him in one of my directories. No phone number, but I have an address for Dr. James Patrick and he's still local. Are you ready?"

"Fire away." Elise scribbled down the address as Courtney read it over the line. "Thank you so much."

"Just remember if things turn ugly, you didn't get this info from me."

Elise's belly fluttered. "Why would things turn ugly? Sean's a cop who needs some information from Dr. Patrick."

"Whatever you say, but be careful."

"Be careful? With Sean?" She'd never felt safer in her life than standing in the circle of that man's arms.

"I saw Lopez's report last night on the news, Elise. Don't you think it's kinda creepy?"

"The fact that his father was set up to take the fall for a string of murders? Yeah, really creepy."

Courtney cleared her throat. "The fact that Brody senior was suspected of being a serial killer and then he took the fall all right—right off the Golden Gate Bridge. And now his son is involved in a similar scenario? Creepy."

Anger, as hot as the red crayon, flashed through her body. "Sean is not creepy."

"No, I'd say Sean is a hot, sexy cop. But he might be a hot, sexy cop with a secret."

"He told me everything."

"After not telling you anything."

"Courtney..."

"I'm just asking you to be careful." She clicked her tongue. "I gotta go. That new client is on the other line."

Courtney ended the call, and Elise ripped the square containing Dr. Patrick's address from the construction paper.

Her friend was right. Sean had kept the whole truth from her, but then what did he owe her? The past had been Sean's personal affair until Ray Lopez had spilled the beans.

Yeah, just like Ty's woman on the side had been *his* personal affair.

The two situations weren't comparable. Ty's secret directly affected her, while Sean's was peripheral to the case. A homicide detective wasn't expected to divulge his personal history to a witness…or buy her dinner, or kiss her.

She dusted her fingers together and reached for her phone again. Sean's phone rang until it tripped over to his voice mail. "Sean, it's Elise. I got the address of Dr. Patrick, and he's still in the city. Call me when you get this message. I'm just leaving school now."

The rap on her door made her jump.

The uniformed cop held up his hands. "Sorry I startled you, Ms. Duran, but the older classes are getting dismissed early today and the school's going to be deserted soon."

"Thanks for the reminder. I'm on my way out."

"I'll wait for you."

True to his word, the officer waited and walked her out to her car. She waved as she pulled out of the school's parking lot.

As her car rolled off the Bay Bridge and into the city, Elise pulled to the side of the road and checked her phone. Still no response from Sean. She called and got his voice mail again. This time she left the doctor's address.

She maneuvered through the city streets and realized the doctor lived on the way to Courtney's. Maybe she should swing by his place and scope it out for Sean.

Courtney would probably be tied up with her pesky new client, and Elise didn't want to rush home to an empty place. She'd had enough of empty places.

Cupping her phone in her hand, she read Dr. Patrick's address aloud. The phone responded and intoned directions to the location.

Elise turned onto Dr. Patrick's street and squinted out her window at the addresses on the row of town houses. She located his address in brass numbers on the outside of a beige stucco building and rolled to a stop at the curb.

Before turning off the engine, she glanced at the clock on the dashboard. Then she plucked her phone from the cup holder and scrolled through her messages—nothing from Sean.

She punched in the number for the station, and a woman answered the phone.

"SFPD Homicide."

"Hello, I'm trying to reach Detective Brody. Is he in today?"

"He's been in a meeting all afternoon. Can I take a message?"

"No, that's okay. I already left him a message on his cell phone."

"He'll get it when the meeting's over, since they usually turn off their cell phones in there."

"Okay, thanks." Elise tapped the edge of her phone against her chin. Should she wait for Sean or just go to Courtney's? He'd piqued her curiosity with that story about his father. What a tragic chain of events.

If Sean's father had been innocent of the crimes, it was all for nothing. *If?* Sean was convinced his father had been innocent, but what child wouldn't believe that of a beloved father?

Her eyes strayed to the front of Dr. Patrick's town house. Would the doctor be able to shed any light on the truth? Even if he implicated Sean's father, would Sean believe him? And if he did implicate Sean's father, would Sean admit that to her?

She gripped the door handle. What did it matter? This was Sean's business.

She folded her hands in her lap. But it wasn't just Sean's

business anymore. There was a killer out there who knew all about Sean's history, a killer who had her in his crosshairs.

After that fiasco with Ty, she'd vowed never to be kept in the dark again, and this situation with Sean was a lot darker than a cheating fiancé.

She grabbed the door handle again and pushed out of the car before she could talk herself out of it. Pausing on the steps to the town house, she pulled out her phone and left another message for Sean letting him know her plans.

She might not want to be kept in the dark, but she didn't want to keep him in the dark, either.

With just fourteen units in the building, Elise located Dr. Patrick's place quickly. A sliding window beside the front door was open halfway across, and the sounds of a game show floated through the mesh screen obscuring the view inside the house.

She scooped in a deep breath and rang the doorbell.

A bump and a scrape resounded from inside, and Elise straightened her shoulders and plastered a smile on her face as if this were the most natural house call in the world. But the door didn't swing open.

She knocked, leaning in toward the window. "Dr. Patrick? My name is Elise Duran. I'm a friend of Detective Sean Brody's. He…we wanted to ask you a few questions about his father, Detective Joseph Brody."

The scraping noise grew louder, and a raspy moan accompanied it.

"Dr. Patrick?" Elise pressed her face against the screen.

A man, leaning heavily against a kitchen chair, shuffled toward the door, one hand holding his left arm.

Elise's stomach flip-flopped. "Dr. Patrick? Are you all right?"

She jiggled the door handle. Another loud scrape and a bump, and then the handle turned. The door opened inward, and the man hunched over in the doorway, his face contorted, a line of drool running from his mouth.

The chair bumped Elise's knees and she realized he was using it as a walker.

"Are you okay?" She placed a knee on the chair. "I'm calling 9-1-1."

Dr. Patrick let out a gasp and toppled to the side.

Elise shoved the useless chair out of the way and crouched beside him, reaching for her phone with a shaky hand. "It's going to be all right. I'm calling 9-1-1 right now."

He clutched her wrist in a cinching vise and pulled her toward him as the phone dropped from her hand. His mouth was working and his dark eyes burned into hers. He strained to keep his chin to his chest, holding his head off the floor.

She ducked, her ear hovering close to his mouth while she felt for her phone on the hardwood floor.

His words rasped from his throat. "Tell him, tell Brody."

Elise's jaw dropped and she froze. "Tell him what?"

"Tell him, tell him…his father…"

Dr. Patrick's eyes rolled to the back of his head and he slumped to the floor.

Chapter Thirteen

As the fog rolled in damp and heavy, Sean narrowed his eyes and watched the EMTs load the gurney burdened with Dr. Patrick's body into the ambulance.

Elise's shoulder pressed against his, and he felt a tremble roll through her slender frame. He took a step to the side. "What the hell were you thinking?"

Her head swiveled around so fast, her hair whipped across her face. A few strands stuck to her damp cheeks. "I didn't cause his heart attack."

"I didn't accuse of you of causing his…heart attack, but what were you doing coming out to his place on your own?" That fact upset him more than the idea that she obviously didn't trust him.

"I was driving back to Courtney's from school. It's not like I have a police escort. I could've stopped off for groceries, dropped in on a friend."

"But you chose to come here."

"Look—" she splayed her hands in front of her "—I had Dr. Patrick's address, you were busy and I happened to be in the neighborhood."

He shoved his hands in his pockets as the ambulance trundled away from the curb. No need for a siren—Dr. Patrick was already dead from the heart attack.

"Why didn't you wait for me? Or why did you have to

wait at all? You left me his address. I could've handled the questioning on my own." He started to shake a finger in her face and made a fist instead.

"Maybe it was fate that propelled me to go in on my own. By the time you got here, he would've been dead."

"I guess fate's not looking out for you too well, since by the time you got here he was dying."

She held up her own finger. "Dying, not dead."

"What does that mean?" He hadn't had two minutes to talk to her alone. By the time he got her message and had driven to Dr. Patrick's address, the cops had already been here and he'd arrived to see the tail end of their patrol car. The EMTs were already wheeling Dr. Patrick out of his town house, and Elise was talking to the neighbors, who were now wandering back to their own lives.

He had no idea what she'd told the cops about her reasons for being here. Had she dragged his name into it?

"It means—" she brushed the hair from her face "—he wasn't dead when I got here. He'd already suffered the heart attack but he was still alive."

"How long did he last?"

"Long enough to talk to me."

He scuffed the toe of his shoe against the sidewalk. "What would he have to say to a complete stranger?"

"I wouldn't say I was a complete stranger." She flicked a piece of lint from the arm of her sweater. "I told him who I was through the window."

"You mentioned my name?"

"Yes."

"What did he say?" Sean sucked in a breath and held it.

She hugged her sweater around her body. "He told me to tell you something about your father."

His lips barely moved in his stiff face. "What?"

"He died before he could tell me."

Sean let out a noisy breath that deflated his chest along

with his hopes. "He knew, Elise. He knew something about my father."

She placed her cool fingers on his arm. "If he knew enough to clear your father, why didn't he step forward at the time? I'm pretty sure your father would've allowed him to break confidentiality to vouch for his innocence."

"Are you implying Dr. Patrick knew my father was guilty?"

"No." Her fingernails dug into his tattoo. "I'm just trying to reason through this with you."

He shook his head. "There is no rhyme or reason. Why did Dr. Patrick have a heart attack today of all days, just when I found out about his existence?"

"Coincidence. Fate, again. It was a heart attack, not murder, not suicide."

"The EMTs verified that to you?"

"Short of doing an autopsy on the sidewalk? Pretty much."

"Damn! Minutes too late. Minutes away from getting to the bottom of this puzzle that has plagued me for twenty years."

Her hold on his arm turned to a caress. "The puzzle, as you call it, doesn't define you, Sean. Whatever your father was or did, you're here now, in this moment."

The tension seeped from his shoulders and he rolled them forward and backward. Then he clasped her hands between his.

She wriggled one free from his tight grip and brushed her knuckles across his tattoo. "And you know it. That's what this is about, isn't it? You're a Phoenix. You've risen from the ashes of your past to create your own present."

As always, he shivered when she touched his tattoo, as if she were touching his soul. "Let's get out of here and get something to eat."

"That sounds great about now, but I don't want you to

get into any trouble because of me. Does your department have any idea you're spending so much time with me?"

Sean clutched the back of his neck to knead his tense muscles. In all the worry about Elise and the drama over Dr. Patrick's death, he'd almost forgotten the meeting this afternoon. "That's not going to be a problem."

"Are you sure?"

"It's not going to be a problem because I'm no longer on the case. It's happening again, Elise."

ELISE STEPPED BACK and placed a hand on her car. "Your department took you off the case? Why?"

"The captain thinks I'm too personally involved." He held up one finger. "And before you get started, it has nothing to do with you."

"It was that reporter's story, wasn't it? Dragging up the past."

He shrugged. "Like I said before, he has a right to report whatever he wants as long as it's the truth—and he told the truth. The department overreacted."

"Sean, what did you mean when you said it was happening again? They don't suspect you of anything, do they?"

"I just meant—" he dug his keys out of his pocket "—they're punishing me because some killer decided to communicate with me. That's how it started with my dad, too."

"Well, it's not going to end the same way."

He reached forward and tugged a lock of her damp hair. "Why are we standing out here in this fog? Follow me back to my place and I'll make some dinner. It's just outside the city, if you don't mind."

"Perfect. I want to get out of the city right now, but I don't want to put you to any trouble. Let me pick up the food this time."

She'd clicked her remote and he opened the car door

for her. “I actually have a couple of steaks in the freezer I’ve been meaning to cook for a while.”

“Then I’ll take you up on your offer.”

“Stay right behind me and I’ll keep my eye on you, but just in case.” He printed out his address on a piece of paper and slipped it into her hand. He shut her door and smacked the roof of the car.

Keeping her gaze pinned to the taillights of his car had the same effect on her as watching him in her rearview mirror—a feeling of safety. After Dr. Patrick died in her arms and the ambulance arrived and the police came, she hadn’t felt safe until she’d seen Sean striding across the street, his gait fueled by fury. His fury fueled by fear.

He cared about her. Whether his concern extended beyond feelings of protectiveness, she didn’t know. Did it matter right now? She needed his strength and he needed hers, too.

He’d been fighting his demons for far too long by himself. He obviously didn’t want to burden his brothers. He had no one right now to confide in, and she knew how that felt.

When the expectations of her small-town life began to close around her, she didn’t know where to turn. So she’d gone through the motions, treading the path that had been laid out for her.

When her maid of honor had dangled the gift of Ty’s infidelity in front of her, she’d snatched it. She knew once she became that runaway bride, there was no going back.

Maybe Sean needed something to hold on to, something to pull him out of his misery. He must’ve turned a corner when he got that tattoo. Now she’d been put here to help him turn another corner.

She followed him closely on the bumper-to-bumper freeway until he put his turn signal on and crawled onto an off-ramp. As she rolled to a stop behind him at the red light, she tapped the display of her phone to call Courtney.

"Hi, Elise. Are you calling because you're going to be late? Because I'm not even home yet."

"I'm going out to dinner, or rather having dinner at a friend's place."

"Turns out I'm going out, too. I'm finally getting together with the guy I met at the Speakeasy."

A shiver ran through Elise. Courtney should be more careful. "What do you know about this guy, Courtney?"

"Uh, he's an investment banker and he's hot."

Elise grimaced. Her experiences over the past few days had made her more street savvy than she'd wanted to be.

"Are you at home yet?"

"No. New client's keeping me busy. Have fun and be careful."

Elise pressed her lips together. She didn't want to tell Courtney about her latest mishap. "You, too."

Ahead of her, Sean's right-turn signal blinked and he swung into the driveway of a small house in a quiet residential neighborhood. He must relish this escape from the big city.

He parked in the driveway and she pulled up to the curb. Tossing his keys in the air, he said, "Miserable traffic."

"This is a nice neighborhood."

"Yeah, my little refuge."

"You need it."

He unlocked his front door and shoved it open for her. "Don't get me wrong. I love my job."

"I know you do. You wouldn't be babysitting me if you didn't."

He tilted his head as he stepped aside, a quizzical look in his dark eyes. "Right."

She stepped into the room and inhaled the scent of cleanliness—furniture polish, bleach, disinfectant.

"It's a good thing my cleaning lady came today." He flipped on a lamp by the door, and it illuminated a masculine room, dark and cozy.

She placed her hands on the back of his couch, smoothing them across the dark brown leather. "Somehow I get the feeling your cleaning lady doesn't have a lot of work to do."

"How much mess can a single guy create?" He spread his arms to encompass the immaculate room.

"You don't know my brothers." She pointed at the kitchen, whose gleaming surfaces were visible even in the darkness. "Do you want me to help with anything?"

"Sure. I'm going to thaw out the steaks and put a couple of potatoes in microwave. I have some fresh asparagus from the local farmers' market. You can wash and trim that."

She saluted. "Got it."

As he covered the steaks on a plate and shoved them into the microwave, Elise ran some cold water over the asparagus spears. "What did they tell you when they dismissed you from the case?"

His fingers paused over the microwave buttons, and then he stabbed them and punched the power. "Said they didn't like killers communicating with detectives, that the killers fed off the high and it could encourage them to commit more murders."

"You obviously don't believe that."

"When a killer communicates with the detective on the case, it tends to yield more clues. There are more chances that he'll slip up, reveal some detail." He grabbed a couple of potatoes from the pantry and slammed the door. "They know that."

"So, it's just you."

"Yeah, it's me. If the killer had chosen anyone else in the department, they'd be all over it."

"Do you think he will?" She took a potato from his hands and held it under the running water. "Replace you with another detective?"

He snorted. "Not a chance. He's fixated on me for some reason—probably because he knows all about my father. He's not exactly a copycat of that killer, but he's close enough. Thinks he's being clever by pulling another Brody into his sick world."

She bit her lip. "No news on anything happening at the bridge today at those coordinates he sent me?"

"No. Those coordinates were for my edification. Who knows what he has planned next, if anything."

He snatched the potato from her, which she'd been scrubbing down to the flesh. "I like a little potato skin on my baked potatoes."

She laughed. "Crime and cooking don't mix."

"Crime and a lot of things don't mix. Let's drop it."

They finished preparing the meal by exchanging small talk, and it almost felt like a normal date. But she'd never dated anyone like Sean Brody before. His intensity always simmered beneath the surface. He ran so hot, he could grill those steaks without the heat.

She stole a glance at his backside, snug in a pair of faded jeans he'd pulled on after shedding his suit. What would it feel like to have all that intensity unleashed in the bedroom?

"Rare or well-done?"

"Huh?" She blinked as he shot her a curious glance over his shoulder.

"Your steak—rare, medium or well-done?"

"I grew up on a cattle ranch. I like mine medium rare and juicy."

His eyes flicked to her chest and back to her face so quickly she might have imagined it. "Juicy, it is."

She dug into his silverware drawer and grabbed a handful of utensils. Had he read her thoughts? Probably just looked at her face, which would forever preclude her from being a professional poker player.

The microwave beeped and he turned from the sizzling steaks. "That's your asparagus. I have some butter over here, unless you prefer something fancier."

"I prefer…butter." She turned and grabbed the bowl of asparagus from the microwave and felt like replacing it with her head. If that's the best she could do at seduction, the only beef she'd get tonight would be that medium-rare steak. She giggled. She'd been hanging around Courtney too long.

"Something funny about the asparagus?"

"Well, there is something inherently funny about the vegetable, isn't there." She plucked a hot spear from the bowl with her fingertips and held it up. "It even looks like a…"

She bit off the end of the asparagus and practically choked on it.

Sean cleared his throat. "Phallic symbol?"

Popping the rest of the spear in her mouth, she nodded. She should've been paying more attention to Courtney over the past year of their friendship. She was pretty sure her friend wouldn't be using asparagus as a tool of seduction.

Sean stabbed the steaks with a long fork and dropped them onto two plates. "I think I got that medium rare. Let me know your expert opinion."

"Actually, I've probably had one steak since hightailing it out of Montana."

"Uh-oh. Is this steak going to bring up bad memories and make you head for the hills?"

"I think I can handle it. Steak sauce?"

"In the fridge."

He stood by his chair until she sat down across from him. "We make a good team…in the kitchen."

She took a gulp of water. She had to get out of dangerous territory. Clutching her fork and steak knife, she said, "I think we make a pretty good investigative team, too. Is there any way we can unseal Dr. Patrick's files now that he's dead?"

Sean didn't seem to mind the shift in topic, and his brow furrowed as he cut into his steak. "That's what's been bothering me, one of many things. If the department knew my father was seeing Dr. Patrick at the time of his…death, I would've thought they'd demand his records."

"Maybe they did."

"But they left everything as unsolved. Those murders are still cold cases. If Dr. Patrick's sessions with my father had proved his innocence or guilt, it would've come out."

"Did you ever ask anyone?"

"I wasn't aware that my father even saw Dr. Patrick until we discussed it this morning." He put down his fork with a piece of meat stuck to the end, a frown still marring his features.

"What is it?"

"Don't you think it's an incredible coincidence that the day I discover Dr. Patrick saw my father, the good doctor winds up dropping dead of a heart attack?"

"Yes, especially since he died at my feet. But what are you saying? A heart attack is a heart attack. Do you think my visit caused his heart attack?" She ran crisscrosses on her plate with her fork.

"Seems like he suffered the attack just before you arrived."

"What's your point, Sean?"

"Heart attacks can be induced."

She dropped her fork. "You think someone killed Dr. Patrick by injecting him with something that caused his heart to fail?"

"It's too coincidental, Elise. It's unbelievable that his death occurred the very day we found him."

"And it's believable that someone killed him? Why would someone want to kill Dr. Patrick before he could tell you anything about your father?"

"I don't know, but I'm going to find out." He picked up his fork and took the piece of steak between his teeth.

"If you don't believe your father had anything to do with those murders twenty years ago and he was never formally charged or convicted, does it really matter anymore? You *are* secure in your beliefs, aren't you?"

He chewed, swallowed, took a sip of water and gazed over her shoulder. Then his eyes tracked back to her face, and she saw the doubt in their depths. "Maybe that's it, Elise."

She had to hunch forward to catch his words, and she caught his hand at the same time. "It's okay to have that uncertainty, Sean. It's not being disloyal. You were a kid at the time."

"I don't want to believe it." He twisted his fingers around hers. "The man who taught me everything, the man I looked up to, couldn't be a cold-blooded killer. He would've had to have been a complete sociopath." Without losing his hold on her hand, he slumped back in his chair. "That's the scary part. I know they exist. I know there are people out there who act just like you and me—who love and laugh and feel pain—but it's all a pretense. They feel nothing at all."

"It's more than just proving your father's innocence to the world. You have to prove it to yourself. I get that."

"How did we get here?" He loosened his grip on her fingers and traced her knuckles with the pad of one finger. "You have a killer sending you notes, launching sneak attacks and you just had a man die at your feet. And you're trying to make me feel better."

"You've done more than enough, more than I ever expected from that moment you sat down next to me in the emergency room. You've been by my side, going beyond the call of duty to protect me." She shrugged her shoulders. "I'm just paying you back."

He lifted one eyebrow. "Is that what you think this is all about? Protection? Securing a witness?"

The pulse in her wrist ticked up several notches. Could he feel it? "I'm the only witness you have right now."

He chuckled in the back of his throat, and the low sound sent a line of tingles racing down to her toes.

"The SFPD is not in the bodyguarding business. We're not going to put you in the Witness Protection Program. It's not like you have the goods on a mobster or anything." He scooted his chair back and tossed his napkin onto the table. "Everything I've done for you has been off the books and off the clock."

She twisted her own napkin in her lap as she tilted her head back to take in his imposing figure. "Why'd you do it?"

"Do you have to ask?" He dropped into a crouch in front of her, like a beast ready to pounce. "You may be a kindergarten teacher from Podunk, Montana, but you're also the runaway bride. You're the woman in my kitchen waving around asparagus and talking about juicy slabs of meat."

She choked. "I…I…"

In one fluid movement, he rose to his full height, catching her under the arms and taking her with him. He supported the back of her head with one hand and pulled her close with an arm wrapped around her waist.

He stared into her face, his lips centimeters from her own, so close she felt the scorching heat of his breath. "I want you, Elise Duran. I've wanted you from the minute I saw you bundled up in that hospital bed, and I can't even explain it."

Her breath came out in short spurts. "Maybe I'm your redemption, the means of redressing your father's sins."

"If redemption feels this good—" he ran a slow hand down the beads of her spine and rested it on the curve of her hip "—I should've gone in for it years ago."

Her lashes fluttered and she parted her lips. If he released her now, she'd fall to the floor.

"Now stop." He kissed her temple. "Talking." He kissed her left eyelid. "About." He kissed her earlobe. "My father." His lips trailed across her throat, and his tongue circled the indentation below her Adam's apple.

She slid her hands beneath his T-shirt and caressed the muscles of his back. Goose bumps raced across his smooth skin in response to her touch.

He nibbled her collarbone, sweeping the hair from her neck. His lips followed along its curve while he hooked a finger beneath her bra strap and top to bare her shoulder. "Your skin is so soft, like the petal of a rose."

She'd imagined making love to Sean many times in the past few days, but she never expected poetry from him.

Her head dropped to the side, and her legs trembled. A very soft sigh escaped from her lips.

He growled in her ear. "I'm not going to take you here among the asparagus."

He was going to *take* her? Before she could process that thought, he swept her off her feet. "Allow me to show you the rest of the house, or at least the most important room."

"You mean the kitchen isn't the most important room in the house?" She dug her fingers into his thick dark hair.

"Only for asparagus."

She buried her face in his warm neck as he carried her to the back of the house. He bumped open a door and she balanced her chin on his shoulder to take in the view. The large bed, low to the floor, dominated the room with black lacquer pieces lining the walls.

He put her down on the throw rug by the side of the bed, and she placed one foot on the mattress. "At least you don't have to worry about falling out of this thing."

"It's a Japanese-style bed frame. Do you want to analyze my furniture or finish what we started?"

She curled her fingers in the belt loops of his jeans and tugged him toward her. "I have an idea. Let's analyze the furniture first, starting with the bed."

Encircling his hands around her waist, he bent his knees and brought her down with him until they were kneeling face-to-face, the low mattress behind her. He dropped his hands and cupped her derriere beneath her thin skirt.

His kiss cut off her breath and sent her heart racing. Everything about him had seemed so hard, but his lips felt soft and supple. His tongue traced the seam of her mouth and she opened it to the demanding pressure.

One hand had bunched up her skirt and she gasped when his rough hand brushed across the silky material of her panties, catching the soft material on the pads of his fingers.

He nudged her down on the bed, and the mattress conformed to her weight and then his as he stretched out beside her. He lifted her blouse, pulling it over her head. He followed the edge of her lacy bra with the tip of his tongue.

Thank goodness she'd donned some good underwear this morning before she'd left for school—about twelve hours ago. Before she'd been chasing kindergartners on the playground and finger-painting with them. Before some stranger died in her lap.

"Wait." She struggled up, propping herself up on her elbows.

His eyes popped open. "You're not going to run, are you?"

She rolled off the bed. "I'd like to take a shower, if that's okay."

"That's fine." With a deft touch, he reached behind her and unzipped her skirt. "But don't think I'm letting you go in there alone."

"Of course not." She gulped, and when she got up from the bed, she left her skirt behind her.

Sean peeled off his shirt and tossed it over his shoulder. When he stood up, he touched a finger to her nose. "You have the best ideas."

She drank in what he'd been hiding under his button-up shirts and tailored jackets. His tattoo snaked up his arm, curling around his biceps. Slabs of hard muscle shifted across his broad chest as he reached down to unbutton his fly.

She swallowed and held her breath. Her friends in Montana had warned her that all she'd find in San Francisco was citified metrosexuals. If they could see her now—or rather see Sean.

Not wanting to appear greedy, her gaze returned to his face as he peeled his jeans from his hips. A quick glance downward confirmed he'd shed his briefs along with his jeans.

He reached out and pulled her against his naked body. She closed her eyes and let out a long breath.

"Why are you still wearing so many clothes?" His fingers fumbled with her bra, and in a matter of seconds they were skin to skin, their bodies meeting along every line.

"That's better." He kissed her mouth and then left her lips throbbing and wanting as he pressed kisses along her throat. Every spot he touched seemed to alight in fire.

She choked out, "Shower."

Taking her hand, he led her to the attached bathroom and cranked on the water in the tiled shower. Water streamed from two showerheads.

She stepped into the warm spray and he joined her. He squirted some liquid soap in the palm of his hand and rubbed his hands together. "Now, what is it that needs washing so much that you had to interrupt my flow in the bedroom?"

She dragged her gaze away from the water sluicing over the planes of his body. "Everywhere."

"I was hoping you'd say that." He flashed her a grin that had her groping for the shower wall for support.

His warm hands, slick with soap, started at her shoulders and quickly descended to her breasts, where he circled her nipples, teasing and provoking them.

His palms rubbed her belly, and she couldn't help the moan that escaped her lips.

"Turn around." His hands cinched her waist and he spun her around toward the bench that extended from the shower wall.

He shifted his attention from her stomach to her inner thighs, and she parted her legs as the spray of water hit her shoulder.

He nudged her from behind, urging her to bend over, his erection spearing her lower back.

She placed her palms flat on the bench beaded with water.

Sean cupped one hand between her legs, and her hips automatically swiveled. She panted. "I thought this was supposed to be a shower."

"And I'm very thorough in my cleaning. Don't want to miss one little spot." His soapy fingers caressed her flesh, and her arms began to shake.

He moved rhythmically against her, his hard, tight erection probing between her open legs. His magic fingers continued their exploration of her throbbing folds. When he entered her with first one finger and then a second, she closed around him.

He cupped her breast, pinching her nipple, and then his

teeth nipped the back of her neck. The contrasting sensations overwhelmed her senses and she exploded.

As she rode the wave of her release, he plunged into her from behind. He was delivering all the intensity that had been simmering beneath the surface. She'd wondered what it would be like unleashed, and now she knew. Overwhelming.

Every time he entered her, he took her to some new height, some realm inhabited by just the two of them. When he pulled out, she felt moments of pure desolation.

He reached between her legs again, and his touch was so electrifying she screamed. Within seconds her muscles tensed and she clenched her jaw. She was almost afraid of the power that gathered within her.

The gentleness of his touch contrasted with the force of his thrusts inside her, and once again she broke. The pleasure that flooded her body melted her and she sobbed, pressing her wet face against her arm.

He whispered her name over and over and it echoed in the shower, surrounding her as he surrounded her. He pounded against her, skin on skin, and when his climax came, it engulfed both of them in its ferocity.

No moaning, groaning or grunting for Sean. He howled. And the sound of his passion, of his possession of her, sent a thrill to her core.

When he spent himself inside her, he covered her with his body. His legs twined around hers, his arms wrapped around her torso, his chest and belly were sealed against her back to the juncture where their bodies remained connected in the most intimate way.

The lukewarm water beat against their entwined forms as they gasped for breath. Slowly, he peeled away from her and slipped out of her. She felt the loss of him in the pit of her stomach, so she straightened and turned in one movement and clung to his chest.

He smoothed the damp hair from her face. "I'm sorry. Did I hurt you? I couldn't…couldn't help myself."

Then she realized tears, not just water, were coursing down her cheeks.

She nuzzled against his chest, the sprinkling of dark hair ticking her nose. "You have nothing to be sorry about. You just took me somewhere, someplace—" she dug her fingernails in his firm buttocks "—I don't know."

He chuckled and wedged a knuckle beneath her chin, tilting her head back. "Would it be too cliché to say 'paradise'?"

"You felt it, too?" She rubbed the water from her eyes.

"You're kidding, right?" He cupped her face in his hands. "Do you think it's every day I howl at the moon during sex?"

The happiness that welled in her chest overcame her, and tears sprang to her eyes again.

He kissed one of her eyelids. "If you keep crying, I'm going to think I'm a brute."

She slapped his chest with her hand. "Are you kidding? Do you think it's every day I break down and cry during sex?"

The smile dropped from his face, and his dark eyes kindled. "It was special, wasn't it? I don't generally go in for the mushy stuff, but you make me feel…mushy."

Her fingers traced the ridges of his pecs. "You don't feel mushy at all."

"You just ruined my mushy moment." He smacked her backside. "Let's get out of here before we both look like prunes."

Sean tucked a towel around his waist and padded out of the bathroom, returning with a fresh towel for her.

He held it out for her as she stepped from the shower. "You do realize that if I towel you off, it's going to ignite that fire down below all over again."

She fluttered her lashes. “Is that a threat or a promise?”

He wrapped the towel around her body. “You do have school tomorrow, right? You don’t want to come in with a sex hangover.”

“I don’t know.” She dropped the towel. “Is that the kind of hangover that can be cured with the hair of the dog?”

Sean made a move but stopped when his cell phone rang in the bedroom. “Oops, that’s my work phone. I’d better pick that up, but hold that thought.”

She gathered her towel from the floor and followed him into the bedroom. He was right. She had to get it together and return to Courtney’s to get ready for school. They’d have another chance to be together. Wouldn’t they?

Despite being half-naked, Sean had already morphed back into the dedicated cop with the phone call. He sat on the edge of the bed, the cell pressed to his ear, his face creased into lines of worry. “Uh-huh. Uh-huh. Do you think I asked him to contact me? Do you think I want it?”

A sick feeling twisted her gut, and she edged out of the bedroom, tucking a corner of the towel in the edge at her chest. She couldn’t take any more, not after what they’d just shared. She wasn’t ready to crash to earth just yet.

She wandered into the kitchen and collected the plates from the table while Sean’s voice rumbled from the other room. As she ran water over the dishes, someone pounded on Sean’s front door.

She dropped the silverware in the sink with a clatter and grabbed a dish towel, twisting it in front of her on the way to the door.

Sean stalked out of the bedroom, clutching his phone in his fist. “Who the hell is that?”

Elise reached the door before he did and peered through the peephole. Her heart galloped in her chest as she fumbled with the dead bolt.

“Wait, Elise. What are you doing?”

"It's Ty." She yanked at the door. "And he's hurt."

"What?"

She got the door open and Ty stumbled into the room, his face battered and pale, a white T-shirt, seeping blood, wrapped thickly around one hand.

She caught him in midstagger and he almost took her down. "Ty, what is it? What happened to you?"

He raised the hand swaddled in the bloody T-shirt and aimed it at Sean. "He happened to me. His henchman attacked me, and then the SOB chopped off my finger. He took my finger."

Ty collapsed face-first on the floor.

Chapter Fourteen

Elise's face took on a shade of green as she swayed over Ty collapsed at her feet.

Sean didn't need two unconscious people on his floor. He took Elise's arm and led her to a chair. "Sit."

Crouching over Ty, he punched in 9-1-1 on the phone still clutched in his hand. He unwound the stained T-shirt from Ty's hand and swore at the bloody mess. He'd been telling the truth about one thing—someone had hacked off his left ring finger.

Why had the idiot come here instead of calling 9-1-1 or driving himself to an emergency room?

"I-is he okay?"

"Passed out from a loss of blood."

"His finger?"

"Gone."

"Oh, my God. Oh, my God." Elise bounded from the chair, but Sean held out his hand.

"Sit down, Elise. There's nothing you can do for him. The ambulance is on its way."

She plopped back down on the chair, knotting her fingers. "Why? What happened? Who did this?"

Given Ty's missing finger, Sean had a clue but Elise didn't need to hear it right now. "If you want to help, bring me a clean dish towel from the kitchen…and my pants."

She looked down at her own towel slipping from her body and jumped up once again. She headed into the kitchen first and returned to the living room, tossing a terry-cloth towel at him. While he loosened the T-shirt from Ty's hand and replaced it with the towel, binding it tightly around the gaping wound, Elise disappeared down the hallway.

Back in her skirt and sweater, she dropped his jeans beside him. He looked up. "If you're feeling up to it, can you hold this towel in place for a few seconds?"

Nodding, she curled her legs beneath her and sat next to Ty.

Sean placed her hands around the towel. "Squeeze as hard as you can."

He yanked on his jeans and tossed the bath towel aside. He squatted next to her and nudged her hands away from the makeshift bandage staunching the flow of Ty's blood.

She slumped back, her hands falling in her lap. "Why did this happen, Sean? This can't be a coincidence."

"I don't think it is." She'd realize just how unlikely a coincidence if she found out about Katie Duncan's finger.

Sirens wailed down the street. "Can you go outside and meet them? I phoned it in, but tell them he lost a finger and a lot of blood."

Elise scrambled outside, and minutes later the EMTs bustled through the front door with a gurney. They peppered Sean with questions as they loaded up Ty.

As they wheeled Ty to the ambulance, one of the EMTs called over his shoulder, "Do you know where the finger is?"

"Nope. Like I said, it didn't happen here." But if Sean could guess, it might be arriving in a package for him soon.

Officer Ashford, the cop who had been quietly talking to Elise, emerged onto the porch. "Can I ask you a few questions, Detective Brody?"

"Of course. Here? Back inside?"

"Here is fine." He jerked his pencil over his shoulder. "Ms. Duran said the victim blamed you for his attack, said you hired someone to assault him."

"Yeah, he did say that. I don't know why he believes that. He passed out before we could question him."

"What do you know about Ty Russell?"

"He's Elise's former fiancé, and he's here to convince her to go back to Montana with him. That's about it."

"And you and Elise are…friendly." Ashford's eyes flicked across Sean's bare chest.

His jaw clenched. "Yes."

Ashford tapped his pencil and licked his lips. "Elise Duran is the first victim of the Alphabet Killer. The case you just got pulled from."

"Yep." Sean folded his arms. If this pip-squeak patrolman thought he could intimidate him with his leading questions, he needed to go back to the academy.

"You haven't been too busy to know he struck again, have you?"

Elise gasped behind him. "Sean?"

"Captain Williams notified me just before Russell showed up on my doorstep." Out of the corner of his eye, he could see Elise creeping closer to him until he could feel the warmth of her presence on his skin.

The cop's face fell a little. Then he puffed out his chest again. "The two victims have last names beginning with C."

"Well, then I guess he's working backward through the alphabet, isn't he?"

"Those victims were also missing their fingers."

Elise sobbed behind him, and Sean lunged for the cop, grabbing the shirt of his uniform. He breathed heavily in Ashford's startled face. "You need to go back to school, son. That's privileged information about this case. We're not revealing that to the public."

Ashford wriggled out of Sean's grasp and stumbled backward off the porch. His face reddened and he blustered, "I'm reporting you, Brody. I may even have you arrested for assaulting a police officer. You detectives think you're something special. You're special, all right. You're neck deep with the Alphabet Killer. Hell, you may even *be* him. A killer—just like your old man."

Sean's eye twitched and his muscles coiled. He felt Elise's warm hand pressed against the small of his back.

He tilted his head back and forth to crack his neck, and then he said, "Whatever."

Turning his back on Ashford, his mouth still gaping, Sean took Elise's arm and pulled her into the house.

"Don't listen to him, Sean." She wrapped her arms around his waist, and his house never felt like such a home before.

He squeezed her tight. "What he says doesn't bother me. What bothers me is that the killer tracked down Ty, and we have two more dead bodies."

"It's awful." She hid her face against his chest. "Two people killed today on six, twelve. Wh-where were their bodies found?"

"Not on the Golden Gate Bridge, so those coordinates were just a tease. The bodies were found in the Bayview area."

"You were right. He was just toying with us." She leaned back to look into his face. "Who were they, Sean? Did Captain Williams tell you their names?"

"A man and a woman this time."

She closed her eyes and her lashes fluttered on her cheeks. "Was that cop right? Were their fingers missing?"

"Just like Katie Duncan's."

"You never told me that." Her nostrils flared as her eyes flew open.

"That was supposed to be confidential information. How that moron found out and why he's spreading it around, I don't have a clue. I'm no longer on the case, as he pointed out."

"Then why did Captain Williams call you at this time of night to tell you about the bodies?"

He left the circle of her arms and paced to the window to stare out at the dark street. "Because the killer left me another message."

"What was it this time?" She pressed her fingers against her lips.

"Elise…"

"Just tell me, Sean."

"He left me the same type of note that he left you at the school, but with slightly different numbers. They're working on it, but the location was a joke last time so we can't trust him."

Two vertical lines formed between her eyebrows. "Where did they find the note?"

He clasped the back of his neck and chewed on his lip. Did Elise really need the visual of a note wrapped around a severed finger and shoved into one of the victim's pockets? "He left a note on one of the bodies."

"What does he want with you?"

"I already know that. The bigger question is what does he want from you?" He tapped on the window with his fingernail. "How did he know about Ty? How did he know about you and me, about our spending time together?"

She knotted her fingers together. "I don't know. He didn't get all that from my purse, or from my house. He must've been the one who attacked Ty. He probably told Ty he was working for you. Where else would Ty get that crazy idea?"

"When Ty regains consciousness, we can ask him. Maybe he can give us a description. How did the guy even approach Ty?"

"It's like he's dancing around me, us. He's playing some kind of game with us that started the night he attacked me."

"And that game has its roots in the past, twenty years in the past." Sean blew out a breath, crossed the room and took Elise's hand. "I'm sorry the night had to end this way. I'm sorry about Ty."

"Me, too," she whispered, and tears welled in her eyes. "For a moment there we pushed it all away, didn't we? For a moment it was just the two of us."

He kissed her trembling lips. "It can be that way again, Elise. This will all be over soon."

She nodded, her eyes widening, and he had a feeling he'd just made a promise he wasn't sure he could keep. Would it ever be over for him? In his gut, he knew it would never be over until he found out what happened twenty years ago in this city.

He stroked her hair back from her face. "I'm going to get a shirt on and see you back home. You still have two more days of school to get through, right?"

"You don't have to follow me back. I'll head straight to Courtney's place and drive right into the garage. It's a secure building. I'll be fine."

He walked into the bedroom and pulled a clean T-shirt from his closet. Yanking it over his head, he returned to the living room and said, "I'm not comfortable with you driving alone at night. It's late."

He scratched the stubble of his beard. This whole incident with Ty Russell had spooked him. How the hell had the killer gotten a line on Ty?

As far as he knew, the only time Elise had seen Ty since he'd been in the city was the day he swooped down on her in front of Courtney's place. He hadn't seen his name in her phone contacts, and he doubted Elise had anything in her house with Ty's name on it.

"Well, I guess I could always use a police escort. I'm obviously not very good about noticing a tail since the Alphabet Killer managed to follow me from the Golden Gate to Chinatown that day."

"He did, didn't he?" The coil in his gut wound tighter. "You said you were careful that day."

"Absolutely, and then when I got close to Chinatown, it was such a big mess because of the parade I had to take a million detours. For each turn I made, I checked my rearview mirror. I even drove down a couple of little alleys—nothing."

"Elise, how many times did you see Ty since he came here?"

"Twice—once on the sidewalk in front of Courtney's place and just now." She combed her fingers through her hair. "Why are you asking? I certainly never told him anything about you or where you lived. I didn't even know where you lived until I followed you here tonight."

"You followed me here tonight." He dug his fingers in his hair.

"Um, yeah."

"There's only one way your stalker could've known about Ty."

"My stalker?"

"He saw him at Courtney's place—with you, with me."

Her head cranked back and forth. "No. That can't be. He doesn't know Courtney. He doesn't know where Courtney lives. How could he? He couldn't be that good, to be able to follow me around the city when I'm on the lookout for him. No way."

"He's not physically following you, Elise. He's tracking you." He barreled toward the coat closet by the front door and reached for the shelf for a flashlight.

"Tracking me? How?"

When he turned with the flashlight in his hand, he almost knocked her over.

Her eyes took up half her face as she grabbed his arm. "How is he tracking me?"

"I have a hunch." He threw open the front door with Elise hot on his heels. "Your car was parked in your garage when he broke in after the attack."

"My car… Yeah." She hooked her fingers in his belt loop. "Oh, God, you can't mean he put something on my car."

"That's exactly what I mean." He nudged her shoulder. "Pull it into the driveway next to mine so we can get it into the light."

Elise dashed to her car as Sean juggled the flashlight from hand to hand. If the killer had put some kind of tracking device on Elise's little hybrid, it would explain so much. It also meant he knew where she was staying and he knew she was here—right now.

His gaze scanned the street of empty cars parked at the curb. One car idled in the driveway, but that one belonged to his neighbor's teenage son who raced up and down the street daily.

Elise parked and exited her vehicle. "Where would he put something like that? Inside the car?"

"Most likely attached to the undercarriage of the chassis." He handed her the flashlight. "Hold this."

He dropped to his hands and knees, rolled onto his back and scooted under the front of the car. His nostrils flared at the smell of oil and gasoline, strong even for a hybrid. He thrust out his arm and wiggled his fingers. "Flashlight."

"Flashlight." Elise smacked it against his palm as if they were performing surgery.

He trailed the beam along the wheel wells and the undercarriage. He knew a bit about cars, and he didn't see anything amiss.

Maybe his instincts were off this time.

He shoved out from beneath the car and walked on his knees to the back. He ducked beneath the vehicle and swept the light back and forth. Rolling to one side, he aimed the beam at the wheel well.

"Bingo."

"What? You found something?" Elise's voice had risen to a frantic pitch.

He wrapped his fingers around the black box and yanked it from the metal, breaking the magnetic force. Gathering his legs beneath him, he rose to a crouch and cradled the device in the palm of his hand.

As Elise drew closer, he illuminated it with the flashlight.

"What is it?"

"It's a GPS tracking device."

She gasped and fell back on her hands. "It's been there since the night of the attack. He's been following me, tracking my every move. That's how he followed me to Chinatown. That's how he knew about my school. That's how he found out about Ty."

"It should've occurred to me sooner."

"That some killer would just happen to have a GPS tracking device handy?"

"He's a clever SOB."

"Sean!" She tugged on his arm, nearly toppling him over. "We have to warn Courtney. He knows where she lives, knows I'm staying there."

"Not anymore you're not. Give Courtney a call. You're staying here tonight, and I'll take you back to her place early tomorrow morning so you can get your things and get to school."

She jabbed her finger at the tracking device. "What are we going to do with this thing?"

"Oh, I have a plan. If the Alphabet Killer likes games, I've got a good one for him."

THE SOUND OF the alarm grated against her eardrums, and Elise sighed and snuggled closer to Sean's warm, smooth back.

She didn't want to move, didn't want to face the harsh world outside. But the alarm was insistent.

Sean growled and threw out an arm, his hand groping for the clock on the nightstand. With one well-aimed smack, he ended the sound that had intruded on Elise's sweet dreams.

She yawned and dug her chin into his shoulder. "You can't wake up to soothing music or wind chimes?"

"Those sounds would never wake me up. I have a hard enough time with that obnoxious noise blaring in my ear."

Elise squinted at the green numbers floating in the dark room. "Ugh, I haven't seen five o'clock a.m. since—since a maniac tried to kill me five days ago."

Sean swiveled around, twisting the covers in his legs, and pulled her against his chest. He kissed the top of her head. "He can't continue at this pace. You don't murder two people and dump their bodies in an alley without leaving a trail of clues."

She burrowed deeper into his arms and inhaled his scent. She wanted to bottle it and take it with her everywhere.

"Are you going to have to answer some questions about Ty today?"

"Of course, but I doubt my supervisors are going to believe I hired someone to mess up your ex-fiancé and then had my hit man tell him it was me."

He stroked her back and she almost purred. They hadn't made love last night after they'd discovered the GPS, but he'd held her all night long and that was almost as good.

"I want to be in on the questioning of Ty, so I hope they grant me that privilege since the guy accused me of chopping off his finger."

Her gut rolled. "I can't even think about that without feeling ill. Ty is going to be devastated when he wakes up and it all comes back to him."

"Ty should be thankful he's alive. I'm sure Katie Duncan wouldn't mind waking up about now missing one digit."

"You're right." She smoothed her hand down his arm, across his tattoo. "He has no idea how close he came to dying."

"We'd better get moving if we hope to collect your stuff from Courtney's and get you to school." He rolled away from her and planted his feet on the carpet. "She's checking into a hotel today, right? I think that's best right now."

"Yes. That girl has money to burn. She'll probably book a suite in some fancy hotel and live it up."

"When is she going back to pack up?"

"Well, since she spent the night with her new man, I think he's going to take her back."

"Have you met this new man of hers?"

"I met him briefly that night at the Speakeasy. He bought us a couple of drinks." She tumbled out of bed and shot him a quick glance. "You don't suspect him, do you?"

"Just covering all bases here."

"Derrick is African-American. I don't think he's the Alphabet Killer."

"Okay, okay. Does this Derrick look like he can handle himself in a fight?"

She hugged her sweater to her body. "Really? You think it's going to come to that? The killer probably doesn't even know who Courtney is."

"Can he?"

"He looks like he could've played football in college."

"Good." He pointed to the bathroom door. "I'm going to hit the shower first because I'll be quick about it."

She longed to hit the shower with him again, but there was no going back to that moment last night. But they'd have other moments—so he said.

An hour later, they stepped outside into the damp, misty air.

Sean tilted his head back. “June gloom is in full swing.”

“Yeah, I pity all those tourists who come out here expecting a sunny California day.”

“Spoken like a true San Franciscan native.” He tossed the GPS device in the air and then clamped it back under her car.

“So what is your plan? You’re just going to let him continue following me around?”

“You’ll see. First stop, Courtney’s condo.”

Elise drove back into the city, and the tracker on her car made her feel exposed and vulnerable. She hated that. Only Sean’s presence behind her made it bearable.

While Sean waited by the front door of Courtney’s condo with his arms crossed, daring anyone to cross the threshold, Elise buzzed around the spare room and bathroom, tossing her stuff into her suitcase.

Joining Sean at the entrance, she took a last look around the immaculate downstairs. “If Courtney’s homeowners’ association was mad about the garlic, just wait until those fine folks discover she invited a killer to their complex.”

Sean loaded her suitcase into the back of her car. “You follow me now. We’re going to take a little detour. You have plenty of time to get to school, right?”

“Uh-huh. It’s an easy day today. We’re taking the kids over to the first-grade rooms to have a look around, and they get to wear their PJs to school and look at their favorite books all day.”

“Wish I could wear my PJs to work and read my favorite books all day.”

“I’d like to see that. What kind of PJs do you have, dinosaurs?”

He winked. “My PJs are my birthday suit, and you’ve already seen that.”

“You’re in enough trouble with the department. Don’t

give them any more ammunition." Elise slid into her car and idled while Sean revved the engine of his Crown Vic.

She followed him across the city in the opposite direction of the Bay Bridge, hoping he didn't plan to take her too far afield.

Her cell buzzed and she answered and tapped the phone for the speaker, without checking the display. "Hello?"

"It's Courtney. Did you get your stuff?"

"I just picked it up. Aren't you the early bird?"

"I want to get home, pack a few suitcases and get the hell out of there. How long has this maniac been watching my place?"

"I'm so sorry, Courtney."

"I'm not blaming you. Hey, it gives me an excuse to get pampered at a hotel for a week or eight. When is your cop going to nail this guy?"

"Soon. Is Derrick going with you?"

"Oh, yeah. That's one silver lining. I get to play the little delicate flower in distress."

Elise snorted. "Yeah, that description fits you to a T."

"Derrick's digging it, so who am I to disappoint him?"

"I can't imagine you disappointing any man."

"Watch it. Don't believe everything you see on YouTube."

Elise laughed. "Take care. I'll touch base with you later. Are you working late?"

"Yes. New clients are running me ragged, but I can't complain. Business is good. One of the new guys said he chose me because of my name."

"Is he Asian?"

"No, but he had an Asian girlfriend, a hand model. He's probably projecting, but it gives us a lot to work with."

"Okay, you take care and let Derrick be the big, strong man."

"Mmm, he is."

Smiling, Elise ended the call and then gulped as Sean made a turn onto the road leading to the Golden Gate Bridge. Why the heck did he want to come here?

He pulled into the fog-shrouded parking lot and rolled into one of the many empty slots.

Elise parked beside him and jumped from the car as he was getting out of his.

"Are you crazy? What are we doing here?"

He put his finger to his lips and strode to her car. He ducked under her car and pulled the GPS from the wheel well. "Follow me and get that jacket out of your car."

Elise snagged a jacket from the backseat and shoved her arms in the sleeves.

They trudged up the path to the pedestrian gate on the bridge. Cars rumbled back and forth across the expanse on their morning commute. A few scattered pedestrians and cyclists dotted the walkway.

"Sean."

He turned toward her and zipped up her jacket to her chin. "Keep up."

They stepped onto the sidewalk on the east side of the bridge, the only side that allowed pedestrians.

Sean took a deep breath. "It's beautiful, isn't it? Even engulfed in fog, it's majestic, mysterious."

"I told you. It mesmerized me from the moment I saw it."

"We used to cross it a lot on foot. My younger brother Ryan used to look over the guardrail and insist he could do a pencil dive and just slice through the water."

She reached for his hand and laced her fingers with his.

Before reaching the midpoint, Sean stopped and faced the water. He plunged his hand in his pocket and pulled out the GPS. He stretched his arm back and flung the black box over the guardrail and into the bay. "Let that SOB track that."

A sharp breeze stirred up the mist, and the moisture caressed her face. "Why here, Sean? Why this spot?"

He gazed out toward Alcatraz, his face a mask. "Because this is where he did it. This is where my father jumped."

Chapter Fifteen

Elise eyed the big clock on the wall as she read the last few lines of the story of Ferdinand the bull, who liked to smell flowers all day. What a life.

Ty was recuperating in the hospital and was demanding to see her. This was one of Ty's demands she was only too happy to oblige.

The bell rang while she and her students were dragging the beanbags and pillows back into the corners of the room. "Last day of school tomorrow. Bring your best smiles for the party and get ready for first grade."

She waved and smiled until her cheeks hurt, and then she packed up her bag.

Viola's husband stopped by, wedging his shoulder against the doorjamb. "You doing okay, Elise?"

"I'm fine. Just wrapping up."

"I heard about the two murders. The boys down in homicide getting any closer to nailing this guy?"

"I hope so." She turned off her classroom light and joined him at the door. "Are you looking forward to going to Alabama?"

He rolled his eyes. "Not at all. I'll walk you to your car since Vi's talking with a parent right now."

She tossed her bag in the backseat and hung on the door of her car. "Thanks for the escort."

"You bet. Take care and tell those boys in SFPD to call us in if they need any help."

"I'm sure they'd take that in the spirit it was meant."

He grinned as she slipped onto the driver's seat and shut the door.

She raced back across the bridge into the city. She'd see Ty alone, but Sean had promised to meet her at the hospital. He hadn't been in on the questioning of Ty, but he'd heard through certain channels that Ty had retracted his accusation against him.

At least his department didn't believe Sean was capable of that.

She pulled into the parking structure of the hospital—the same one where she'd met Sean less than a week ago, although it seemed like an eternity. How had they gotten so close so fast?

For some reason, the killer had targeted them both and that had given them some sort of shared purpose. Would that connection end when the killings did? She didn't want to be bound to Sean through some sick individual's obsession.

She joined a group in the elevator and rode up to the lobby of the hospital. From there she took another elevator to the fourth floor and checked in with the nurses' station.

"I'm here to see Ty Russell. Elise Duran."

The nurse at the desk tapped a few keys on the keyboard and nodded. "Four fifteen, down the hall to your right."

Elise thanked her and made her way down the antiseptic-smelling corridor, her running shoes squeaking on the shiny floor. When she reached Ty's room, she peered through the glass at him reclining on the hospital bed, watching TV.

She rapped one knuckle against the window, and his head jerked up. He beckoned to her with his right hand—the unbandaged one.

Lifting the door handle, she pushed through with her hip. "How are you, Ty? You look a lot better. Got your color back."

"I'm just great." He lifted his heavily bandaged left hand. "Except I'm missing my finger."

"I'm so sorry. That must've been horribly painful, but why in the world did you head to Sean—Detective Brody's house instead of the emergency room?"

"I don't know." He muted the TV. "I was in shock. I was in a rage."

"You couldn't possibly have believed that Detective Brody would send someone after you and that person would then reveal who hired him."

"I guess it's pretty stupid now that I think about it."

"Were you able to give the police a description?"

"Didn't the detective tell you? The man that attacked me was wearing a black ski mask over his face, and a bulky jacket. He was shorter than me and a lot heavier. If he hadn't ambushed me, I could've taken him."

"I feel terrible that you got all mixed up in this. You should've never come out here."

"Really, Elise? When your landlord, Oscar, called me and told me what had happened, how could I *not* come out?"

She sighed and wound a strand of hair around her finger. "Ty, I'm not your concern anymore."

"Are you worried about the finger? It's just my ring finger. I can't wear a wedding ring on the hand, but at least it's not my index finger or thumb."

"The finger—that means nothing, but I can't believe you're talking to me about wedding rings. If we were so great together, you never would've cheated. It's over between us, Ty."

"It's that cop."

"It is not that cop. How many times have I told you

this past year that I had moved on?" She patted his knee beneath the sheet. "You should, too. Give it a try with Gina. You must've seen something in her to risk our engagement."

His mouth dropped open. "Gina? She's a waitress at the Cozy Café."

She raised her eyes to the ceiling, remembering all over again why she'd had her doubts about him. "I can't help you there, Ty."

She snatched her hand back and rubbed it against her jeans. "I'm curious and you've probably already told the police, but how did you get Sean's address?"

"He gave it to me." Ty studied his bandaged hand. "The Alphabet Killer gave it to me."

A chill zigzagged down her spine. "Go home, Ty. Go back to Montana."

They chatted a bit more about home until Ty's pain meds kicked in and his eyelids began to droop and his words began to slur.

Elise tiptoed out of the room and practically ran into Sean coming around the corner at the nurses' station.

Grabbing her shoulders to steady her, he said, "I was hoping to run into you."

"And you did—literally."

"You look washed out, although it could just be the lighting. Are you okay? Did Ty give you a hard time?"

"Not really. He started the conversation still believing there was a chance that I'd go back to Montana with him, but I think he's getting the picture now."

"He's probably halfway in shock. That was a nasty business, and he was just in the wrong place at the wrong time."

"You know the killer gave him your address?"

"The detective questioning him told me."

"Do you think he knew your address before he tracked my car there?"

"Probably." He tapped her head. "Don't get it into this thick skull of yours that you led him to my place."

"Was there any evidence with the bodies?"

He cupped her elbow. "Let's get something to drink in the cafeteria. We can't talk here, and I'm not even supposed to be hanging around Ty's room. I'm off the case, remember?"

They took the elevator down to the lobby and crossed to the other side of the building to the hospital cafeteria. They both filled up sodas from a self-serve machine and snagged a table in the back of the noisy room filled with clattering plastic trays and hushed conversations.

"So, what do you know?"

Sean took a long sip from his straw. "Only what I got from Curtis. It's a lot different when you're not on the scene."

"I can't believe they're keeping you away. You know more about this case than anyone."

"If anything, they were justified in their actions today when Ray Lopez showed up and started wondering aloud why the lead detective wasn't at the crime scene."

"How did Lopez even know it was the work of the Alphabet Killer?"

"He didn't. Just fishing." He jiggled the ice in his cup and tilted it toward the soda machines. "I'm getting a refill. How about you?"

"Diet."

He returned with the cups topped off.

"Sean, was that cop last night right? Did the victims both have names that started with the letter C?"

"Yes. They were a married couple."

She bit down on her knuckle. "That's awful. Wh-where are their fingers?"

"I'm not discussing this with you, Elise. You don't need

to know the details, and don't get all in my face and tell me you have a right to know. I'm not falling for that."

"I'm not going to play that card." She folded her hands on the table in front of her. "But I would like to know what was in the note. That can't be too gory, can it?"

"The note." He plucked a napkin from the metal dispenser and lifted a pen from his pocket. He scribbled as he spoke. "Fifty-one plus fifty equals 187. Forty-two plus fifty-eight equals 187."

Elise cocked her head. "Makes no sense at all."

"He's just yanking our chain."

"Have you tried to decipher it yet?"

"Haven't given it a lot of thought. It's not my case, remember?"

"Even though he sent the note to you?"

"It's not like I can run around and investigate the case on my own. I'm not like my brother Judd."

"What does your brother Judd do?"

"He's a P.I., a private investigator. He follows a different drummer. He could never report to anyone. He's a rebel who distrusts authority."

"Where does he come in the line of Brody brothers?"

"He's my youngest brother."

"That makes sense. He probably remembers your father the least and has the most flimsy connection to him. Sounds like he might have grown up distrusting authority."

"Wow, are you picking up tips from Courtney or something?"

She stirred her ice with her straw. "Some things don't take a degree in psychology. They're just obvious."

"Well, you're probably right about Judd. He doesn't see what the big deal is. He can almost accept that his father was a serial killer and move on."

"But you can't."

"Never."

"He didn't know him like you did. How old was he when your father jumped?"

"He was six years old."

"A baby, like my kids."

"Yeah, he missed Dad and would cry himself to sleep when he was gone, but he didn't really understand what was going on."

"Reminds me a lot of my kids. So many of them come from broken homes or they never knew their fathers, and their moms are busy supporting the family. In many ways, it's just best if they move on, find another father figure."

"That's what Judd did. He's a carefree SOB. Wish I could be more like him."

She traced the grooves of his knuckles. "You were the oldest. You were his father figure, and you couldn't afford to be carefree."

"Not then, but maybe I should move on, too." He crossed an ankle over his knee. "Is Ty going home?"

"As soon as the hospital releases him. I think he's had enough of San Francisco."

"I'm sorry he got caught up in this." He turned his hand over and captured her fingers. "It's interesting that the killer has taken the index fingers of all his victims, but he chopped off Ty's ring finger. Do you think that has some significance?"

She tapped her cup. "Funny you should bring that up. Ty was talking about how he couldn't wear a wedding ring anymore. It's almost like the Alphabet Killer knew about our situation, almost like he was protecting me from Ty."

Sean slapped his palm against the table. "I'm glad you see that, too. That's exactly what I was thinking. He seems to have fixated on you, Elise."

She hunched her shoulders. "I don't want him fixated on me."

"Of course not, but in a way it makes me feel better. I

don't think he's going to hurt you. It's almost as if once you escaped from him, he developed some respect for you and is putting on a show just for you."

"Yuck. I wish he'd stop. I've had enough." She tapped the table in front of him. "Does the note mean he's going to kill again?"

"I don't see how he's going to keep up this pace. A killing takes a lot out of someone—emotionally, physically. He's already killed three people this week. Some serial killers go months between kills."

"He's going to screw up. I just know it. Attacking Ty like that was totally out of control."

"It feels like he's heading for some kind of climax."

"Sexual?"

"That's also something curious about this guy. So many serial killers rape their victims. The victims haven't shown any signs of molestation."

"Of course, that would just leave more evidence like DNA. He's very careful, isn't he?"

He sucked down the rest of his soda, slurping at the end. "Sorry. Do you want another?"

"I've had enough caffeine. I'm going to have a hard enough time getting to sleep tonight."

He grabbed her hand. "You're staying with me, right? That's decided."

"Courtney invited me to join her in her fabulous suite."

"Would you rather be with Courtney in her fabulous suite, or with me in my not-so-fabulous house?"

She ran her tongue along her bottom lip and stared deep into his dark eyes. "Your house was about the most fabulous place I've ever been—especially your shower."

"Such impure thoughts from a kindergarten teacher." He wiggled his eyebrows up and down. "Do you need to go back to your place or Courtney's to get anything?"

"Probably not a bad idea to drop by my place even

though I packed enough the first time around to get me through the week."

"You know—" he ran his knuckles down her forearm "—it might not be a bad idea for you to get out of the city when school's over. Did you have any plans before all this broke?"

"I was actually just going to take a week or so and drive down the coast—you know, through Monterey, Big Sur and maybe as far south as Hearst Castle. I've never been to any of those places."

"That's a great drive. You'll love it. Can you do that sooner rather than later?"

"Are you trying to get rid of me?"

"Trying to keep you safe."

She hunched forward. "Sean, tell me you're going to catch this guy."

"Me?" He jabbed his chest with his thumb. "I'm not allowed to catch him. I'll be picking up other cases and leaving the Alphabet Killer to the task force—the task force I'm not on."

"That's crazy."

Sean's eyebrows collided over his nose. "Fifty-one fifty."

"Huh?"

"The call for picking up someone mentally unstable—fifty-one fifty."

"Okay, if you say so."

He shoved the napkin in front of her. "Fifty-one fifty. It's in the note."

"Is he telling us he's crazy? We already know that." She folded up one edge of the napkin as she studied the other numbers. "Could this be a coordinate again?"

"I don't know, Elise. Could be anything and could be a total red herring like the coordinates for the Golden Gate Bridge."

She tapped some ice from the cup into her mouth. "I wonder what he thought when he tracked my GPS right into the bay."

"I hope he realized two can play stupid mind games." He rolled up the napkin and stuffed it in his pocket. "He loves those mind games."

"And fingers."

"Is Ty going to be okay?"

"He'll get over it. Like you said, I think he's beginning to realize he's lucky to be alive."

"And he's beginning to realize it's over between the two of you? Is it over?"

"Of course. Did you think I'd feel so much sympathy for his finger I'd go back to him?"

"I think he was hoping you would."

"I set him straight."

Sean pushed back from the table. "Unless you want to eat hospital cafeteria food, let's get going."

"I'm in the parking structure below."

"Not a great idea, Elise."

"We got rid of the GPS. He's not tracking my movements anymore."

"We don't know what he's up to." He patted his pocket with the napkin. "He's obviously on the hunt for a new victim."

"Does the task force have any idea how he finds his victims?" She dropped her cup in the trash. "Any idea how he found me?"

"We…they're looking into everything, Elise." He glanced up and pointed. "That guy can tell you more than I can now."

Detective Curtis was barreling into the cafeteria and didn't notice them until Sean raised his hand.

Curtis's eyebrows jumped. "You didn't drop in on the vic, did you?"

Sean placed his hand on her arm. "She did. Don't worry—I stayed well away."

"Was Ty able to tell you anything, Detective Curtis?"

"You can call me John." He skimmed the top of his short hair with the palm of his hand. "He couldn't tell us much. Guy came at him out of nowhere."

"Are you heading up the task force now?" Elise shifted from one foot to the other, brushing Sean's arm. He seemed to be taking his removal from the task force well, but his body still seemed tight and tense.

Curtis shot an apologetic look at Sean. "Yeah, the captain has me running the show. Hey, did you see Jacoby wandering around? I thought he was coming down to get prints on the vic. Sorry, Ty."

"I didn't. Why, did you find a finger?"

"Not yet. I hope it doesn't wind up in the mail to you."

"What is this guy's obsession with fingers, anyway?" Elise shoved her hands in her pockets.

Sean snorted. "Who knows? Maybe he got sick of people pointing fingers at him and decided to lop them off."

"It's sick and weird."

"And right now, it's Curtis's problem." Sean grabbed her hand. "Let's get the rest of your stuff and move it to my place."

Curtis coughed. "Elise is staying with you now?"

"I told you, her friend's place was compromised. Her friend's in a hotel, and I think Elise would be safer with me."

"You know there's going to be hell to pay when the captain figures out you tossed that GPS device into the bay?"

"Had to do it. Do you think we would've gotten anything from it? The Alphabet Killer is too careful with his fingerprints, and if he's that careful with his prints he probably knows to file off the serial number on any device he uses."

"You're right, Brody. That's why you should be heading up this case."

Sean smacked him on the back. "You'll do fine, Curtis, but in the meantime Elise is coming home with me, and you can tell the captain that, too."

"The captain doesn't have to know everything." He winked and then rubbed his hands on his way to the hot-food counter.

Elise turned to Sean in the elevator and said, "I can't figure out if John is happy he's got the task force or upset."

"Probably a little of both. It's always good for your career to lead a task force, but he's worked in my shadow for a long time."

"Do you think he resents that?"

"John?" Sean stabbed at the elevator button for the parking garage a few more times. "He's too good-natured for that."

"Still, I get the impression that you're the superstar detective in the homicide department."

"I've solved a few big cases, but it's all a team effort. I couldn't do my job without all the support people."

"With all the little people?"

The elevator doors trundled open on the second floor of the parking garage, and Sean wedged his shoulder against one side of the opening to hold the door open for her.

"Is that how it sounded to you?"

"Not at all. You sounded very modest, but I just wonder if everyone sees it that way."

"Curtis knows the score. He's good at some things and I'm good at other things."

She clicked her remote. "Where are you parked?"

"Out front. Give me a ride to my car and I'll follow you back to your place."

"My place. I don't even know where that is anymore."

WHEN THEY'D COLLECTED her things and returned to Sean's place, he stepped over the brownish spot on his carpet where Ty had collapsed. "I don't think that stain will ever come out. I'll have to get the carpet replaced or forever be reminded of Ty accusing me of hiring someone to attack him before passing out on my floor."

"Ty was crazy with shock and confusion. Obviously the guy planted that in his head."

"You know that accusation made my blood boil even though I knew there was no chance that you or anyone else would believe it. I'd fight to the bitter end to clear my name if someone unjustly accused me of a crime." He shoved his hands in his pockets. "I just can't understand why my father didn't do the same."

"You just can't know what was going through his head, Sean."

Elise dropped one of her bags in the corner next to the only plant in the room, making its leaves wave.

Sean snapped out of his reverie. "Hey, watch it. That plant's barely alive as it is."

She flicked her fingers at it as if to dismiss it. "Looks like it's doing as well as the plants in my classroom. Just one more day of school."

"And then you're going to take that trip down the coast?"

"Maybe." She tossed her hair over her shoulder. "Do you think he'll stop sending you messages when he knows you're off his case?"

"You haven't been watching Ray Lopez. I think everyone in the city knows I'm off the case. He's not going to care about that."

"I guess not, since he left you a message with the bodies last night."

"Exactly."

"Fifty-one plus fifty. Fifty-one fifty."

"Uh-huh."

"Forty-two plus fifty-eight. That can't be a date. He's not going to commit a murder on April second and tell us about it today."

"Tell *us?*"

"You know what I mean." She reached for her purse. "That's my phone. It's Courtney." She picked up the call. "Hey, did you get checked in?"

"It's like a minivacation. You can join me if you like."

"I'm good where I am." Her gaze wandered to Sean, checking the messages on his phone.

"I'll bet you are."

"Thanks so much for letting me stay with you. I'm sorry I led a killer to your doorstep."

"How were you supposed to know the creep had bugged your car? Are you going to stay there with Detective Tall, Dark and Handsome until this guy is caught, or what?"

"I'm thinking of taking my vacation a little early."

Without looking up from his phone, Sean flashed her a thumbs-up.

Courtney concurred. "I think that's a great idea. Oscar should be home next week and I think that he'll be around all summer, not that he would be much help in an emergency, but at least you won't be coming home to an empty house."

"Maybe it'll be safe by then."

"Oops. Hold on a minute. The restaurant where I just ordered my dinner is calling me. They forgot to take my address." The phone beeped on the other end and then Courtney came back on the line. "Four twenty-five, eighth floor."

"What?"

"Oh, sorry. Wrong line."

"You sound busy."

Courtney huffed out a breath. "It's that needy new client. I'm seeing him after hours again."

"Well, you go figure out his craziness. I'll talk to you later."

She ended the call and pointed her phone at Sean. "Anything new?"

"I called for the autopsy report on Dr. Patrick."

"And?"

"Preliminary report suggests heart attack."

"Then maybe that's all it was—a heart attack and bad timing."

"A heart attack and an incredible coincidence." He stretched and perched on the edge of a bar stool. "Is Courtney working late tonight?"

"Yes, her demanding new client."

"That's a whole lotta crazy I couldn't handle."

"And that's from someone who gets a package with a finger in it."

"Come here." He crooked his finger at her.

She eased out of the chair and sauntered toward him, his dark eyes drawing her like a magnet.

He drew her between his open legs and pinned her. "I'm glad you're here. I'm glad you're safe."

"I don't know what I would've done without you, Sean." She rested her hands on his thighs and leaned in to kiss his lips.

His legs tightened around her thighs. "Let's go out and get something to eat. It's getting late, and we both have to work tomorrow."

Nodding, she slipped away from his clinch, missing her opportunity to ask him about their future. She didn't want to push him into anything. Right now they needed each other, but when that need ended, what did they have?

"You okay?" He chucked her under the chin.

"Greek."

"What?"

"I want to try that Greek restaurant, if that's okay with you and if it's still open this late."

"Greek it is. I think they stay open until eleven for dinner."

An hour later they were sitting at a corner table in a noisy establishment in North Beach.

"I can't believe it's so crowded at this time of night—and on a Wednesday." Elise leaned across the table. "Are they going to start breaking plates?"

"Do you want them to?"

She scooped more tapenade onto her plate. "That's okay."

Sean checked his phone for about the third time since they sat down to dinner.

"Are you expecting a call or a message? Something about Dr. Patrick?"

"I sent my brother—the FBI agent—a text about Dr. Patrick."

"So, let me get this straight. You're a homicide detective, you have one brother who's a P.I. and another who's FBI?"

"That's right."

"What's the fourth one?"

"Actually Ryan is the third one, and he's the police chief of Crestview."

"I guess the Brody blood really does run blue. Is there something the FBI agent can do in his position to get more information?"

"Not sure, but I'm asking."

She felt in her purse for her own phone. "Courtney was going to check in with me when she finished with her client."

She checked the display, but Courtney hadn't called or texted.

"Did she call? She's more than welcome to join us for dinner. We haven't gotten to the main course yet, and her office is close by, isn't it?"

"I'll invite her if she ever finishes up with this client. She hasn't called yet."

"She sure goes all out for her patients, doesn't she?"

"She comes across as a party girl, but she's really very serious about her work and very caring. And since she's a therapist, she calls them clients instead of patients."

"She can't prescribe medication, but I'm sure she has some clients that need it, right?"

"She refers them to a doctor she works with. She's had a few certifiably crazy clients, and she ended up transferring them to a psychiatrist she knows."

"Must be hard to deal with the really crazy ones."

"I don't think *crazy* is the term the professionals use." She bit into her cracker and dabbed her mouth with a napkin.

"Well, that's the term cops use." Sean drew his brows over his nose. "You did say Courtney's office was nearby, right?"

"Yeah, the address is forty-two something or four, two, something on Market."

Sean balanced his fork on the edge of his plate. "What floor is she on?"

His voice was so low it barely cut through the din, but the urgency behind the words had her looking up from her plate sharply.

"Floor? I don't remember." She gave up trying to stab the olive with her fork and pinched it between her fingers instead. "Why are you asking? Are you suggesting we bring the food to her?"

"No, I..."

She snapped her fingers. "Wait. She was getting food delivered to her office, and she thought I was the delivery guy and she rattled off her address and floor number. It was four, two something and the eighth floor, but I don't think she needs…" She trailed off, her gut twisting at Sean's tight face. "What is it?"

"The message, Elise. The message from the Alphabet Killer. Fifty-one plus fifty equal 187. Forty-two plus fifty-eight equal 187."

She blinked and gulped some water to wash down the sour taste of fear. "I don't get it."

"We already guessed that the fifty-one, fifty might mean crazy, as in the type of clients Courtney might see. If her address is four, two, five on the eighth floor—forty-two plus fifty-eight—we have a problem."

She'd already shoved back from the table. "You mean Courtney has a problem. She's in danger."

Sean pulled out his wallet and dropped several twenties on the table. "I'm going to call this in, but let's head over there now."

Elise kept stabbing at the redial button on the way out of the restaurant, but the call rolled over to Courtney's voice mail every time. When they hit the sidewalk, Elise took a deep breath after Courtney's recorded greeting. "Courtney, it's Elise. I don't want to freak you out or anything, but once you're done with your client, don't see anyone else and just wait in your office with the door locked. Sean and I are heading over there right now. It's about ten-thirty. Call me as soon as you get this if we don't see you first."

By the time they reached Sean's car, Elise's breath was coming out in short spurts.

Sean buckled his seat belt and chucked his phone against the dashboard. "They won't come. The lieutenant on duty thinks it's a wild-goose chase and is refusing to send a patrol car."

"What about John?"

"He's off duty. I tried him at home, but he's not there or he's not picking up."

"Hurry, Sean. It's not that far. Maybe she's still with a client. I told her to stay in her office and lock the door."

Sean's tires squealed as he shot into the street, horns honking in his wake.

"Elise, did Courtney ever tell you anything about this new client of hers, the one who was so demanding?"

She clamped down on her bouncing knees. "No. Why are you asking me that?"

But she knew why. The same thought had been niggling at her brain since Sean started putting together the puzzle of the note.

"She started seeing that guy right after you were attacked, right after you moved in with her."

Elise doubled over, sinking her face in her hands. "He found her because of me."

"Maybe. This is all just supposition right now."

She shot up, pain pounding behind her eyes. "Courtney did mention something about him today."

"Description, name?"

"She wouldn't break that confidentiality." She stared unseeing out the car window. "She told me how he picked her out."

"How?"

"Her name." She dug her fingernails into Sean's thigh. "He chose her because he liked her name, Sean. Courtney Chu. Two Cs. He's still on the Cs."

With this last bit of news, Sean whipped around the next corner and tossed his phone at her. "Try calling Curtis again. Leave him a message. Tell him we're on our way to Courtney's and give him the address again."

Elise followed his instructions and by the time she ended the call, Sean had pulled up in front of Courtney's office building.

Elise scrambled out of the car before it came to a complete stop. She grabbed on to the two long silver handles of the glass doors and yanked. They didn't budge. She pressed her face against the glass, her eyes searching the lobby.

Sean joined her and picked up the phone to the right of the doors. "This is SFPD Homicide Detective Sean Brody. We're trying to get into the building to see Courtney Chu on the eighth floor."

He listened for a minute and then replaced the receiver. "That was security. They're sending someone down."

Elise kept hold of the door handles as if that could make them arrive sooner. "It's dark, it's locked up. Maybe Courtney left already. Maybe she's out with Derrick. It's so late."

"Here's the security guard." Sean opened his ID and pressed his badge against the glass.

The doors clicked, and the security guard swung one open. "Is there a problem?"

"We're here to check on Courtney Chu, eighth floor. Have you seen her? Has she left for the night?"

"I know Ms. Chu. She had some food delivered a while back, but I haven't seen her since."

"Did anyone come to the office to see her? Anyone you had to let in?"

"No, sir. We lock the doors at ten o'clock. If she had a client before then, I wouldn't have opened the door for him or her."

"Okay, thanks. We still want to check on her."

"Sure thing." He swung the door open wide and they stepped into the building. "From this point, you can go on up to the eighth floor."

"Can you come with us in case we need to get into Ms. Chu's office?"

"I have my rounds, but—" he pulled a key from his keychain "—this is the master and it'll get you in."

"Thanks." Sean took the key and pounded the button for the elevator. "One more thing."

The security guard stopped at the door to the right of the elevators with his hand on the doorknob. "Yes?"

"Has anything unusual happened tonight? Anything out of the ordinary?"

The guard cocked his head. "As a matter of fact, yes. An emergency buzzer sounded for one of the side doors about an hour ago."

Elise swallowed and curled her hand around Sean's arm. "What does that mean?"

"Means someone left the building by way of an emergency exit. Who knows? Maybe it was Ms. Chu."

"H-has she ever done that before?"

The security guard shook his finger. "That Ms. Chu likes to break the rules."

As they rode up to the eighth floor, Elise said, "Maybe that's it. Maybe Courtney's not even here."

"Maybe."

The doors opened, and Elise tugged on Sean's sleeve to steer him to the right. The silence enveloped them, and Elise held her breath. When they got to the door of Courtney's office, Elise let out a breath on a whispered prayer. "Please, God, let her be safe."

Sean tried the door handle first. Then he pulled out the key the security guard had given him and shoved it into the lock. He turned the lock and pushed the door at the same time, staggering into the small waiting room.

Elise had been in here once before and it looked the same—undisturbed. Courtney had fanned out the latest magazines on one low table and had stacked others in a holder on the wall. Two fake plants bobbed in the corners, and someone had left an indentation in one of the leather love seats.

The needy client who liked Courtney's name?

Elise marched toward the door to Courtney's inner sanctum, but Sean put out a steadying hand.

"Wait."

He drew his gun from his holster and crept toward the same door. Shoving Elise behind him, he eased open the door.

More silence.

Elise's nostrils flared and the blood thrummed in her eardrums.

Sean aimed his gun at the three closed doors off the hallway and whispered, "Which one is her office?"

The whisper sent a chill up her spine, but she shook off her fear and pointed to the first door on the left.

"Stay back."

Sean twisted the handle of the door and inched it open. He'd stepped into the office, but Elise was no longer watching him.

A slight movement on the floor to her right caught her eye. Her gaze darted to the tile in front of what she knew was the bathroom floor.

A trickle of dark liquid meandered from the crack beneath the door. As if in a trance, Elise stepped over it to push open the bathroom door. The door swung freely and then stopped.

She heard Sean's voice coming from the office, words she couldn't comprehend, words coming at her in a fog.

She opened her mouth and managed a small sigh. She ran her tongue along her teeth and tried again.

This time she managed a scream, a scream so loud it echoed and bounced off the walls of the small bathroom where Courtney's lifeless form couldn't hear her at all.

Chapter Sixteen

Sean shot a worried glance at Elise, slumped in the leather love seat in the waiting room, her eyes glassy, a grayish pallor to her cheeks.

Curtis was yammering at him. “You figured out the next victim was Courtney Chu from that cryptic note?”

Jacoby slapped Curtis on the back. “Brody’s the best. Get used to it, Curtis.”

“So you got some prints this time?”

Jacoby smiled and patted his bag. “If he was posing as a client and he’d been here before, maybe we’ll get lucky.”

Sean swung around on Melvin, the security guard. “Did you get the video from the cameras?”

“We’re collecting that for you now, Detective Brody.”

“But you didn’t notice the guy coming in tonight?”

“Nope. The only one I saw was the delivery boy from the restaurant.” He pointed at Curtis. “And I gave Detective Curtis the name of the restaurant.”

Curtis held up his hand. “I’m on it. We’re going to bring the kid in for questioning.”

“The killer has to be on camera. I’m hoping we can get a good look at him on those videos.”

Curtis lowered his voice and moved closer to Sean. “Sorry I wasn’t available when you called, and there’s going to be hell to pay for Healy for refusing backup.”

"I don't know if it would've helped. Judging by the—" he slid a glance at Elise, who was sipping some water "—condition of the body, I think we were too late anyway."

The coroner had arrived and Sean slipped away from the crush of people and crouched in front of Elise, taking her hands.

"How are you doing?"

She raised her blue eyes, flooded with tears. "It's my fault. I brought him into her life."

He squeezed her hands. "It's his fault, Elise. His and no one else's."

"She was so full of life. I can't even imagine her silent forever." She pressed a hand to her forehead. "Has anyone notified her brother? Has anyone told Oscar yet?"

"They're working on that."

A tear crested on her lower lid and rolled down her cheek. "He screwed up, didn't he? Dan Jacoby told me he got a lot of prints. There has to be video of him coming in and out of the building as a client of Courtney's. He can't have come and gone through the emergency door every time he saw her."

"We'll get him. I promise you that. There will be justice for Courtney and the other three victims, too. Justice for you."

She dashed the tear from her cheek with the back of her hand. "How am I going to make it to the last day of school tomorrow? It's already past one-thirty."

"Take the day off. Everyone will understand."

"But the kids."

"You can see them next year when they're first-graders. I know you're a wonderful teacher, but they'll be so excited for the last day of school they won't be sad for long that you're not there."

"Maybe. I feel so awful. I don't even know if I can get up from this love seat."

"Sean!"

He twisted his head around and answered Curtis. "What is it?"

"Lieutenant Healy wants you down at the station—now."

"Are you kidding me? Don't tell me he's mad because I found the Alphabet Killer's victim."

"He's mad about a lot of things. I suggest you head down there."

Sean rose to his feet and brought Elise with him, tucked against his side. "Technically, I was on a date."

Curtis cleared his throat. "Technically, you were on a date with a witness, which is another one of his points of contention."

"I'm not leaving Elise stranded, and I don't want her going back to my place alone."

"Your place?" Curtis rolled his eyes. "Yeah, the LT doesn't even know about that, but he could add it to his list when he chews you out."

Elise pressed her shoulder against Sean's. "It's okay. There are a million cops here, and my guess is they'll be here for a few more hours. I can just stay here and wait for you."

Sean glanced at the coroner's stretcher in the hallway. "I don't want you hanging out here, Elise. You're exhausted."

"I'll tell you what." Curtis smiled at Elise. "You go have your confab with the lieutenant, and I'll take Elise out for coffee to wait for you or back to my place, or we can even go back to your place."

"Hot chocolate."

"Huh?"

"Elise likes hot chocolate with whipped cream." He hugged her close. "Is that okay with you?"

"Yes, of course. I don't want you to get into any more

trouble because of me." She sniffled. "I don't want to be the cause of any more trouble for anyone."

Sean gave her a quick kiss and didn't care who saw. "Hang in there, kid. I'll be with you as soon as I can."

She bobbed her head once and sank back down to the love seat.

"Take care of her, Curtis." Sean glanced over his shoulder at Elise one more time before leaving the crime scene.

When he got to the station, it looked like one o'clock in the afternoon instead of one o'clock in the morning. And Lieutenant Healy was presiding over all the controlled chaos with a tight rein.

When he saw Sean, he barked, "Brody. In here now."

Sean sat tight-lipped as the lieutenant dressed him down for consorting with a witness, for conducting an investigation on his own and even for continuing to thrust himself into this case when he'd been removed from it.

At the end of the tirade, he praised Sean for his good detective work and was personally inviting him back on the case.

"I'll deal with the captain tomorrow. He can't really believe you don't have something important to contribute, but—" he held up one crooked finger "—Curtis will still be lead. And if you have a problem…"

"No problem with that, sir."

"Good. Now let's head over to the situation room. The security office at the victim's building turned over the tapes. We have the victim's phone and appointment book, so we're going to try to match up some appointment times with the videos."

"I'm in."

He and the lieutenant and one of the junior detectives hunched over the laptop and fast-forwarded through people walking in and out of Courtney's building.

Sean tossed down his pencil in frustration. "There are a

lot of offices in that building and a lot of foot traffic. Elise Duran told me there were a few nights this week where the victim saw this new client later in the day. Let's concentrate on the video for those times when there aren't so many people."

When the videos were loaded, Sean peered at the grainy images on the laptop monitor. They stopped the video and captured and printed pictures of every man who came through the door.

When he had a stack, he said, "I'm going to run these by Elise so she can see if any of these guys look familiar."

He studied in particular a stocky man with a cap pulled low over his face, which he kept turned away from the camera. He could even be wearing a gray jacket, like the man who attacked Elise.

Rubbing his eyes, Sean checked his watch. He'd been here for almost two hours. He wanted, no, he needed to see Elise.

He grabbed the printouts and cruised down the hallway to the lab. Lieutenant Healy had the techs hopping in here, too.

Sean waved the papers in his hand. "I need a few of these blown up. Do we have anything on the fingerprints from the office yet?"

Kwan looked up from his computer. "Fingerprints? We don't have no stinkin' fingerprints yet."

"Jacoby hasn't been back here with his treasures yet? I thought he'd be gleefully running prints about now."

"Jacoby does love him some fingerprints, but he hasn't come back from the crime scene."

"Are they still out there?"

"Oh, yeah."

Sean furrowed his brow and smacked the printouts down on the counter. "Okay, can someone work on these?

I'm going to check in with the LT, and then I'm outta here. Call me if something comes up."

Sean returned to his desk to file some notes and then started for the lieutenant's office. His heart stuttered when he saw Curtis through the glass talking to Healy.

Had he brought Elise here?

He stalked to the office and pushed open the door. "Where's Elise? Did you bring her down here?"

Curtis turned and leaned against the lieutenant's desk. "No, I had more work to do at the crime scene and then the lieutenant called me back here."

"Where is she? You didn't leave her alone, did you?"

"Relax, loverboy." Curtis shifted a quick glance at Healy and grimaced. "I left her with Jacoby. He said he'd take her back to your place and stick around until you got there."

Jacoby. The adrenaline continued to course through Sean's body and he charged out of the lieutenant's office and back to the lab.

"Have you singled out those stills from the video yet?" Sean had punched in Elise's cell phone number, but it had tripped over to voice mail.

Kwan's mouth dropped open. "Dude, you just dropped off the printouts. We haven't had time to match them on the video yet."

Sean pulled out a chair at one of the computers and opened the portions of the video they'd marked. He scanned through and stopped at the image of the man in the baseball cap. "Kwan, come here."

Kwan hovered over his shoulder. "What?"

Jabbing his finger at the screen, Sean asked, "Doesn't this look like Jacoby to you?"

Adjusting his glasses, Kwan leaned in. "Could be, same shape, but Jacoby's built rock solid. This guy looks a little heavyset to me."

"That could be the jacket, right? A guy with big muscles might look heavy in a puffy jacket."

"Sure, but what are you saying? Jacoby was in that building? I mean, he could've been—dentists, lawyers, hell, even steroid docs. So what?"

"Fingers. Fingerprints."

"What the hell, Brody?"

"How come there hasn't been one set of prints to come out of any of these murders? Not even a partial."

"The Alphabet Killer wears gloves. He's careful."

"He knows police procedures."

"Jacoby's weird, but he ain't that weird."

Sean's head jerked to the side. "What do you mean by *weird?*"

"I don't know." Kwan wiped his mouth with the back of his hand. "With the ladies. He trolls those online dating forums but can never get up the guts to make a move."

The blood was roaring in Sean's ears now. He stormed out of the lab and interrupted Curtis and Healy. "Where's Jacoby?"

Curtis smirked. "Why? Do you think he's moving in on your woman?"

Sean smacked his hand against the doorjamb. "This isn't a joke, John. I think Jacoby might be our killer."

Both men stared at him, but they weren't laughing.

"That's crazy, Sean."

"Brody, unless you have some hard evidence, you'd better put a cork in it."

"Here." Sean drilled his fist into his gut. "I feel it here."

"You're a good enough detective to know that's not good enough." Healy had sat back down in dismissal.

"Fingers, the guy loves his fingerprints." Curtis scratched the stubble on his chin. "What do you need, Sean?"

Healy glared at them from beneath his eyebrows. "You two can take this outside my office."

When the door shut behind them, Curtis turned to Sean. "What do you need me to do?"

"Look at his schedule, John. See where he's been at the time of the murders. Review that video for me. One of the guys walking in that building looks like Jacoby." He grabbed his shoulders. "Did he ask to watch over Elise?"

Curtis squeezed his eyes closed. "Sort of. Let's just say he was eager to take over the job when I got called away."

"Damn. Where'd they go? What kind of car does he have?"

"We can look up his car here. He told me he was taking her to that twenty-four-hour coffee shop near the park."

"Thanks for your help, John. I know you can get in trouble for this if it's all in my head."

"I'll bet on you every time, Brody."

Sean yelled over his shoulder as he took off toward the elevators, "Keep me posted."

When he got to his car, he punched in Elise's phone number again. This time when he got her voice mail, he left her a message. "Elise, where are you? Call me as soon as you get this message and don't trust Jacoby. If you're with him, make some excuse to get away and then—get away. Run away from him as fast as you can."

He cranked on his engine and swung out of the parking garage. His phone buzzed in the cup holder, where he'd tossed it, signaling a message, and he grabbed it. He blew out a breath when he saw Elise's name on the display.

He balanced the phone on the steering wheel to click on the message. Then he slammed on his brakes, sending his car into a fishtail as he read the message: Elise is busy. Thirty-seven plus forty-nine plus 122 plus twenty-eight equal 187.

The coordinates for the Golden Gate Bridge.

ELISE COUGHED AND gagged as Jacoby dragged her from the trunk of his car—a different car than the one he'd had at their first meeting.

He shoved her in front of him, prodding her back with

the barrel of his .45. "No running away this time, Elise. Guns are not my weapon of choice—too much evidence in the form of ballistics and blood spatter. You see, I'm just as good a detective as Brody."

She licked her dry lips. "Where's your phony English accent?"

"The same place as my phony cast, beat-up car and fake beard." He nestled close to her side and she gagged on his cologne. "You have to admit that was a pretty good disguise. Nothing even registered for you when I came to your house not twelve hours later. Of course, I didn't think it would since you wouldn't expect a homicide field tech to be a killer, would you?"

"Something about you rubbed me the wrong way from the beginning."

"Yeah, yeah. That's what they all say. Keep walking."

"Where are we going?" But she didn't have to ask. Even though he'd parked his car in the gravel parking lot on the other side of the tourist center, the Golden Gate Bridge soared above them, just peeking from the early morning fog that swirled around it.

He clicked his tongue. "Just trying to make small talk, Elise? You know where we're going."

"W-we can't go onto the bridge. It's closed to pedestrians at this time of night."

"It's actually morning, but who's counting?" Smiling, he showed her a black, square device in his hand. "I'm sure I mentioned that I'm a cyclist, and we get special privileges for the bridge."

Elise shivered but plodded on ahead of Jacoby. Would he force her to jump? He'd have to shoot her first. She'd never jump off that bridge. Maybe he just planned to slice her up as he did the others. As he did Courtney.

She hugged herself. She should've never gone with Jacoby when John had to leave. She could've just stayed at the crime scene or waited with security at the building until Sean came back for her.

"Sean's going to know it's you. Why else would you take off with me?"

"Well—" his feet crunched on the gravel behind her "—I thought of that and figured I could just tell him I took you back to his place and had to leave myself. I'd be beating myself up about leaving you alone, but you'd still be dead."

"He'll never believe you. You're leaving too many clues, too much evidence."

"Ah, evidence. I'm quite good at covering up, but I have other plans for Detective Sean Brody."

Elise's heart jumped. "You're not going to hurt him?"

"What is it about all that dark brooding masculinity that drives women wild? I believe you'd die for him. Would you, Elise? Would you die for him?"

"Shut up."

"You must get that level of maturity from your kindergartners, like that little Eli."

She whipped around on him. "What do you know about Eli?"

"Enough." He shoved her and she tripped. "Now get moving."

Her teeth began to chatter as the chill seeped into her bones. Just like that other night. Would she wind up in the bay again?

He clicked his remote control device, which unlocked the security gate to the pedestrian walkway. He pushed it open and left it ajar.

"Won't the cyclists be suspicious about an open gate?"

"Happens more than you think. Besides, I'm expecting company."

Again, her heart lurched in her chest just as her feet hit the pavement of the walkway. Would any cyclists be crossing at this time of morning? It had to be getting close to three o'clock. The walkway opened at five to pedestrians.

But something told her they wouldn't be here at five.

"Stop."

She slowed her steps and grabbed a lamppost. "What are we doing?"

"Waiting. Have you ever wondered how it would feel to jump, Elise? Four seconds. They say it takes four seconds to fall before you hit the water. That's a long time to change your mind."

"People must be desperate, lonely."

"Or guilty." His gun hand wavered. "I get lonely sometimes. Does it fascinate you, Elise? This bridge? It fascinates me. Always has, and I grew up here."

"It's beautiful. Maybe that's why they choose to have their last moments here."

He snorted. "You know nothing of depression or desperation. The last thing on your mind is beauty."

"Why don't you just turn yourself in, Dan?"

"You remember my name? Seems like you only had eyes for Brody."

"Of course I remember your name, Dan. C-Courtney liked you, too. She told me about her new client. She liked you."

"Courtney is beautiful."

"She would've helped you, Dan."

"She tried. She wanted to."

His aim had slipped, and she tensed her muscles. Could she tackle his legs?

"Elise!"

She jerked her head up to see Sean jogging toward them on the pedestrian path. How had he found them?

The smile spreading across Jacoby's face told that story.

"Perfect." Jacoby grabbed Elise's arm and dragged her closer, the gun leveled at her head. "Stop where you are,

Brody. This time I was telling the truth about the coordinates."

Sean's chest heaved and every breath pained him. What did this psycho plan to do with Elise? "It's over, Jacoby. When I saw your car in the parking lot, I called it in. How did you expect to get away with this?"

"Does this spot look familiar to you, Brody? Do you know this spot on the bridge? Have you been here before?"

"It's where my father jumped. It's where they found his things."

Elise sobbed, her face a pale oval in the mist.

"Exactly. And now you're going to do the same thing."

"No!" The fog swallowed Elise's scream.

"You're going to murder the lovely Elise, and then the Alphabet Killer is going to jump, just like his father the Phone Book Killer did."

Sean ground his teeth. "My father was not a killer."

"That's funny. My mother never believed he did it, either."

"What?"

"We lived in the city then. It was the Phone Book Killer who got me interested in police work, in homicide. I always thought he did it, but my mother claimed nobody that handsome could be a killer." He shrugged his massive shoulders. "You Brodys live charmed lives."

"Yeah, really charmed."

He yanked Elise's hair. "Do you want mine instead? My father was a petty thief and pimp, in and out of jail. Your father even arrested him once for domestic battery. How about that?"

"You have a good life, Jacoby. You're respected in your field."

"*My* field isn't *your* field. I wanted to be a police officer. I wanted to be a homicide detective." He shoved Elise against the guardrail. "I didn't pass the background. Now, how is it I couldn't pass the background with my father but you could with yours?"

"Maybe it was your psych eval, Jacoby. How much do you think you can hide?"

"How much can you?"

"I never tried to hide anything. Is that what this is all about? You're jealous of my wonderful career and life, so you went on a killing rampage."

Jacoby slapped Elise across the face, and Sean clenched his fists and took a step forward.

"Not really, Brody. I just like hurting people. I guess I am like my old man, and you're going to be just like yours."

"But I'm not." Sean rolled up his sleeve. "Is that why you got the tattoo? You wanted to blame all the murders on me?"

"Nice touch, wasn't it? Of course, it was just a temporary one I got in Santa Cruz that washed right off."

"You're dreaming, Jacoby. You can't pull this off."

He rested the barrel of his gun against Elise's temple. "You're going to jump off the Golden Gate Bridge, or I'll shoot Elise in the head and dump her over. Then I'll shoot you and dump your body over. Is that clear, Brody?"

"If you do it that way, it's going to spoil your little scenario."

"One way or the other, you'll both be dead. Who knows? You might survive the jump. I hear you need to go in feet first at an angle. You're even wearing heavy boots."

"Sean, don't even think about it."

Jacoby smacked Elise's other cheek and Sean almost went for him.

"Or I can slice and dice Elise while you watch, leave her body on the bridge and then shoot you. I'll figure it out, but it would be easier for you if you just jump. Now."

Sean took a step toward the guardrail. The wind lashed

his face. He'd make the SOB kill him here, unless he could get the gun away from him…and off of Elise.

"Sean, don't." Elise twisted away from Jacoby.

Jacoby raised his weapon, but Elise scrambled on top of the guardrail, throwing one leg over.

"Elise! What are you doing?"

Jacoby crowed and trained his gun on Elise straddling the guardrail. "I knew she'd die for you."

"If I jump, it's just you and him, Sean. And you're a superstar cop. He's just a guy who takes fingerprints."

And then she rolled over the edge.

Sean bellowed and rushed Jacoby, who'd lowered his weapon in momentary shock. Sean drove his shoulder into Jacoby's iron chest and twisted his arm back.

The gun dropped from Jacoby's hand and skittered across the cement. They both lunged for it, but Sean was taller with longer arms and reached it first. He tensed his body, waiting for Jacoby's attack, but felt nothing but cool air.

Gripping the gun, he rolled onto his back—just in time to see Jacoby go over the guardrail.

Sean staggered to his feet, sobs building in his chest, taking his breath away. Why had Elise done that? Why had she sacrificed herself for him?

"Sean!"

His stomach dropped. "Elise?"

"I'm down here, on the ledge."

Sean leaned over the guardrail. Elise was huddled on the two-foot-wide ledge. Warm relief poured through his body and he reached over the rail for her.

"My God, what did you do?"

"I knew the ledge was here. When I rolled over, I grabbed for these pipes to hold myself up and pulled myself to the ledge."

"Jacoby?"

"He went right over me. I hope he saw me before he started flying."

Sirens wailed in the distance.

"Now they get here." He extended his arms. "Hold on to me and I'll pull you over."

He clasped her arms and pulled her up until she was folded over the guardrail. She rolled onto the ground from there.

Sean sat down next to her because he didn't think he could stand another minute. He wrapped his arms around her and pulled her into his lap. "You plunged me into the deepest darkness I'd ever known before."

"I knew it would distract him enough for you to get the upper hand."

"A bit drastic, but then you go for the dramatic."

"I didn't see any other way." She snuggled against his chest as the sirens drew closer.

"You seem drawn to the bay, one way or another. Must be fate."

She placed her cold hands on each side of his face and pressed her lips against his. She whispered, "This is the only fate I want."

Epilogue

The music grew frenzied and someone smashed a plate.

Elise lightly scraped her fingernails across Sean's tattoo. "You told someone to do that."

He grabbed her hand and kissed her fingers. "You jumped off the Golden Gate Bridge for me. I can arrange for a few broken plates. But I've got a question for you."

"Fire away."

"Did you ever sign up for one of those online dating services?"

Her cheeks sported a pleasing pink. "No. Why would you think that?"

"The two other women who were murdered had profiles on Lovelines."

Elise wrinkled her nose as she spread more tapenade on a cracker. "Not unless..."

"Not unless what?"

"Courtney was teasing me about being dateless one night and threatened to register me." She put down her cracker and dropped her lashes. "Maybe she did it as a joke. It's something Courtney would do."

He brushed his fingertip across her cheek. "I'm sorry, but it looks like Courtney may have steered Jacoby into your life before you brought him into hers."

"It doesn't make it any better."

"I know. When you lose a friend, especially like that, the pain will come out of nowhere and strike you."

"And you know all about that."

"My pain has been fading a little more every day—because of you."

He cupped her face with one hand and nibbled on her earlobe.

Two of the waiters approached them and dragged them onto the dance floor, where they joined half the restaurant in a Greek dance that nobody knew.

Ten minutes later, laughing and breathless, they collapsed in their chairs. "Two months ago, you would've never seen me out there."

"If you hadn't brought attention to yourself by all that PDA, they never would've singled you out. You'd better learn the ropes. Sometimes, you're just asking for attention."

"And you know all about that, Runaway Bride. How's Ty doing back home?"

"He's fine. He has an amazing story to tell all the ladies and a missing finger to prove it, so he's lapping up all the attention."

Sean's cell phone buzzed in his pocket, and he pulled it out.

Elise touched his arm. "Everything okay?"

He held the display out to her. "It's my brother, Eric, the FBI agent. He was able to order some additional toxicology reports on Dr. Franklin, and he had a trace of some chemical in his bloodstream."

"Sean, that's great—I think. Is it great? It might prove someone murdered Dr. Franklin and it might have something to do with your father's case."

"Maybe it will, but my life isn't on hold anymore. I'll help Eric if he needs it, but right now I have some living to catch up on."

She grabbed his hands. "Great. Then let's get started, because there's something I've been wanting to do with you for a while now, and it's only eight o'clock, so we still have time."

"Really?" He gave her his best wicked grin.

"I want to take a walk with you on one of my favorite places in the city."

He tilted his head. "Let me guess—the bridge."

She nodded, her big blue eyes wide. "Are you in?"

"Let's go, but no jumping and no swimming in the bay."

"Got it."

Later, when they walked hand in hand across the bridge, the lights of the city twinkled in the mist and a boat skimmed beneath them.

Whatever drove his father, Sean knew he had a different destiny—and the brave, fearless woman beside him would be a part of it every step of the way.

* * * * *

Carol Ericson's BRODY LAW *miniseries continues next month with THE DISTRICT.*